THE PARTISAN
HEART

THE PARTISAN HEART

Gordon Kerr

MUSWELL
PRESS

First published by Muswell Press in 2019
This paperback edition published in 2020

Typeset in Bembo by M Rules
Copyright © Gordon Kerr 2019

Gordon Kerr asserts the moral right
to be identified as the author of this work.

Printed and bound by
CPI Group (UK) Ltd, Croydon CR0 4YY.

A CIP catalogue record for this book
is available from the British Library

ISBN 9781999313593

Muswell Press
London
N6 5HQ
www.muswell-press.co.uk
team@muswell-press.co.uk

For Diane, Lindsey and Sean

Lasting from September 1943 to May 1945, the Italian Civil War was a brutal conflict contested by the Italian resistance movement and elements of the former Italian Army, fighting on the side of the Allies against the Axis forces. During the hostilities, around forty thousand partisans and former soldiers lost their lives and tens of thousands of civilians were tortured, killed or deported to Germany.

All of the events and characters of The Partisan Heart are fictional, as are several of the place names. The majority of the action, however, takes place in a real valley – the ruggedly beautiful Valtellina.

1

10 October 1999
Beldoro
North Italy

A woman screamed.

The noise startled several pigeons dozing on the telephone wires that snaked between the buildings above the square. The birds took off, wings slapping, before lazily settling back where they had started. The streets had been hushed until then, the only sound the crackle of the dry leaves being chased in small circles by the brisk wind. It was autumn, after all, and the town of Beldoro was bedding down for winter. The large palm trees outside the big hotels on the lakeside had been wrapped in sacking material, to protect them from the chills of the coming months and the boats in the marina were wearing slick coverings. The wind was keeping people off the streets and the square was empty.

The scream was brief and ended abruptly, as if it had been silenced. In fact, its final moments were muffled and the sleepy stillness that had enveloped the square outside, before the scream had momentarily splintered it, returned immediately.

Above the square, Alfio Bonfadini had heard it, though. He had been on his way to the toilet when the sudden noise had stopped him in his tracks. He listened, unsure if he really had heard such a sound, pulling the lace curtains of his bedroom window to one side to see what was going on. His overweight body was naked, having just got out of the bed where the dozing, full figure of a woman still lay. She was called Silvia and the noise had failed to stir her, tired as she was after their lovemaking.

Alfio pulled the curtain across his face so that he could not be seen and watched as a grey van appeared from around the corner at the far end of the square and roared up to the pavement in front of the bar that occupied part of the ground floor of the building. His immediate thought was one of panic. What was going on? *Christ!* Maybe it was Silvia's husband! She was the wife of a man named Ignazio Mazzini, but there was little love in their marriage. On the first occasion she and Alfio had crept upstairs, pulling at each other's clothes, she had told him that Ignazio had not slept with her since the night of their wedding five years previously. Nonetheless, it was well documented – mainly in the files of the local *carabinieri* – that Ignazio could be a violent man with a temper that was easily roused.

My God, how could I be such a fool as to take up with such a woman? he thought, his heart beginning to pound and a sick feeling starting to worm its way into his stomach.

It had all seemed so easy and so comfortable. She worked part-time in the shop with him. In the middle of the morning, every couple of days, when the first rush of business – or, at any rate, such a rush as one could expect in a shop selling

2

wool and ladies' underwear – had died away, they would put a notice on the door and would sneak upstairs to his bedroom and make love for an hour. An hour and no more. On the stroke of twelve they would return to their chores and no one would be any the wiser. Or, at least, they thought no one knew, but it was common knowledge that there was no point trying the door of the shop between eleven and twelve on every second day. But, blissfully ignorant, once they were back behind the counter, Alfio and Silvia did not speak of it. It was as if it were two other people who made love in that room, with the lace curtains swaying gently in the breeze and the sound of mopeds and cars seeping in through the gaps in the window frames.

Alfio watched what was becoming frenzied activity down below. A man jumped out of the van and rushed round to its rear, throwing open the back doors, out of which two other men jumped and ran into the bar below, next door to his shop. Almost immediately, from the bar came a scrum of bodies. The three men re-appeared, half-carrying, half-dragging a blonde-haired woman whose legs appeared to have lost any of the properties that made them useful.

'Mad*oooo*nna!' whispered Alfio, his surprise elongating the expletive.

The men all wore black balaclavas, with holes for eyes and large, round holes for their mouths, just like the Basque Separatists or the IRA men in Ireland that he sometimes saw on the TV news. Not that there was anyone around to see them though. The square slept on.

They were struggling, but not because the woman was protesting. Rather, it was because she had become like a rag doll, arms flailing and legs collapsing underneath her. Finally, one of them grabbed her around the middle and threw her over his shoulders, running the last few steps to the van and dropping her in heavily, before climbing in himself. His colleagues followed and the doors slammed shut as the van sped off around the square, slamming through the gears, and down Via Costanza towards the mountains.

Bonfadini was confused as he hurriedly pulled on his trousers. He also felt a deep sense of relief that it had not been Ignazio. That could have been very bad. He resolved then and there to bring his relationship with Silvia to an end. He would tell her he could no longer afford her wages. Then he would wait a while and re-advertise the job. He could take on a widow or, better still, a younger woman with no husband. He could return to his mid-morning breaks without being concerned about having his kneecaps broken.

He fastened his trousers quickly and dragged a t-shirt over his head. Naturally nosey, he wanted to see what was going on. He ran downstairs into the backyard from where he could get to the street via a short alleyway, loudly shouting 'Get dressed!' to the stirring Silvia as he went. He just had time at the bottom of the steps to hear two police cars arrive from different directions, sirens wailing and blue lights flashing, before he ran into a wall, hearing his nose splinter and feeling it spread across his face. At least, it felt as if he had run into a wall. His body folded and crumpled to the ground, his eyes filling with water, and the pain beginning. It started somewhere at the back of his head, undertaking an inevitable journey towards the middle of his face where it would, he knew, explode into something memorable. As his body slumped to the floor, blood gushing from his smashed nose, he caught a glimpse of the tall figure of Ignazio, Silvia's husband, stepping back into the shadows at the bottom of the stairs, a baseball bat hanging limply at his side and a slow, satisfied smile beginning to crease his dark features.

2

3 November 1999
Dulcino
The Valtellina
North Italy

'Michael!'

Night falls in layers in the Valtellina, especially as autumn shakes off its sprinkling of brightly-coloured leaves and the valley adopts the greyness of winter. The arrival of darkness seems to exonerate each day, no matter what has filled it, no matter what indiscretion, what cruelty, what moments of doubt have distinguished it from all the other days that have gone before or will follow relentlessly, after.

For Michael, however, these last few days had been empty. His eyes, too, were vacant, although they should, at that moment, have been focused on the view of the valley from the balcony on which he stood. It was a view for which tourists would pay good money.

It consisted, in the near-distance, of a town, its thin, weak lights just beginning to flicker in the growing twilight. Into the far-distance, in either direction, villages were strung along the length of the valley like the pearls of a necklace.

The Valtellina, unlike the other valleys that dangle longitudinally from the arc of the Alps, stretches east to west, about a hundred kilometres in length. Once its settlements had been sparse, groups of houses gathered round the few bits of grazing land that fed the cattle that kept their owners just above subsistence level. But as times got better and as roads began to connect the farthest flung corners of the valley with the outside world, so people had moved towards the mouth of the valley, where it and its neighbour, the Valchiavenna, descended into plains that led to the glittering waters of Lake Como.

Tourism had opened up the valley. The *Milanesi* had arrived in their Alfa Romeos and Porsches, building chalets and renovating old, run-down houses, turning the cattle sheds on the ground floors into garages for their gleaming chariots, and the villages had rapidly grown into towns, while new settlements grew where before there had been nothing. Supermarkets arrived, things of wonder to people starved for centuries of the luxuries enjoyed by the inhabitants of the bigger towns and cities.

Michael watched columns of smoke rise from chimneys the length of the valley. Drifting into mist, miles away to the west, Lake Como lay in oriental stillness, its gleam just visible beyond the red roofs of the countless villages. At this hour, seven o'clock, steamers would be making their final incisions of the day in the lake's glass-like surface, late commuters and tourists huddling at the rails like notes on a stave as the evening's gentle breeze began to stir the flags on the grand hotels and restaurants on the far side of the lake.

'Michael!'

Renzo, Michael's brother-in-law, had been standing in the doorway for what had seemed to him like an eternity, one foot in the real world and one hesitant foot in the uncertain world in which Michael seemed to have become immured. It was a world from which Renzo felt excluded and one which he did not fully understand. Nor did he wish to. Renzo was a much younger man, but seemed somehow older, Michael always thought. He was so different from his sister, Rosa, Michael's wife. He took life seriously; the old adage about life not being a rehearsal seemed to have been specially coined for him. In fact, for Renzo life seemed to be a command performance in which he constantly had to give his all. He gave it to his village, Dulcino, on the edge of which his house stood. He was mayor and had represented the village on all sorts of committees and councils since he was old enough to do so.

'You should come in now, Michael. It's getting cold out there. It gets cold quickly in the Valtellina at this time of year.'

'Why do you respect the dead so much here, Renzo?' Michael said, without turning. 'You seem to be in awe of them . . . or maybe you're just afraid of them . . . I don't know.' The tired voice faded into nothing and the eyes, briefly filled, emptied again.

Renzo stared at Michael for an instant, as if he did not understand and then stepped back through the doorway, back into the real world.

Outside, night continued to slide down the sides of the mountains.

He came in shortly afterwards, shivering as he stepped through the doors that divided the darkness that now enveloped the valley from the electric light that illuminated the interior of the house.

'Michael, at last.' It was Giovanna, Renzo's wife, wiping

7

her hands on her brightly-coloured apron as she emerged from the kitchen. She was the possessor of the darkest eyes Michael had ever seen. They had an opaque quality that belied her warm, generous nature. Giovanna and Michael had become good friends and confidants overs the years. She always listened patiently to his troubles without criticism – even when he knew it was well deserved. In such circumstances, he would almost prefer to turn to her rather than to his wife who would rapidly become impatient with him and tell him to stop being so self-indulgent. The aromas of cooking followed Giovanna into the room. She walked over to him and took both his hands in hers.

'I thought you were going to stay out there all night!' She shivered, clasping his cold hands. 'Oh, but you're freezing. Come over and warm yourself.' She led him over to the fire that blazed in a corner of the room and sat him down on the long sofa that stretched in front of it. Voices interspersed by bursts of music came from a television. At this time of day, it was constantly switched on, providing a noisy backdrop to the routines of the household. She turned to face him on the sofa, a serious, concerned look on her face.

'We don't want you getting ill, Michael. You have to take care of yourself, especially when you go home, when you're on your own again.'

'You don't have to worry, Giovanna. I can take care of myself.'

'I know that, Michael, but I also know that it's time you went home. I know it feels soon, but you need to start getting on with your life. You're thirty-three, not that old. You've got your career. You need to get busy again.'

'You're absolutely right, Giovanna. But I just need to think about it all a bit more . . . You know what I'm like.' He smiled, a rarity lately.

They were interrupted by a sudden high-pitched yell that came from a far corner of the house. At the same time, they both turned their heads in the direction from which it came.

'I told the children to finish their homework and that doesn't sound like homework to me!' She sighed and began to rise. 'I'd better see what's going on.'

She bustled off towards the back of the house and within a few seconds came a stream of angry Italian, in the middle of which he heard his name.

He sat back on the sofa, sinking deep into its generous upholstery and stared at the ceiling as if there was something of great interest up there. Gradually, the television intruded on his concentration, however, and he turned his attention to it as an advert in which a faded American actor to whom he was unable to put a name was attempting to sell dog food. It came to an end and the urgent tones of the music that introduced the evening news filled the room.

The first item was the same one that had filled Italian TV screens for three-and-a-bit weeks now – the kidnapping in broad daylight of Teresa, the thirty-five-year-old daughter of the Italian industrialist, Luigi Ronconi. The kidnapping had great local interest, firstly because it had happened in one of the towns that lined Lake Como and, secondly, because Luigi Ronconi had been born in a Valtellina village, not far away from where Michael now sat, but was now one of Italy's wealthiest men. Added to that, he was a war hero and a ruthless businessman. Nothing had been heard of the woman or the kidnappers since the incident and, lacking anything new to say, the programme raked over the ashes of the case, showing old and familiar footage: the shots of the bar where the kidnapping had taken place, the interview with the bar owner who had been powerless to intervene and the testimony of the valiant shopkeeper, Alfio Bonfadini, whose nose had been broken by what was described as a ruthless and vicious gang as he tried to stop them. He was now a hero and the papers were full of pictures of him, face black and blue and plasters crisscrossing his swollen, broken nose.

That item concluded, the news drifted into yet another story about a government official who had been caught up in corruption. Michael wondered why they were surprised. It was a way of life in this country, after all.

He searched for the remote control and killed the television, the newsreader's sculpted hair momentarily turning a shade of iridescent purple as the screen shut down.

That night, it seemed to Michael as if he was beginning to re-enter the world. Sitting at the dinner table with Renzo, Giovanna and their two children, passing plates of bresaola and pasta and salad, entering once again into commerce with the day-to-day business of the world. The meal passed in an uncharacteristically quiet manner, however; the children, as they had done for the last few weeks, treated him like a ghost, not daring to speak, afraid, almost, that just one word would make him fall to pieces. Renzo and Giovanna tiptoed around things, and were selective in their topics of conversation.

For his part, he was conscious of their needs as a family, their need to trade in the events of their day, to exchange conversation like currency, maintaining a knowledge that made them whole, that bound them together.

Consequently, he made his excuses early and fled to his bedroom. Once there, he stared out into the blackness of the valley, seeing nothing, before closing the shutters. A whole world was carrying on out there, but he sensed none of it. He threw off his clothes and crumpled onto the bed, lying there in the dark, listening to the muffled voices coming from the other side of the house, their sounds interrupted by the hoot of an owl or the bark of a dog on the far side of the valley, a bark echoed along its length as if a message was being passed from one to another. Now and then there would be the laughter of a group of kids passing on the lane in front of the house, but to him it was all like radio waves from another planet, another world. A world that he had once inhabited.

Eventually he drifted into sleep, carefully keeping to one side of the bed as if an electric current ran down the other.

Blue.

Blue was all he could see at first. A sea of dancing blue whose waves crashed against the walls and splashed against the ceiling.

Then, slowly, more began to leak into his cracked vision. A desk, a few feet from the bottom of the bed, and on it a thick, leather-bound book. A jacket – his own? – hanging over the back of a wicker chair in the corner.

Just on the edge of his vision he sensed something massive and silent. Painfully – the pain was in his neck and shoulders – he turned his head and discovered the oppressive bulk of an ancient armoire, the possessor, it seemed to him, of many dark secrets which lay like hidden bodies behind its massively mirrored doors.

The blue was draining out of the room now, seeping under the door and oozing through the slats of the shutters which lay fast against the light of the sun to his right.

The ceiling began to shimmer, as if light were being reflected onto it from the surface of a swimming pool. From outside came the sound of water lapping gently against stone.

He began to feel as though he was watching rain fall on a watercolour. His vision dripped in long, slow elongations down the page of the room, and just as he became aware that somewhere, in someone else's dream, he knew this room, a

11

car – a blue car – drove silently and, somehow, miraculously, without dislodging bricks or plaster, through the wall directly in front of him. Oddly, the sound he heard was not that of an engine revving but rather, wings flapping, the sound getting louder and louder.

Meanwhile, on the car's bonnet, like an insane marionette, sprawled the body of a woman – his wife.

He woke sitting bolt upright, rivulets of sweat dripping down between his shoulder blades. And yet it was cold. It was November and, as Renzo had told him, the nights quickly became chilled. The stones no longer held the warmth of the day long after dark as they did in late autumn, and windows and shutters had to be closed tightly. He groaned and held his head in his hands. The clock on his bedside table showed that it was only twenty past two and he realised that the night stretched before him like a desert.

He lay back on his pillow, rubbing his tired eyes.

She was gone. Rosa was dead. They had buried her a few days ago. From now on, he thought, he would miss her hand on his as they landed at Milan's airport. A descent that he had often likened to sliding down the spirals of a coiled spring. One minute you are tiptoeing across the Alps, the next, arcing round and round in sweeping curves down over the flickering metropolis. She always alleviated his fear of flying with this laying on of hands, somehow conveying a part of her calmness to him.

He remembered, too, how she had often observed that he attached himself to things, limpet-like, and crumpled like a paper bag at any sign of their departure. Parting always felt like a little death to him, and death, well, it felt as if a giant hand hovered over his small life, ready to crush it as if on a whim. Now this, the only person in the world who had seemed to be entirely one with him – she, too, had become part of his terror and it seemed as if a vastness stretched in front of him he could not possibly fill.

You get to know so much about a person, he thought. You invest your understanding, the very shell of your existence in them, sense things about them that they have yet to feel and then they are gone. A light goes out and never comes on again. A door closes on a darkened room in which no one will ever again set foot.

As his mind stumbled slowly towards sleep, his memory began to freewheel. Unrelated images flooded through it in a torrent. A slide show of their relationship flashed on his cerebral cortex; but it was an art-house version. Light seeped into and out of the edges of each frame – some moved slowly, some at speed. He saw them walking along the cliff edges of the Dorset coast, saw them entwined in their bed, laughing uproariously; saw them arguing across that same bedroom – about nothing, as is often the case – and finally, trying to push the images away, trying to replace the sequence of events, saw them walking down the track from Renzo's house, talking about nothing, really; saw them cross the road; saw her stop at the side of the road, looking through the lens of her camera at the mountains, while he went into the shop – for some sweets for Renzo and Giovanna's children, for God's sake; and he heard the dull thud and then the racing engine that made him turn around, dropping his money to the floor. Seeing the blue car, he was unsure what make or model, a bird, he thought, depicted on its rear bumper, disappearing around the corner. It was colourful and not very big, painted or stuck onto the left-hand side of the vehicle's boot as he remembered. Its wings seemed large, its head tiny. But he could not be sure. He caught sight of it – no more than a fleeting glimpse, really – but, just then, everything was moving so fast, and yet so slow at the same time. At that exact moment, his thoughts were only for Rosa whose broken body lay awkwardly at the side of the road.

Finally, he saw himself a few days later throwing a handful of dirt into her grave in the little Italian cemetery, heard it rattle on the coffin lid like shrapnel.

He woke while the house still slept, a dull ache throbbing in his head. He had a cold coming on, perhaps from standing too long out on the balcony the previous evening. In the kitchen he was searching for headache pills as Renzo walked in, yawning and running his hands through jet-black, poker-straight hair, his slippers dragging noisily across the floor tiles.

'Good morning, Michael. You're up early. Couldn't sleep?' He reached for the kettle.

'Oh, I slept on and off through the night, Renzo, but it's just, you know, difficult to really shut out the thoughts.' He dropped two tablets into a glass of water. They began to fizz and he stirred and prodded at the mixture to break them down more quickly.

'I understand, Michael. We all do. We miss her, too. I just can't get used to the idea that I won't see my big sister again. It's almost more than I can bear.' He put a sympathetic hand on Michael's shoulder and then began to take plates for breakfast down from the cupboard above the sink.

'But at least I've made a decision, Renzo. I'm going home today, if I can get a flight.'

Renzo stopped laying the table and looked up. 'Really? You know you don't have to, Michael,' he said. 'You know you're free to stay as long as you like. Are you sure?'

'I'm really grateful, Renzo. You've all been very kind to me, you've always been kind to me. But it's time. I need to get back there to start dealing with it, get on with stuff. And

14

there are people to see, things to take care of. Insurance, things like that, you know? And my job. They told me to take as long as I liked, but I've been gone more than a month. I should get back.'

'You know what's best for you, Michael, but remember you can come back here any time you want.' He laid the plates on the table and Michael swallowed the diluted pills and retreated once again to his room.

He got on the phone and succeeded in booking a flight from Linate airport for the late afternoon. He started packing, moving like a ghost from wardrobe to bed, throwing his own things into his suitcase, but apart from the rolls of film she had shot in the days preceding her death, he left Rosa's belongings behind – he was unable to face that yet.

Later, after a hurried lunch as dark clouds stalked the sun around one, Michael kissed Giovanna and the children farewell and could almost feel the relief descend on the house as Renzo drove him away down the long driveway, carefully taking a detour to avoid passing the spot, festooned with faded flowers, where Rosa had been killed. They travelled along the side of Lake Como, through long tunnels, water running down their insides, past hidden villas, then through Milan's suburbs to Linate airport.

Before long he was being pushed back in his seat as the plane spiralled upwards in its long slow climb towards an altitude sufficient to take it over the Alps and then on across France, landing at Heathrow in the rainy gloom of early evening.

3

The flat seemed to have taken a deep breath in his absence. The air hung heavily above the few bits of furniture that he and Rosa had spent long weekends choosing in markets and in huge furniture warehouses back when they had moved in together. Each piece was like a time capsule to him, speaking to this future self that he had suddenly and reluctantly become.

He placed his suitcase by the door and bent down to pick up the pile of post that lay on the mat, a month's worth of circulars, free papers and bills. He walked into the living room, switching on the light and putting the detritus from the mat on a table. He looked around, as if he had walked into a strange hotel room and was sizing up its possibilities.

For a moment it seemed no longer to belong to him. Its relevance to his life had been stripped away in his absence and he had the sudden desire to be rid of the whole place and everything in it, to start anew. But, he thought, it is, after all, only bricks and mortar and a few chairs and tables. What would he do but replace this collection of bricks and mortar with another one more or less the same, only in a different place? And, in any case, was he ready to become involved with estate agents and solicitors and the whole enervating rigmarole of moving house? He thought not.

The bedroom had always been dark, overlooked as it was by some very large trees whose branches sometimes came crashing down in winter storms. Indeed, a branch had once exploded through their window in the middle of the night, like a giant arm come to lift them out of bed. They had instinctively reached towards each other, even in their half-slumber.

He could not sleep in their bed tonight. Instead, he rolled the quilt up in his arms and carried it awkwardly into the living room, dropping it in a heap on the sofa.

He felt as if he had to shut down this world and its attack on his senses and his memory. Everywhere he looked, he felt as if a dart was being pushed into him. Vases, pictures, tables, chairs, carpets – each of them assumed a life of some sort as his eyes fell on them, each of them dredged some instance or other out of his memory and played it like an old family video in his head.

He went to sleep without even unpacking. After all, he had the rest of his life to unpack things.

Before very long, he woke once again, in that blue, rippling room and once more there was the sound of flapping wings before the wall was burst asunder by the bonnet of a blue car, Rosa's body lying limp and broken across it.

'Michael. I don't know what to say.'

John Appledore had been Rosa's closest professional, and

probably also personal, friend during the last few years. They had shared the rent on a studio in a run-down part of East London and had fed off each other's work. That their relationship was anything other than purely professional, Michael had no fears because John was gay and happily ensconced in a long-term relationship. A good-looking, funny man, he was also a brilliant photographer. While Rosa's work had become increasingly commercial, appearing more and more regularly in newspapers and magazines in the last few years, John had been gaining a reputation for innovative and, frankly, startling photos. His work had begun to appear in upmarket magazines and next year an exhibition of his work was due to be held in New York, a city in which he was spending ever-increasing amounts of his time.

They embraced on the doorstep and Michael winced at the thought of how many times in the coming weeks he would have to endure the well-meaning words and sentiments that followed.

'I was devastated ... well you probably know from that awful phone call I made to you. I'm sorry, I should have thought of you and how you were feeling, but I couldn't help it. It's just ... just so unbelievable that she's gone.' He broke down, putting his hand to his eyes, wiping away the beginnings of tears.

'I know ... Come on, John. Let me get you a drink.' Michael put one arm around John's shoulder, leading him into the kitchen and sitting him down while he poured two over-large whiskies.

John took a sip, shuddering as the spirit caught the back of his throat.

'You know, I do wish you would have let us come to the funeral. It can't have been easy for you to handle on your own.'

'Actually, I think if you had come it might have been even more difficult for me to handle. Don't ask me why . . . You just make these decisions . . . I thought that if you and Steven or any of our friends had been there, it would have made it all seem somehow even more final.' He held his head in his hands. 'Christ, at times like that you make the strangest decisions for the strangest reasons. None of it makes any sense. It probably never could.'

John lifted his glass to his lips once again, draining it and reaching for the bottle which stood between them.

'God, I don't know why I let you poison me with this stuff,' he said, grimacing. 'It makes me feel sick when I drink it and makes me feel sick after I *stop* drinking it.'

'Yes, but you should really stop after the first bottle,' Michael said and they both smiled. How many times had he, Rosa and John drunk themselves into helpless giggles in this room over the last few years? And how many times was he going to have to relive the events of his life with Rosa in the familiar places in which they occurred? Would it always be like this?

'How are you feeling, anyway?' John asked, as Michael filled his glass again. 'I mean really.'

'Oh, I don't know, John. How am I supposed to feel? Exhausted, empty, sad, sorry for myself . . . all of that and a whole lot more.'

'You do know that if there's anything Steven and I can do . . .'

Once again, the feeling that these were words that he was going to hear a great deal during the next few weeks.

'Thanks, John. I'll be fine. But look, there is actually one thing you could do. I have the last few rolls of film that Rosa took.' He stood up and picked up a plastic bag containing rolls of film that he'd placed on a table. I wonder if you could . . .?'

'Of course, Michael. I'll develop them for you.' He beamed. At last there was something he could do to be helpful. 'Were they taken in Italy?'

'I think so, although I'm not really sure. She disappeared quite a lot during the six days before the accident.' He swallowed hard as he said the words. 'I'm afraid we argued about it. She took the car we'd hired and I was stuck in the house with nowhere to go until she got back. More stupid, bloody arguments. What a waste of precious time.' He thought of them arguing quietly across their bedroom in Renzo and Giovanna's house so that no one could hear them. Observing the niceties – a very English habit.

'Had you been arguing a lot, then?' There was reluctance in John's voice as he asked this question. It felt like he was about to get in too deep and he did not want his view of this relationship between two of his best friends to be altered, especially as it was now gone forever. He would rather preserve it as he had known it. However, the question had to be plucked out of the air where it had been left hanging by Michael.

'As you've seen often enough, Rosa and I were always at each other. It was just the way we were. I suppose, though . . .' He hesitated, recalling the pain of their last few weeks together. '. . . we had been arguing a bit more than usual. That was one of the reasons we decided to go to Italy. We'd both been under quite a bit of work pressure – she was doing the book and trying to earn some money and I was up to my eyes in political shenanigans for the *Post*. To be honest, we'd hardly spent any time in each other's company for weeks, maybe months. We thought that being with Renzo, Giovanna and the kids again would bring us back to ourselves, bring us back to where we had been. And a little taste of her Italian homeland might be relaxing for her.'

21

'And it wasn't working?' John reached for the whisky bottle and helped himself to another drink, filling Michael's glass at the same time.

'No, I don't think so. She had kind of climbed inside herself.' Michael sipped at his drink. 'I'm sure you've seen that in her, John. You know, all her life people took Rosa to be a calm person, unflustered by crisis, totally centred, when all around people were losing themselves in panic. I think it probably paid off for her in her work. Some of those pictures she took in Ireland – remember, the ones of the kids throwing stones at the army – they had something about them, something calm and focused in the eye of the beholder. It often worked like that. But she told me it wasn't calm. It was what she called nothingness – she said, just nothingness. Those words stuck in my mind, John. She was irritated by the lack of it in others and when she encountered that she would simply throw the 'off' switch. Frankly, she could become strangely emotionless for one who was normally so sensitive.' He felt a sharp pang of guilt as he said it, but continued: 'She once told me how when her father died and her mother's life was in tatters, she felt as if she was watching it all take place on a roll of film. Naturally, I expect she evolved, as ever, into the steady fulcrum at the centre of the drama, the organiser, the maker of tea, the acceptor of wreaths, the recipient of doorstep whispers from caring friends and relatives.'

Michael explained how she would afterwards have to face her own coldness, how she would burn herself on the icy edge of her emotionless being and, as she had confessed to him with tears boiling up at the corners of her dark eyes, could not even find the words to ease her mother's pain of loss.

John leaned forward.

'Look, Michael, we can't help what we are. We're the sum of our lives and no more. Of course, I've seen this in

Rosa, but remember, she was also an immensely talented human being who used that distance to create terrific work. The obituaries in the papers – you may not have seen them; remind me to send them to you – spoke of her as a lost opportunity for photography, a great loss. She was a fabulous artist. Her work is a testament to that and, believe me, it'll be remembered.' He looked down, momentarily saddened. 'But all that aside, Michael, I'll just miss having her around, her sense of humour . . . and the invaluable advice she used to give me back in the day about my mad love life!' They both laughed. 'But she hadn't been herself in recent months. She told me it was the pressure of putting together the book, but I began to wonder if maybe there was something else going on that she wasn't telling me.'

Michael shook his head and said, 'Nothing that I'm aware of, John.'

After a moment's silence, John asked, 'So, what about the book? Will it still happen; can it still be finished?'

Michael had tried not to think too much about it. It meant travelling back inside himself to a landscape that he did not yet feel ready to visit. The book that was due to be published the following year had been a large part of Rosa's life for the past three years and the trip to Italy, as well as being an attempt to re-awaken their relationship, was also meant to be the opportunity for her to put the finishing touches to it, including the addition of a few final pictures to the magnificent portfolio of landscapes that she had constructed.

'I really don't know yet, John. It was almost done, as far as I know.' And then, feeling tears fill his eyes, 'I can't really get to this just yet.' He wiped his hands across his face and breathed deeply. 'I guess that's something else I need to do – get in touch with the publishers and find out what they want me to do.'

They both stared into the middle distance, not really having much more to say to each other. They both knew instinctively that there was simply an emptiness in their relationship that would never again be filled. John knew that he would drift apart from Michael, that Rosa had been the mortar in this friendship and without her, it would inevitably crumble.

'I'll develop these rolls tomorrow and send you the contact sheets so that you can let me know which ones I should do more work on,' John said, standing at the door, Michael's hand grasped tightly in his own.

'Thank you, John.'

'And remember, Michael, if you need anything, if I can help in any way just give me a call,' he said, turning as he walked down the steps to the road where a taxi was waiting. Guiltily, he felt a sense of relief as he sank into the back-seat of the cab and waved to Michael, smiling as reassuringly as he could.

Michael, too, felt relief as he closed the door and walked back into the lounge. He poured himself another drink – one too many, he thought – and sat down on the sofa, where within a few minutes he had fallen into a deep and, for once, thanks to the whisky, dreamless sleep.

Michael pulled back the curtains and watched a leaf drifting slowly down onto the lawn at the back of the house. There was something odd about it and it only struck him as it settled gently on the grass that it was quite a way from any trees and yet was falling in a vertical manner as if it had fallen from heaven rather than from a tree on earth. He smiled to himself at the thought and turned towards the kitchen to make a cup of coffee. His head felt thick from the whisky of the previous night and his neck was stiff from the position in which he had lain on the sofa. The cold he had felt developing in Italy was beginning to make its presence known and he searched for a piece of kitchen roll to blow his nose and clear his head.

It was seven-thirty and today he would go into the office to pick up whatever pieces he could. He worked in the newsroom of the London *Evening Post*, a competitive arena in which the time he had spent in Italy could spell trouble for him. Stories had come and gone during his absence. He knew the longer he had been away, the more difficult it would be to get back into the best assignments. These thoughts were worrying him as he walked into the living room and caught sight of the pile of post where he had placed it on the table in the corner. All day yesterday he had ignored it as he busied himself around the flat. He decided he had better sort through it to see if anything demanded his immediate attention.

After sorting through the free newspapers stuffed with leaflets and flyers, he had to take a deep breath before dealing with the post. Rosa's name was on the front of a number of the envelopes and it was hard for him. Bills – electricity, phone, gas. A couple of attempts by credit companies to get him and/or Rosa to take out loans or open accounts with them. He sorted them into piles – those that would go straight into the bin and those that would have to be dealt with in the next few days. There was a letter from an old friend of his who lived abroad and, with the outline of part of a footprint on one side of it, a card from the Royal Mail with Rosa's name on the front, saying that it had tried unsuccessfully to deliver a parcel to her. It said he had twenty-eight days to collect it from the sorting office or it would be returned to sender. He checked the date and discovered that he only had one day left before the deadline.

It was bound to be something that Rosa had ordered from a photographic catalogue, but his curiosity was aroused and he resolved to go down to the sorting office as soon as he was dressed. It wasn't far and the air would do him good after spending the whole of the previous day mooching around the house and then drinking far too much whisky last night.

The sorting office had a 1950s feel to it. It resembled a school building and reminded Michael a little of the large comprehensive school he had attended what seemed like another lifetime ago.

He followed a sign directing him to 'Collections', walking through a swing door into a dingy room with a large counter at one end.

In this obviously neglected space, Michael stood feeling similarly neglected. No one came and there was not a sound from anywhere. Behind the counter was a low partition beyond which there were rows of wooden shelving with pigeon holes filled with parcels of all shapes and sizes.

Soon a woman appeared and Michael explained he was collecting a parcel for his wife. The woman absently took the card, checked the address and disappeared into the dinginess behind the partition. She returned after a minute or so with a large brown paper parcel, about a foot by one-and-half feet in size. A typed, white label showed Rosa's name. Michael showed the woman his driving licence for ID, signed a form and left the office clutching the parcel.

It was soft to the touch and sealed so completely with brown packing tape that, when he got home, he was forced to hunt down a pair of scissors to open it. Inside, wrapped in a piece of thin clear plastic of the kind dry-cleaners use to wrap clothes, he was surprised to find a man's jacket. He searched for a letter or a note accompanying it and found one in an unsealed envelope, its letter-head denoting that it was from a hotel, the Lighthouse Inn, in Dumfriesshire, Scotland. Puzzled, his eyes quickly took in the short message written on it:

Dear Mrs Keats, we are delighted to be able to return to you a jacket found in the room you occupied during your stay in our hotel in September. We hope to see you again at the Lighthouse Inn soon.' It was signed *'J. Stewart, Manager.*

Michael's eyes returned to the jacket. It was light brown with a faint check of a darker hue stitched through it. *Expensive*, he thought, looking at the label, which displayed an Italian name of which he had never heard. But that was no surprise to him. Fashion and clothes had never been much of an abiding interest with him.

He put the jacket on, approving of the lightness of its cloth, but found that its chest size was at least a couple of sizes bigger than his thirty-eight. The sleeves hung down below his fingertips and the shoulders dropped a couple of inches too low. The owner was undoubtedly a big chap, he thought, eyeing himself in the long mirror that formed one of the doors of a wardrobe in the bedroom. *Shame*, he thought. *I might have just hung on to it had it fitted.*

This was obviously some kind of mistake. Rosa had not, to his knowledge, been in Scotland recently. She *had* gone away in September, the month that the note claimed she had been at the Lighthouse Hotel, but that had been a trip to Newcastle on a photographic assignment for some magazine or other.

Certain that a mistake must have been made, Michael pulled off the jacket, laid it on the bed and resolved to ring the Lighthouse Inn later that day to let them know that they were mistaken and that he would post it back to them.

As he got ready to head into town, however, it nagged at him, tugging at his thoughts. Whenever he tried to push it to one side it would return, like one of those irritating flies that can plague you in a hot climate. You swat them away and within a minute or two they return to buzz around your food or drink. How had the hotel come to connect Rosa with this item of clothing? It was unlikely, after all, that there was another combination of names like hers in the country – Rosa Keats – and, apart from that, how would they have come into possession of her address?

'Hello, Lighthouse Inn, Mary speaking. How may I help you?' The voice was soft and musical. He asked to be put through to 'J. Stewart' and explained the reason for his call.

'Well, Mr Keats, the thing is . . .' – there was hesitancy in J. Stewart's voice because the delicacy of the situation had suddenly made itself very apparent to her. Husband receives man's jacket in post. Jacket doesn't belong to him but has been left behind by male companion of his wife. '. . . The point is, we were quite certain the jacket belonged to Mrs Keats's companion because we had the room refurbished shortly before their stay, but found out after they left that the plumber had made a right mess of some of the pipes and water was leaking down onto the ceiling of the room below. When the bed was moved to lift the floorboards, we found the jacket.' She hesitated, before adding nervously, 'But, of course, there might be some other explanation.' There was a silence at the other end. 'I'm sorry,' she said, eventually.

Surely not, he thought. *Oh, Rosa, surely not*. There must be some kind of mistake. Ten minutes after he had hung up, he was staring out of the window watching the world go about its business as if nothing had happened, as if everything had not just taken a step in the wrong direction. He had been too embarrassed to pursue the matter further with 'J. Stewart' and sensed that she was relieved when he brought the brief conversation to an abrupt close.

They had her address. She had evidently given them that, unashamedly; had had no fears at all about being found out. God, she had been having an affair! What a quaint, old-fashioned way of putting it, he thought – 'an affair'. Someone else, the owner of this fine, expensive, Italian-tailored jacket, had been screwing his wife.

His first instinct was to pick up the phone and speak to someone, find someone who would tell him what he wanted to hear, that he was being paranoid, that this was all some silly mistake. He started to dial John's number, but stopped after his finger had angrily pushed three numbers and replaced the receiver, realising that it would mean nothing. What could John do to reassure him? No. Even if he was just being paranoid, he somehow had to prove it. Tears of sadness and frustration began to form in the corners of his eyes. As if the grief and the hurt of her death had not been enough, now he was losing her life as well, was losing all the intimacy of the time they had spent together.

He pressed his face to the glass of the window, his breath spreading mist across it, and moaned like a sick animal.

'Oh, dear God, Rosa, how could you . . .?'

The cold November rain splintered on his windscreen, the wipers sweeping furiously from side to side, but failing to make much of an impression on it. The heavens had opened up at Preston and he had been slowed considerably. Lorries, whose sides shouted about the glories of frozen chips or nappies, sped north showering his BMW with spray every time he overtook them, adding to the tiredness that was making the drive so difficult.

He hardly knew why he was doing this, driving to Dumfriesshire in the hope that he could prove that it was all some kind of mistake. It was so important to him that he prove that this was, indeed, the case. If he couldn't, then the last few years of his life would be completely invalidated. The relationship into which he had invested a vital part of himself would crumble into dust and where would that leave him? Just the thought of it filled him with horror.

The alternative was, of course, to just let it go. Put it down as some bizarre error. Some confusion of identity. Some mistake on his part. Or some miscalculation by Rosa. Perhaps someone had stolen her credit card. Sure, she had not told him it had gone missing, but, of course, she didn't tell him everything. Perhaps she had just forgotten. They were busy people. There were days when she would be working at the studio until late into the night and he would be fast asleep by the time she came home and flopped into bed. His hours were equally unstable and they had often been like ships that passed in the night, or kissed on the stairs, one coming home, one just going out. Perhaps in the midst of this frenetic existence she had just forgotten to pass on the tiny domestic detail that her card had been stolen in the underground or she had left it at a restaurant and now someone else was using it fraudulently.

This thought had sustained him from Birmingham to Manchester, to the extent that he had come close to turning the car round and heading back to London. But it was no good. He knew she would have cancelled it if it had been lost or stolen and, therefore, it could not have been used by anyone else. No, he had to somehow make it certain in his mind one way or the other. To go back home and have to live with this doubt was unthinkable.

He had left the motorway some miles back and, after following the A75 for a distance that made him think he had gone too far, he came to the small town of Annan. Traffic was bad – it was early evening and the road was filled with people returning home from their day's work. He should have been doing the same himself, of course, but had phoned Harry, his boss at the *Evening Post*, this morning to say that he could not get back for another couple of days. Harry had reassured him that it was fine, but Michael had picked up just a tinge of irritation in Harry's voice. *Probably just having a tough day*, he thought, but just the same he reckoned it would be unwise to push his luck. At Annan he stopped to get petrol and peered in the dark glow of his interior light at a hotel guide that gave directions to the Lighthouse Inn. He pulled out of the petrol station, rain still spattering on the car windows and followed the sign for the coast road.

About seven miles later, the village he wanted was sign-posted to the left. It was dark by now and the road was narrow, barely wide enough to take two cars abreast. At least the rain had eased off, however, and the sky was beginning to clear, revealing a bright quarter moon scudding between the clouds.

He came to a village, which consisted of little more than a few houses and a shop, as far as he could see, and then followed the road along what appeared, in the dark, to be a rocky coastline. Then he saw a sign bearing a line drawing of a lighthouse with a beam spitting out of it on all sides. It announced that the Lighthouse Inn was one hundred yards further down the road on the right.

The Lighthouse Inn was an old sandstone building with an empty car park outside. It stood alone, staring grimly out to sea, its slightly lighter outline showing through the darkness. He took his overnight bag from the back of the car, the wind pulling at the car door as he struggled to shut it. He bent into it and ran the few paces to the hotel entrance.

31

The roar of the wind disappeared suddenly as he closed the door. He placed his bag on the floor and stood there gathering himself, running his hand through his wind-tousled hair.

The Lighthouse Inn took its name seriously, indeed. Its walls were covered in framed photographs and paintings of lighthouses of every description. The window ledges held models of lighthouses, large and small. In the far corner was what he took to be the workings of an old light – huge cogs interlinked and levers stuck out at irregular points. Ropes hung the length of the walls and had been stuck onto the bannisters of the stairs. The overall effect was that of a concept carried too far.

He approached the desk which, like every other surface, was edged with rough rope. The only sound was the cracking and spitting of a large fire, which roared into a huge chimney to his right.

'Hello?' He said hesitantly, before repeating it, almost shouting. 'HELLO!'

He then turned and surveyed once again the bits of lighthouse that surrounded him.

A distant door opened and the sound of a familiar piece of music emerged – the theme tune to some TV soap or quiz show, he couldn't quite remember. TV wasn't really his thing.

'Good evening, sir, welcome to the Lighthouse Inn.'

She was about twenty-five or so, attractive with blonde hair tied back in a pony-tail and wearing a blue skirt and a similarly-coloured jumper. Her skin had a slight glow about it, the glow that comes from sitting too close to a good fire.

'Good evening. I'd like a room, please.' He put his bag on the floor and rubbed his hands together to get some feeling back into them after the iciness of the wind outside.

'Would that just be for the one night, sir?' she said, handing him a form on which were spaces for his name, address and credit card details.

'Yes, I think so,' he replied.

'Well, if you change your mind and want to stay longer, it won't be a problem. We're a wee bit quiet at the moment.' Her Scottish accent was soft and precise and she had a slow, lambent smile that, when it flickered across her face, struck him as being well worth the wait.

'Is Mrs Stewart in tonight?' he asked, handing her the completed form and reaching into his pocket for his wallet so that she could swipe his credit card.

'Oh no, Jacquie went home ages ago, but she'll be in early tomorrow morning.' She handed him his key, directing him to the first floor and added. 'Enjoy your stay . . . Oh, and if you're hungry or want a drink, the bar's open.' She indicated a doorway to his left, under the stairs. 'The restaurant's closed tonight, but I can do you a toasted sandwich and some salad, if you want.'

'Thanks, I think I might just take you up on that,' he replied, smiling. 'Give me fifteen minutes to freshen up.'

'See you in fifteen minutes then,' she said, filing away his form and letting another of those smiles drift across her face.

The hotel had an out-of-season atmosphere. It felt as if it were in hibernation. Needless to say, his room persisted with the lighthouse theme. The walls once again provided a photographic record, it seemed, of every lighthouse in the world and the window was round like an enlarged porthole. Nonetheless, it was clean, comfortable and quite spacious.

He emptied his bag, laying the jacket he had been sent carefully on the bed. He showered quickly and changed into a fresh shirt and pair of black jeans before heading downstairs once again in the direction of the bar.

The girl was behind the bar, pulling at one of the pumps

and emptying the results into a slops pail that stood in the sink. The walls around her were decorated with still more pictures of lighthouses and mysterious brass items – pieces of the workings of lighthouses sat on shelves.

'Hello!' she said cheerily as he entered, 'I hope everything's alright with the room?'

'Oh, yes thanks, absolutely fine,' he replied. 'A bit heavy on the lighthouse theme, but I can live with it.'

'I know what you mean.' She laughed as she spoke. 'You should hear the locals about it! It's not as if there's even a light-house for miles around! Now, if you'd like to choose a filling for your sandwich, I'll get you a drink. What would you like?'

He looked down at a hand-written menu she had handed him. 'Cheese and ham would be fine and a pint of . . .' He surveyed the unfamiliar names on the pumps and selected one at random. 'A pint of that, please,' he said, indicating his choice with a nod of his head.

She poured it, her face a mask of concentration and her tongue sticking out of the corner of her mouth. He got the impression that this was not a part of hotel work with which she was totally familiar.

'And will you join me?' he asked, pulling out his wallet.

'Oh, I shouldn't really, but . . . well go on then!' she laughed. 'I'll have a gin and tonic, if that's alright.' She put the pint of beer down in front of him. 'I think I deserve it. I've been on duty since the crack of dawn and the guy who was supposed to be doing the bar tonight phoned in with flu, so I'm here until the death.'

'The joys of the catering industry, eh?' He said taking a long draught from his glass.

'Yes indeed. I've just about had enough of it.' she replied. 'Now, cheese and ham you said, didn't you?' She disappeared in the direction of the kitchen to prepare his sandwich.

He climbed onto a stool at the bar and began to eat his sandwich there when it arrived. She polished glasses and sipped intermittently at her gin.

'Business?' she asked.

'Pardon?' he mumbled through a hot mouthful of ham and melted cheese.

'Is it business that brings you here?'

'Oh, erm, yes. Well, business and coincidence, really.'

'Coincidence? What do you mean?' she asked, becoming curious. He had prepared his story as he had showered and it came out, he thought, like the truth.

'Well, it's a bit complicated. You see, my sister stayed here a few months ago, with a friend of hers and it seems this friend left a jacket behind. Your Mrs Stewart sent the jacket to my sister's address and ... well ... the truth is, my sister died a month ago and I don't know who the jacket belongs to. If she was close to someone, I'd really like to meet him.' It sounded quite plausible, he thought.

'Oh, I *am* sorry,' she said, and he realised with relief that she actually had no reason not to believe what he was saying. 'I mean to hear about your sister's death, and all. That must have been a blow. I presume she wasn't that old.' She stopped polishing the glass in her hand and put it on the bar-top.

'Yes, it was, and she wasn't,' he sighed, 'It was very sudden,' he added, warming to his subject. 'And then to find that she had been here seemingly with a friend, a male friend at that, that none of us knew about ... well, it was a bit of a surprise, as you can imagine.' He had been staring at his knotted fingers and looked up at that moment partly for effect and partly to gauge whether she was, in fact, buying his story. She was, however, nodding sympathetically, with a concerned look in her eyes. 'We were close – she told me everything – so I thought at first that some kind of mistake had been made,' he went on. 'Anyway, long story short, I happened to be passing on my way to Glasgow and decided to come here to see if I could find out anything about this shadowy friend. At the very least I could let him know what has happened to her if he doesn't already know.'

He felt guilt at this fabrication, but it seemed to be having the desired effect. Her interest was well and truly aroused.

'Oh, but perhaps I could be of help. When did she stay here?'

'It would have been in September.'

'And her name?'

'Keats . . . Rosa Keats, and her companion would have been a big guy, if his jacket is anything to go by. I have a photograph of her, if that would be any help.'

He fished out of his wallet the photo of Rosa that he had always carried with him. It had been taken in a restaurant before they had married. She had been caught laughing at something, holding her head in that peculiar way of hers, angled to one side like a puzzled bird, her dark hair, as ever, cascading down over her shoulders. He thought he could smell it, even now, as he handed over the photo.

'Och, yes, I remember this lady. What a shame. She was lovely.' She smiled sadly at him, holding the photo. 'What I should say really is that I remember the chap she was with. He wasn't all that young – in his fifties, I would think – but, God, he was really good-looking. In a kind of well-off way, you know? You know the way that rich people's skin glows in a funny way?'

He evidently did not.

She laughed again. 'You know, it's like the money oozes out of their pores; they look tanned all the time without having gone anywhere.' She smiled at the bewildered look on his face. 'Och, you know what I mean.'

'Okay, I think I do.' He smiled faintly. 'But tell me, did they have two rooms or did they share? I was wondering, erm, just how close they were. I may have this all wrong and he might just have been a business associate.'

He asked as nonchalantly as he could, but this was a question he would rather not ask, a question for which he would rather there was no answer. Nonetheless it was the question that he had travelled all this way to find the answer to. Whole lives can sometimes pivot around key moments. These are usually decisions that one makes – to decide on the spur of the moment to go to a party where you meet your soulmate; or to open a newspaper at a certain page and see a job that inalterably changes your life; or to step into a road that looks clear but, unknown to you, hides a juggernaut which is balling round a blind corner in your direction. Sometimes, however, hearing a single sentence that appears to the speaker quite innocent can move your life to another place entirely, in the same way that chaos theory asserts the familiar cliché that the innocent flap of a butterfly's wings in China can set off a chain of events that ends in an earthquake on the other side of the world.

'Oh, they shared, if I remember rightly. Yes, they had a double room.' She casually picked up another wet glass.

Michael felt the ground shift beneath his feet. His heart was riven by pain that was beyond the physical. If a soul could hurt then his was hurting greatly. The last few years unravelled like a film falling off a spool. The images in the frames seemed to slip out, fall to the floor and shatter. He grasped the edge of the bar to steady himself.

'Between you and me they seemed to be very much in love,' she went on. 'I waited on them in the restaurant – it was the waitress that phoned in sick that time – and they held hands and stared into each other's eyes all the way through the meal. She was so busy looking at him that she hardly ate anything. I remember that because Chef was bloody furious. He was all for going out and asking if there was something wrong with the food ... hey, are you alright?' she asked, looking curiously at him and noticing that something had changed in him, perhaps the colour draining from his face. 'Oh, I'm sorry, I'm being stupid, forgetting how difficult this must be for you; let me get you another drink.'

He asked for a Bowmore malt whisky with a little water, reviving slightly as the smoky liquor slipped down his throat.

Just then some locals entered the bar and she went off to serve them, exchanging noisy stories about the excesses of the weekend and leaving Michael alone with thoughts he would rather not have. Indeed, they were thoughts that several more malts failed to quell.

Eventually, the locals drifted off, noisily making their fare-wells, leaving Michael and the girl alone again in the bar. He was by now seated at a table and she came over to join him, sitting down with a sigh.

'He was Italian,' she said after a moment had passed.

'What? You mean ...' He ran his hand through his hair in exasperation. 'Italian?'

'Yes, your sister's friend, he was Italian. I heard them speaking Italian together and when he ordered his food, he had an accent. He was Italian. I thought you should know.'

'Oh, thank you. Thank you very much.' His words were quiet.

'But I'm afraid I don't know his name,' she went on.

'No?' he asked, disappointed, beginning to come to his senses and becoming curious.

'No. I'm afraid your sister signed the register as Mrs and Mr Keats and *she* paid with *her* Mastercard. I checked.' She got up and disappeared behind the bar for a moment, returning with a bottle of Champagne and a couple of glasses. Jacquie . . . Mrs Stewart . . . said I could help myself to a bottle for staying on late tonight and locking up. 'Like to join me?'

'Why not?' he replied, smiling.

'It's Helen, by the way. Helen Matthieson,' she said holding out a hand to him.

'And I'm Michael, he said shaking the hand.

'I know. I already checked it out on your registration card. Michael John Keats, to be precise. Very poetic. Would you be kind enough to do the honours?' She handed him the bottle and he removed the foil and the wire from around the cork. He was no expert at opening Champagne bottles, but he managed it without losing too much of the contents. He filled the two glasses she had brought and they raised them in a toast.

'To lighthousemen everywhere,' he said.

'To lighthousemen,' she replied, laughing and adding, 'Long may their lights shine!'

'I'm not sure it's a good idea for me to be drinking this, given that I've already had a pint and a few generous malts. You know what they say about mixing the grape and the grain.'

'Och, Champagne's absolutely the best idea there ever was,' she replied. 'Anyway, *carpe diem*, Michael. *Carpe diem.*'

There were a few moments of silence between them.

'How long were you married, then?' she said quietly, breaking the silence as she raised her glass to her lips, looking directly at him.

He had been lost in the sound of the wind raging outside, driving squally rain against the windows.

'Sorry?'

'Ah, Michael. That look in your eyes when I told you that they shared a room, Rosa and her companion. That wasn't the look of a brother trying to find a friend of his dead sister's.

39

That was the look of a lover wronged. For a moment you looked utterly destroyed.'

He looked at her, the feeling of devastation momentarily returning.

'Well? I'm not wrong, am I?'

A pause. He smiled.

'How old are you, Helen?'

'Oh, twenty-five going on sixty, my mother says.' A smile spread across her face. She had cut through the facade of his secret like a knife through rice-paper.

'She's not wrong, your mother,' he sighed. 'Yes. You're right. Rosa *was* my wife. When she was here, I thought she was actually in Newcastle on a photographic assignment. She was a photographer ... and ...' The alcohol, tiredness and the emotion of the last month took hold of him. 'I'm sorry.'

'It must be awful. I understand.' She reached across and squeezed his hand. 'You obviously had no idea ...'

'None at all. I think that's what's making it so hard.'

And he told her the whole story, the shifting sands of their marriage, the photography, the trip to Italy, the blue car. She listened intently, the rain hammering on the windows of the bar.

He finished and felt like he had emptied himself. He felt, somehow, better for having shared his story with a virtual stranger.

'So, what now for Michael Keats?'

'Who the hell knows, Helen. I need to get back to work, I suppose. But I need to know, too, about this guy who's barged into my life, who was seeing my wife. I'd like to find out more. How long it was going on. I'd also like to find the driver of the car that killed Rosa. The Italian police don't seem to be getting very far. Those two things would close the circle for me and I think I could kind of get on with my life.'

'That would mean going back to Italy for a while?'

'Possibly . . . I guess, yes.'

Helen yawned across the table from him.

'But look, you're knackered. When did you start work this morning?

'Oh . . .' she stifled another yawn. '. . . about six, I think.'

'So, time you went to bed, then!'

They both stood up.

'Breakfast is from seven o'clock. I'm on duty again.'

'You need to find another profession! But, thanks for the Champagne and for listening. I didn't mean to burden you with all my problems.'

'Sometimes, you know, all you need is to talk to someone.' She touched his arm. 'Goodnight, Michael. See you in the morning.'

As he climbed the stairs, he realised he had drunk a little more than he should have. He managed to get the key into the lock at the second attempt and entered the room. The jacket lay on the bed where he had left it on his arrival. He picked it up and held it at arm's length, swaying slightly from the cumulative effects of the beer, whisky and Champagne.

'Bastard! Bastard! Bastard!' he hissed, hot tears beginning to roll down his cheeks. He held it against his body as if he were in a shop trying on a jacket with a view to buying it and once again put it on, as if somehow that would make him feel better. The sleeves still dangled three inches below his fingertips and he wiped the tears from his cheeks with one of them. *This was one big bastard*, he thought. He put his hands into the pockets and eyed himself in the mirror. He looked like a little boy trying on his father's clothes. All at once, however, the passion left his body, his shoulders fell forward and he sighed and began to remove the jacket. He was about

41

to throw it back onto the bed when he felt something inside the lining at the hem, something rectangular and hard, like a small piece of card. He felt in the pockets and sure enough there was a hole in one. That'll teach you to put such fine lining on a jacket, he thought to himself as he folded it back so that he could reach two fingers down into the bottom corner where the card was lodged.

His fingers found it and lost it a couple of times before he was able to pull it out. 'Got you!' he breathed, looking at a business card. He mouthed the words written on it as he read them. 'Massimo Di Livio, Via Broletto No. 110, Milano.' There were simply those words and a phone number.

He stared into space wondering who this Di Livio character was. It need not necessarily be the same man who was having a fling with Rosa. It could be a business associate, anyone. But it was a start, a clue. He put the card carefully in his wallet, folded the jacket and climbed out of his clothes, kicking them off carelessly onto the floor, before crawling into bed. Before too long, the room stopped spinning and he drifted off into a shallow sleep.

Outside, rain had begun to rattle on the window once again and the waves beat against the coastline like a warning.

4

Fifty-six years had made a substantial difference to the valley that Michael Keats surveyed from Renzo's balcony in 1999.

In 1943 the villages were smaller and the distances between them greater; each did not possess its own urban sprawl. Instead, the houses huddled together as if for warmth, and the roads that ran between them did not shine blackly in the glare of the late afternoon sun as they did in 1999. Rather, back then they were mainly tracks, rivers of mud in winter and dust bowls in the searing heat of summer.

In fact, the valley possessed an altogether different colour back then; a greyer, darker tone hung over it and was present in its houses, as well as in its undergrowth and in its people. The style of construction made a large contribution to this difference in atmosphere. The walls of the buildings were

43

of dark stone and the roofs were of local slate, not the red, Mediterranean slates of factory-produced regularity that became fashionable in the nineties. In 1943 they were dark and ragged-edged in design, hewn by hand in the quarry. And even then, these buildings looked ancient, spilling out their insides and, in some cases, pursuing a centuries-long collapse into rubble, as if being swallowed up by the earth from whence they came.

In the distance the lake glowed as ever, on its shores two different stories being played out. On the Italian side, desperate people clutched suitcases. The Jews from Milan and Rome waited in a kind of purgatory, ready to escape through the mountain passes that in previous centuries had served as corridors for armies from Central Europe moving in one direction and armies from eastern Italy marching in another. For the Alps had, through those centuries, separated this part of Italy from the major shifts of European political and economic life.

On the other side, life went on in a more or less normal fashion, albeit a normality coloured by the shifting sands of the war. The air was rent by suspicion: suspicion of everything and everyone. Motives were always suspect and in these latter days of the war, this was wise, as fortunes were made quickly and, sometimes, lost even more quickly, as the future of the world was carved and laid out on tables in expensive restaurants.

Much had changed. The Allies had landed on mainland Italy during the first weeks of September, 1943 and by early October, they were in control of the whole of the south of the country. It was just the beginning of a grinding slog up through the rest of the country. Meanwhile, Benito Mussolini's rule of Italy had ended in July 1943 when the Italian Grand Council of Fascism had passed a vote of no confidence in his leadership. He had been replaced by Marshal Pietro Badoglio and arrested. The Kingdom of Italy – in reality, the southern part of the country – had signed an armistice with the Allies in September.

After his arrest, Mussolini was transported around Italy, firstly taken to small islands in the Tyrrhenian Sea, but by September was being held at Campo Imperatore in the Gran Sasso massif, high in the Apennine Mountains. It was from there, on the 12th September, that he was rescued by a detachment of Nazi commandos, under the orders of Adolf Hitler and flown to Munich, where he met with the Nazi Fuhrer. Hitler made him leader of a new puppet state – the Italian Social Republic, created from the northern part of Italy that the Germans still controlled. The state was popularly known as the Salò Republic, because it was run from the town of Salò on Lake Garda where Mussolini lived. But even though he was installed as *Duce*, he was no more than a pawn in the hands of the Germans who were still in charge in the north.

About a hundred and seventy kilometres from where Mussolini was pretending to be important again, eighteen-year-old Sandro Bellini's eyes were itching from the rubber eyepieces that were attached to the lenses of a pair of binoculars. For two hours he had been lying in almost the same position, high up the side of the valley, stretched uncomfortably across a large rock. Another, flatter slab of stone that had probably slid down the side of the mountain centuries ago sheltered him from the rain that had been falling for days and also hid him from view. The object of his rapt attention was a bend in the road a few hundred feet below him, as, indeed, it had been for the last week. Each morning he had risen from bed at four and, after washing down a piece of stale bread with a cup of water, had gone out into the wet darkness, walking the ten miles to his position, all the while climbing steadily into the skirt of mists worn by the mountains.

Every morning he would curse the weather and his jacket, which had long ago lost any capability of keeping him dry. His boots had also seen better days — unfortunately, long before they had come into his possession. Even the birds seemed to be under cover in these rainy, early winter days.

By the time of his arrival at his eyrie, the sun would have risen and he would take the opportunity before beginning his task to take in the view of this valley he loved so much. A small town sat in the distance, dominated by the bulk of the parish church of San Giovanni, centuries-old dwellings huddling around it in the early morning chill. His eyes moved to the right, to the bell tower of the church of San Pietro, in the village of Dulcino, five kilometres to the north and higher up the valley side. In their house just outside the village, his mother would have been awake for a couple of hours by now and would be preparing food and busying herself with the many chores that made up her day. His eyes strayed across the grey, uneven rooftops above which the smoke of early morning fires was beginning to rise and drift, towards another house no different to all the rest in the village of San Marco. He raised the binoculars to his eyes and the house grew in his vision, but not sufficiently for him. He put the glasses down and wiped the rain from his brow.

Now it was almost ten o'clock. For two hours there had been a silence broken only by the tapping of rain on the boulder above him and the occasional wing beats of a bird, but now that silence was ended by the sound of a powerful car engine in the distance. It was, however, still some way off.

He pulled the binoculars from his eyes and, for the hundredth time that morning, wiped the rain from his hair and forehead. Raising them again, he swept them across the bend in the road that was the object of his attention.

A minute later, the engine noise growing, a German staff car turned the corner, moving at speed, accompanied by a lorry filled with German infantrymen with rifles trained on the surrounding hills. The car swept past a long way below Sandro's outpost and disappeared in the direction of the town of San Marco, its occupants oblivious to the attentions of the observer in the hills above.

At last, Sandro was able to remove the binoculars from his eyes. He rolled over on the damp grass and stretched his aching body, looking up at the vast expanse of the sky. The morning was warming up and the clouds that had brought rain since first light were slowly beginning to break up.

God, how he loved this country. The valley stretched out in front of him, its mountains delineating his entire experience. He had walked them when he was younger, obsessively, for hours on end, rising at dawn, as he had this morning, wrapping some cold meat and cheese in a cloth and stuffing it in his knapsack, before quietly opening the door and stepping out into the half-light. Those were the very best moments, when few were stirring. True, people rose early in the village, but he always tried to be first, to make his mark on the morning, like making the first footsteps in freshly fallen snow. Upwards he would climb, out of the village and off the road, following whatever direction took his fancy.

Other times he would take rather more food and a blanket, tied in a roll, and would stay away for a night, or sometimes two or even three, often crossing to the other side of the valley and exploring it. And at those times, he would sometimes find himself on a promontory, staring back at life across the valley, knowing his mother would be, as ever, busy in the house or in the yard tending their few scruffy chickens and the goat that they owned. His father would be in their small vineyard, fussing with the branches of the vines, or pulling up weeds. Or he would be in the trees above the village, chopping wood to be stored against the extreme cold of winter.

At times like that, and even now, alone beneath the vastness of the mountain sky, he would wonder what was going to become of him, where life would lead him. Back then, before the war, only a few short years ago, his life had held promise. That promise was of a life very different to the harsh and difficult lives led by his father and the generations of valley-dwellers who had preceded him. When he could and work at home allowed, he went to school and did very well there. He read books, devoured the classics, in fact, and was considered by the priest the brightest child to have passed through the school for many years. He was a likely candidate, even, for university down in Milan, if the money could be found to support him.

The war had changed everything, however, and the school had failed to survive its vicissitudes. His teacher was Jewish and had fled to Switzerland in the early days of Italy's involvement. Sandro had not known what Jewish meant until then. He, himself, would have had to join the bedraggled Italian army if he had not decided to throw in his lot with the partisans fighting in the mountains, causing as much trouble for the Germans as possible.

He had considered all kinds of possibilities in the last couple of years. War brought lots of things to an end and shattered everyone's life, but if those shattered pieces could be put together once again, perhaps not in the same shape or form as before, of course, how would they look, he asked himself, what would they make? He felt himself to be on the very edge of just such a new shape or form, felt as if he could fashion any kind of life he wanted, as soon as this was over and the world had once again rearranged itself. As long as he could survive.

He sat up. The sun was climbing towards its highest point in the sky. All around him the trees, grass and rocks were hushed, expectant. The world was dozing, but he had to be on his way, to rendezvous with what Dino, his closest friend, called his 'foolishness'.

Angela was a year older than him, but both were young. She, however, had been married for three years and was the mother of a child – the reason for the marriage – conceived in the woods above the village in the high heat of summer when she knew nothing of life.

Her husband, Luigi, eight years older than her, had been smitten with her since he had, with pumping heart, watched her dance at a cousin's wedding, aged fourteen, spinning like a top, her head of long, jet-black hair thrown back, laughter spilling from her mouth like sparkling wine from an over-filled glass. He had watched her from afar over the intervening years – in the market, helping her mother in the small garden of their house, playing with friends and, as she got to her mid-teens, gathered on the small village's one street, giggling and pouting. He, of course was of another world, another generation and did not even figure in her world.

Eventually, however, he had taken her in a clearing in the trees above the village when she had not long turned sixteen. He had manufactured an accidental meeting during one of the walks that he knew she was partial to taking after lunch. Afterwards, she cried with pain and he knelt beside her, hot tears laced with guilt searing his cheeks and apologies spewing from his mouth. He expressed his love to her, told her how she made his life complete, how if he could not be with her he would rather die. Finally, as the pain diminished and

49

she returned to herself he promised to talk to her father and ask for her hand in marriage.

He did not, however; for that night and every night for weeks after, his love for her had leaked out of his body like water from a sieve. He saw her in the street looking at him imploringly and where once just a glimpse of her head across the crowded church on Sunday had sent a shaft of pain through his heart, now he felt nothing but emptiness. It was like a corner of a room in which a much-loved piece of furniture had long stood, but where now there was only a patch of carpet coloured differently to the rest and, somehow, no longer fitting.

He was horrified, therefore, when Angela's father summoned him to their house one night and calmly informed him over a glass of grappa that Angela was pregnant and, having confirmed that Luigi was, indeed, the father, he was expected to do the decent thing – inform the priest immediately and arrange the wedding.

Of course, there was no escape from such a situation, save to flee, but Luigi could not bring himself to do that. It was thus that he found life closing in on him, in a marriage to a beautiful child who was terrified of him for what he had done to her that hot day amongst the trees.

He was made very welcome, however, by Angela's family and soon after the wedding, their lives settled into a rhythm of sorts which was not entirely unpleasant. Even Angela began to accept her lot and when the baby arrived a few months into the marriage, a strong, big-lunged little boy with Luigi's sharp nose and her lovely, sensuous mouth, she seemed suddenly to become a woman, accepting of her place in the scheme of things, even though it was a place not of her choosing.

She opened herself to Luigi, tried her hardest for him. She

50

learned how to cook, spent hours in the kitchen with her mother, perfecting her skills with polenta and sausage-making and stews of hare or stag and cheese-making. These were some of the best times of her life; the bond between mother and daughter strengthened, became as taut as a metal wire, the mother passing on the collected knowledge of centuries of mountain women. This collected wisdom had been leavened by her own experience during her years of marriage, by the knowledge teased from the commentary provided by her husband throughout those years – 'That could use a bit more *basilico*' 'More salt in this', I don't like that'. That was the marriage of Angela's mother and father, their relationship defined to a certain extent by food, herbs and condiments. For he spoke little, Angela's father. In fact, the night he had informed Luigi of his daughter's situation, those were virtually the only words he uttered to him. He was a silent man, a silent man at the end of generations of increasingly silent men; men who grubbed at the dirt without protest, shifting huge boulders on steep terraces to plant vines, lettuces and leeks, to tend peach trees and tomato plants, to feed the mouths of generations of boy children who would grow up to do the same and girl children who would provide the boys to cultivate, in their turn, the crops of the mountain people's gardens and small holdings.

It was from this subsistence that it had been thought Sandro would be the first of his family and one of the few in the entire history of the mountain villages to escape by choice and not because of war or death. His mother had pushed him, and cajoled him; she taught him to read even before he went to school. She, herself had been taught to read – unusual for a woman in these villages – by a solicitous priest. Sandro's father looked on silently and it was impossible to know what he thought of it all or even if he understood what it all meant – another silent mountain man.

Some of his silence, however, was caused by pain. He had been ill almost all of Sandro's life. He was unable to eat properly and experienced terrible stomach pains that would suddenly drain the colour from his face and render it almost impossible to communicate with him. He would disappear deep inside his pain and leave Sandro and his mother somewhere outside, looking in.

The war had dashed Sandro's ambition, however. His teacher had fled, his mother was preoccupied by the illness of her husband and Sandro's interest in books dried up as did his supply of them. As his father would disappear into his pain and his mother would attempt to follow him down that path as far as she could or he would allow her, so Sandro would disappear more and more and for longer and longer into his beloved hills and forests until his parents had almost forgotten that they had a son.

Then one day it happened.

Angela, too, had taken to wandering in the hills above the village. After Luigi had eaten lunch and chucked baby Antonio under the chin and had finally, awkwardly, bade farewell to Angela, she would listen to his footsteps fading down through the village towards the garage that he and his father owned down on the main Sondrio road. She had grown to recognise those footsteps so well, had grown to understand them like another language. Walking home at night slowly through the village's one street, tired footsteps seeking rest. Shuffling footsteps late at night as he returned from the bar that sat next to the garage, picking up custom from eastbound travellers as well as locals. Two or three times a week Luigi would frequent it, the grappa and card games having got the worst of him both in terms of the amount he drank as well as financially. She hated those nights – his drunken fumblings at her clothing and his rough version of love, at first intimidating her and then, ultimately, after many repetitions of the same scene, alienating her. Unnecessarily, too, for she would willingly have given herself to him; she was determined to make her life work, for her child, for herself and, yes, even for the man she had married. They were bound together now, by marriage and by this tiny, demanding bundle of flesh and bone that had come from both of them. She had wanted to make it work. But those fingers clumsily unfastening the buttons of her dress were also undoing the ties that bound them together.

She began to escape, both in her mind and in reality. She would disappear into the trees above the village, where Luigi had first laid his rough mechanic's hands on her flesh. Only for an hour or so at a time, the baby cradled in her arms, but it was her hour and no one else's.

She wondered why she was different from the others, for the other women did not seem to need this, did not share her burning need to escape. She would meet them in the village, converse with them as she fetched water or hung out washing, but not once did she feel that any of them wanted any more than the life that they had – a life of drudgery enlivened by rare moments of happiness.

Those rare moments came to her in the free and heady air of her own time wandering in the forest. It was still very close to the village, admittedly, but far enough away to create a distance and an illusion of another life in her mind, a life of golden, wide, tree-lined avenues; of furniture rich in colour and generous in its provision of comfort; of restaurants, filled with exciting diners and purveying exotic food and above all, a life full of people. People who could hold conversations about all manner of things; not just the latest village gossip – this one hasn't spoken to her husband for a month, that one has a roving eye, this one drinks too much, that one is sleeping with her husband's brother. No, instead weightier matters would be talked about, such as the drift of the war or the affairs of film stars. It was the stuff of the magazines that she saw now and then. They were ancient, dog-eared and torn by many fingers by the time she saw them, but they filled her with ideas and thoughts and, above all, dreams.

It was during one of her meandering walks that Sandro entered her life.

It was a fine winter's day. Everything felt brittle, as if it were just about to snap – the clouds, the trees, the birds. She was trying to push Luigi from her mind. The previous night he had been even drunker than usual and had, consequently, hurt her more than usual. At lunch time he had been contrite, but had become angry at her silence as she put his food in front of him and had left the house angrily without his usual few words to Antonio. He had slammed the door and walked angrily down the hill towards the garage. She read his anger in his footsteps.

That fateful day, she rounded a boulder that guarded a small clearing just as Sandro approached from the other direction, coming downhill after two days in the mountains. His legs were tired and his stride was long and careless. The descent had taken over his progress and his boots were skidding off boulders, sending showers of gravel down in advance of him.

He struck her and the baby full on, sending her to the ground with a sickening thud that temporarily drove the air from her lungs. Some sixth sense, however, made her cling to Antonio as she fell and, although he was unscathed, she immediately began to feel the stiffness and swelling of what was undoubtedly a large bruise forming on her hip where it had struck a small rock that jutted upwards from the ground.

When she had found her breath once again, she opened

her eyes to see, kneeling beside her a man, or a boy, really, on the verge of manhood. His handsome, weather-darkened face wore a worried frown and his concerned eyes looked into hers, looking for a sign that she was not badly injured by her fall.

'Ah, *Dio*, are you alright? ... are you hurt? ... I didn't see ...'

She sat up, pulling twigs and fallen leaves from her long, black hair and examining Antonio who merely gurgled at her and blinked those dark, brooding eyes.

'Oh ... yes ... I'm ... fine ... we're fine ...' The words came in gasps, her chest heaving. 'I did not ... expect to bump into ... anyone.' And then she realised what she had said and laughed a little laugh, raising her hand, as was her habit, to cover her mouth as she did so.

Sandro, smiling, noticed this motion, the raising of the hand and loved it, loved her for it. He sat back, leaning on the boulder and reached into his knapsack, taking out a water-flask, filled several hours previously at a waterfall high up on the mountain.

'Please, have some water.' He extended the flask towards her. 'It might help.' His voice, she noted, was solicitous, involved, unlike the usual distant, unengaged manner of the men who lived in these mountains. She drank and the chill mountain water immediately made her feel better.

They talked for perhaps another fifteen minutes during that first encounter and found out a little about each other. They learned that they lived in neighbouring villages and yet they had never met, to their knowledge, or even set eyes on each other. This was not surprising, however, for each village in the valley was different to the next; each was like a little closed world. They even spoke almost different languages, distinct dialects that had developed over centuries.

Eventually Sandro and Angela parted, formally and, on his part, apologetically. He stood aside and watched her climb into the trees, admiring her body, the swing of her hips and the gentle swell of her breasts, across which her baby lay.

The swing of her hips was, of course, deliberate. She knew his eyes would be on her as she climbed away from him; indeed, she felt them drilling into her back and deliberately did not turn to wave as she rounded a stand of fir trees and disappeared from his sight.

But, she was married and he immediately tried to cast her from his mind on that account. That night, however, exhausted though he was by his days in the hills, he lay awake and she floated through his mind like a ghost: her face, her hair, the swing of her hips, drifting across his eyes like a piece of dust that he was unable to remove. He tried to disperse the thought of her, to dilute it with other things, as wine is diluted with water to lessen its strength; he tried to swat it away like one would a fly, but there she would remain, looking up at him from the forest floor as if she had just emerged from the earth, with her dazed, beautiful eyes. When, finally, he drifted off to sleep, she appeared there, too, with her baby clasped to her breast like a piece of her.

She, too, carried away a lasting impression of their meeting. It became almost a magical event to her, as if he really did not exist, that she had dreamed the whole thing and for the next few evenings, sitting across from the taciturn Luigi at dinner, she felt a pang of loss for the sparkling, caring eyes of this boy, Sandro, as he leaned over her, a pang of loss for those fifteen minutes that would never happen again, that now faded back into the past as she drifted on with her existence in this dreary home over which hung the spectre of drunken violence. In her mind she compared those fifteen minutes to the violence, the uncontrollable lust that had filled Luigi's eyes in the clearing those few short years ago – those few short years that had seemed to consume several of her lifetimes, one after the other.

Independently of each other, they both returned to the clearing guarded by the huge boulder at the same time of day as their original meeting, but not on the same day. Gradually, as the days and then the weeks drifted past, they both sank back into the realities of their respective existences; she, caring for baby Antonio and putting food in front of Luigi and awaiting, with dread, his shuffling footsteps returning from the bar; he, beginning to help his ailing father more and more in cultivating the few fruit trees and vegetable plants that provided them with an existence. Opportunities for taking off into his beloved mountains became fewer and only rarely could Sandro find the time.

One day, however, he was returning to the village by way of the boulder and the clearing, as was his habit now, and, suddenly, there she was again, just entering the clearing from the other direction. This time they did not collide, but he gasped and she let out a small cry and it was as if they had each seen a ghost.

She raised a hand to her breast as if she could still the pounding of her heart. Here again were those eyes that had begun to appear to her everywhere she went. Now and then, when she closed her eyes in search of sleep, Luigi's deep snores resonating beside her, those eyes had seemed to float across the insides of her eyelids, settling there as if becoming one with her own eyes.

'*Buongiorno*, Angela!' he exclaimed, his face reddening, as he said it.

She felt a pulse of satisfaction that he had remembered her name after all these weeks.

'*Buongiorno*, Sandro,' she replied. 'Walking the hills again, I see.'

'Oh, I don't do it as much as I'd like to,' he replied, and he told her about his father and how he was finding work difficult and how he had to help. They picked up their easy conversation as though all those weeks had not intervened. He remarked on the growth of baby Antonio, even in that short time, the increase in his size and the greater thickness of his jet-black hair.

And so, it started. The next day, when she arrived at the boulder in the clearing, there he was, leaning against it, rolling a thin cigarette, a broad smile splitting his handsome features. That day, however, Antonio was grizzling from an attack of cholic and she was unable to stay very long. In the days after, she would stay longer and they gradually began to share their dreams with each other.

She hung on to every word of his description of the one and only time he had left the valley, to visit Milano in the company of his teacher. Her eyes widened and her heart pounded as he spoke of the magnificence of the station *Il Duce* had built, the splendour and graceful beauty of the cathedral with its massive, vaulted, Gothic ceiling and the kaleidoscope of colours spilled onto the floor from the diffusion of the sun by the rose window. He told her all this once and then the next day she asked him to repeat it in every detail, missing nothing and when he did, she reminded him: 'Oh, you missed the description of the spires' or, 'what about the beggars in the station?' She drank it in and lay in bed at night, her head spinning with the wonder of it all.

In her turn, she spoke of things of which she knew little, of life beyond the valley and, indeed, beyond Italy. He would listen with a smile on his face, marvelling at her tremendous naivete, but loving her sheer enthusiasm for life. He was falling in love with her innocence of the world, her trust in the good in everything. But as she spoke, he picked up hints of darkness in her life, unhappiness in her house in the village.

On the first day of the second week of these clandestine meetings, Sandro awoke and smelled the rain before he heard its steady drumming on the roof of the house. He and his father were unable to work in the vineyard, and, after helping to fashion new fence posts in their small lean-to shed for most of the morning, he excused himself, claiming a need for fresh air. He climbed through the steadily falling rain to the clearing.

The rain dripped down from the leaves of the trees and its steady rattle on bark and greenery filled the clearing when he arrived.

Time moved on and he was rolling his second cigarette without there being any sign of Angela. It must be too wet, he thought. She could not bring Antonio out in such weather. But, suddenly, she was there, bursting into the clearing through the damp bushes and branches that hid it from the view of the outside world, had there been anyone abroad on such a day to look in. She was breathless and flushed and her long hair stuck to her face and dripped water.

She was alone, he noticed as she stood with her hands on her hips, her legs apart, her body bent forward, breathing in the damp mountain air.

He removed his waterproof jacket and threw it around her heaving shoulders as she gasped, 'I have left Antonio with . . . my . . . mother-in-law . . . I was afraid . . . you would be . . . gone . . .' He drew her over to the boulder and sat her down under its overhang where there was a soft carpet of lush grass that had been protected from the rain.

She turned to him and raised a cold, wet hand to where

his hand reached around her shoulder, wrapping his jacket tightly around her. Her fingers touched his and she looked up into his eyes, those same, soft eyes that had haunted her for weeks, wherever she was.

She offered her lips to him as if it was the most natural thing in the world, as if it had always been written that she would inevitably do such a thing, that they would do such a thing.

Once again, she found herself making love in a clearing, staring at the canopy the trees threw over them. The first time, all she had felt was pain and fear. This time she felt pain again, but it was the pain of loving too much. Her body opened and something from deep inside her broke free and soared over the mountain peaks that guarded the valley.

As for Sandro, there came a moment when he could swear her body was melting beneath his touch and his, too, seemed to be fusing with hers until they were one.

A few feet away, the rain exploded on the earth, scattering fir cones with its force and running in tiny rivulets towards the edge of the clearing.

5

Michael had spent the morning staring into space.

The weather on the return journey from Scotland had been even worse than the drive north. Rain had slanted onto his windscreen, necessitating his wipers to go at double speed all the way while his car went at half speed. He had, at least, enjoyed company on the journey. As he had been putting his bag in the boot of his car, Helen Matthieson had emerged from the hotel, swinging a bag.

'Any chance of a lift?'

'Where you headed?' he asked, thinking she was just making the short journey into Annan.

'Well, New York'd be great, but I'll settle for London.' She smiled.

'So, you've realised that catering isn't the correct career path, then?'

'I guess so. I've worked non-stop for the last few months and need a break. Jacquie's a bit annoyed with me, but that's tough. Anyway, I've got an old friend in London who's had a baby and I've been meaning to pay her a visit. So, what do you say? I'll pay half the petrol.'

'No need for that. Chuck your bag in the boot.'

And so, they talked most of the journey and the time passed quickly as they cut through the morning traffic and skirted Birmingham by early afternoon. He dropped her off around four at a tube station on the outskirts of London.

'Give me a call, Michael,' she said, leaning in the window of the car. 'It'd be nice to see you again, when you've got everything sorted, I mean.'

'I will, Helen. You have a good time.'

She leaned into the car, kissed him on the cheek, smiled and was gone, lost amongst the commuters.

Now he sat in the flat, deliberating what to do next. The trip to Scotland had left him even more confused than before. He had come home and searched through the file that contained all of Rosa's bills and receipts, ready to be passed to her accountant at some future date. My God, but she was organised, he thought, as he removed the rubber band that held together the papers that related to September.

He was searching for her credit card statement, just to confirm once and for all that she had, indeed, stayed at the Lighthouse Inn.

His heart raced as he found the bill. There it was; a receipt for £180.46 debited to the Lighthouse Inn. So, there was absolutely no doubt. She had stayed there. It had been her.

He had lain down on the bed and that was where he remained, staring at the ceiling, the minutes passing. Eventually he looked down at the statement once more, as if hoping that there had been some mistake, as if he perhaps had misread it first time. But no, there it was in black and white. His eyes strayed up and down the column, taking in the account of a part of her life during those last few months. Petrol, clothes, all laid out with their cost tidily totted up beside them. Another entry caught his attention, however. It was a charge for £650 from Rogerson & Gilchrist, the very upmarket jewellers in Kensington. What was that for? She had not talked to him about such a purchase and surely she would have, if she had bought something costing that much. Although they were certainly comfortably off, that was still a substantial sum and she would have told him about it.

Ninety minutes later he was in a shop doorway on Kensington High Street, ringing a bell on the door of Rogerson & Gilchrist.

The shop front was like a remnant of another century. Around it were the cloned fascias of the typical nineties high street – identical shops filled with exactly the same items at exactly the same prices occupied streets the length of the country. That was what made Rogerson & Gilchrist so unique. Elegantly carved dark wood surrounded the windows on which the name of the proprietors was painted in gold. Above the door a brass plaque announced the shop name quietly and confidently, as if to say, *if you have to ask you have no right to be here.* And it was not a shop into which just anyone could wander. A doorbell had to be rung and the door opened to let a prospective customer enter, this presumably only after perusal by a hidden security camera.

A dark-suited, bald man opened the door to Michael. He, himself, looked as if time had forgotten him, as if it were still the late eighteenth century within the confines of this shop. His suit looked as if it longed for tails and his shirt collar was starched and shiny. A thin, dark blue, silk tie hugged his throat and he seemed to bend at the waist unconsciously.

'May I enquire as to the nature of your business, sir?' he asked, eyeing Michael's leather jacket and jeans suspiciously over the top of a pair of small spectacles that hung precariously on the end of his nose like a fence at the edge of a cliff.

'I wish to purchase something, but, erm, it is a little delicate. May I come in and explain to you what I require?'

'Why certainly,' said the bald man, not at all happy to be letting Michael come in, but rendered curious, all the same, by the hint of delicacy. 'Please follow me.'

He led Michael through what turned out to be a foyer, lined with leather chairs and with glass tables on which society magazines were carefully laid out. The wallpaper was heavily striped and a small chandelier threw light dimly into the corners. An upmarket waiting room, thought Michael.

They entered a large, high-ceilinged room beyond in which there was a desk in each corner. The desks were highly polished and ornate. At one of them sat another dark-suited, dark-tied, grey-haired man, busily writing. He barely looked up as Michael and the bald man came in.

'Please take a seat,' said the bald man, going round to the other side of his desk. 'Now, you say it is a delicate matter, sir . . .?' He left the sentence hanging, unfinished.

'Well, it is a *little* delicate. I've placed myself in a rather difficult situation and I'm hoping you can be of help.' The bald man shifted in his chair and looked at Michael even more sceptically. 'I hope I can trust you to be discreet . . .?'

The bald man raised his eyebrows, put his head to one side and spread his hands on the table. 'Of course, sir.' he said.

Michael continued, 'I am married, to a wonderful woman. However, I have been having a . . . how can I put it . . . a liaison with someone else. My erm, friend sent me an item of jewellery purchased from you, but my wife found it before I had a chance to open the packet, read the accompanying note and threw it out of the car window at eighty miles an hour on the M4. My problem is that I have to see my friend tomorrow night – she has been away – and she will expect me to thank her for what she gave me and even to be wearing it. As I never even got to see the item, I have no idea at all what it was. What I want to do is buy another one and then she will be none the wiser. So, I was wondering if you could check your files to find out what she bought and I will simply buy another of the same, if you have one.'

'I see, sir. I understand the, erm, delicacy of the situation, but I'm afraid we may not be able to help. You see, Rogerson & Gilchrist is not like a high street jeweller, mass-producing items of jewellery. Most of the items we sell are unique, hand-crafted.'

'But would it be possible for you to just check for me? Please? Even if I knew what it was, everything might be alright.' Michael looked at him imploringly.

'Well, it is a bit irregular, sir.' His gaze shot over Michael's shoulder, presumably to his colleague, scribbling away at the other desk, 'but, given the delicacy of the situation in which you find yourself, I think we can certainly try. Now, if you could provide me with the date of the purchase and the name?'

Michael gave him the information he needed, trying not to sound too precise with the date as it might seem suspicious if he knew the exact details.

The bald man took a pad from a drawer in his desk and wrote on it. 'If you will excuse me, sir ...' He stood up, pushing his chair back and went through a side door into an adjoining room. At this point there was a loud buzzing from downstairs – another client seeking entry into this sanctum.

The other dark-suited man stood up, said 'Excuse me, sir' in Michael's direction and left the room.

The bald man returned two or three minutes later, clutching a sheet of paper.

'We keep full records of every purchase made so that we can be of as much help to our clients as possible,' he said sitting down and pulling his chair closer to the desk. 'Now, this would appear to be the only purchase ever made from Rogerson & Gilchrist by Ms Keats,' he said, his eyes darting to the paper in his hand for confirmation of the name.

'A lovely piece that your ... friend purchased for you. A diamond-studded tie-pin, sir. I have a photograph of it.' He removed a paper clip and detached the picture from the sheet of paper. 'At Rogerson and Gilchrist, we retain photographs of each item we sell for our own records, sir, as well as for insurance purposes for our clients.'

It was, indeed, a beautiful piece, but certainly not something that Michael would ever consider wearing, even on those rare occasions that he wore a tie. It took the shape of a golden vine leaf, in the centre of which lay a cluster of small diamonds.

'24-karat gold, sir, with a cluster of small diamonds set in the centre. A French piece and, I am afraid, sir, as with most of the pieces we sell, one of a kind. I regret, therefore, that I am unable to supply you with a replacement for the one which has been so sadly lost.' A look of satisfaction spread across the bald man's thin face, as if he were rather pleased that Michael had been mired in this situation and there was no way out.

As for Michael, he was delighted that there was no other example of the vine leaf tie-pin. He had feared that he was going to have to shell out £650 for it, had Rogerson & Gilchrist been able to provide one.

'Oh, well, I suppose I will just have to face the music,' said Michael, pushing back his seat and beginning to rise.

'Er, there is just one other thing, sir. The address to which the tie-pin was delivered, sir. According to our records it was sent to an address in Italy, and not to an address in England. Do you live in Italy, sir?' The bald man put his hands together in an attitude of prayer, resting his chin on them.

Michael stared at him, blinking and attempting to come up with an answer. Could he carry it off, he wondered? The address of Rosa's boyfriend must be on that piece of paper lying across the desk from him. He had to get it somehow.

'Oh God!' He slumped back into the chair and held his face in his hands. 'Oh God, I'm sorry. It's just ... she ... my wife ... she's been having an affair ... I can't stand it anymore. I had to ... to find out ...' Amateur dramatics, he thought, but perhaps it would be enough. He looked up, his eyes moist, where he had rubbed them furiously with a finger while his face was covered, but unable to produce tears. He was not that good an actor. His antics were having an effect, however. The bald man had sat bolt upright in his chair, shocked at such a show of emotion. Michael buried his face in his hands once more and began to sob. Was he overdoing it? Perhaps not, because he heard the chair across from him being pushed back on the pile of the plush carpet.

'I'll ... I'll ... get you some water, sir.' Michael looked between his fingers and saw the retreating back of the bald man heading for the door. As soon as he was out of sight he reached across the desk and grabbed the piece of paper that lay across it, hurriedly reading its contents. There it was at the bottom. Delivery address: Box 98432, Milano Centrale, Piazza Duca d'Aosta, 20124 Milano MI, Italy. Damn! A box number at the post office in the main station of Milan.

He stuffed the piece of paper into his pocket as the bald

man's footsteps returned. Lifting his head from his hands he saw him enter the room, a glass of water in his hand.

'Oh, there'll be no need for that,' said Michael rising from his chair, apparently miraculously recovered from his emotional collapse. The bald man stood with his mouth wide open as Michael walked past him saying, 'Don't worry yourself, chum; I'll see myself out.'

A box number. For a moment in that musty old room he had thought he was at least going to have a name to put to this anonymous man. Somehow that would have given him some satisfaction. Now, he was no further forward – but he was not even sure whether he really wanted to be any further forward.

He turned down Kensington High Street and headed in the direction of the offices of the London *Evening Post*.

Harry Jones's office bore witness to an amazing career in news journalism. The walls were lined with his great stories, yellowing in frames and, indeed, they were the world's great stories. He had given Londoners their version of history for nearly forty years, spending that entire time with the same newspaper, the last twenty as news editor. Rumours suggested that he had been offered the editorship of the Post – and a number of other papers – on numerous occasions, but would not leave his beloved newsroom, with its banks of hardened hacks banging away on typewriters and latterly on word processors. It was a sight he often described as the most beautiful thing he had ever seen.

Harry was on the phone as Michael was shown into the office by his secretary. He beckoned to him to come in and sit down while shouting down the line at some poor, benighted journalist who seemed to be signally failing to understand the story Harry wanted.

'Christ, Michael, it would be easier if I were to write the bloody articles myself,' he said in his rich Welsh voice, putting the phone down. 'How are you, lad?'

'Oh, I'm alright in the circumstances, Harry.'

Michael's relationship with Harry had always been an easy one. He had rarely given him occasion to lose his ragged temper at him and they had bonded early on in Michael's career over countless whiskies in anonymous hotels, as they tried to record the boredom of party conferences or the corruption of local councillors.

'Very sad, Michael, very sad. Life can be so bloody cruel.' He blinked at Michael and Michael thought Harry was about to burst into tears, his Welsh sensibilities getting the better of him. It passed, however. 'What are you planning to do then, lad? When are we going to have you back, giving us the benefit of that fine purple prose of yours?' Harry asked, reaching for the cup of coffee on his desk.

'Or . . .' looking straight into Michael's eyes, 'perhaps you're not coming back?'

Suddenly, Michael realised that Harry was right. He was, indeed, not coming back to these offices. Rather, he was returning to Italy to pursue the golden tie-pin and its owner. Why he wanted to do that and when he had made the decision, he did not know, but that was what he was going to do.

'No, I'm not, Harry.'

Harry stared at him. 'I feared as much. What are you going to do then? Spend the bloody insurance money?' He was rattled that his prediction was true. He also found it difficult to imagine anyone not wanting to work anymore in his beloved newsroom.

'Well, not exactly . . .' replied Michael, a little taken aback by Harry's outburst. 'There's Rosa's book to finish. Perhaps I'll write one of my own. You know I've always wanted to.'

'But to give up on this, Michael, to pack in your career. I have to admit I've been a little peeved at the time it's taken you to return and I was half afraid that when you did finally get back into the land of the living – and I use that term completely unadvisedly – you wouldn't like it and would try to make your exit. You're good. I don't want to lose you. These kids I'm forced to employ these days, some can write, I'll give you that, but there aren't many that come along who have that extra spark that you have, that can invest a story with a bit of spirit, with the stuff that makes the punters want to come back for more. You're good, lad, you're good. If it's money . . .'

'No, Harry, the money's irrelevant.' Michael leaned forward in his seat. 'Look, I've always been straight with you. Let me explain what's really going on.'

And so, Michael recounted to Harry what he had discovered about Rosa's relationship with the unknown Italian. He explained that he had to find out more about her life in the last few months. 'And, of course, I *do* also need to get her book finished. I'm meeting with the publisher this afternoon. I just feel it will be a lasting memorial to her.' He looked down at his shoes, musing on his lack of anger. 'Her work deserves it, in spite of what she might have been doing to me personally.'

Harry sat back and shook his head. 'My God, lad! That's terrible. Terrible.' His Welsh accent drew out the first syllable of the word 'terrible' as if it were a mussel being pulled from a shell on the Anglesey coast. He looked at Michael, shaking his head. 'You're sure of this? You know you've been through rather a lot in the last few weeks.'

'I'm not going mad, if that's what you're hinting at, Harry.' And then, a little angrily, 'I'm not bloody paranoid. That's what has been happening and I want to go back to Italy to

70

find out who this guy is that Rosa was having a thing with. I need to find out why it happened and learn how I could be so stupid as to not see it happening right under my nose.'

Harry leaned back in his seat and was silent for a moment. 'You know, old Leo Tolstoy once said something very interesting, Michael. He said: 'All newspaper and journalistic activity is an intellectual brothel from which there is no retreat.' An *intellectual brothel*, Michael . . .' He left a space in the conversation for emphasis.

Harry often spouted quotes – Michael suspected he devoted some of his time to learning them at weekends, so that he could impress young staffers with his erudition. However, he often misunderstood their meaning, as at this time. 'But you can generally walk out of brothels, Michael – a little unsteadily, mind you . . .' He smiled as if at some distant memory. '. . . but just the same . . . If you are good at this work – as *you* undoubtedly are, Michael – there will be no escape. You will end up writing for some newspaper somewhere. And that will piss me off something rotten.' He paused, thinking for a moment. 'Look, here's a thought. *I* want you to carry on working for me. *You* want to go to bloody Italy. We can make this work for both of us, make a virtue out of bloody necessity, as it were. You know that kidnapping? The Ronconi daughter? It was not far, I believe, from where your family live, down by Como, somewhere. Old Luigi Ronconi has heavy links with all the right people in Italy, as well as – if we believe the whispers, Michael – all the wrong people. The trail has gone completely cold and the Italian police are beginning to look even more stupid than they usually do. Why not go freelance for me and see what you can dig up? It would make those cretins upstairs happy. They're trying to persuade me to get everyone to work on a freelance basis. Where's the bloody loyalty, I keep asking them?'

'Well, I hadn't really thought . . .'

'Oh, come on. At the very least it will give you the opportunity to speak to me every now and then. You can tell me
about the sunset over the Alps or whatever the bloody mountains are over there. What do you think?'

Michael considered the offer for no more than a moment.
'Alright, Harry. You're on. I'll see what I can dig up. I'll do it.'

'Great, lad, great!' said Harry as a sharp knock on the door
was followed by his secretary walking in.

'His Lordship rang down asking if you would just pop
upstairs, Mr Jones.'

'Bloody hell. What does he want now?' he asked, shaking
his head.

They both stood up.

'I'll get someone to organise a freelance contract for you,
Michael.' He extended his hand and they shook across the
ash-dusted desk. 'You take care of yourself, now, you hear?'

He wanted to leave almost immediately. Walking out into
the street, he felt as if London had virtually ceased to exist for
him. He crossed the road and entered Kensington Gardens
and watched pigeons clustered around a ragged looking
woman who was feeding them crusts of bread. Their wings
beat against each other in their furious haste to get as close
to her outstretched hands as possible. A smile of utter bliss
was etched on her face and she was completely oblivious to
the fact that the worn velvet hat she wore was slipping from
her head.

Once it would all have meant something to him – the
uniformed nannies pushing expensive prams through the
park, the red buses making their way along Bayswater
Road – none of it mattered to him anymore. All that mattered . . . Well what did matter? Rosa's infidelity was a fact.

Perhaps getting away and throwing himself into her book and this kidnap story would help clear his head of it all. A drive down to the Channel and then through France – that would help. Long straight French roads, hyphenated by plane trees, the bark peeling from them and that characteristic white necklace of paint a few feet from the ground. That had always helped.

By the time he returned home it was set in his mind. Tonight, he would pack and he would leave for Milan first thing in the morning. He would not tell Renzo and Giovanna. He really did not want to see them so soon, and felt that he should create some distance between himself and the bad time of the last month. Making contact with them would only put him back in the midst of it all once more.

He fell asleep early, at last in the bed he had shared with Rosa. He felt apprehensive. As he drifted off to sleep, he wondered where he would be at this time the following night and through which wall the blue car would come crashing with the limp body of Rosa crucified on its bonnet once more.

He awoke early and felt refreshed. It was the most sleep he had enjoyed in weeks. He had had the dream, of course, but, having wakened with the first intimations of daylight, he gulped down a glass of cold water, pulled the quilt around himself and had fallen asleep again almost immediately.

Around eight he stood, looking out of the kitchen window, drinking a coffee. Everything was ready – bills paid, a post-card sent to John to let him know he was off on a job, but not indicating where he had gone, windows locked, electricity switched off.

As he carried his suitcase to the door around eight, a large envelope fell through. He recognised John's handwriting on the address label and realised it would be the contact sheets from the rolls of film he had given him a couple of nights ago. He picked it up and put it into the zippered pocket on the outside of the bag, waited until he heard John's car drive off, opened the door and stepped out of the house.

6

November 1943
Southern slopes
The Valtellina
North Italy

Sandro shivered as a breath of wind rounded the side of the mountain and found its way between the buttons of his coat. Every now and then he would start as a small animal skittered through the undergrowth. From behind him came the soft murmur of deep voices and the occasional crackle as a pocket of gas in a piece of wood on the fire exploded amidst the flames. The smell of meat cooking on the fire drifted towards him and he longed to be closer to the heat of the fire instead of staring into the deadness of this dangerous black night.

Towards the end of the summer of 1943, as the time rapidly approached when he would be called into the bedraggled Italian army, he had instead joined up with a group of local men who, earlier in the year, had taken up arms against the occupying Germans. It was difficult, however. Everyone had expected that the Allies would be sending money, arms and advisors to help defeat the Germans, but, so far, they had sent nothing. All because in Milan and across the rest of northern Italy, they were busy arguing amongst themselves. Communists were arguing with non-Communists and other factions, some of whom were no more than thieves and killers, added to the Allies' perception of chaos. Consequently, they were unwilling to provide the necessary back-up that would really give the Germans something to think about and the groups had to make do and mend with stolen weapons and their own initiative rather than a strategy concerted by the OSS or the British Secret Service from their headquarters in Berne.

Thus, it was an old pre-war rifle of his father's that Sandro nervously raised to his cheek as he heard a noise behind him.

'You must get warmer clothing,' a gruff voice said out of the darkness. 'I think I have an old greatcoat I could let you have, or perhaps we can get you one tomorrow off the body of a dead German. German coats are the best, you know.'

Sandro could barely make out the shape of Luigi moving up the slope towards him, the darkness was so profound. There was no moon tonight and the stars were hidden behind stormy clouds.

'Here, have some food. It might warm you up.' He was carrying a metal plate on which was a piece of chicken which had been roasted on the fire at the mouth of the cave in which they were going to spend the night. 'Only another hour or so and I'll send Dino up to relieve you.'

Once again Sandro felt guilt well up in him, as it always did when he talked to Luigi. Angela and he now met and made love on a very regular basis. It had been going on over a period of nine months and had continued even when, with his father's help, Sandro had joined this group, which was commanded by Luigi Ronconi.

'Oh, th ... thank you.' He was barely able to speak, it was so cold, and he welcomed the warmth of the plate as he grasped it.

'It will be difficult tomorrow, you know,' said Luigi, turning to look out over the valley. 'We must take von Stoltenberg alive or it is just a waste of time. Although I guess, even if he is killed, we will have achieved something, although he would undoubtedly be replaced almost immediately and we would have to start all over again.' And then, turning solicitously to Sandro; 'It'll be your first real piece of action, Sandro. How do you feel?' Sandro felt Luigi's big hand clasp his shoulder. The guilt was almost making him sick. 'Tell me, do you think you're up to it?'

'Yes, of course, of course, I'm ready to do what has to be done. It's why I joined in the first place.'

'Good lad. It's not easy to go to sleep knowing that when you wake up you are likely to kill a man. A man who may have a wife and children, who is loved by people and will be missed by them. You have to know that you're doing it for the right reason. That's what separates us from them, the Germans. Our fight is a just fight. Theirs is evil. Tomorrow just do what I tell you. Stay close and use your ammunition wisely. Make every bullet count. And no heroics, remember. Keep your head well down. And remember what we're fighting for – our freedom and the freedom of our loved ones.'

He removed his hand from Sandro's shoulder, smiled, turned and walked back down towards the cave entrance and the warmth of the fire around which the hushed voices of their comrades could just be heard. Over his shoulder he called out: 'And keep your eyes peeled.'

The night passed slowly. Sandro's friend, Dino, who had joined this group at the same time, relieved him, as promised by Luigi, with a grunt and a yawn but Sandro, back in the cave and wrapped in a blanket borrowed from his own bed at home, was unable to do more than doze for short spells. He smelled the smells of his own house from the blanket – he tried to identify them; the cooking smells of the kitchen, herbs and game and cheese, mingling with the scent of mothballs from his father's wedding suit, which hung in the ancient wardrobe in the corner of his room – so strange out here in the mountains, mixed with the scent of pine needles and damp earth. During the few times that he did drop off, he found himself in the midst of dreams that were exceedingly vivid at the time but completely forgotten on waking. All he could remember was that they had been deeply unsettling.

He opened his eyes from one of these snatched periods of restless sleep to find the sky at the mouth of the cave light and his comrades stirring. They crawled out from beneath their blankets, yawning and cursing. One stood at the mouth of the cave, urinating into the morning, whistling a familiar tune.

'Let's be having you then,' growled Luigi, already up and checking the workings of his rifle, which lay across his knees. 'Check your weapons, make sure everything is in working order. Let's have a drink – Sandro, there's a bottle of my father-in-law's grappa in that bag over there – have a slug yourself and pass it round. It'll warm you up, lad, put lead in your pencil.' The other men laughed and began to pack away their blankets.

Sandro uncorked the bottle and, taking a long draught of the clear liquid, felt its warmth slipping down his throat and into his stomach. He shivered, passed the bottle to one of his comrades and began to get his kit together, rolling his blanket and tying it to the top of his rucksack.

Twenty minutes later, they were spread across the hillside above the stretch of road that had become so familiar to Sandro in recent weeks, their eyes trained on the bend in the road, their ears straining for the sound of an engine. They had felled a tree and it lay across the road, blocking further progress by any approaching vehicle. Once stopped, the car and the lorry would be unable to turn on the narrow road and would be sitting ducks. Beside Sandro, a couple of yards to his left, Dino lay, eyes straining to see round the corner on which their attention was focused.

'Dino!' Sandro whispered his friend's name.

'Sandro. What's up?'

'It's incredible, isn't it?'

'What's incredible?

'All this, us, fighting the war, when just a few years ago . . . well, we were at school, wondering what would become of us.'

'Oh, you mean like whether we would be adulterers, Sandro. Is that what you mean?'

'Oh, don't start on that again . . .'

'What do you mean – 'don't start on that again'?' he hissed. 'You're the one who started it and you are the only one who can finish it. I don't know how you can look a good man like Luigi in the eye. It's a terrible thing you're doing.'

Sandro rolled onto his back, his rifle lying across his chest, his eyes fixed on the sky from which a light drizzle was beginning to fall, a light drizzle that seemed to have been falling for weeks now.

'Oh, Dino, you . . . you don't understand. I *can't* just stop it. I love Angela too much. When I even think of stopping it, of not seeing her again, it hurts so much. And she loves *me*. Not Luigi. Anyway, when this is all over we're going to move away from here, she, me and Antonio. We'll go to Milan or to Rome.' He rolled onto his side, his head resting on the palm of his hand, wishing he had never confided in Dino.

'You're a fool, Sandro,' Dino growled and then added

with even more anger, raising his body up and resting on his elbows: 'It's not going to happen! She's married to Luigi! *Madooooonna*, she is the mother of his only child, she can't leave him. And anyway, do you think Luigi would let her leave? He would track you down, Sandro, and, in the meantime, if he finds out, he'll kill you. *And* her. I fear for you. Believe me, I fear for you and for Angela.'

Footsteps approached from behind them.

'*Basta, ragazzi*! *Basta*! Enough! – gossiping like a pair of old washer women at the river!' Luigi knelt beside them, a cigarette dangling from his lips. His steely gaze never left the bend in the road to their left. 'Concentration, lads, concentration. Not long to wait now and then there'll be little enough time to gossip. What are you two getting so excited about? The girls that gather in the *piazza* on a Saturday night? Although, I tell you, there are a couple of those beauties that I wouldn't mind taking into the cemetery and lying down on a gravestone with, myself!'

Dino smiled complicitly, but Sandro stared ahead, unsmiling, disgusted by Luigi's comments.

'Now, let's be having your full attention on the job in hand, *ragazzi*. It might just save your life.' He moved away, crawling through the boulders towards the others. Dino shook his head in Sandro's direction and resumed his surveillance of the road.

An unnatural silence seemed to descend on the hillside. They could almost hear each other's hearts beating and the occasional screech of a bird made them start. It was uncomfortable. The drizzle of this chilly and damp November was now steady and seemed to have set in for the morning. Sandro took in the familiar view, diminished though it was by the low clouds and the rain that fell from them. What would she be doing now, he wondered? She was in that part of her life of which he knew little, in which he took no part – the only time he was part of her life was during the brief, snatched hour or so after lunch every second or third day when their feelings for each other would remove them from reality for a short time. Why was life so complicated? Why could he not just have her, for always?

He was stirred from his reverie by the sound of a stone rolling down the hillside, dislodged by Dino as he tensed.

'Sandro! Can you hear it?' he whispered. 'They're coming!'

The low murmur grew in the distance. Sandro looked across at his friend who had closed his eyes and was crossing himself. He followed suit, pleading with God to let him get through this, not that he really believed, but because it seemed the right thing to do. With trembling fingers, he checked his rifle and his ammunition, laid out beside him. He raised the rifle to his cheek and stared down the barrel towards the bend as the sounds became more distinct as the engines of two vehicles. His insides began to churn and he prayed that he would not be sick.

It seemed like an age as they waited for the car and the truck to round the bend. The world was split into two. The sound of the engines in the distance and the quiet around them. The forest below them wore a cloak of impenetrable silence and only the hiss of the rain tied their senses to the earth and the moment they were in.

Suddenly, it was there. First, its bumper and then its bonnet and then the rest of it, green and shiny with the rain, slowly climbing the hill, the protests of its diesel engine shattering the silence. Behind it, the lorry emerged from the corner, a tarpaulin roof rolled halfway up the side of the lorry providing cover for the troops inside – estimated at usually no more than six by Sandro during his long days of watching.

They held their breath. Luigi's instructions had been to

81

wait until he gave the order to fire, but it seemed never to be coming, that command. *Surely he should be telling us to open fire now,* they all thought. A stream of tension linked them, almost visibly. They had trained as much as possible for this exercise, but most of them had before they joined the partisans been used only to shooting rabbits or the occasional deer, if they were lucky. To fire on men, they had found, was different: exciting and horrific at one and the same time.

The driver of the staff car saw the tree trunk stretched across the road in front and stopped. He then seemed to be trying to reverse and turn in the road at the same time, shouting out of his window at the lorry behind. But his gears crunched as he searched in vain for reverse. And anyway, his efforts mattered little because Luigi chose that moment to scream '*Fuoco*!' and a fusillade of shots ripped into the front of the car and into the lorry. The car lurched forward and came to a crunching rest against the tree-trunk, while bodies scrambled out from under the tarpaulin and hid behind the lorry, leaning out to fire blindly into the boulders that littered the hill facing them. Meanwhile, the car engine roared, the driver's lifeless foot jammed on the accelerator.

Dino and Sandro fired round after round at the unseen targets that were crouched down behind the lorry. Everything was happening at twice normal speed. They shifted positions to get a better angle on their targets, fired at shapes moving behind the felled tree. Leaves danced on the damp ground as bullets ripped into them. The air was alive with gunfire and the whistling of bullets grazing the boulders that sheltered them.

'Make your ammunition count!' Luigi screamed. 'Don't waste it!'

Sandro rolled over onto his back to reload his weapon. His heart was pounding like a piston against his chest and he could hardly breathe. He had somehow gone beyond fear. Rather, he was exhilarated, enlivened and almost liberated from the earth by this experience.

Rolling back onto his chest, he caught sight of a German trying to crawl into the forest behind the lorry, no doubt attempting to circle around to the side of them to take them by surprise. He was in full view of Sandro for a moment. Sandro hesitated before raising his rifle to his cheek and letting the sight at the end of the barrel fall on the middle of the German's back, between his shoulder blades. He squeezed the trigger, as his father had taught him when he was ten years old. The report from the rifle sounded almost insignificant, too quiet and ineffectual to do any harm. It seemed to occur outside the other noises going on around him – the reports of rifles and shouts of men – but the body of the German arched the moment it was unleashed, arched and then fell forward, his hands reaching out to grab a fistful of wet leaves. Then it fell still, crucified against the ground.

Sandro lowered his rifle and stared at the body he had just dispatched.

'Well done, lad! Great shot!' It was Luigi behind him, with a huge smile on his face as he crawled along to get a better shot at the Germans still hiding behind the lorry.

Sandro lifted his rifle's cold, damp stock to his cheek once more and resumed firing on the Germans who remained alive, as did his comrades, a barrage of shots raining down on the truck and ripping holes in its tarpaulin and its metal sides.

The two remaining Germans lasted only a few minutes more before throwing their weapons out from behind the lorry and waving a white handkerchief of surrender.

'Okay, lads,' shouted Luigi, standing up. 'Let's go down and get the general. He's on the ground behind the car. Take no chances with these bastards, though.'

They all stood up and began to make their way gingerly down the slope towards the two Germans who had emerged from behind the lorry. On approaching, Sandro was amazed at how young they were. They could have been not much older than him and their eyes were filled with fear. They looked like the terrified young of a deer that Sandro had once shot dead a few years ago on a hunting trip in the mountains. He had come upon them sniffing at the dead body of their mother and they had looked up at him as he approached, staring at him in abject terror before fleeing into the trees to goodness knows what fate.

'Damn!' A shout came from the direction of the staff car where one of the partisans, Carlo, was leaning in through the open door.

'*Cosa*, Carlo? What's wrong?' shouted Luigi.

'The bastard general's only fucking dead, that's what's wrong.' Carlo replied, looking across the roof of the car towards Luigi.

'Ah, shit!' exclaimed Luigi, kicking the side of the lorry hard.

It was at this point that Sandro noticed that Dino was not with them. He sought the familiar, slightly overweight figure of his friend amongst the men who stood in a semi-circle around the lorries.

'Dino!'

'What?' asked Luigi, now leaning again the side of the lorry, a look of the utmost anger on his face.

'Where's Dino? He's not here.' He turned and ran up the hill towards the boulders behind which he and his friend had been sheltering, his feet sliding and scattering small stones and boulders as he scrambled towards them.

His worst fears were realised as he rounded the boulders. Dino was stretched out on the ground, his breath emerging in gurgling sounds from his throat. A dark stain was spreading across his chest.

'Dino ... ah, *Dio*, they got you.' Sandro knelt down and took his friend's head in the crook of his arm. Dino's eyes fluttered and then opened. They were filled with fear. He smiled up at his friend.

'Ah ... Sandro ... when will this ... rain stop ....eh?' He squeezed the words painfully between his teeth. A shudder then seemed to pass through his body and his head rolled to one side, the life leaving his eyes. Sandro grabbed at his head, cupping it in his hands and shaking it as if he could bring life back to it.

'Dino, Dino. No ...'

He felt a hand on his shoulder and Carlo was pulling him away from the body.

'He's dead, Carlo. They've killed him.' He buried his head on Carlo's shoulder and began to sob.

Suddenly, however, a shot rang out from down below them.

'What ...?' Sandro lifted his head as a second shot echoed through the forest. Looking down, he saw Luigi emerge from the forest, putting his pistol back in its holster at his waist. The two young Germans were nowhere to be seen.

'Carlo ...?' He looked imploringly into Carlo's eyes.

'They would have done exactly the same to us, if they had caught us, Sandro.' Carlo grabbed Sandro's shoulders.

'But, we're not animals like them, Carlo. This is what we are fighting against, this kind of barbarism.'

'This is a war, Sandro. Not a debate about morals. The fewer there are of those pigs the better for all of us.' Saying this, he turned and walked back down the hillside to where his colleagues were collecting guns and clothing from the dead Germans. A good pair of German boots was a unit of high currency in the Valtellina these days.

Sandro stared across the valley, wiping the rain from his face where it had mingled with tears for his dead friend.

A peal of laughter came from down below and he looked back to see Luigi slapping one of the others on the back, his mouth wide open in a huge grin, his teeth gleaming in the rain.

7

8 November 1999
Talimona
North Italy

Even when Ignazio Mazzini was a boy, he had been huge. By the age of twelve he already stood six inches taller than his father and they were calling him *il gigante*. He was a man amongst little boys when he played with his friends and he often hurt them as a result, more often by accident rather than design. He simply did not know his own strength, had not had the opportunities offered by experience to try it out in different situations, to understand the extent of his control over it. Consequently, he garnered a reputation as a bully. He would fall on top of one of his friends during a bit of rough and tumble, the friend would run home in tears to his mother complaining about *il gigante* Ignazio and the mother would brand him a bully.

So, he grew into the mould created for him by others as a rather frightening and short-tempered man. Being as large as he was – by the time his body had decided to stop growing, he measured six feet eight inches – he attracted the wrong sort of attention from drunks and hard men throughout the valley. Night after night in his late teens and early twenties he would be called upon to dispatch a couple of likely lads in a display of strength that became something of a freak show and which drew crowds from miles around. The owners of bars would vie for his custom, knowing that he would attract a good crowd in anticipation of a fight.

Of course, Ignazio soon grew tired of it all and retreated into himself, not even emerging when his family married him off to a not very bright girl called Silvia, in whom he lost interest on their wedding night.

He remained, however, an imposing figure of a man who still cast a longer shadow than anyone for miles around and when it fell across the desk of *Sovrintendente* Cosimo d'Annunzio, it felt to the policeman as if the sun had been switched off.

The station sergeant had been dozing over some paperwork which had ceased to be urgent some days ago when it had been due to be completed. It was cold and damp outside as it had been since autumn. The one bar electric fire that heated the room was hardly adequate, but it was the best they were going to provide him with in this little village police station in which he had to spend three hours every second day, providing a police presence for the scattered local community.

At first, he thought he must be dreaming. In front of him stood a giant cradling a baseball bat in his arms like a baby. The giant's nose had been broken in a long-forgotten brawl and it rose out of the centre of the huge face like a broken-backed mountain soaring out of a valley.

'*Buongiorno,*' the giant was saying. '*Buongiorno, Sovrintendente.*' D'Annunzio blinked.

'Ah, *buongiorno, signore.*' He shifted his body in his seat and sat up, adopting a better angle from which to view this man mountain.

Ignazio wore his customary clothes – in fact, his only clothes – a suit that had seen far better days. The trousers shone and the jacket was stained. His large head was topped by an unruly tangle of jet-black hair and his unshaven face was etched with lines that the weather had carved into it over the years he had worked the land. It was a difficult face to love and, indeed, Silvia had never loved it, even before their relationship had descended into silence on the first night of their marriage.

'How may I help you, *signore?*' asked d'Annunzio, his eyes flickering nervously from Ignazio's face to the baseball bat.

'I wish to confess to a crime, *Sovrintendente.*'

'A crime?' D'Annunzio's eyebrows arched in surprise, but he truly felt a sense of relief that this was not, as he had first feared, a madman, come to beat him with the bat he held in his hands. Still, he thought, he should not relax too much – he was still carrying it.

'I can no longer stand it,' growled Ignazio, becoming suddenly angry, slapping the end of the baseball bat into the palm of his left hand.

'Calm down, now, *signore*. We don't want you committing another crime, do we?' d'Annunzio replied with a laugh, immediately regretting the attempt at humour. 'Now, if you don't mind I'll take some details. Please, sit down.' He gestured with a hand to a seat on the other side of the desk at which he sat.

The giant seemed to take an age to lower his huge body onto the chair and when he did, his body spilled over its edges and seemed to swallow it up.

'Now, some details first. Name?' his pen poised above the form that began all official conversations.

'Mazzini, Ignazio.' he said with a sigh.

'Address?'

The giant began to calm down, slumped in his chair, giving the mundane details of his life. Only when d'Annunzio turned the page and asked for the particulars of the crime to which Ignazio wished to confess did he come to life once more, his eyes blazing with anger.

'I hit him! Not the kidnappers. With this bat. I . . . I can't stand to see him on television, being treated . . . being treated like some kind of a hero when it was *me* who waited in the alley and got him. It was me!' His voice rose and he sat forward in his chair. 'I wanted to get both of them when they came down, but there was only him and I didn't even kill him. I should have struck him again when he was down . . . but I heard the sirens . . . I thought they had come for me . . .'

'Ah, *signore*, wait, slow down.' D'Annunzio waved his hand for emphasis. 'I can only write so fast. Start again, please. Who did you hit with the bat and who has been kidnapped?' *Perhaps he is, after all, a madman*, he thought to himself.

And so, Ignazio slumped against the back of his chair and explained in more measured tones how in a bar one night someone had told him that the relationship between Silvia, his wife, and Alfio Bonfadini, her employer, was something more than the normal employer-employee relationship. It had become well known all over the village that there was little point in trying to buy a ball of wool or a pair of knickers between eleven and twelve every few mornings because the couple who worked in the shop were, as the informant delicately put it, 'otherwise engaged.' He had been furious and wanted to go round to Bonfadini's house immediately, but thought better of it, deciding to wait to take his anger out on them properly. Consequently, next day he had loitered in the alley that ran down the side of the building. He heard the commotion outside the bar, but decided that whatever was going on was none of his business and was about to climb the stairs to Bonfadini's flat when he heard someone coming down. When he saw Bonfadini running towards him he stepped out of the shadows and swung the baseball bat, hitting him full in the face. He had then heard sirens in the distance and, fearing someone had seen him and reported him to the police, took off over the wall at the back of the building. Later that day, to his horror he had seen Bonfadini claim on the television news that he had been struck by the kidnappers who had been at work in the bar next door as he tried to save the girl they were kidnapping. Bonfadini was a hero now and had been on television a further dozen times. Worse still, there were rumours in the town that he was going to receive a large reward from the father of the kidnapped girl for the 'valiant efforts' — that is how they were described in the newspaper — he supposedly made to save her.

'You see, I was driven to it. They were making a fool of me, people were laughing at me. I admit I wanted to kill them *both*. But now, I just want the truth to be told about that *bastardo*. *I* hit him! *I* smashed his nose! He is no hero!'

D'Annunzio's swivel-chair creaked in protest as he sat back in it. He had become increasingly galvanised by Ignazio's story as it unfolded.

'You understand you are likely to be charged with assault, *signor* Mazzini?'

'I wish I could be charged with murder! I would give anything not to see that *buffone* acting the hero on TV again!'

D'Annunzio put down his pen and reached for the telephone.

'A moment, please *signor* Mazzini.' He cleared his throat, as if he were a small-town politician about to give an important speech: 'Ah, yes, I would like to speak to the *Commissario* please?' It came out as a question. Not at all the way he wanted it to sound.

This could indeed be embarrassing for the hero of Beldoro, he thought, as he waited for the voice at the other end of the line.

8

10 November 1999
Beldoro
North Italy

Michael drove down through northern and eastern France and onwards into the more enticing mountainous region that abutted onto Italy. He had been a traveller on this road many times and in many different guises – as a hitch-hiker when he was a teenager, heading south to meet up with whatever fate he could find, selling leather bracelets in sunsoaked markets the length of the Riviera or picking grapes near Béziers; with Rosa, a few years later, in an open-topped car, heading for the silver beaches of the south, wiping with the back of their hands the peach juice running down their chins, lust colouring their every move; later still with Rosa, cooler, better off, much older, it seemed, and more assured, taking several days to get there, good hotels booked *en route,* silk handkerchiefs with which to soak up the peach juice still glistening on their chins.

This time he approached the journey in a business-like fashion. He noted only perfunctorily the mountains beginning to rise on the horizon as he headed towards the French Alps. He listened to Puccini and Bruce Springsteen on the car stereo and stared straight ahead at the road that glistened in an endless, shiny black strip into the distance.

By seven in the evening he had crossed the French–Italian frontier – cold-looking soldiers waving a long, slow-moving snake of cars through with hardly a glance at passports and faces within – and his eyes had begun to ache with the strain of the drive. He stopped at a town about thirty kilometres into Italy, a town that existed solely for that purpose. Consequently, he had a choice of any number of inexpensive hotels, picking one that seemed very modest from the outside and did not betray that particular notion inside. Still, it was clean and a place to lay his head. He ate pasta and drank a small carafe of red wine at a restaurant in the middle of the town's one street before calling it a day around ten.

Next morning dawned crisp and sunny and he was speeding along the motorway to Turin long before the other travellers had even breakfasted. He breezed past Turin but got hopelessly lost a few hours later on the motorway that skirted the northern edges of Milan, finding himself in a spaghetti-like tangle of roadworks and missed signs. Eventually, he extricated himself from it and had soon joined the motorway to Lecco and Como, a road with which he was very familiar from his visits with Rosa to this part of the world. It led, if you stuck to the direction of Chiavenna and Sondrio, around the eastern side of Lake Como. Michael took the wrong junction, however, and found himself on the road along the western side of the lake. Never mind, he could take the ferry to his destination, Beldoro, from the small lake-side town of Menaggio.

A few wispy clouds punctuated the blue sky, but, in the distance, over the mountains which enclosed the lake, the clouds were gathering and starting to look angry. The petrol gauge on the BMW was registering about a third of a tank as he pulled into a tiny one pump petrol station to fill up and check the map. Beldoro would be a good base for his investigations. It was there that the kidnapping had taken place in the bar next to the shop belonging to that character, Bonfadini, who had become a hero. Luigi Ronconi, father of the kidnapped girl also lived close by, in what could only be described as a palace overlooking the lake and the small town.

He arrived at the ferry at 3.20 p.m. to discover there was not another crossing until 3.55. The afternoon was getting chilly as the wintry sun began to slip down towards the mountains, whose jagged peaks were topped with snow, and he decided to give himself some energy for the last part of his long journey by drinking an *espresso* at the large hotel that overlooked the ferry. He left his car second in the ferry queue and walked the short distance to the hotel. Its frontage was grand, but the bar was surprisingly small. A television set was switched on with the volume turned up very loudly. A large, masculine-looking woman stood behind the bar and at a table in the corner sat another woman and a baby. She was talking to a man he took to be the hotel chef, judging from his white top and checked trousers, and both were making cooing noises at the baby in between remarks. He sat down at the only other table, which was right in front of the television and was soon taking his first grateful sip of the bitter black coffee and reading the headlines of the *Gazzeta dello Sport,* which lay on the table in front of him. But the loud voices booming out of the television almost immediately wrestled his attention away from the latest problems facing the over-paid stars of Inter Milan.

The programme on the TV was coming to an end, the credits rushing underneath the main action as the host brought it all to a close, giving way to adverts, loud and brash, selling pasta, washing powder and cars. These were followed by an insistent theme introducing a local news bulletin: a dapper middle-aged man with unnatural, bronze-coloured hair staring at the camera and announcing the main story of the day – the exposure of Alfio Bonfadini, the hero of Beldoro, as a liar.

A man, by the name of Ignazio Mazzini, had confessed to assaulting Bonfadini because Bonfadini had been having an affair with his wife, who worked in Bonfadini's shop. Film of a strangely smiling Ignazio being led in handcuffs into the main police station by police officers over whom he towered was followed by a picture of Alfio's shop. Police were considering, said the announcer, whether to bring charges against Bonfadini.

'That's a turn-up for the books,' said the large woman who was polishing glasses behind the bar.

'Oh, Bonfadini was never any kind of a hero. I could have told the police that. He's a weakling, an idiot. He spends his life selling wool and knickers, remember.'

'Judging by some of those rich bitches in Beldoro, probably *woolen knickers* sometimes, too!' The woman behind the bar laughed as she said this and the others, Michael included, joined in. Moments such as this reminded him how good it was that he had learned Italian a number of years back.

His coffee finished, he wandered back out and leaned on the railing that ran along the side of the lake. The ferry, a small craft capable of carrying about ten cars, was approaching, cutting a line through the faultless surface of the water.

A turn-up for the books, indeed, and one about which the police will not be at all happy, he thought. He had planned on talking to this Alfio Bonfadini, had thought it might make an interesting sidebar to the kidnapping story, the elevation of this shopkeeper into a national hero. This new twist on the story, however, was even better and he would try to talk to this new man on the scene, Ignazio Mazzini. The first piece he wrote would be about this particular blind alley in which the police now found themselves.

The ferry arrived, unloaded a couple of cars and with an efficiency rare in any activity carried out in Italy, filled up again with the four who now waited alongside Michael's car. Within a few minutes he was staring back at the hill that rose above the multi-coloured buildings of Menaggio as the ferry engines throbbed beneath his feet on the way to the next stop before it zigzagged back across the lake to Beldoro.

Once again, he recalled making exactly this journey a few years ago with Rosa. They had eaten sandwiches at the rails of the ferry with the wind pulling at their hair, but had stayed on and returned to Menaggio where they had left their car. He felt a stab of pain as he remembered that crossing and reminded himself that he would have to get to Milan. He had called into a post office before leaving London and had sent an express letter to the box number that he had discovered at Rogerson & Gilchrist. In the letter, he had enigmatically told the recipient that he had something of great interest to him and suggested that if he wished to find out what it was he should meet him at the bar in Milan's Stazione Centrale at noon on the 12th of November.

How beautiful Beldoro had looked when he had last seen it with Rosa — as the ferry approached, he saw that it still was. The hotels that clustered around the lake-front were painted in a variety of shades of ochre, topped by red slate roofs. The tower of the church climbed up above the red roofs in the centre and pine trees clothed the hill that rose behind the town, sheltering it from the worst of the winter weather. Large buildings hid amongst the trees there, but standing proudly out on its own and hiding from nothing and no one was a large orange building, which he recognised from photographs as Palazzo Ronconi.

He carefully drove his car off the ferry and turned into the road that ran along the lake. Hotels lined the streets, looking closed for the winter as indeed the majority of them were. He had consulted a Michelin guide on the road through France and had selected the appropriately named Hotel del Lago, phoning ahead to ensure that it remained open during the off season. It was across from this establishment that he parked his car, staring up at the hotel's weather-beaten, orange-coloured frontage.

He waited an age at the front desk – this was, indeed, the close season for visitors. Eventually, a man appeared, clad in paint-spattered overalls. He apologised for the fact that the hotel was undergoing some refurbishment, which meant that Michael's room was located at its furthest extremity. It was no more than a cupboard and to get to it he had to clamber over rolled-up carpets and furniture that belonged elsewhere.

'*Mi dispiace, signore,*' the paint-spattered man apologised all the way through the seemingly endless corridors. In all honesty, Michael did not care and when he threw open the shutters, none of it mattered anyway. His small room looked out on the lake, the magnificent view taking in Menaggio and the mountains on the far shore, the peaks of which were beginning to dissolve into mist in the early evening light.

Naturally, in this state of disrepair, the hotel had closed its restaurant for the winter – it was only open for breakfast – which meant that, after showering in a bathroom so small that he could hardly turn round in it, Michael walked the streets to find somewhere to eat, settling finally on a busy, steamy-windowed bar full of noisy card-playing workmen that was able to cook him a steak that he could wash down with his customary half carafe of red wine. Such was his relief at having stopped travelling and at being anonymous amongst all these people living out their existences in this town on the banks of Lake Como that he ordered a second small carafe, knowing he would regret it in the morning. He drank it, watching them talk, argue and laugh at each other, an outsider looking in on the life of a town and happy to be so.

At eleven o'clock he got up and staggered through the deserted narrow streets of Beldoro, his footsteps echoing in the darkness. As he entered the hotel, he looked back across the lake, which stretched like a black sheet towards the lights of Menaggio. A light flashed in the distance, probably on the ferry landing stage. Above it, lives were being played out, lives from which he felt for the moment divorced. Somehow, he had to get back into that world, he thought, stopping for a moment in the doorway.

When he went down to breakfast at around eight-thirty next morning, he discovered he was not alone in the hotel, after all. There were four others – three elderly Germans, a man and two women, obviously on holiday and dressed for walking in stout boots and thick clothes. There was also another man, an Italian, it seemed to Michael, probably here on business. A travelling salesman of some kind, he thought, from the practised manner in which he dealt with the complexities of the self-service breakfast bar.

He rapidly lost interest, however, as he drank his coffee and planned his day. He never slept well when he drank a lot, and having wakened early this morning, around six-thirty, he had watched the television news and was surprised to learn that Ignazio Mazzini had been released from custody late the previous night. Alfio Bonfadini, it seemed, was unable to stand the embarrassment of going to court with this case and had decided not to press charges. The police, therefore, had had no choice but to let Mazzini go free. The newsreader noted, however, that the police had not yet decided whether to charge Bonfadini in relation to the lies he had told about the kidnapping.

Perhaps, thought Michael, it was time to talk to these two men, Alfio Bonfadini and Ignazio Mazzini.

The Bonfadini shop was just off a medium-sized square with a church dominating one side of it and shops occupying the other three, which served as the centre of town. Michael made his way there around eleven, as the streets began to fill with the increased bustle of late morning.

The shop itself was dowdy, its one window filled with lack-lustre displays of wool and faded knitting patterns on one side and industrial sized women's under-garments on the other. Bonfadini's customers were evidently of the matronly sort.

The lights of the shop, however, were off and the sign on the door had been turned around to the side that announced that it was closed.

Next door, as Michael already knew from press reports about the kidnapping, was the bar in which it had actually taken place. It was long and small, with a chrome-surfaced bar running down one side. Michael entered and ordered a *caffè macchiato* from the barman, who was absently cleaning glasses and staring out through the doorway as if expecting someone extraordinary to walk in at any moment.

'So, he's closed, next door?' asked Michael, lifting the small cup to his lips.

'*Cosa*?' The barman had been far away.

'The wool and knickers shop. Is it closed?

A smile played across the dark features of the barman.

'*Si, signore, chiuso*. He is closed, but the widow that works for him is most definitely *open* for business.' He laughed, creases appearing around his eyes.

'You mean . . .?' Michael also smiled.

The barman leaned forward, his elbows resting on the bar, as if he were sharing a great secret.

'It's well-known, *signore*. Every day, when the widow is in, from eleven until twelve, Alfio Bonfadini likes to enjoy a little, how shall we say, *siesta*. He is very good to his employees because he allows them to share his hour off.' He leaned forward even further and began to speak very quietly, even though there was only one other customer – an elderly man, reading a newspaper at the other end of the bar. 'The Mazzini woman wasn't the first, you know, although she was certainly the youngest.' He then stood up straight again, picked up his tea towel and began to dry another glass.

'So what kind of women does he usually go for?' Michael smiled conspiratorially, humouring him.

'Usually they are older, widows or spinsters who are just glad to have some tender loving care.'

'What is it now then, Widow or spinster?'

'Oh, it's the widow Briganza. She's fifty, lost her husband fifteen years ago. As I say, hungry for a little TLC.'

'And how long before he opens for business again?'

The barman looked at his watch. 'He will be in for a coffee and a brandy on the stroke of twelve, *signore*. But, hey, who wants to know all this. You a journalist?'

'Yes, I am. From London.'

'Once, you know, that would have been some kind of big deal round here, but we've had them in here from all over the world – the States, Australia, Scandinavia, you name it. I've been on TV all over the world. My cousin in Sydney saw me being interviewed.'

'So, you were on duty then, when the kidnapping . . .?'

'Actually, no, *signore*, but most of you reporters really didn't care. It was my brother Claudio who was on duty that day, but he is a little camera-shy, so I have been standing in for him.'

The man at the end of the bar signalled for a refill and the barman went over to serve him. Michael picked up a copy of *La Stampa* from a nearby table and lost himself temporarily in the affairs of the world.

It was fifteen minutes later, at exactly twelve, as the barman had predicted, that Alfio Bonfadini came in. It was not too difficult to work out that it was him because of the scaffolding of plasters and bandages that covered his nose.

He was a plump, balding man whom Michael estimated to be in his early fifties. He had something almost feminine about him; his walk or his posture, Michael was unsure. Bonfadini ordered a coffee and a brandy and stood at the bar, lifting the tiny coffee cup to his mouth, a cigarette between the fingers of the same hand and his little finger crooked delicately like an English aristocrat.

'*Signor* Bonfadini?' Michael had gone to the bar and ordered a beer. He couldn't drink another *macchiato,* as it generally played havoc with his digestion if he drank more than one cup of Italian coffee.

'Maybe. Who wants to know?' He changed the position of his foot on the chrome foot-bar that ran along the base of the bar, turning towards Michael.

'Michael Keats of the London *Evening Post*.' Michael extended his hand.

'*Un altro giornalista meschino!*' he said, ignoring Michael's outstretched hand. 'Look, I have nothing to say to the press. Nothing that has not already been said.'

'But we would all like to know what you really saw of the incident, *signor* Bonfadini. You must have seen or heard something.'

'Look, *signor* . . .'

'Keats.'

'*Signor* Keats. Most of the time during which this incident took place I was flat on my back with my nose spread across my face. I've already told the police a hundred times what I saw and heard. I heard the scream, then saw the van pull up, watched three guys get out . . .'

'Hang on a second, *Signor* Bonfadini. You just said you heard the scream and then saw the van arrive on the scene. Is that right? That's not exactly what you've been saying up till now, is it?'

Bonfadini suddenly looked worried. He began to stammer. 'Erm . . . I . . . I'm not sure . . . perhaps . . . perhaps not.' And then angrily, collecting himself again. 'I can't remember. I was knocked senseless. My nose was smashed by that thug, Mazzini.'

The barman returned to the bar from wiping some tables outside and Michael took Bonfadini by the arm, guiding him to a table in the corner where they could not be overheard.

'*Un altro cognac per signor Bonfadini, per favore,*' he called over his shoulder to the barman, pushing the other man into his seat and taking a seat opposite, both elbows on the table, looking hard into Bonfadini's face.

'Look, *signor* Bonfadini . . . Alfio . . . I am not concerned about whether your nose was broken by Ignazzio Mazzini or by a kidnapper. What is important is what happened just before that. So, concentrate. What came first – the scream or the van?'

Bonfadini was visibly shaken, reaching nervously with a shaking hand to the bandages across his face as if their very presence provided him with confirmation that all was well with the world.

'I . . . I am not sure. I was walking past the window,' he was looking at the table, his eyes screwed up, going through his actions carefully in his mind. 'I had to pee; you know how it is when you have been making love?' Something approaching a leer crossed his face.

'Yes, and . . .?'

'Ah, *signore*, I remember now. Silvia – that's the wife of that ignorant farmer, Mazzini . . .' A faraway look came into his eyes. 'Oh, *Madonna*, what a body, *signore*. The body of a . . .'

'Okay, Alfio, I get the message.'

'Sorry, *signore*. I heard the scream, as I say, as I was making my way across the room and I remember I pulled the curtain back to see what was going on. It was then that I saw the van come down the street and stop out there in front of the bar.'

'So, you *did* hear the scream before you saw the van.'

'I suppose I must have. I heard the scream and then looked out of the window to see what was going on.'

Michael sat back to consider this. If the scream happened before the van arrived then surely it was obvious that one of the kidnappers was already in the bar. Why had the police not worked that out?

Bonfadini threw back the cognac that Michael had bought for him and made as if to go.

'Now I must get back to work, *signore*.'

'Just one more question, Alfio, if you don't mind.' Michael grabbed his arm as he stood up.

'Okay, but please make it quick.' He looked at his watch.

'How many men got out of the van when it arrived?'

104

'Three. Definitely three. Two from the back and the driver.'

'And how many dragged Teresa Ronconi out of the bar?'

'Again three. But, look, *signore*, I have to go. My shop . . .' He stood up, shrugging his shoulders at Michael and bustling off in that slightly effeminate way of his towards the door of the bar.

So, the action had actually begun in the bar before the van arrived, Michael thought. However, according to what he remembered of the press reports he had studied, there had been no other witnesses apart from Alfio and the barman.

'Your brother, is he around, *signore*?' he asked the barman.

'Claudio? Oh, no. All of this . . . he has taken it very badly. As soon as the media started to arrive in town he took off. He's the delicate sort, you see.' He smiled contemptuously at the thought of his brother's delicacy. It was obvious to Michael that it was a source of some tension for the two men.

'Oh, and where did he take off to then? Milano? Roma?'

'Oh no, *signore*, he couldn't go that far. I don't think Claudio has been to Milano more than twice in his entire life— he certainly only went further than that when he did his military service in Firenze.'

'So where . . .?'

'He's gone up the mountain.'

'Up the mountain?'

'*Sì*. Like a lot of people round here, our family has a little chalet up in the mountains. In the old days they took the cattle up there in the summer. These days we rarely go up there. I want to sell the damn place, but Claudio won't agree. Anyway, at the first sign of a TV camera, he was off.'

'So where exactly is this chalet of yours? How can I find it?'

The other man smiled. 'No, *signore*. You don't quite understand. My brother doesn't wish to speak to you or any other journalist. That's why he's gone up there, to get away from all of you.'

His eyes fell to Michael's hand, in which was clasped a wad of notes. Michael began to slide them across the bar.

'There's two hundred and fifty thousand *lire* for you if you'll give me directions to the chalet. And the same for Claudio for a half hour conversation. Come on, how many *macchiati* do you have to pour to make that much profit?'

'Look, *signore*, my brother and I may disagree about a lot of things, but I still would not betray him. You won't find out from me where he is.' He turned away from Michael and walked to the other end of the bar.

Michael shrugged his shoulders, picked up the fistful of notes and walked out into the street. He was walking slowly in the direction of his hotel, wondering what to do next when he heard a voice behind him.

'Hey, *inglese*, wait.'

An elderly man whom he at first failed to recognise, was limping breathlessly behind him.

'Ah, *signore* . . .' He stopped in front of Michael, breathing heavily from his exertions and removing his cap to wipe his sleeve across his sweat-covered brow.

'*Signore*, I was in the bar . . .' Michael recognised him now. He was the man who had been standing at the other end of the bar. '. . . and I overheard your conversation with Franco, the barman. I wondered, is your offer open to anyone?'

'Offer?'

'I mean the two hundred and fifty thousand for directions to Claudio's chalet in the mountains?'

'It might be. Do you know . . .?'

'Indeed, I do, *signore*. I am a friend of the family. I used to go up there hunting with the boys' father.'

The road was hardly a road at all. It switched back and forth up the side of the mountain. For a half mile or so the precipitous drop fell away on his right and then for the next half mile it fell to his left. The valley down below became increasingly distant and then disappeared from view entirely as he drove over a ridge, deeper into the mountains.

Every now and then he would pass a track leading off the road with a small, usually hand-made sign announcing the ownership of whatever property lay through the trees at the end of the track.

The air was very pure and he opened the car windows to let it circulate.

The man with the limp had given him precise instructions as to which road of the several that led up into the mountains he should take. He had told him that the place he was looking for was at the very end of the road he was now on and that it was signposted 'Casa Scatti', Scatti being the surname of Claudio and Franco.

'It is a long way up, *signore*, about three hundred metres beyond the end of the road. It's the highest chalet. You have to leave your car and walk the last part. It's a steep climb.'

He had, indeed, been climbing for about thirty minutes on a track that became ever more precipitous and ever less smooth. The track began to narrow and branches began to brush against the sides of the car. Then up ahead he saw a scruffy, old, red Cinquecento parked against a wall of trees that signalled the end of the road. To the right, a footpath led off upwards through the trees and a wooden board nailed to a tree with a painted arrow underneath it told him that Casa Scatti lay at the end of the path.

Michael took his shoulder bag, containing his tape machine and spare tapes and batteries, locked his car and set out on the footpath. It was clearly cut through the trees and bushes, but the grass and ferns growing across it showed how little used it was. Above him, the trees closed in and he was able to see only patches of sky between the overhanging branches. There was complete silence apart from the dull sound of his footsteps and his increasingly heavy breathing.

At last, he broke out of the trees into a grassy clearing and there in front of him stood the Casa Scatti: a small, stone building with a wooden roof and a raised porch at the front, accessed by a wooden staircase of four steps. There was a deathly hush in the clearing; not even the movement or call of a bird shattered the silence. Above the house, the jagged peak of the mountain rose into the clear, blue sky, the first snow of winter clinging to its steep, rocky slopes.

'*Buongiorno!*' Michael paused at the foot of the steps up to the porch. No sound or movement came from within. 'Claudio!' He shouted now to the forest around him, thinking that perhaps Claudio was walking or climbing nearby. Still nothing.

He waited a moment and then climbed the steps. Arriving at the door, he raised a hand to knock upon it, only to find that it was actually slightly ajar.

'Hello!' he called, more nervously this time, gingerly pushing the door open and peering into the darkness within. The curtains were closed. He stepped cautiously inside, his eyes becoming used to the dark. It was furnished very simply: just a table, some chairs, and a sofa, but the chairs had been upended and as he took a step forward, Michael felt and heard the crunch of broken glass beneath his feet.

There was an odd smell. Like food gone rotten and left for a week. There was also a sound, a deep humming, seeming to come from behind the door to his right.

His hand grasped the door handle and began to slowly turn

it. At the same time, he said once more, but more quietly this time, '*Buongiorno*? Claudio?'

The door opened and he was hit by a sickening stench that invaded his nostrils, seeped down his air passages and ended in the pit of his stomach, pushing up the coffee and beer that he had drunk earlier in the day.

There before him, slumped in a bath, was the body of a man he presumed to be Claudio Scatti, bathing in his own slowly congealing blood. Around his head he wore a hood made up of hundreds of buzzing flies, frenziedly investigating a gaping wound in his neck, which he wore like a second smile. Claudio's eyes stared sightlessly straight at Michael in the doorway and his mouth was frozen for all eternity in the midst of a silent scream.

Michael's legs momentarily began to fold under him, as the horror of the sight invaded his mind and the smell his senses. Then he turned and ran, gasping for air and gagging. He banged painfully into the doorjamb and then stumbled and fell down the four steps that led down to the lush grass of the clearing, landing on all fours at the foot. He retched dryly and painfully, inhaling great lungfuls of clean mountain air between each crisis of his body.

'God!' Tears ran down his cheeks, partly from the exertions of retching, but equally from the shock of the hellish sight that he had just witnessed.

Clambering unsteadily to his feet, he staggered back into the shady comfort of the trees, plummeting through the branches and bushes that threatened to eventually swallow the path entirely. He reached the car, got in, locking the doors immediately and sat back, his head burrowing deep into the headrest, his eyes screwed tight shut.

'Jesus Christ!' he squeezed the words like toothpaste between gritted teeth. 'Jesus Christ!'

*

It had been a difficult few hours. He had driven back down the mountain recklessly, almost losing control several times on the steep, switch-back road. On returning to his hotel room he had locked the door and had drawn the curtains, peering out between them, as if expecting to see someone staring back up at him from the street outside.

It seemed pretty obvious to him now that Claudio Scatti had been involved in some way in the kidnapping. If Alfio Bonfadini's memory was right, and there was a scream from the bar *before* the arrival of the van, it could only be that Claudio, alone in the bar with Teresa Ronconi, had been involved, had begun the action.

And now, he was dead.

Michael realised it was foolish, but he had decided not to go to the police. He gambled that Scatti's body would remain undiscovered for some time and that, in turn, would give him some time to investigate further and put together a more comprehensive story. And, anyway, there was not very much Michael could do for him now.

It had not been difficult to find the Mazzini farm; the television news had given the name of the village near which it was situated. About five miles from Beldoro, having climbed even more switchback roads with precipitous edges, he came upon a group of houses – it could hardly be called a village – and had been directed along a dirt track road by an old woman who stood in the road watching him drive off, shaking her head at what he presumed she thought was the foolishness of Ignazio Mazzini getting his shame paraded on television and brought these foreigners to visit him.

Not far along, this track had widened into a small plateau and there in its midst stood the stone farmhouse to which an unwilling Ignazio had brought his equally unwilling bride, Silvia, five years ago. The house gave the impression of having grown out of the earth. Either that or it was tumbling back into it. It was difficult to make out if its walls were actually walls or just piles of large stones onto which a roof had been thrown. Old, rusting farm machinery added to the overall impression of disintegration and neglect.

As he pulled up on the uneven ground, however, a snarling dog came running towards him, teeth bared and eyes red with fury. Foamy saliva now ran down the car window where the dog's sharp-toothed mouth had jumped up. Michael instinctively pushed down the locks and leant inwards away from the muffled growling. The dog now stood about three feet away from the car, snarling and barking at him. Its fury showed little sign of abating until the door on the farmhouse slowly opened and a huge figure stepped out, a figure Michael recognised from the television as Ignazio Mazzini.

'Hoh! *Via!*' he growled at the dog which immediately started whimpering and backing away from the car, its tail between its legs.

Ignazio stood at the door staring in Michael's direction. He wore what appeared to be the same scruffy dark suit that he had been wearing as he walked into the police station on television and on his head was a small, trilby-style hat of the kind the men wore in these mountains. His dark face was etched with deep lines and his eyes sank deep into their sockets.

Michael gingerly opened the car door and stepped out, but the dog was sufficiently cowed by Ignazio's voice to do nothing but yelp in a shame-faced way, wagging its tail and looking at him with large eyes.

'*Buongiorno,*' he walked towards the house, more confident now that the dog had been ordered to leave him alone.

'*Signor* Mazzini?'

'*Sì.* I am Ignazio Mazzini. And you are . . .?'

'*Signor* Mazzini. I'm Michael Keats and I'm a reporter. I

work for the English newspaper, the London *Evening Post*. I'm very pleased to meet you,' he stretched out his hand, which was received somewhat unwillingly in the massive, calloused hand of the farmer. 'I wondered if I could talk to you about Alfio Bonfadini and the events of the last few weeks?' He had decided that there was little point in beating about the bush with Ignazio and he also counted on the early mention of Bonfadini raising the hackles of the big man.

'Ach!' Ignazio leaned forward, hawked and spat out a ball of green phlegm, which hit the wall beside the door and began to slowly run down it. 'Don't talk to me about this man. He is as good as dead if I ever see him again. He *would* be dead if only I had had the courage to hit him just once more ...' His eyes were blazing with anger. He seemed so angry he could not talk.

'Perhaps we could go inside and you could tell me about you and Bonfadini? I expect you'll be happy to see the truth being told about this business, rather than let anyone go on believing Bonfadini's lies?'

'*Sì!*' There clearly was no doubt in his mind. He certainly wanted that. 'Please, come in.' He pushed the door open and stepped to one side, ushering Michael into the house with his hands. 'Please ... excuse the ...' He failed to finish the sentence, casting his eyes around the kitchen as he walked in and shaking his head. 'My wife ... you know, she has ... gone.' This last word, '*fuggita*', was difficult for the big man to say and he said it with such tenderness, such sadness, Michael thought.

The kitchen, however, was in a terrible state. Food lay all over the place and greasy plates were piled up in the sink. Coffee that had been spilled – goodness knows when – on the work surface had congealed into a shiny stickiness. A faintly rotting smell pervaded the atmosphere and Michael felt as if he did not want to touch anything. Especially the table at which Ignazio beckoned him to sit.

'She left immediately Bonfadini was taken to hospital. She knew it was me who had hit him, knew what a liar and a coward he is, that he didn't do what he claimed to have done.' He pushed some plates around the table to clear a space for Michael's tape recorder.

'You have no objection?' Michael asked, moving a heavy green ashtray piled high with ash and cigarette ends to one side and gingerly placing the machine on the table's sticky surface.

'No, none whatsoever. After all, I spent most of yesterday talking into one at the police station. What do you need to know?'

Michael spent the next forty-five minutes teasing Ignazio's life story out of him – the poor childhood spent on this farm; the loneliness of his adolescence followed by the humiliation of the times when he was treated like a circus freak and a target for bullies and drunks from both sides of the lake. Then he spoke of the anger he had felt on realising that once again he was being humiliated, how he had been told by a Beldoro man about his wife's dalliance with Alfio Bonfadini.

His story told, he slumped back in his chair, his eyes cast downwards, his mind struggling with the idea of living on with so much pain inside.

Michael took his leave of him, looking back in his rear-view mirror as he pulled away and seeing Ignazio standing staring after him, unmoving, sadness oozing from every pore.

The next day, Michael would be making the two-hour train journey to Milan and would be calling in at the *Post's* Italian sister paper to send the first part of his story through to London. He also wanted to send the photograph that Ignazio had given him, showing him and Silvia on their wedding day, standing awkwardly side by side, he in a dark suit that might even be the one he now wore every day; she, clutching a posy of flowers, wearing a white wedding dress that spilled out from her waist in copious folds; on both their faces an expression of complete incomprehension. And behind them the ever-present mountains rising accusingly towards the blue sky, the last remnants of winter dusting their peaks.

He was in two minds, however, about Claudio Scatti. It would make a fantastic scoop. But something made him hesitate. He should tell the police, of course. There was a man dead up there in the mountains. But, he knew that as soon as he told them, his story would become public property. The job, therefore, was to write the story, send it to London and then inform the police. There might be a spot of bother about holding the information back for a little while, even a charge of some kind. But it would be worth it. This story would blow the whole kidnapping wide open.

He finished writing the first part of his piece at around nine-thirty. He had sent out for a pizza from the local pizzeria about an hour-and-a-half before and he was now very thirsty and in need of a change of scenery. The paint-splattered receptionist had told him that, even though the rest of the hotel was closed, the bar remained open and so he thought he might as well go downstairs and have a couple of beers. With the intention of taking his mind off the task in hand, he picked up the book he had started reading weeks ago, left his room and negotiated the debris that littered the corridors of the hotel.

The bar was small but untouched by the refurbishment. The faded grandeur of the hotel was present in all its glory. At one end of the room stood an ornately carved mahogany bar, bottles and glasses glinting in the mirror that lined the wall behind it. Large paintings that were in need of cleaning hung on the cream walls and the ceiling above it all was like the icing on a wedding cake. In the centre hung a large chandelier, which threw light across the room in the same casual way as it had probably done for the last century.

There was no one behind the bar, but at one end of it, sat on a stool, with a glass and a bottle of whisky in front of him, sat the man who, at breakfast, Michael had thought to be a travelling salesman of some kind, although there was now something about him which suggested otherwise. His suit looked too good for that.

'*Buonasera.*' he said, looking up from the newspaper that rested on the bar in front of him. 'I'm afraid you'll have to help yourself. Paolo, the barman, is trying out his skills as a painter and decorator on the fourth floor this evening. He says we can drink what we want as long as we settle up with him in the morning. So . . .' he said, standing up. 'What will it be? Let me get it for you.'

'That's very kind of you. I'll just have a beer, please.' said Michael slipping onto a bar stool.

The other man walked around to the other side of the bar, bending to pick a bottle of beer out of the cold shelves at the bottom.

'Now, where is . . . ah, yes, here it is.' He reached down below the counter and brought out a bottle opener.

'Not often you get the run of a hotel bar, eh? Like letting a junkie loose in a pharmacy!' He opened the bottle and handed it to Michael along with a glass. 'I'm Vito Pedrini, by the way,' he went on, holding out a hand to Michael.

'Michael Keats,' said Michael, shaking Pedrini's hand.

'Ah, you're English?' he asked, not quite sure.

'Yes, I am.'

'I wasn't certain for a moment, there. I thought you might be

American. Or Canadian, even. That's a very different accent, you know, the Canadian accent. I lived there for a couple of years, I should know. But, hey, you speak good Italian.'

'Thanks. I learned it at university and I am . . . I *was* married to an Italian.' Michael took a long drink of the glass of beer in front of him. The pizza he had eaten had given him a thirst.

'So, you are here on business . . . Michael. I hope you don't mind if I call you . . .?'

'No, of course not. Please do. Yes, I am here on business of a kind. I'm a reporter.' He sat on a stool a few feet from the man.

'Ah,' Pedrini said, as if understanding a great deal. 'The Ronconi kidnapping. But, you're a little late, are you not? The journalistic community was out in force a few weeks ago when the kidnapping took place. I was passing through then as well. If I hadn't known Paolo here, I wouldn't have been able to find a room in all Beldoro!'

'I've come to follow up on the case. You know this story about the shop-keeper lying? I'm, as it were, applying some local colour to it.'

'I see. And have you found out anything of interest since you've been here?'

'No, not really. I've spoken to the farmer who beat up the shop-keeper, though. That was very interesting.'

'Really?' The other man leaned forward on his stool, his steely blue eyes full of interest. 'Did he tell you anything new?' Michael was for some reason suddenly suspicious of this man and immediately reined himself in from saying too much – although why would it be too much? The story was in the public domain, to the extent that it would probably be read by three quarters of a million Londoners tomorrow, or the day after, if the paper was already full.

116

'Oh, nothing you don't already know.'

He managed to pass the remainder of the half hour or so that he spent in Pedrini's company in inconsequential talk about Italy and England, and at ten-thirty, after two beers, he made his excuses and left in the direction of his room, where the work of the day engendered a good night's sleep, preparing him for an early rise in order to catch the train to Milan.

Mattresses hung drunkenly over the balconies of brightly coloured modern tower blocks as the train slowed on its way into the city.

Michael shifted uncomfortably on the leather seat and recalled making this journey with Rosa many years ago. They had gone to see Leonardo's *Last Supper* at Santa Maria delle Grazie and he remembered how they had been amazed at the simplicity of it. It had seemed to them not at all like one of the greatest pieces of art in the world, but just as it had actually been intended – wallpaper in a refectory, a piece of decorative adoration. They had both been deeply moved by just that simplicity and had left the building, walking in silence for a while before returning to their senses or, rather, having their senses returned to them by the bustle and the oppressive heat of Milan.

The train took an eternity to arrive at the station. It crawled over points at an achingly slow pace, accompanied by a metallic chorus of shrieks and screams, passing huts in which Michael could see blue-jacketed workmen enjoying their coffee and probably the finer points of the weekend's football. At last, it pulled into the station and squealed to a grudging halt.

The station bar was quiet. The waiters lounged at the till, talking to each other, glad of the rest. The gap between breakfast and lunch seemed, to some of the old-timers, at least, to get shorter every year and soon they would again be gliding across the stone floor, trays carrying impossible quantities of drinks, hands dealing out change like lightning and placing receipts on tables, or pulling the tops off bottles, always with their eyes looking in another direction, searching out the next order or the nearest short skirt.

Michael sat at a table close to the wall with a good view of the entrance to the bar and ordered his usual *macchiato*. 'Dirty coffee,' Rosa used to call it. To make identification possible, he had asked, in his letter to the man who had been with Rosa, that he carry a copy of each of two newspapers – *La Gazzetta dello Sport* and the London *Times*. This was a mixture he felt was unlikely to be found very often. The place was so quiet, however, that this fussiness seemed slightly redundant.

There was a huge clock on the wall behind the bar. The hands moved laboriously, with a loud clunking noise. It was, indeed, as if time had become audible, as if it could be heard passing.

Ten to twelve . . . clunk, clunk . . .

Seven minutes to twelve . . . clunk, clunk . . . The hands moved as if passing through something viscous and heavy. Michael began to sweat, in spite of the fact that it was chilly in the vastness of this huge edifice.

With four minutes remaining before the appointed time for the meeting, he regretted having sent the letter. He regretted having gone to Rogerson & Gilchrist, he regretted his trip to the Lighthouse Hotel. He began to feel very warm. What was he going to say to this man, anyway? 'So, you're the chap who was screwing my wife? Pleased to meet you.' It was not going to be the easiest conversation. He fought for the right words, but his mind was confused and nothing of any sense was rising to the surface. Most likely, he was going to walk away without saying a word, but, somehow, for some unknown reason, he felt he had at least to see him.

Three minutes to twelve . . . he lifted his coffee cup to his lips only to find his mouth filling with the bitter dregs from the bottom of the cup.

Two minutes to twelve . . . A man came in carrying *La Gazzetta* and Michael sat up, but there was no English paper and he turned round and walked out again just as soon as he came in.

Three minutes past twelve . . . He checked his watch, but the bar clock was indeed correct.

Ten minutes past twelve . . . His eyes darted to his watch again and his heart sank and rose at the same time. He need not find out the truth, need not confront Rosa's secret life.

Twenty-three minutes past twelve . . . Positive joy at the thought of not having to deal with this, of being able to luxuriate in the idea that it might not be true; he may, in fact be wrong about what had been happening in the most important part of his life.

At half past twelve he stood up and negotiated a path between the tables to the door and out through the main section of the station towards the massive exit.

He failed to notice the figure leaning on the wall just outside the bar who pulled the collar of his heavy jacket tight around his neck, threw a darting glance to his right and his left and then fell into step about twenty yards behind him.

There was a constant hum in the room. The murmuring and sometimes shouting voices were accompanied by the sounds of fingers hitting computer keys. Men and women with phones pinned between their ears and their shoulders, talked and typed, occasionally taking their hands off the keys and gesturing with them.

Increasingly, newsrooms were beginning to look the same all over the world. This one was no different. True, the language was not the same, but close your ears and it could have been the *Post's* main news office in London, with black cabs and the ladies of Kensington crawling past outside instead of the luxurious cars and fur-coated women of the capital of northern Italy. Michael felt a stabbing pain of envy for all these journalists in their ranks of desks and cubicles, so comfortable in this, their scheme of things. They fitted where he no longer did. They had a purpose that he no longer did. He felt as if he was here in this country on false pretences, outwardly to write a story, but inwardly he knew very well that he was here to expunge a part of his life that he once held as dear as anything in the world. What kind of purpose could that truly be? It was as if he were about to destroy his own past and, in so doing, perhaps also destroy himself.

'Michael!'

His train of thought was interrupted by a plump figure making his way between the rows of desks. Bruno Barni and Michael had spent time in each other's company on several occasions. Most memorably, they had travelled together across America with Bill Clinton's cavalcade of journalists and hangers-on for the last month of the 1992 American election campaign. They had spent many nights carousing and bemoaning their journalistic fates in small town America and, as is always the case in such circumstances, had, on their last night in each other's company, sworn eternal friendship. Since then they had exchanged the occasional postcard, but had always failed to meet up whenever Michael had visited Italy or when Bruno had come to London.

'Michael, how are you?'

'All the better for seeing you, my old friend.' They clasped

120

each other in a bear hug and then Bruno stepped back, holding Michael by the shoulders.

'I was so sorry to hear about your wife, Michael. I couldn't believe it. I still can't.'

'Me neither, Bruno. As you can imagine, it's not been easy.'

Bruno put an arm around Michael's shoulder, walking him back the way he had come.

'Come on, let's get out of this dump and grab some lunch. I'll just get my jacket.'

They had almost finished their first bottle of red wine before the food arrived at the table. Michael had explained everything to Bruno and Bruno now sat shaking his head and running his hand through his thinning black hair.

'You mean you had no idea?'

'None whatsoever, Bruno.' He smiled at the apparent absurdity of it. *Surely you can tell when someone has fallen out of love with you? Surely you know when that someone is dreaming of a life with someone else?* 'Hey, I know what you're thinking. How come I didn't realise? Well, Bruno, it seems you just don't.' He smiled at Bruno and reached for the bottle, sharing the remnants between both glasses, at the same time indicating to a passing waiter that they were in need of another.

'Ah, Michael.' Bruno shook his head and stared into Michael's eyes. 'But, hey, you remember what we used to say whenever we hit one of those small towns in the States in ninety-two?'

They said it together, smiling at the memory: 'It don't get much worse than this!'

'But look, you say you don't know who this guy is . . .?' Bruno said this between hungry mouthfuls of *cotoletta alla Milanese* and Michael recalled just how much Bruno had loved his food in America. He would start the morning with a huge pile of pancakes and maple syrup and work his way

121

through whatever food he could get his hands on as the day wore on. Michael, a sparing eater at the best of times and especially when on the road, would look on in wonder and sometimes even disgust, as steaks, ice cream, waffles, and hamburgers would disappear in ever larger quantities into that grinning mouth. 'You have no idea . . .?'

'Well, I know he's Italian. I know he wears a size forty-four jacket. I know he has expensive taste. Oh, and I think I have a name that has some kind of connection to him.' He put down his knife and fork and searched in his inside pocket for his wallet. From it he fished out the card that he had discovered in the jacket pocket that drunken night at the Lighthouse Inn and handed it to Bruno. 'Or it could even be him, for all I know. I found that card in the pocket of the jacket I was sent.'

Bruno, in turn placed his knife and fork on the table and took the card from Michael.

'Massimo Di Livio, Via Broletto No. 110, Milano.' He read from the card and then turned it over in his fingers like a playing card with which he was performing a conjuring trick. 'I'm sorry, I don't know the name, but I know the street. To live in Via Broletto it helps if you have a lot of money in the bank. This guy is pretty well off.' He sat up, as if a thought had just occurred to him. 'But, hey, here's an idea. Why don't I run his name through our computers back at the office and have a word with a few people? Even if this isn't your man, he may at least be able to point you in the right direction.'

Michael concurred. 'Well, if it's not too much trouble . . .'

'It's no trouble at all, Michael. To tell you the truth, I'd like to help you get to the bottom of this. You seem a little, how do you say . . . dislocated from things, my friend. Understandably so, I might add.'

'Yes, you're right, Bruno,' Michael replied, nodding and

smiling slightly. 'I think I need what our American friends would call *closure*.'

They finished the meal talking about the old days and took leave of each other, agreeing to speak by telephone later in the day once Bruno had made his enquiries.

Michael walked unsteadily back to the *Stazione Centrale* and, even after drinking a bitter *espresso* at the bar in which he had waited in vain earlier in the day, he dozed all the way back to Beldoro, waking with a start as the train pulled into the station. He had intended to finish his piece at the office, but he had drunk way too much and would need to sleep it off before he could concentrate sufficiently to put together something cogent.

His shadow in the heavy jacket who had followed him to the newspaper office and sat at a corner table of the restaurant, slowly eating a dish of pasta, watched him climb onto the train before walking purposefully in the direction of a phone box at the exit to the station.

'Michael! I *so* enjoyed our lunch. I am just sorry it couldn't have taken place in happier circumstances.'

Michael's head felt fuzzy. He had lain down and almost immediately fallen asleep on the bed when he had returned to his room. Just before the telephone's shrill ring had jarred his senses around seven, he had once again found himself in the blue room with Rosa's flailing body speeding towards him, but never quite reaching him, on the bonnet of the blue car.

'But let me tell you, I've found something on your Massimo Di Livio. Something very interesting.'

'Yes, go on, Bruno. What have you got?' He rubbed the sleep from his eyes, making himself comfortable against the headboard of the bed.

'Now look, Michael, you said that this man was a big man?'

123

'Yes . . . the jacket was a size forty-four. I don't know what that is in European sizes . . .'

'Oh, don't worry, Michael, I've bought clothes in England. Forty-four is a substantial man. Not as substantial as me, of course, but that only comes with a lot of practice.'

Michael smiled.

'No.' His voice turned serious now. 'This Di Livio character, he *is* known to us. In fact, he is known also to the police; perhaps a little more intimately than *we* know him.'

'What do you mean, Bruno?'

'Well, I asked around – as you know I have some friends in the police – and I also had a look in our archives and came up with some interesting stuff about *signor* Di Livio.' There was a moment's silence and Michael guessed that Bruno was probably taking a sip from a glass of the bourbon he had grown to like so much in the States and which had been the cause of so many hangovers during those few weeks. 'For example, in 1968, he was suspected of being one of the henchmen of a guy running a protection racket in Turin. Three of his colleagues went to prison. He walked.' Another pause, another sip. 'In 1973, he was charged with rearranging the face of another character in the same line of business. Again, he walked – this guy has good lawyers, believe me. He stayed clean for ten years and then in 1979 he did time for some very tricksy financial dealings. His crime had gone legit,' – Bruno enjoyed using the argot of the American crime novels he loved so dearly – 'but *signore* Di Livio hadn't. He did three years and since he came out he seems to have kept his nose clean. He is very careful.'

'Good God, Bruno. That's unbelievable! How could Rosa get mixed up with such a man?' Michael was by now sitting bolt upright on his bed.

'That's just it, Michael. I've asked around and I also found some pictures. This is a seventy-year-old man who is as thin as a string of spit and is no more than five feet five inches tall. And if that wasn't enough to convince you, well, let me just say that from the conversations I have had, Di Livio's proclivities lie on the more, erm, muscular side, if you get my drift. No, believe me, Michael, this is definitely not your man.'

9

March 1944
Near Val Masino
The Valtellina
North Italy

Sandro nodded to a man whose name he did not know as he left the camp in Luigi's footsteps.

There were now some thirty-five men in the group of which Sandro was a member. They lived in these mountains over which they had total control, only visiting their families under cover of darkness or when they were absolutely certain of their safety.

In the early months of 1944, the politicians in Milan and Rome seemed finally to have come to some sort of agreement amongst themselves as to who the real enemy was and the Allies, from an earlier position of doubt, had gradually begun to understand the value these groups of fighters, no matter their political colour, could provide in blowing up bridges and sabotaging troop movements. At the same time, men had been flocking to join the nearest partisan group as the Germans began to send fit Italian men to do war work in Germany. Even if they escaped the dire consequences of transportation to the Fatherland, they still faced the possibility of being called up by Mussolini to support the Republic he had set up in Salò. Many of the partisans were also deserters from the Italian army and other groups contained American, British and Canadian soldiers, prisoners of war who had escaped from the Italian camps and whose fighting experience was proving invaluable in this guerrilla warfare.

The atmosphere in the camp was nervous. Operations in the valley had recently been very successful and had hurt the local German garrison very badly. They were having to throw more and more men into the fight against the partisans, distracting them from the even more serious threat of the Allied invasion from the south, which signalled the beginning of a push planned to take the Allies relentlessly to Berlin.

There were reports drifting back from the valley that the Germans were beginning to take steps against the local population. The slightest infringement of the stringent laws the occupying army had introduced resulted in harsh punishments for young and old. Thus, many of the men feared for their loved ones and guiltily prayed that it would be someone else's family that would suffer.

Sandro was no different. He was a hardened fighting man now. He had taken part in many actions, had done his share whenever it was required. His face, too had taken on a toughened look, had become weather-beaten and sharp. He had the air of someone older than his years. Lack of sleep and long hours staring down the barrel of his gun had carved an experience into his countenance that would have otherwise taken years to achieve.

His hardness, the cold, expressionless way in which he

went about the business of waging war on strangers, mostly as young as, or even younger than him, had not, however, eroded his thoughts and feelings for those he loved.

His father was dead. He had at last succumbed to his long illness before Christmas – and Sandro now had only his mother to worry about. She would be alright, however, and was unlikely to find herself in trouble, even from this occupying army who found trouble in a gaze in the street that lingered a few seconds too long.

He worried constantly, however, about Angela. He saw her infrequently, still in their clearing amongst the trees. She seemed almost happier these days, no longer having to listen for the language of Luigi's footsteps every night, no longer having to anticipate his mood and whether it was going to cause her pain, for he, of course, like Sandro was living in the mountains, moving camp every few nights to evade capture, although the Germans now ventured rarely into the higher slopes of the mountains, so tightly did the partisans control them.

Therefore, the group acted almost as it pleased and struck at the Germans frequently and effectively. Money, too, was coming in to help their efforts and it was to ease the transport of money to another group that Luigi and Sandro were walking back along the side of the valley towards Chiavenna.

They were to meet up with members of a squad from the valleys to the west who had accompanied from the Swiss border an Englishman bearing a large sum of money, which would furnish a brigade further along the valley with a war chest. Luigi and Sandro had orders to guide the Englishman to the edge of the territory that they patrolled by tomorrow evening, when they would be met by the other group.

The smell of a wood-fire alerted them to the proximity of the other partisans and a great deal of back-slapping and hand-shaking took place following their arrival in the clearing where the others had been waiting.

'*Falcone*!' – this was the *nom de guerre* that Luigi had adopted, as all did to avoid any casual connection of their names with espionage activities – 'good to see you. How goes it in the Valtellina? Come and have something to eat and tell us how many Germans you've killed.' They all laughed.

In the valleys of North Italy, Luigi – '*Il Falcone*' – had by now gained a brutal reputation for dispatching the enemy in a fairly unceremonious fashion. Since that day on which Dino had given up his life all those months ago, and on which Sandro had cried for the two terrified, young Germans that Luigi had executed in the trees, he had witnessed Luigi's ability to turn his heart icy cold on many occasions. In fact, he had become immune to it, the more frequently he had experienced it. So, he listened to Luigi's immodest recounting of recent actions and his lurid details of the deaths of tens of Germans without much interest.

Meanwhile, the Englishman sat apart from them, studying maps and scribbling in a small notebook. He was slight of build, with thinning hair. A pair of round, wire-rimmed spectacles on the end of his nose gave him the air of an academic. Sandro speculated that he had probably been a school-teacher or something similar before the war.

He walked over to the edge of the clearing where the Englishman was sitting.

'We weren't introduced,' – Luigi had deemed Sandro too unimportant to introduce properly to the group – 'I'm *Lupo*.' Sandro, too, had another name by which the war knew him. It was as if they all wished to divest themselves of their true selves for the duration of this conflict, as if their actions during these times could be considered to have been carried out by people who were not actually them. They were like performers, actors on a stage, taking on the roles of these soldiers, these killers.

'Ah, *Lupo*. A good name, indeed!' The Englishman's Italian was impressive, with a strong southern accent. 'Sorry I don't have as romantic a name as you. Captain George Bright of the SOE.' He put down the notebook and the maps and shook Sandro's hand. He then removed the spectacles from his nose and rubbed his eyes, at the same time yawning. 'I think I've been living the good life in Berne a little too long. I'm completely exhausted after walking for a couple of days.'

They talked for quarter of an hour and Sandro learned something about George Bright's life. He had not been too far wrong about his pre-war occupation. He had, in fact, been a lecturer at a small college in the south of England, married with one child, a girl of ten whom he had not seen for almost a year and whom he obviously missed more than words could express. It was easy to tell just how much he missed her from the look that entered his eyes when he showed Sandro a photograph of her – a blonde, curly-haired child with a smiling face: 'Smile for Daddy a long way away,' he could hear voices saying on the other side of the lens.

Eventually, Luigi stirred himself from his conversation. Throwing a piece of rabbit bone down on the fire and wiping his greasy lips with the sleeve of his coat, he announced that it was time they set off, so that they could get in a couple of hours' walking before darkness fell on the mountains. They made their farewells and left.

They walked in silence, Luigi leading, the Englishman in the middle and Sandro bringing up the rear. After a couple of hours, they stopped for the night beneath a rocky outcrop, which sheltered them from the slight drizzle that had begun to fall. After eating some cold meat that they had brought with them, they lay down to sleep as best they could, surrounded by the mist that had begun to envelop the mountains.

Next morning, as Sandro rolled his blanket and tied it to his rucksack, Luigi came over to him, drinking from a pewter hip flask.

'Ach!' he shivered as the liquid hit the back of his throat. 'Want some?' He held the flask out to Sandro.

'No thanks, *Falcone*.' Sandro had grown to hate this habit of drinking *grappa* to kick-start the day. It only made his head fuzzier and it upset his stomach.

'You know, I've been thinking, lad.' Luigi wiped his mouth after taking another hefty slug from the flask. 'In this weather the Germans aren't going to be out in the hills.' He looked out across the valley, or rather, he looked in that direction, but the mist and the relentless drizzle that accompanied it, meant that he could see little but a hanging greyness that clothed the entire valley. 'I really don't think there's any need for you to come any further.'

Sandro was confused. 'Why? What do you mean, *Falcone*?'

'I mean, we're not far from your village. Why don't you go and visit your mother, see if she's alright?' He smiled. 'I can manage the remainder of this journey on my own. We're only about fifteen miles from the meeting place. We should be there in about four or five hours, if the Englishman can keep up.' He sneered in the direction of Captain Bright, who sat on the edge of a rock, wiping his glasses with a grubby handkerchief. 'And I *do* know where I'm going.'

'But, no. It wouldn't be safe, *Falcone*.' Sandro was elated and reluctant to argue too vehemently in favour of staying with Luigi and the Englishman. The thought of seeing his mother and maybe even Angela, filled him with anticipation and no small amount of guilt that Luigi was giving him permission to once again wrap his arms around his wife.

'Oh, of course, it would be safe. In fact, it might even be safer without you. One less pair of boots blundering through the undergrowth might make less noise. Go! Go and see your *mamma*. And enjoy some home cooking. That, *Lupo*, is an order from your *comandante*!'

A huge smile creased Luigi's features and he laughed, slapping Sandro on the back and knocking the wind out of his lungs.

Indeed, it *was* wonderful to be back in his own house with his mother busying herself around the range on the fire-place, cooking for him as if that was the purpose for which she had been put on the earth. She had cried when she saw him and threw her arms around him.

Later, towards midnight, he stood outside, leaning against the wall of the house, blowing the smoke from the last cigarette of the day into the night. The mist had cleared as the day had progressed and the night was now clear, with a three-quarter moon illuminating the village below his mother's house and making the shadows of the far side of the valley just discernible.

He was thinking of the detour he would make tomorrow to visit Angela on the way back to the camp – Luigi had told him he did not have to be there until nightfall. His heart thumped against the wall of his chest in anticipation of stroking her skin and of feeling her warm, moist breath drying on his face.

Suddenly, however, he was stirred from his dreaming by a sound emanating from the trees to the right of the house. His body stiffened. It could be a deer or a stray dog, but there was the unmistakable sound of twigs cracking underfoot. His rifle was inside the house, he was fully illuminated by moonlight and, consequently, there was little he could do as the sounds came closer.

A shape emerged from the trees and Sandro awaited others to join it, fully expecting this to be a German patrol, alerted to the fact that there was a partisan in the vicinity. Already playing in his mind were questions: *how could they know? Who had told them? What would happen to Mamma?*

'Sandro!' The voice was lenten and hoarse. 'Sandro! It's me ... Luigi ...' The shape then crumpled to the ground amongst the leaves that had lain there since autumn. His father would normally have cleared them, but by the time autumn had arrived he had been dying and the leaves had remained there throughout the winter, a reminder of his absence.

Sandro threw his cigarette down and ran towards the dark, fallen shape of Luigi.

'Luigi! What's happened?' Sandro cried, and looking around, he asked 'Where's the Englishman?' Sandro helped him up and, putting Luigi's arm around his shoulder, he half-carried and half-dragged him into the house.

'*Mamma! Mamma!*' She emerged from the next room, clad in a night-dress, a frightened look clouding her face. He said urgently, '*Mamma!* It's my *comandante*. He's been hurt ... shot!' He was looking at Luigi's shoulder. The whole right side of his body was shiny with blood, as if he had dipped his arm in a vat of wine. But the hole in his coat showed where the bullet had entered, a similar hole on the other side showing that, fortunately, it had also exited. 'Quick, *Mamma*, he's lost a lot of blood.' His mother put a pot of water on the fire as Sandro removed Luigi's coat and tore his shirt at the shoulder to get at the wound. Luigi's face was drained of all colour and he was shaking, as if chilled. 'He's in shock, *Mamma*. We need to keep him warm.'

His mother busied herself with cloths and boiling water as Luigi drifted in and out of consciousness.

'We were almost at the meeting place.' Luigi grimaced

as a wave of pain shook his shoulder. 'We were early. I will say one thing for that English *capitano*, Sandro, he was brave. I could tell he was finding it hard going, but he carried on without complaining.'

'Here, try some of this.' Sandro held a cup of broth to Luigi's lips and he drank from it.

'But we were almost there and, you know, I sensed something wasn't right. I could almost smell it. We rounded the side of a small hill just above Cerese and they were waiting for us. The Englishman was felled by the first volley. I fell back at once, heading off the trail, but a stray one caught me.' He winced, shifting position on the bed on which he lay. 'I didn't really notice it because I was so preoccupied with getting away from them. But when I stopped to get my breath back I knew all about it. It hurt like hell.'

'The Englishman . . .?'

'Oh, he was a goner. I could see as soon as he hit the ground. He took a lot of bullets, poor man. They were on the track in front of us. I thought the only thing was to try to get back here to your mother's house. Christ, I thought I'd never make it.'

A little later, Sandro went back into the bedroom to see how Luigi was, all thoughts of going to see Angela having disappeared from his head.

'Sandro, I am feeling better,' he said hoarsely, 'but there is one thing that is worrying me.'

'Yes, what is it, Luigi?'

'Well, you know I sent you back here because I figured you hadn't seen your *mamma* in quite some time and I know your father, God rest his soul, is only recently deceased. I did it with the best possible intentions and I really didn't think the Germans would be out and about in such weather. What we were doing was a piece of cake.'

'Yes, and I feel guilty as hell for not being there.' said Sandro, shaking his head.

'Exactly, Sandro, my lad. And I'm worried now that there will be repercussions. The English *capitano* was carrying a substantial sum of money and that is now lost to the Germans. I could get into serious trouble with headquarters for being casual in my approach to this exercise.'

'I'm sorry, Luigi, I should have insisted . . .'

'Unless . . .' said Luigi, looking steadily at Sandro.

'Unless what?' said Sandro, guilt lacerating his mind.

'Unless we just forget to tell anyone that you were not there?' He smiled now, smoothing down the blankets in front of him.

'Forget?'

'Yes, forget. After all, what difference would it have made if you had been there? The Germans would still have been waiting for us. The Englishman would still be dead. In fact, you might be dead also and, yes, it is terrible that the Englishman is dead, but it would be worse still if a good partisan were also out of action.'

Captain George Bright's bespectacled face entered Sandro's head at that moment and the smiling face of the daughter he had not seen for so long and who he would never see again crossed his mind.

'Well, if it'll help. I suppose it wouldn't really have made that much of a difference if I had been there.'

'Exactly, lad. Exactly. Now we will just forget that you weren't there. Eh?' He lay back on the pillow behind his head, closed his eyes and drifted into sleep once more.

Once again, Sandro leaned on the wall beside the front door, smoking a cigarette. There was something gnawing at the back of his mind like a dog with a bone, but he had no idea what it was. He feared that he no longer trusted the man who was sleeping in the room behind him, feared that he had never trusted him or his humanity, ever since Angela had told him about the beatings that she took from him, ever since he had disappeared into the trees with those two young Germans. And even now. He had no reason to doubt what Luigi had told him, but there was something inside him warning him that he should take everything this man said with a pinch of salt, that Luigi somehow saw himself standing outside of the rules by which other people lived.

There were moments, he realised, when he considered Luigi to be as much the embodiment of evil as the Nazis.

Waging war, taking lives, places blinkers over your eyes, he realised. You enter a tunnel that is walled by violence and death. At no point do you step back, step outside the cycle of death and violence to weigh up exactly what is going on, exactly who you are killing and what this killing is doing to those who are wielding the weapons. The valley, the Valtellina, still existed, its walls climbing up towards jagged peaks. The tracks that he had walked as a boy still led to the same places on either side of the valley. But so much, so much had changed and would never again be the same.

He went back into the house, put a flask of water in his pack, picked up his rifle and said to his mother, 'I am going out for much of the day. I think he will sleep. If he wakes up tell him I will be back before nightfall.' He could not bring himself to utter Luigi's name.

She nodded and returned wordlessly to the pot that was boiling on the range.

As he climbed towards the track that Luigi and George Bright would have taken, he calculated the time that they had been *en route*. His years, as a boy, of tramping across these mountains gave him a unique and innate ability to work out how long it would take to get anywhere.

He considered Luigi's wounded stumble towards his mother's house and added it to the time at which they had separated, high on the valley side. Eventually, after walking with measured steps for five hours, he arrived in an area that felt right to him, that by his calculations should be where the ambush had taken place yesterday.

The trees were skeletal and regular, as if they had been placed in the ground as part of a plantation. The earth was russet with the leaves that had remained there since last autumn and above it all, the sky was cobalt-blue. It was cold in the early morning, but it was at least still, without any wind. Later, it would probably even become quite warm, he thought, bringing the first intimations of the heat of spring.

He started to make a sweep of the area around the track, in long strips, zig-zagging back and forth, his eyes darting from right to left, in search of anything that looked at all unusual. He indicated each strip with a wooden marker and reckoned he could carefully search about ten feet on either side as he walked.

He had stopped for something to eat at about eleven-thirty in the morning and sat on a stone, sweating, wondering what on earth he was doing, what he was hoping to find. Or was this all about hoping not to find anything?

Three hours later, however, he did find it. It was about twenty feet from the main track, on the south side of it. He saw it from a distance, hoping it was something else, but knowing that it was not. A pile of leaves, a beautiful golden-brown heap, bathed in spots of sunlight that sprinkled down between the branches of the trees.

He walked up to it and bent down to brush the top layer of leaves away, tears falling from his eyes onto them.

The dark English uniform had mud splatters on it from the

hike through the mountains and the face was grubby from the leaves that had lain on it for a day.

George Bright wore a surprised look on his face, his eyes staring out in an almost quizzical manner and his mouth open as if in the process of saying 'What . . .?'

As Sandro tried to lift the Englishman's head he felt, with a sinking stomach, his finger disappearing into a space in the back. He bent down to have a look, turning the already stiff neck, and found a small, round hole in the back of the head, just above the neck.

He uncovered the rest of the body and examined it for other wounds, but, as he had feared, found none.

'*He took a lot of bullets, poor man. They were on the track in front of us.*' Luigi's words reverberated in his head.

Captain George Bright had taken only one bullet and that was in the back of the head.

It had been dark for several hours by the time Sandro returned home. He had sat for a very long time in the forest, thinking about what he should do, but continually revisiting the guilt he felt about Angela. But he also had an overwhelming desire to see her again. He felt he could hardly do that if he were to have her husband killed, which was, in effect, what would happen if he were to tell the *Comitato di Liberazione Nazionale*, the body who controlled all partisan activity, what had really happened to George Bright. Against this, of course, was weighed the photograph of the Englishman's daughter, smiling out at a world filled with hope and promise and not the world filled with death and despair that Sandro felt he now occupied.

He walked into the house still undecided, but, within moments, heard himself saying to the figure that lay on the bed, 'Luigi, my friend, how are you? Is it any easier?'

*

139

Sandro's boots left a trail of dark prints on the snow that dusted the rocks across which he walked. There had even been a fall of snow down on the valley floor. That meant that it would be even heavier up amongst the higher peaks. which for the last few days had been shrouded in impenetrable cloud.

It was without too much fear of discovery, therefore, that Sandro descended the side of the valley with the intention of once more falling into Angela's arms under the familiar rock overhang. It was cold, but these days the partisans were well-clothed. The Allies had provided coats, warm clothing and boots before Christmas and Sandro no longer had to rely on the unpleasant necessity of plundering the bodies of dead Germans. It didn't stop some of his colleagues, however.

From high up its northern slope, the valley looked wonderful this particular morning. He rarely found time now to wander at will like this, as he used to, but a number of the group who had taken part in several operations recently had been stood down for two days and they were all making their way to visit loved ones. Sandro was hoping to meet up with Angela. She went to their clearing after lunch each and every day just in case he somehow was in the area. In the last few months they had met only twice and even then for a very short time, in which they held each other so tight that the breath had almost deserted their bodies.

His anticipation increased the closer he came to the clearing. He had found, during the last six months, that the very thought of Angela was his saving grace. She entered his head and cleared it of all the misery of the war, all the conflicting feelings that he endured. He thought of her as he lay down at night, attempting to sleep, wrapped in layers of blankets as protection against the mountain chill; fantasised about a different life with her and baby Antonio, in another place far from the Valtellina; imagined going home to her each night; felt, even in the cold mountain air, the heat of her embrace beneath blankets in a warm bed.

As he rounded a small hill close to her village, however, he experienced a familiar feeling. It was a feeling of dread, of danger. It was almost as if he had developed a sixth sense over the past months and could smell danger like the smell of a wood fire from a distance.

And, in fact, the first confirmation he had that something was actually wrong was the smell of burning wood. His nostrils twitched and then his eyes widened as he rounded the hill above the village in which Angela lived. A plume of dark smoke climbed out of it, drifting lazily into the sky.

He stopped dead in his tracks, trying to control his muscles. His hands shook and his knees trembled as if he had just climbed a steep slope. Then he started out again, increasing his pace, coming down the hill. His fear for Angela and Antonio was almost tangible. A foreboding within him told him that it was already too late, that this was the end of the best thing that would ever happen to him.

He heard someone moving towards him on the same track. He or she was moving at speed, crashing into branches and bushes. He stepped to one side, fearing that it might be a German.

Suddenly, around the corner ran an elderly woman, clutching a baby to her chest. Her eyes were wild, looking in every direction and her breath was being dragged out of the very corners of her lungs.

Sandro stepped out in front of her, his arms open wide to halt her headlong rush.

'*Madonna, cosa fai* . . .?' she gasped, knocking Sandro back a few paces.

141

'*Signora*, what's wrong? *Calma ... calma*. Why are you running ...?'

'The Germans ...' she gulped in oxygen and slumped to the ground, clasping the child to her even more tightly. 'They came about an hour ago ... herded us all out of our houses like cattle ... and started setting fire to them. Old Salvatore Pezzo protested and they shot him. They just shot him! He did nothing ...'

'Easy ... *Calma* ...' He knelt beside her, holding her shoulder and shaking it. 'Why did they come? Why did they do this?'

'I don't know. They're starting to hurt us for what the partisans do. Two days ago, they took hostages in the next village to ours and shot a dozen of them.'

'Did they take anyone from your village?'

'Yes, but I don't know why. They only took one. I don't know what she had done ...'

'Who was it?' he asked, knowing full well what the answer was going to be. 'Who was she?'

'She has done nothing. She has a baby ...'

'Who? What was her name?' His voice rising. He knew already.

'Ronconi. It was the Ronconi woman. The wife of Luigi who has the garage down on the Sondrio road. They took her and her baby. The baby was screaming and she was shouting at them. I ran with my daughter's baby. I don't know what they're doing to the rest. I was at the back of the crowd of villagers and I sneaked away. Ohhh ...' She collapsed into torrents of tears, her fists bunched into her eyes as if to rub away the sight she had just witnessed. 'This damned war! When will it end?'

'Come with me. I'll take you to my mother's house.'

He half-carried the old woman and her granddaughter the few kilometres to his mother's house and by the time they arrived there she was exhausted by both the walk and the events she had witnessed.

Sandro bade his farewells to his mother and returned to the burning village.

He slid like a shadow along the sides of the buildings on the outskirts, rifle at the ready – it was carried at all times now – heart pounding, concerned that there would still be Germans in the village. Smoke billowed into the sky from a few of the houses, but a ghostly silence reigned, as if the world had been emptied of birdsong and the everyday sounds that held the houses together like mortar between the bricks – the echoing sing-song voices and the sounds of cooking implements; the shrieks of children and the deep-voiced grunts of the men, home for lunch.

He looked out from behind one building and there was the village square. The church, a dilapidated dark grey building with an imposing front door stood on one side. Houses looked out from the other sides, smoke drifting lazily from the windows of one of them. In the centre of the square lay a body – the old man, Salvatore Pezzo, no doubt, of whom the old lady had spoken – but apart from that there was not a movement.

Reckoning that the Germans had departed, Sandro walked out towards the body, his gun still at the ready and shouted, 'Ho! Is anybody there?'

Not a sound. Again, he shouted:

'Ho! Anyone!'

There was a movement behind him and he turned swiftly, his finger tightening over the trigger of his rifle. But it was a young woman with a child. Then to his left, an elderly couple appeared and following them an entire family of men, women and children; all shuffling out of their homes silently, staring at him in terror.

*

Angela shifted position again. The old man to her left had fallen asleep and his head had come to rest on her shoulder. She shivered as she felt it roll uncomfortably against her collar bone. He smelled awful; his breath was rank and his body stank. But then, she probably did not smell very good either, she thought, letting her head fall back against the wooden slats of the carriage, staring up at the roof.

The train had not moved now for many hours. It had stopped in the last hours of the night and the hundred or so souls in the carriage had watched the first shafts of light begin to splinter the gaps between the planks of wood that made up the walls and roof of the carriage.

At first it had been good to stop moving. The endless bumping of the carriage across the tracks jarred bones and stretched already aching muscles. After the silence of the night, the light had instigated a fresh round of sounds from the huddled group, like a human dawn chorus. From one corner a woman had talked endlessly, a stream of words in a language that Angela could not understand, words that seemed to have no gaps between them. She imagined a long, thin stream of paper being pulled from the woman's mouth, covered in the strange letters of an unknown alphabet. From other corners came the sound of weeping and the deep, gruff sounds of men's voices trying to calm their sources.

Gradually as the morning had worn on and turned, she presumed, into early afternoon, an eerie silence had descended on the carriage. She looked at the faces around her. They were grey and dirty. Children stared back at her with sunken eyes. They stared at her but saw nothing, helplessness and hopelessness forming cataracts over their vision. They earthed themselves in their parents, clinging desperately to them as if in the grip of a huge wind that was going to tear them away, lifting their tiny bodies into the sky like paper kites.

Antonio slept in Angela's aching arms. For the two days she had been in the carriage, she had held him to her breast as if she were trying to force him between her ribs to make him a part of her. He had cried with hunger yesterday, at first angrily and, gradually, more and more hopelessly, staring into her eyes, pleading for something to eat. Eventually, his tears had dried into dirty, salty streaks on his face and he had gone silent, resigned to this new feeling of constant hunger.

In the middle of the night, they had been given water, which had been passed around in silence, politely almost, as if they had been sitting round a kitchen table, eating dinner.

At last there were shouts outside: the harsh vowels and consonants of the German language and the train shuddered into movement once more, slowly at first and then faster.

Angela stared at a hole in the roof, through which she could see dark, rain-bearing clouds passing up above. These were alien clouds, however; not the clouds of her homeland, the clouds that hung as if on strings above the mountain peaks of the Valtellina. She knew she would never see them again. She would never see Luigi again. She would never again burst through the bushes into that clearing above the village and see Sandro rolling a cigarette between his slim fingers, a smile spreading across his handsome face like the sun across the valley floor in the morning.

She fell asleep once more, hearing the crackle of rain on the roof but dreaming that it was the sound of rain on the overhanging rock that sheltered two lovers entwined in each other's arms on the side of a mountain.

10

13 November 1999
Talimona
North Italy

Michael was surprised to find a number of police cars parked in front of Ignazio's house. *Carabinieri* in their dark uniforms and men in plain clothes were busy around the house and a further group was milling about over in the small vineyard that hugged the side of the cliff to the right of the property.

'What's happened?' he asked a policeman through the window of his car.

'And you are, *signore*?' the policeman answered the question with another and quite aggressively. Without waiting for a response from Michael, he followed with a curt, 'Please get out of the car.'

'My name is Michael Keats; I'm a journalist, from the London *Evening Post*.' He closed the car door. 'I'm writing about the Ronconi kidnapping for my paper and interviewed Ignazio Mazzini, the owner of this farm, a few days ago.

I've come to ask him a few more questions. Where is he?' he added more forcefully, looking around at all the activity. 'What exactly is going on?'

'I am afraid, *signor* Keats, that there's been an accident. Please come with me. My boss will want to speak to you.'

The policeman led Michael up the steep incline towards the vineyard.

The explosion of growth that had made the branches of the vines heavy with dusty grapes had been months ago and the vines now resembled gnarled, brown sticks that had been stuck into the earth as if they were part of some kind of modernist artistic installation. It was a small but tidy vineyard of perhaps a few hundred vines and had been planted on a sloping south-facing plateau that clung to the side of the mountain. Still, it had furnished Ignazio and his antecedents with enough wine for their own consumption for many generations.

Michael was led over to the edge of the cliff where a man in a dark suit, a detective, no doubt, was in discussion with a colleague. In the distance, several hundred feet below where Michael stood, a hydrofoil tore a silver strip out of the surface of the lake, separating the water between Menaggio and Verdanno.

The policeman who had brought Michael up interrupted the conversation, nodding towards Michael as he spoke to him.

'It's a steep climb, eh, *signore*?' said the second policeman, turning to face Michael, putting one hand on his hip and wiping the sweat off his forehead with the other.

'Indeed it is,' replied Michael.

'I am *Ispettore* Coloni. My colleague tells me you are English, *signore*? A long way from home, eh? What brings you here?'

Michael repeated the explanation he had given a few minutes ago and asked once more what was going on.

'Ah, you are a journalist, *signore*. Well, you will certainly have this story before anyone else, I think. I am very sorry to have to inform you that it will not be possible for you to ask *signor* Ignazio Mazzini any more questions. You see, *signor* Keats, his body was found down there on the Beldoro road earlier this morning.' He gestured in the direction of the road some three hundred feet below. 'It would appear that he fell, or possibly jumped – who knows? – from where we are standing, to his death. A truck driver found him in the middle of the road. His skull was fractured and his neck was broken. Regrettably, there was nothing that could be done for him. So, if you spoke to him recently, you may well have been one of the last people to see Ignazio Mazzini alive, *signor* Keats.' Michael's surname sounded odd in Coloni's mouth, as if he were chewing something that was too large to swallow. He came up to stand beside Michael at the side of the cliff and looked down, shaking his head.

'What would drive a man to do such a thing? Eh? If, indeed, he did jump, that is. Such a man would have to be pretty desperate, don't you think?'

'Desperate indeed. I'm not the greatest judge of human nature, *Ispettore*, but I would never have described Ignazio Mazzini as a desperate man, and certainly not as a man who would throw himself off the side of a mountain. Not from my discussion with him. He was an unhappy man, I will admit, but he was consumed with a desire to revenge himself on that shopkeeper who had been having an affair with his wife. That's the kind of anger that gives a man a reason to live, not to die.'

'Ah, you may well be right, *signore*, and don't worry, we shall certainly be talking to Bonfadini, the shopkeeper. But, nevertheless, I think I agree with you – it somehow doesn't feel right – a man who has lived the life that he has lived, throwing himself off a cliff, committing suicide. He would have seen that as an act of the purest self-indulgence. These people up here in the mountains, you know–' he swept a hand around the circle of jagged-topped mountains that bordered the lake, 'they live like animals. Survival is all. It always has been. Up here they don't understand the kind of angst and stress that drives those poor bastards in Milano and Roma to take their own lives because a share price has dropped a couple of points. Sure, they have their problems, but . . .' He shook his head sadly. 'I, too, must admit that I find it hard to accept that he would have killed himself, but . . .' he shrugged his shoulders and stared off into the distance, 'that is for the judge to decide. Anyway, we are jumping to conclusions. It may all have been a terrible accident. Perhaps he was stepping back to admire his work in the vineyard and suddenly found his foot reaching out into space. Oh, I know, it seems unlikely, but in my line of work we do have to consider every possibility. In fact, nothing can be ruled out until we are certain the evidence is overwhelmingly *against* it happening. However, *signor* Keats, I apologise. I am wasting your time and mine with my idle speculation. We shall, of course, require a statement from you. Oh, and we will also need to know where you were yesterday and early this morning. Purely routine, you understand. Why not go down to Beldoro now and we can get it out of the way? Please, would you be kind enough to wait while I find an officer to accompany you to the police station?' He bustled off towards a group of policemen who were examining the earth with great attention.

As he waited, Michael gingerly approached the edge of the cliff. He had never been very good with heights and the drop was sheer, without even an outcrop to break a fall. Down below, the asphalt strip of the road stretched like a shoelace in the direction of Beldoro one way and towards Milan the other.

Had Ignazio Mazzini really taken his own life? Had he taken a break from his pruning and stepped to the edge to admire the view, the view to which he had awakened every morning? Had he, breathing in the enormity of it all and realising the smallness of his own existence, limited by the land he worked and the peninsula on which he lived, stepped closer to the edge and leaning over, seen the nothingness below, the yawning empty space? Had he felt a desire for that space as he had never felt a desire for anything before? Had he looked back behind him and seen the crumbling walls of his own home, sensed the empty rooms within it, the shifting of a dirty dish in a sink, the scratching of a rat beneath the floorboards, the silence of a spider at the centre of its web?

Had he then taken a step into that space he desired more than anything, a step into that mirror of himself, a smile creasing the weathered lines around his eyes?

Michael closed his eyes, standing at the edge of the cliff, and said a silent prayer for a small life that had perhaps finally given up the unequal struggle. He then took one final look at the beautiful view that had been Ignazio Mazzini's last and turned away.

'It was his Lordship's doing. Sometimes he has his uses, you know.' Harry Jones's guttural, smoke-damaged laugh gurgled down the telephone line from London.

Michael had returned to his hotel room after giving his account of his conversation with Ignazio to a policeman in the little police station in Beldoro. As he left he had been asked not to stray too far from the area just in case they needed some more information from him. 'Purely routine', of course, but he had no doubt that there were suspicions about him. It made him realise that it was now even more impossible for him to say anything about Claudio Scatti's body rotting away in that chalet high above the valley.

On returning to the hotel, the receptionist/decorator gave him a fax from Bruno in Milan saying that, not knowing where Michael was staying, Harry had called his newspaper and asked for Michael to be told that he wanted to speak to him. And so Michael was seated by the window of his room, watching dark clouds threaten the mountain tops, laughing with Harry on the phone, happy to hear his Welsh accent. He was even more delighted to hear that the *Post's* aristocratic owner had used his connections to arrange an interview with Luigi Ronconi. It would be the first interview with the old man since the kidnapping and it was to be with an English paper.

'He bloody hates the Italian press, apparently, even though he's owned most of it over the years. So, he is perfectly happy to well and truly piss them off by giving the story to a foreign paper,' Harry gleefully added, before giving Michael details of who to contact to arrange the interview.

'Before I go – I hope you don't mind me asking – how is everything else, Michael? Have you found anything out? About Rosa, I mean.'

'I'm no further forward, to be honest, Harry. I'm not really sure what to do next.'

'How about coming back and getting on with your life, boyo? I've got a job here as Deputy News Editor that has your name on it, should you want it.'

'Give me some more time. I'm not quite ready, but if I haven't found out any more soon, I'm going to pack it in and get back to reality. I promise.'

'Good lad. Now must dash. Mustn't keep his Lordship

waiting. You take care now, and let me know what happens with Ronconi. He's supposed to be a difficult old bugger from what I hear.'

'Bye, Harry. I'll let you know.'

Michael put the phone down. He had not told Harry about Claudio Scatti, had not voiced his suspicions. It was hard to know why not. He still had not got it right in his head and wanted to be sure of it before sharing it with anyone. He was like that.

He ran a bath, wondering idly if he was, indeed, as he had said to Harry, ready to get back to reality. What was reality, anyway? Anything that was real had evaporated, had fallen between his fingers like sand as soon as he had discovered that Rosa had been dishonest with him. Even if he did return to reality, it would have to be a different version and perhaps that meant that he, too, would have to become a different version of himself.

It had turned unseasonably warm and even quite muggy as the morning had lengthened towards eleven, the time of Michael's appointment at the Palazzo Ronconi, and he had been happy to walk the couple of miles from Beldoro to the gates of the palazzo. However, he thought longingly of his car's air conditioning as he walked slowly up the steep drive-way with sweat dampening his hair. The gate had swung open electronically for him after he had spoken his name into the grill on the gate-post and now the full glory of the palazzo began to appear in front of him from amidst the trees that screened it from curious eyes on the road that ran past it or from the town below.

Or, at least, its full lack of glory. He was almost disappointed by the simplicity of the building, a simplicity that belied the term 'palazzo'. It was very large, however, a square, ochre-coloured building with a red tile roof. It was not, in fact, very old, Michael had read this morning. It had been built by an Italian-American millionaire philanthropist in the fifties to house a college in which young, affluent Americans could study Italian culture. Luigi Ronconi had acquired the building in the seventies when he had decided to return to the area of his youth after spending many years with Rome as his home as well as the centre of his business activities.

Luigi Ronconi was an enigmatic figure, if ever there was one. A man who, if he could be bothered, could count his fortune in hundreds of billions of lire, a fortune earned from his many industrial plants around Italy and the world; a man who had, many times since the war, been rumoured to be one of the power-brokers in Italian politics, moving politicians around like pieces on a chess board to create coalition governments; a man who, at one time, had controlled, through his network of companies, huge swathes of the Italian media and, consequently, influenced the opinions and thoughts of his fellow countrymen.

And yet, this was a man about whom not much was really known, as Michael had discovered from the fax that he had been sent by the *Post* this morning. Three pages to sum up one of the most influential European lives of the second half of the twentieth century.

He was born in the tiny Valtellina village of Dulcino in 1916; he became a car mechanic before the war; he distinguished himself in the partisan movement towards the war's end; then little is known until 1950, when he appeared from nowhere to buy a small factory near Naples. The rest is history, really. Ronconi cashed in on the economic boom of the mid to late fifties, supplying engine parts to the major car companies from a network of factories across the country. He became an industrial puppet-master, a genius at making money and now he had one of the largest private fortunes in all of Italy and was, in fact, one of the richest men in Europe. Yet, he had never been interviewed on television and few photographs of him existed. Those that did were from the sixties when, for a few short years, he could be spied hobnobbing with the beautiful people of Europe. This was mainly because in the early nineteen-sixties, he fell in love with and married a Swedish model – Agnetha Dorland. The marriage, however, had not lasted longer than the time it had taken to have a child – Teresa, the victim thirty-five years later, of the Beldoro kidnapping.

Michael had read how peerless Ronconi's record in the war had been. As '*Il Falcone*', he had been a ruthless scourge of the German garrison in the Valtellina, charismatic and inspirational leader of what turned out to be a doomed group in countless operations, but his wife and young child had been taken by the Germans as a reprisal and he had left the valley and had spent the next few years fighting with other partisans before disappearing from view, presumably seeking the fortune that eventually was to be his.

While he had been earning his fortune, he was also investigating the fate of his son, Antonio, and, indeed, Antonio was miraculously found, living with a German family just a couple of years after the war. He returned to live with his father and grow up to learn the family business. It was Antonio Ronconi – half-brother to Teresa and twice as old as her – that Michael had to meet with first.

The door was opened as he approached and he was welcomed by a young woman, dressed for business in a blue, two-piece Chanel suit. She spoke to him in English.

'Good morning, Mister Keats.' Her accent had an American inflection to it, as if she had been left behind by the college that used to occupy this building. 'How nice to

155

meet you.' She reached out her hand. 'I am Anna Trabucchi? *Signor* Antonio's personal assistant?' She spoke in questions, betraying her American education. '*Signor* Antonio apologises. He is just completing an important telephone call and will be down directly? May I get you something, a coffee or perhaps some water . . .?' As she said this, she was ushering him into an office that was located to the right of the main door. As he entered it he took stock of the luxurious decor of the entrance hall. Lush, floral wallpaper that looked almost too heavy to stay on the walls; large gilt-framed oil paintings depicting classical scenes; a long, sweeping, red carpeted staircase leading to the upper floor; a sparkling chandelier with tears of crystal dripping from it. The road that Luigi Ronconi had taken to this from a small village in the Valtellina represented something of a miracle.

'Water would be great, thank you. It's warm out there,' replied Michael, taking in the room he had entered – book-lined walls, a seriously hefty and inordinately tidy desk in front of the large French windows, which opened onto a beautiful vista down through the trees to the ever-present lake, gleaming in the midday sun.

She was not for small talk, this woman. 'I'll have someone bring it?' she said, bustling out of the room in search of someone to bring his water.

A few minutes later she returned, accompanied by a woman carrying a tray on which were three decanters of different flavoured juice, a bottle each of sparkling and still water and a couple of glasses. The woman placed it on the table under the bustling direction of Anna Trabucchi, who then proceeded to pour a glass for Michael. He had just taken a long, refreshing draught of the ice-cold water, when the figure of a large man appeared in the doorway.

Antonio Ronconi was, as the magazines were always at

pains to point out, a handsome man. He was tall, powerfully built and his hair was very dark and surprisingly long for a man of his age – around fifty-eight years old. His skin gave off a healthy, tanned glow. Sun-lamp or the beach, Michael would have been hard-pressed to say. He wore tiny, round sunglasses, tight-fitting black jeans and a leather jacket.

'Anna, I never want to talk to that idiot again. He knows nothing. See to it that he never gets through to me.' His words were in rapid Italian and he seemed to be angry in a very controlled way. Michael sensed a capacity for fury in this man, however, from just those few words. But when he turned to face him, his anger was immediately replaced by a disarming charm as he changed to speaking English. He held out his hand, speaking very fluently.

'Mister Keats! How lovely to meet you. I know your newspaper well from my many visits to London. It's a good paper.'

'Thank you, *signor* Ronconi. It is kind of you to say that. And very kind of you and your father to see me,' replied Michael, taking the proffered hand and feeling a strong, firm handshake. He was unnerved, however, by the hard stare that he received from Antonio Ronconi, as if the man were trying to read what was going on in his mind. But he quickly shook off the odd feeling of familiarity he experienced.

'Of course, I get to London very rarely these days. My father hasn't been well for several years and I spend most of my life behind this damn desk with the telephone glued to my ear. Or, increasingly, stuck in front of this computer. Aren't computers the curse of modern life, Mister Keats, or do you mind if I call you Michael?' He sipped from the glass of water that Anna Trabucchi had poured for him before leaving the room, closing the door quietly behind her.

'No, not at all. Michael's fine. I must say in my line of work, I find computers very useful.'

'Ah, well, each to his own, I suppose,' Antonio said, sitting down at his desk. 'Now, tell me, regarding the kidnap of my sister, are you finding anything new? It seems to me that the media is tiring of it already. We have our public relations people working on ideas to keep them interested. I know, it's ridiculous,' he sat back in his chair and shook his head. 'My sister has been kidnapped – she may even be dead, although I think she is most definitely alive – and we have PR people working on ideas to keep the story in the news! Yes, it is ridiculous! We market even our own grief these days, it seems, Michael.' He spun round in his seat and stared out of the French doors at the lake, shining like a polished mirror in the distance. Then, he seemed to shake himself and drew his hands across his face as if wiping away all the words he had just uttered.

'Anyway, you're here to talk to my father. I don't know what his lordship or your editor told you, but I fear that you are not going to be able to spend an awful lot of time with him. Luigi Ronconi has had a tough life, you know. People ask why they don't know more about him, why he isn't accessible to the press every minute of the day. What they should remember is where he came from – a small village in the Valtellina, about forty kilometres from here. The people of that village and all the villages around it, had been nowhere. Think of it. For centuries, man, they had been *nowhere*.' He fell into the rock idiom like a man falling into a vat of wine – comfortable and secure. 'In those days, you know, Michael,' he went on, leaning forward in his chair, folding his large hands in front of him, 'you didn't travel far.' He stood up, facing the doors leading out into the garden and sweeping his hands across the panorama they offered. 'You were lucky if you could boast of travelling more than twenty kilometres from your home in your entire lifetime. Until the wars, that is. Wars change everything. They change people. But they not only change people; they also change their expectations. The last one certainly changed my father. In 1939, he was a mechanic working in a garage; a couple of years later, he was married with a young child – me; another couple of years later, his wife and son had disappeared, had been taken to Germany, to certain death, it seemed; he, by this time, was killing Germans as if he had been born to it, as if it was the most natural thing in the world; then he was wandering across Italy like a vagabond; and then ... well, you can see it all around you; his *success.*' Michael was surprised by the emphasis that was placed on the last word. Antonio hissed the word, rather than spoke it.

In the last two minutes, it seemed to Michael, the man in front of him had experienced a range of emotions. Antonio seemed to be under an inordinate amount of stress; he was a man in *extremis*, a man at the end of whatever tether he had made for himself.

'But ... anyway, you know most of this.' He walked towards Michael, suddenly emanating *bonhomie* and warmth, throwing an arm around Michael's shoulder, guiding him to the door and saying, 'Come on, let's go visit the old man. But let me warn you, he recently had a ... how do you say it in English ... *un ictus?*'

'A stroke,' Michael obliged, knowing the Italian for the illness of one of Rosa's aunts.

'That's it! A stroke!' Guiding Michael through the door, towards the stairs. 'Such a strange way of putting it, but English is such an odd language, don't you think? Anyway, you never know how he is going to be and his speech ... well he was never the world's greatest talker – the Valtellina is famous for producing men of few words – but, his words often lose themselves somewhere between his brain and his tongue. He gets very frustrated, but there's nothing to be done. I shouldn't tell you this – you being a member of the Fourth Estate and all – but I think you are a man of honour, even though you are a journalist! My father will almost certainly suffer another stroke soon. The doctors don't know how soon or how serious, but it won't be long, they think.'

They climbed the long, sweeping staircase, past oil paintings from which colour glowed as if they had been illuminated from behind. Heavy gilt frames surrounded each one and they, too, shone. At the top of the stairs, they turned right into a long corridor which was similarly lined with expensive-looking art. Antonio stopped in front of a door and whispered to Michael, 'Let me just go in first to make sure he's okay.'

A moment passed and then he returned, beckoning Michael into the room.

The 83-year-old *Falcone* was over by the window of a large, dark room. He sat in a wheelchair, in front of a huge bay window, the curtains of which were drawn closed apart from a three feet gap in the centre of the window. It was in front of this gap that he sat, a shaft of bright sunlight slicing into the room and creating a halo around his head. Motes of dust tumbled lazily in the light above his head and his oiled, still-black hair gleamed.

'*Papi*. I have Mr Keats, the English journalist here to see you for a moment.' Antonio took the chair by the handles and pushed it round so that Luigi's face came into view.

The handsome, angular features of the twenty-seven year-old Luigi Ronconi could just about be made out, if, indeed, you had known him back then. But his cheeks had become sunken and his eyes had lost the deep colour that had made them seem iridescent and had attracted the opposite sex when he was young. They had become grey and flecked here and

160

there with white. His body, though stooped in the wheel-chair, was still large and powerful-looking for a man of his years.

Michael stepped forward and held out his hand.

'*Signor* Ronconi. It is an honour to meet you. Thank you very much for seeing me.'

'Ah you can thank his Lordship for that.' The voice was harsh and deep, the accent was still recognisable as the one which coloured the words of Rosa's family, the accent of the Valtellina. His speech was slightly slurred, mainly because his mouth was pulled down at one corner, probably, Michael surmised, by the stroke he had suffered. 'We go back a long way.'

Antonio beckoned Michael to sit on a leather sofa in the centre of the room and pushed the wheelchair over to it.

'I hope you don't mind answering a few questions for me, *signor Ronconi*?' He gestured to the small tape recorder he had taken from his pocket and was now placing on the coffee table that was in front of both of them.

'That is why you are here, I believe, so, please, ask away.'

'Not too long, though, *Papi*.' Antonio interrupted.

'Oh, you fuss too much, my boy. I am feeling fine today.'

'So, *signor* Ronconi, I am interested in knowing who you think might have kidnapped Teresa. The newspapers have speculated that it might be the *mafia*, or business rivals or even Eastern European gangsters. Who do *you* think kidnapped her?'

'I wish I knew, *signore*. Antonio thinks it is local gangsters. I don't know.' He sighed. Speaking was not easy for him and the words came out in staccato bursts at the end of each of which he seemed to gather himself for the next burst. 'Of course ... I have enemies. You don't get all this,' his eyes swivelled, taking in the whole room, as he drew in a deep breath, 'without making enemies ... What is the phrase ...

161

You can't make an omelette … without breaking eggs?' A slow smile crossed his face. 'I' Another deep breath, 'have made rather a large omelette … don't you think?' His eyes twinkled, but then they clouded over again. 'Ah, Teresa … She is a lovely child, you know. So open … and honest. And with a fighting spirit … just like her mother.'

'Does she work here, for you, *signore*?'

'No, she doesn't.' It was Antonio speaking. He was seated in a chair across from them. 'She has her own work, her own studies.'

'Ah, what is she studying?'

'She is a … lepidopterist … you know … butterflies,' said Luigi.

'She is obsessed by them.' It was Antonio now, interrupting his father. 'Always has been, since she was tiny.'

'She would chase them around the garden … when she was small. She was like a little butterfly … herself, back then,' Luigi now, with a wistful look in his eyes as he cast his memory back over the years. 'This place, you know … is a veritable haven … for butterflies and Teresa … Teresa has learned everything … everything there is to know about them.'

'Before you leave I will show you her room and her study. You have a camera with you, I presume?' Antonio rose from his seat. 'I think that is enough, *Papi*. I don't want you getting over-tired.'

'Okay, okay. *Signor* Keats …' Luigi reached out a shaky hand to Michael. 'It was a pleasure to meet you … Please give my regards … to his Lordship.'

Antonio wheeled the chair back to its former position in front of the window and they left the room filled with the laboured sounds of the old man's breathing. The interview was over too quickly for Michael.

'You were lucky. *Papi* was very lucid today. There are days when he is less clear about who he is talking to and he wanders a great deal in what he says.' Antonio was leading Michael to a room towards the rear of the ground floor of the *palazzo*. He opened it and stood to one side to let Michael go in.

'This, as you can see, is Teresa's office.'

The room was like any office – computer, desk and sofa against the far wall.

'But she slept here as well. Next door is her bedroom – she wanted always to be close to her butterflies – and through here . . .' He walked towards a door to the left of the room. '. . . through here are . . .' He threw open the door with a flourish: 'the butterflies!'

Michael walked into a small foyer with another door a few feet inside, allowing an area for viewing what lay beyond. What lay behind it was a large, conservatory-like construction which had been added, it seemed, to the back of the house. Inside were butterflies. Hundreds, perhaps thousands of butterflies, landing on plants and taking off again, bumping up against the glass through which Michael and Antonio were looking, coloured clouds of silently flapping wings.

'It's marvellous, isn't it?' asked Antonio, shaking his head.

'My God, yes. There must be thousands of them.' answered Michael, his eyes taking in the extent of this butterfly-infested room.

'Actually, around five thousand. This is her laboratory, her study, her workshop. She breeds them and studies them.'

A woman walked through a door to the left of where they were standing, smiling at Antonio and then walking to the rear of the building.

'She has a number of assistants. They have been wonderful in the last few weeks in keeping the whole place going.' He looked at his watch. 'But, I am afraid I must leave for Milan very shortly. If you wish to take some photographs here, please do . . .'

'I will, but I wonder,' interrupted Michael, 'if I might actually take some shots of Teresa's bedroom. Some real human interest may be just what you need, if as you say, you want the newspapers to take an interest in the story again.'

'Well, it is a bit of a, how do you say it, a tabloid approach, in a way, but . . . oh what the Hell, why not. It's through here.'

Michael had dropped the film into the Beldoro photographic shop as he passed through town on his way back to the hotel. He had then stopped at a bar and relaxed over a beer and a sandwich before making his way back to the hotel to start transcribing the tape and writing his story.

'*Signor* Keats, there is a letter for you.'

The receptionist/decorator stood in his paint-spattered overalls, waving a small manila envelope at Michael as he climbed the first flight of stairs.

'A letter?' Who would be writing to him? No one knew where he was. He was even more puzzled to see that it had a local postmark on it. '*Grazie*.' He took it and headed off to his room to open it.

'*Gentile Signor Keats*,' the letter began. The envelope was old. It was brown, of the kind used for business communications and only half of the glue on the flap had worked, so that it was half-open. The paper inside was a small, lined sheet, yellowing around the edges, as if it had taken years to be delivered. Ignazio Mazzini – for it was from him and Michael had given him his hotel details when he talked to him, in case he recalled anything else – was not the sort of man to have supplies of fresh stationery around the house and there was every chance that this sheet had been sitting in a drawer for decades before he had found a use for it.

The writing was painstaking. Each letter sat alone, as if it had been chiselled out of the paper. Each was bold and had been pressed deep, even going through the paper on a couple of occasions.

'Please forgive me for taking the liberty of writing to you there is something I have remembered that I didn't tell you I told it to the policeman who came to see me not long after you left. Rinaldi was his name.' The punctuation, or almost total lack of it made it necessary to concentrate on what Ignazio was trying to say.

'When I stood waiting for il porco, *Bonfadini, and my whore of a wife, I overheard voices from the front of the bar a voice said,* 'Mi dispiace, la mia farfalla.' *I hope this can be of use to you the policeman was very interested.* Distinti saluti.'

The signature that followed was laboured, like the handwriting of a ten-year-old. Still, Ignazio had had little occasion to pick up a pen in his lifetime, Michael surmised. 'I am sorry, my butterfly'? Why did someone say that? Michael was puzzled.

'Rinaldi?' answered the voice at the other end of the telephone. 'I'm sorry, there is no one of that name here. Are you sure you have the correct name, *signore*?'

'Thank you, I must have made a mistake,' replied Michael, replacing the receiver.

He had spent the last hour phoning every police station in the area and even a few outside the area, trying to locate the policeman who had visited Ignazio Mazzini a short time after he had. Every time he had received the same response. No one of that name worked out of that police station. The conclusion had to be that there was, in fact, no policeman of that name.

Michael stood up and went to the window, instinctively peering out from behind the curtain down into the street in front of the hotel, as if he expected to see this phony police-man staring back up at him. The street was, of course, empty. It was lunch time, the sacred hour in Italy.

Michael let the curtain fall from his hands and walked over to the tiny table on which his laptop sat. He felt uneasy. Had he been followed to Ignazio's farm? It would not, of course, take a genius to work out that Ignazio might have some important information. But had they thought that he had found out something that no one else had and that was why he had been talking to the late farmer?

There were a number of possibilities. The main one that occupied Michael's thoughts as he stared at the screen was that this Rinaldi had, in fact, killed Ignazio. Of course, he may have killed himself, but it seemed very unlikely. And surely there was no way that he could have fallen? He had worked that land all of his life. It would have been as familiar as a sitting-room carpet to his feet.

But, why would Rinaldi have killed him? What did Ignazio know that was so critical? Could it be something to do with his recollection of the words he had heard on the day of the kidnapping as he waited for the shopkeeper's footsteps?

Michael reached over to the bed and picked up the yellow-edged letter that he had left there. He peered at it, running his finger across the badly punctuated words. '*Mi dispiace, la mia farfalla.*' – 'I'm sorry, my butterfly?' An ironic reference to Teresa Ronconi's studies, no doubt. Those words were the only thing about which the police had no knowledge, because Ignazio had not repeated these words to them. Could those four words be the reason that he had been killed?

Again, he stood up, feeling nervous, and made his way to the window. The street was now beginning to fill up again as the lunch hiatus came to an end. Mopeds were spluttering into life in the distance and cars were revving up. Voices filled the silence that had previously enveloped the town.

He, too, now possessed this information.

They may have thought that Ignazio had already shared it with him during his interview. No matter, though. He knew it now. And, more importantly, he presumed they knew that he knew it.

He pulled the curtains closed and returned to the seat at the table. He stared, unseeing, at his laptop which gazed bluely back at him, the cursor winking at him from just to the right of the last letter he had typed.

Still nervous, he waited until the sun had sunk behind the high peaks and light began to seep out of the town before leaving the hotel to collect his photographs.

He had also arranged for a courier to collect the photos from the hotel in an hour and take them down to Bruno in Milan, from where they could be transmitted electronically to London. There was no internet here at the hotel and anyway he wanted to ensure that the quality was good. He had already e-mailed several thousand words to Harry. He was back in business and happy to be so.

He walked briskly to and from the photography shop, keeping to the centre of the narrow streets, cheered by the fact that the mild weather had encouraged people out to look in the windows of the shops or just to stroll. He had ducked into a small grocery store and bought a bag of crisps and a six-pack of beer and was just opening one of the bottles back in his room when Rosa's face jumped into his mind, unbidden. Her dark eyebrows were raised in a quizzical way and the downward pout of her lips seemed to give her a critical look, as if there were something of which she did not approve. It was precisely at that moment that he remembered the envelope of her contact sheets that he had stuffed into the side pocket of his bag the morning he had left for Italy.

He hauled down his bag from the top of the wardrobe and searched in the side pocket. It was empty. He stood up, scratching his head and took a step back from the bed on which the case lay, looking around on the floor, expecting it had fallen out as he lifted it down. But it was not there.

He was certain he had put it in there. He thought back to that morning, only a few days ago, taking himself through everything he did before leaving his house. He saw himself bending to the floor, picking up the envelope and putting the bag down to unzip the pocket and put it in. He saw himself closing the zip, picking the bag up, opening the front door and leaving. It had been there. There was absolutely no doubt.

Had he taken it out and forgotten he had done so? He searched the room, under the bed, behind the dressing table. Still, it was not to be found.

Had someone taken it? Had someone come into his room? It was inconceivable. He took a large swig of the bottle of beer, wiped his mouth with the back of his hand and sat down on the bed.

Why? What could anyone possibly want with Rosa's photographs of ruined, abandoned churches and farms?

Shortly before seven o'clock, the time the courier was due to pick up the envelope containing the photographs of Palazzo Ronconi, Michael collected himself once more, realising that the photographs needed to be annotated in some way so that the office in London would know what it was looking at. He opened the package containing them and started to number them, cross-referencing those numbers with a number on a piece of paper and providing a few lines describing each.

Some of the shots were good and a number were very definitely usable. *Not bad*, he thought, considering he was not a photographer, although, naturally, he had learned some tricks of the trade from Rosa over the years.

He came to the four or five shots he had taken of Teresa Ronconi's bedroom. It was a large room, which adjoined the butterfly sanctuary that took up the rear of the house. In contrast to the fairly grand manner in which the rest of the house was decorated, it was quite simple. The walls were painted in a quiet, pastel shade, instead of groaning under the weight of several decades of hefty wallpaper. What was most striking was the fact that every surface was covered with photographs in frames, large and small. What he presumed were her family were frozen in time, playing on ski slopes, cavorting for the camera on yachts. The lives of the rich and famous, indeed.

He had taken a photograph of one table, the surface of which was hidden by the sheer number of photo frames and he now peered at it in close-up to enable him to describe it properly. The photos in the foreground of the shot were of a younger version of her father and a blonde woman, most probably her mother seated at a restaurant table, smiling at the camera during that brief moment of happiness they had enjoyed together. Beside it were pictures of people he did not recognise, but at the edge of this group was a framed photograph of a younger and thinner Antonio Ronconi, a posed photograph that was a little like a publicity still of an actor. He sat, leaning forward on a stool, with his legs crossed and his chin resting on his hand. He was smiling and could easily have been the hero of an American soap opera. At the bottom of the photograph were some hand-written words. Michael could not make them out and wished he had a magnifying glass to find out what this brother had said to his sister.

It was then that he remembered Rosa's glass, her linen

tester. He had thrown it into his bag just before leaving their room in Renzo's house and had not taken it out of the bag when he had been at home. So, it must still be there.

He fumbled around in the corner of his bag and there it was. Unfolding its stand, he placed it over the photograph. It took a moment for his eye to adjust to the glass's magnification, forcing him to lift his head from the glass, blinking a few times, before returning to it.

The handwriting was flowery, with dramatic up and down strokes. *A dream for a handwriting expert*, he thought, trying to focus on the letters.

'Con i migliori saluti, la mia farfalla - tuo fratello, Antonio.'

His eyes widened over the two words – *mia farfalla*. It was what Ignazio had heard one of the kidnappers say to Teresa as they manhandled her from the bar! *Mia farfalla* – Antonio's name for his sister. It was too much of a coincidence that a stranger would use the same term of endearment, no matter how ironically.

Just at that moment, there was a knock at the door.

'Damn!' said Michael, realising it was probably the courier, here to collect the photos and bike them down to Milan. He looked at his watch and saw that he was fifteen minutes early. *Bloody Italians and their relaxed approach to time. They're either too early or too late. Never bang on time*, he thought.

He stood up and walked to the door.

When he opened it, he briefly saw two men standing there. One of them quickly stepped towards him and grabbed him round the middle, pinning his arms to his side. He struggled as a cloth of some kind was pushed into his face by the other man. There was a pungent, chemical smell that caught at the back of his throat. Michael kicked out, catching one of the men hard on the shin, but the fight started to go out of him as whatever chemical was on the cloth started to take effect. His vision became blurred and then there was just an echoing silence.

11

April 1944
Upper northern slopes
The Valtellina
North Italy

It had been sixteen days since Luigi, *Il Falcone*, had disappeared. He had left the camp to go and meet with another group and had neither met them nor returned.

Sandro had learned of his non-arrival at his rendezvous with a profound sense of dread. In the days immediately following his disappearance, it was thought that he must have been taken by the Germans *en route*, and even as they spoke, was probably being tortured for information. As the days had passed, however, it had become increasingly obvious that something else had befallen their leader. The Germans would certainly have made propaganda out of their capture of such an important figure. He would have been paraded before the local people and would probably have been publicly executed. The Germans knew *Il Falcone*, of course. All of North Italy knew him. His exploits were recited by children in the villages of the Valtellina.

The reason for Sandro's dread was the increasingly erratic behaviour that Luigi had understandably demonstrated in the last few weeks since his wife and son had disappeared from their village. Sandro had spent the first few nights with him after word had come back that, indeed, they had been transported by train out of the valley, presumably north to Germany. Luigi had drunk himself senseless and had fallen into a coma-like state. He had then repeated the process for three days and nights, distraught when awake and raving when asleep, the demons of guilt haunting the passageways of his mind like drunks staggering through empty midnight streets. Then on the fourth day, he became lucid, frighteningly lucid.

'Someone informed on me.'

Sandro awoke to a pair of hands tugging at his lapels and shaking him.

'Someone informed on me.' A louder hiss. A wild look in his eyes, the look of a man who was on a journey through hell and had only bought a one-way ticket.

'*Falcone* . . . Luigi . . . What . . .? I can't breathe . . .'

He let Sandro's head fall to the ground and covered his face with his hands. A deep, almost inhuman sob emerged from behind his interlocked fingers. He took his hands away from his face and wiped his nose with the back of a sleeve, gathering himself.

'Don't you see? Someone, someone from this camp must have told the Germans that I am *Il Falcone*, that Angela is my wife. As far as they are concerned – if they were concerned at all – I was killed fighting in the Italian army eighteen months ago. Someone *must* have told them.'

'But Luigi, it could have been anyone. It could have been a neighbour, someone in the village who knew.'

'No. They do not know. As far as they know, my wife is a widow and my boy is fatherless. *Dio*, I haven't set foot in the village for eighteen months. It has to be someone in the camp. It isn't the first time either. Look at San Giorgio. No one outside of this camp knew about that, no one.'

Several weeks previously, a band of partisans had been ambushed as they went to the hillside village of San Giorgio to carry out an attack on a German barracks. As the partisans were making their way through the forest above the village, they had found the Germans waiting for them in force and seven partisans had lost their lives in a vicious fire-fight. Luigi had escaped along with half a dozen others and, although suspicions were mooted, they were too unpalatable and it was decided, finally, that the Germans had simply struck lucky by stumbling into the operation.

'That was pure luck, Luigi. We discussed it.'

As he said this, Sandro recalled his and a number of his colleagues' doubts at the time. There had been too many Germans and they had been too well prepared. Quite simply, they had been waiting for the partisans, and on the exact route they were taking. It had been no coincidence.

Everything was risky now, as the war went on. In the south, the Allies were making slow, but relentless progress, pushing the occupying German army further north and it was only a matter of time, unless the Germans threw every man they had into the battle, before the Allies took all of Italy. Still, German divisions poured through the passes in the mountains to bolster the exhausted troops retreating from Rome. People were becoming mercenary as they anticipated the end-game. Anything was possible. Even the unthinkable — one of the partisan group, seeing the end of the war, deciding to play for high stakes; a reward from the Germans to give him a good start when peace finally broke out. Yes, it was entirely possible.

'Ach!' Luigi hawked up a lump of phlegm and spat it out as if he were ridding himself of the evil thoughts he had been having. 'It had to be someone who wasn't on that raid.'

'But, Luigi, this is impossible. These men wouldn't do it. *Madonna*, I wasn't on the San Giorgio raid, remember? You're saying that it could have been me!'

'The swine could have been any one of you!'

He stared into Sandro's eyes for a second and then stood up suddenly and lumbered away into the trees that lined the clearing in which the group had made camp.

Sandro once again felt doubt swell up, the doubt he pushed to the back of his mind each time it arose. The face of George Bright came back to him, seated on a rock, squinting at the sky as he polished his spectacles, and the photograph of the Englishman's daughter, smiling expectantly at the camera. With Luigi so unstable and capable of anything – as, indeed, Sandro feared he had been with the Englishman – there was danger hovering around him. He wore it like an overcoat. It defined him and it drove him.

Adding to the confusion were Sandro's feelings for Angela – lost now, it seemed to him, lost in the vastness of this war, as were so many things and so many people, scattered like autumn leaves in the wind, across Europe. He slumped back, his head resting uncomfortably on the earth beneath it. She was lost forever and he still had not acknowledged the fact. In fact, he refused to acknowledge it. As far as he was concerned, she was still waiting for him in their clearing surrounded by trees, leaning on the rock with Antonio gurgling in her arms.

After a while, it had seemed to Angela like she was walking beside herself. This realisation had been a gradual process. At first she had come back to her body after only a minute or two, after suddenly noticing how odd it was that she was no longer part of that original body and that she could even look at herself, walking along to the left of her. That was the strangest part of it. She had felt that she was not alone. Of course, she was not alone because there were hundreds, perhaps even thousands treading the same circles that she walked. Their walk had definite boundaries. Those boundaries were delineated by the wire fences that marked the edge and the end of the world and, in fact, everything may well have ceased to exist beyond those wires, for all any of them knew, prisoners or guards. For Angela, who all her young life had dreamed of worlds beyond her own in the Valtellina there was a certain irony in this. Her world seemed to be becoming smaller as her life progressed and her dreams, once large and all-encompassing, were now also shrinking, shrinking until they occupied only the few hundred feet on which her circle of exercise took her. One day they would be so small that they would disappear altogether and life would no longer be worth living.

It was, indeed, far from the promenading of her youth in the square in her village, she thought, as she slowly and with great effort, placed one foot in front of the other; the teen-aged girls, arms linked conspiratorially, hands to their faces, pushing the giggles back between their lips, hips swaying in an exaggerated fashion, knowing and yet, at the same time, ignorant of, the great themes of their young lives. The boys, huddled on corners, smoking and affecting nonchalance, their deep, quiet, Valtellina souls troubled with love and longing, their eyes following the shadows of that longing as they circled the square.

She feared to look to her left where her other self, that other version of her walked. She sensed it there. Sensed the shaved head, cut and scabbed from the rough slashes of the razor that had separated her from her thick black hair. She had cried as she watched it fall from her head to the floor to mingle with all the other clumps of shorn hair. Sensed the red-rimmed eyes, underlined with black shadows that looked as if they had been painted there by an expert make-up artist at La Scala. Sensed the face that would, inevitably, like the faces of all the other women who surrounded her, be shrunken like that of a woman thirty years her elder; like theirs, her face would gradually be taking the shape of the skull that formed its framework, as if a building were to take on the shape of the scaffolding that held it up. It was as if her body were being turned inside out, as if she were beginning to wear her bones like clothes.

Someone was singing as they left the clearing high in the mountains that held their camp. It was an old song of the valley, one that Sandro recognised. He remembered his mother singing it as she hung out wet clothes to dry when he was a lot younger, she unaware that he was listening, innocently stopping for a rest, putting her hands on her hips and staring up at the peaks, the words of the song spilling into the silence around her. Now it hung in the damp, heavy air of the late spring afternoon, as if it were caught up in the fine drops of the steady drizzle that was falling onto their hats and down their faces.

There were seven of them and they were on their way to a rendezvous with another group who were relaying ammunition to them. This was one of the more mundane tasks in which the groups of partisans had to engage. Every month or so this meeting would take place and would involve a lot of walking and a good deal of carrying. It was never, therefore, the most popular of duties. Sandro was especially unenthusiastic on this occasion. A flu epidemic had rampaged through the camp and he had spent the past three nights soaked in sweat. This morning, however, he had awakened feeling better, if still a little weak.

He trudged along at the rear of the small column, almost pleased to be going somewhere other than the perimeter of the clearing that was about as far as he had gone while ill.

'I wonder where old Luigi is right now?' It was Carlo, dropping back to have a word with him. He blew cigarette smoke into the drizzle and it hung over them as they walked as if it had been trapped in a bag which was being held at the end of a string.

'I just hope he's alive,' Sandro replied. 'Two weeks without any sign of him – it's not good.'

'You may be right. But, the *tedeschi* normally make a big show out of capturing someone like Luigi. Even if they were still questioning him – and may God help him if they are – they would let it be known that they had him in custody. To frighten us all off.'

'As if they would succeed in that,' said Sandro, looking up, hoping to see a break in the grey sky that would signal the end of this spring rain. 'You've heard how they're on the run in the south. It's only a matter of time.'

'Let's hope so,' grimaced Carlo, pulling up the collar of his heavy jacket and throwing away his sodden cigarette. 'Let's hope so. Or, at least if it isn't, let's hope the damned rain stops.'

They trudged on, heading in a westerly direction towards the slopes above the town of Chiavenna. The paths they were following were becoming more and more difficult to walk on. The rain had now been falling for two days and was rolling down the sides of the mountains. In places it flowed like small streams and the dismal thought of returning to the camp carrying heavy ammunition lent a dejected air to the walk.

Finally, they stopped, as the light was beginning to fade.

The sun had sunk invisibly below the high horizon of the mountain peaks at least half an hour previously and it was becoming chilly. Mercifully, the rain had finally stopped, but their clothes were soaked through and they were very cold as they slumped down against the trees that hugged the side of this part of the mountains, the place where they always stopped for the night before walking the next morning for a few more hours to arrive at the rendezvous.

A fire was quickly lit and they huddled close to it, eating the cold meat they had brought with them and passing a couple of bottles of grappa from mouth to mouth in an effort to restore some warmth to their shivering bodies. As the heat of the fire reached into their damp coats, steam rose into the darkness as if they were being cooked.

Later, Sandro lay wrapped in his blanket, shaking, his flu having returned with a vengeance, exacerbated by the dampness of his clothes and the effort of the day. He realised he should have stayed back at the camp to recover more fully. He opened his eyes and stared up at the sky. At last it seemed as if the flat greyness of the past few days had broken and stars winked between the clouds. The moon, too, was visible once more, racing like a ship across the sea of the heavens.

At first he thought he was delirious. There were noises around him. The scuffling of boots on earth and gruff foreign accents.

'Good evening, *signori*! As you can see, you're surrounded! There are more than twice as many of us as there are of you. So, there are several guns pointing at each of you.' The man's Italian was slightly stilted.

They were all around them. Sandro turned his head to one side to see Carlo, trying to get to his knees, only to be returned swiftly to the earth by the point of a boot striking his nose with great force.

'I said don't move! Stay very still and you won't get hurt.' Sandro tilted his head slightly backwards and saw a German officer with a handgun trained on the recumbent figure of Carlo whose hand was held to his face, blood smearing out from between his fingers. 'At least, not just yet.' The German officer smiled as he said this and the dozen or so men who stood around him with machine guns and rifles trained on the partisans also smiled.

Sandro immediately felt a surge of fear paralyse his body as if an electric current was running through it. This was the moment he had feared for months, the moment when finally it would not be a matter of blowing up hydroelectric plants, or of firing on Germans from a distance so that they meant nothing, were rendered barely human by that distance. The moment had arrived when he was face to face with the men he had been intent on killing all through these winter months and they had the upper hand, the power of death over him and his colleagues.

His neck hurt as he arched it to watch the German officer walk amongst them, looking down at each of them, one by one.

'You know, you've been a pain in the arse for some time now. So, we were very grateful for the information that has led us to you. You see – and I think there is no harm in telling you this; in fact, I think you should know – a good friend of yours, and, of course, now equally our good friend, let us know about this regular little piece of activity.'

Luigi, thought Sandro. It could surely be no one else.

'He even let us know where you would be spending the night. A bit foolish that, really, not to vary your stopping place. Tut-tut. Perhaps you're not as clever as you think you are!' The officer laughed. A high-pitched laugh that seemed unfamiliar to him and that almost seemed to surprise him.

'However, my only wish is that there were more of you to share the pleasure of our meeting.' He stopped above Sandro, his boots about six inches from his head. Sandro could not help noticing how brilliant their shine was in between the splashes of mud that coated them. 'Still, perhaps you can help us to make that possible, facilitate a little meeting.' A stream of German then followed and several of the German soldiers rushed forward with rope and began tying the Italians up, dragging them into a circle ten or fifteen feet from the dying embers of the fire. They did not dare look at each other. The only noise was the heavy sound of Carlo's breathing. His nose had been reduced to a bloody pulp by the shiny boot of the officer.

'Now look, *meine Herren*,' He spoke standing in front of them, legs apart and hands behind his back, the German words incongruous amongst the Italian: 'there are only a few hours until dawn. You *Valtellinesi* are reputed to be deep thinkers, I believe.' He walked from side to side in front of them. 'I want you to exercise some of that talent for philosophy during these next few hours, with a view to giving me directions to your camp.' He stopped and smiled at them. 'So that I can meet your friends, perhaps share a few reminiscences with them. Remember. At dawn we'll have some fun together.'

He turned his back on them and went to join the others around the fire. Two Germans were allocated guard duties, although that seemed hardly necessary, given that the partisans were completely immobilised by the tightly-knotted ropes.

The rest of the night was endless. Sandro was both cold and hot, shivering as if he had just awakened on a cold winter's morning to find all the blankets had fallen off him. The others were motionless. Each man was left with his own thoughts.

Meanwhile, the Germans sat around the fire, talking quietly and occasionally throwing their heads back, laughing at something. How ordinary they seemed, thought Sandro. They were boys, mainly, boys brutalised by the war and turned into machines that ate, slept and killed. Machines that also expected to be killed. Like he and his partisan colleagues, life for them did not stretch effortlessly towards middle age, going through the numerous stages through which a man's life passed. It stretched only as far as the next exercise, the next piece of this war in which they would play a part. They had all, these young men, seen so many people killed. And not just strangers, but friends, men they had got drunk with, women they had kissed and made love to; shot, killed next to them. They had been covered in their blood, they had held their hands to their friends' torn bodies, pushing their innards back in through tattered skin, as if somehow they could make them whole again. They had felt the whisper of dying breath moisten their cheeks.

The German soldiers talked quietly by the fire, laughter occasionally shaking the branches of the trees.

Over on the far side of the fire, a lone figure lay with his back to a tree. It was the officer in charge. He held a cigarette lighter in his hand, an unlit cigarette dangling from his lips. The flame of the lighter illuminated his face. He was a good-looking man, with clear skin and almost gentle blue eyes. Sandro peered into the darkness and saw him extend his left hand horizontally above the flame and then down towards it. He held his hand there for a full fifteen seconds, in the flame, the red glow reflected in his eyes which watched without expression, as if they were watching someone else do this. Gradually, he withdrew his hand, blowing on it and sheathing the flame in the lighter's cap. He looked at his palm and smiled, and then laughed to himself, his shoulders heaving against the tree. His head fell back and Sandro noticed tears slowly beginning to fall from his eyes and trickle in straight, symmetrical lines down his cheeks, darkening the lapels of his uniform.

12

15 November 1999
Lago di Como
North Italy

Blue.

Blue was all he could see at first. A sea of dancing blue whose waves crashed against the walls and splashed against the ceiling.

Then, slowly, more began to leak into his cracked vision. A desk, a few feet from the bottom of the bed, and on it a thick, leather-bound book. A jacket – his own? – hung over the back of a wicker chair in the corner.

Just on the periphery of his vision he sensed something massive and silent. Painfully – the pain was in his neck and shoulders – he turned his head and discovered the oppressive bulk of an ancient armoire, the possessor, it seemed to him, of many dark secrets which lay like hidden bodies behind its massively mirrored doors.

The blue was draining out of the room now, seeping under

the door and oozing through the slats of the shutters which lay fast against the light of the sun to his right.

The ceiling began to shimmer, as if light were being reflected on to it from the surface of a swimming pool. From outside came the sound of water lapping gently against stone.

He began to feel as though he were watching rain fall on a watercolour. His vision fell in long, slow elongations down the page of the room.

Michael waited for the inevitable conclusion to his dream – the usual dramatic last act, the flapping of wings with the car miraculously appearing through the brickwork, his wife's body spread-eagled on its bonnet. But this time it did not happen. The ceiling continued to ripple with the reflection of water from somewhere outside.

He sat up. He was lying on a bed and was surrounded by the paraphernalia of the dream. The wardrobe was huge and solid and was matched on the other side of the room by a dressing table with the wicker chair and his jacket reflected in its large mirror.

His head hurt and his eyes stuck together as if he had been unconscious for some time. His watch had gone from his wrist and there was a pungent chemical smell in his nostrils. As his head began to empty of sleep it all began to come back to him. Or, at least, all that was to be remembered.

He recalled being in his hotel room, looking at the photographs he had taken at the *Palazzo Ronconi* and writing on the backs of them. Then there had been a knock at the door and when he opened it ... well, what exactly had happened? All he could remember about opening the door was a cloth of some kind heading for his face. And a smell, the same pungent smell that was now in his head. A chemical of some kind. It had rendered him unconscious and he had been brought to this place, wherever it was.

He put his feet on the floor, his legs reacting to the commands of his brain slowly and stiffly and gathered himself before standing up and walking to the door. As he expected, however, it was locked. He went over to the window, which had wooden shutters half-closed and padlocked. The reflection on the ceiling was a shaft of light that cut between the two shutters. He peered between them, the light at first hurting his eyes and could see water, the lake and its far shore, shimmering in what appeared to him to be bright afternoon sunshine. He thought he recognised Menaggio across the lake. That would mean he was probably somewhere between Verdanno and Beldoro, in one of the buildings that is hidden down by the shore, usually by large palm trees and thick, high walls.

He returned to the door and started to bang on it with his fists, continuing to do so for about a minute, until his hands started to ache. He then stopped and listened, putting his ear to the crack between the doorjamb and the heavy, wooden door. Silence. The silence that screams down long, empty corridors. Only the sound of the water from outside, kissing the shore.

'Ho!' he shouted, hesitantly at first, but then louder. 'Hey! Is there anybody there!' Again, he persevered for a minute or so and then stopped to listen. And again he was rewarded only with silence. He went back to the window and looked out, but realised that there was no point in shouting out into the vast emptiness of the lake.

He returned to the bed and sat on the edge. He then swung his legs up onto it and began what he feared might be a long wait.

They came as it began to get dark. There was the sound of a door opening in another part of the house and two sets of footsteps approaching briskly and noisily on the tiled floor.

Michael stood up beside the bed and stared intently at the door handle, as if an angel was going to turn it and enter the room. The footsteps approached the door and then stopped for a beat before there was the sound of a key turning grudgingly in the lock. The door swung open and two figures in dark suits were outlined from behind by the sun pouring in through a window at the other end of a long corridor.

One was inches taller than the other and much younger. He was very well-built and that made his suit seem almost too small for him. His hair was very dark and cropped short, exposing a large expanse of tanned forehead above a pair of hard-looking eyes.

The other was a man that Michael recognised – the man from the hotel bar. What was his name?

This man began to speak in English.

'Mr Keats ... Michael. Nice to see you again.'

'What the hell are you playing at? Why have you brought me here?' Michael shouted. *Pedrini*, he remembered. That was the name he had given. Rico ... Mico ... Vito. That was it. Vito Pedrini.

'It's Pedrini, isn't it?'

The other man stiffened, evidently ready to calm Michael down, if necessary.

'Oh, Michael, please, don't be like that.' He was speaking now in Italian. 'You must understand, we had no choice in this matter. You were getting very close to finding out some things that we ... well, we would rather you didn't know. That knowledge might have interfered with our plans. And there was no way we could let that happen.'

'What plans? What knowledge? I've no idea what you're talking about!' replied Michael, stretching out his hands, palm upwards, as if to emphasise his ignorance. At that moment, Ignazio Mazzini's large, dark face appeared in his head like a warning. Were these the men who had thrown the giant farmer over the edge of the cliff?

'Oh, come now. We know you've learned certain things, you've spoken to certain people. You have certain evidence of a photographic nature.' The photographs, Rosa's photographs. Oh why had he not looked at them before they had been stolen from his room?

Michael looked at them, shaking his head. What were they talking about? It must all tie in with the kidnapping of Teresa Ronconi.

'Our big problem now, however, is what are we going to do with you?'

The other man reached down to the floor where there stood a black leather briefcase that Michael had not noticed he had been carrying. He walked forward and put it on the table, opening it, taking out a hypodermic syringe and a small phial of clear liquid. He stuck the needle into the plastic top of the phial and withdrew the plunger of the syringe.

'I think it best that we all sleep on it, don't you, Michael?' said Pedrini with a smile as the other man handed the syringe to him. 'I hope you won't mind if we give you a little something to help you sleep. Please roll up your sleeve.'

'Piss off! I'm not rolling ...' The other man placed the syringe on the table and stepped forward with an almost bored look on his face. He drew back his hand and with the back of it, struck Michael hard on the right side of his face. Michael fell back onto the bed, stunned, his head spinning and the side of his face stinging. Dazed, he felt his sleeve being roughly rolled up his arm. There was the sharp sting of the tip of the needle puncturing the skin of his forearm and then there was just the lapping of the water on stone outside and the blue seeping back into the room through the window and under the door. The ceiling shimmered and the wardrobe hid countless secrets. He waited . . . waited for the sound of the wings and the car . . . waited for the sight of its bonnet . . . waited to see a body of a woman sprawled on it once more like a marionette . . . he waited for the comfortingly familiar sight of Rosa's body.

Somewhere in the distance there was a sound. It was beyond the water's gentle teasing of the shoreline and lay outside the roar of silence that filled the corridor stretching behind the door.

He moved his head and the whole world seemed to him to move with it. His eyelids were heavy as if they had been stapled together and any feeling in his body started to fade halfway down his legs and arms. There were no reflections on the ceiling. Only darkness fell through the half-open shutters to his right.

The sound was there again. It came from directly in front of him, beyond the foot of the bed. It was, he realised, the sound of a key in the lock, turning slowly and carefully. The lock turned all the way, settled into place and the door began to open. He could only sense this, because the darkness threw a black curtain across that end of the room.

Someone entered, carefully and silently. He saw a shadow approach. Still, he could not move, could not even lift his head. A rising sense of panic overcame him and he wanted to cry out, but only gasps emerged from his dry throat.

The shadow hovered over him and then a hand covered his mouth, stifling his attempts to shout for his life.

'Sssssh!' The sound came from the darkness close to his face. And then in a whisper, 'Michael, it's alright, it's alright.'

It was a woman's voice, speaking in an urgent, quiet whisper. Through his stupor, he realized it was somehow familiar.

'What have they done to you?' She put a hand behind his

head and lifted it. 'Can you get up? Can you stand? Let me help.'

She pulled his legs round onto the floor and put a hand behind his back to keep him upright. He shook his head, trying to clear it of the fog that swirled through it.

'Come on. Stand up. We have to get out of here.' She whispered. 'I'll help. Try to be as quiet as you can.'

She helped him to his feet, his legs buckling once beneath him, before she pulled his right arm around her neck, placing her left arm around his waist.

'Please help me Michael,' she whispered. 'Come on, one foot in front of the other. Concentrate on that. It's not far.'

He focused as hard as he could on lifting each foot and then placing it on the stone floor as quietly as possible. He was coming to a bit more and began to remember what was at stake. She breathed hard as she bore his weight at every step.

Light blazed out into the darkened corridor from a doorway ten feet ahead of them and the voices of a couple arguing on television raged from inside the room. Suddenly another voice, a voice in the room, not on television, erupted into a deep smoker's cough. She stopped dead, froze in mid-step, her next breath caught in her throat and staggered slightly as Michael's forward momentum almost brought them both to the ground. The cough continued and there was the chink of glass, the sound of a bottle pouring liquid and then another, shallower cough and an agitated clearing of the throat before once more only the sounds of the voices on the television could be heard, quieter now, the argument waning.

They turned away from this into another corridor, at the end of which they entered a kitchen in which the lights were on. At first she feared that someone was in there and hesitated before entering. She let Michael lean on the wall a few feet from the doorway, praying he would not slide to the floor, and crawled carefully along the cold plaster to peer in. No one. On the table, however, lay a large brown envelope with what appeared to be photographs sticking out of the top. She stuffed it inside her jacket. There was a small revolver on the table. She stuffed that carefully into her jacket pocket. She then stole carefully through the darkness and opened the door at the other end of the room before returning to Michael, who had begun to slump towards the floor.

Once again, she coaxed him to his feet and manhandled him to the outside door of the kitchen where a slab of cold night air hit them. It seemed to revive Michael slightly. He lifted his head and inhaled deeply, filling his lungs.

Moving forward, they started to descend a couple of flights of rickety, wooden stairs. It was the most difficult part, so far, of their traverse of this house. The stairs were noisy, creaking underfoot and Michael almost fell headlong down them on more than one occasion.

The sound of the lake's small waves came closer as they got to the bottom of the stairs. They descended the last step and found themselves on a shingle beach. What light the moon threw at them from between the passing clouds, showed that behind them was a high wall from which the kitchen steps emerged under a small arch. The wall had the legend 'Hotel Royal Victoria' stencilled on it in large but faded letters above an iron gate that led back into the garden of the building, brooding darkly behind. A memory of a different time. This was the only means of escape from the beach, apart from the way they had just come. She set Michael down on a large rock that lay in the middle of the beach and he watched her or, through the double vision that the drug still gave him, watched her and her twin perform a perfectly synchronised walk to where the water met the beach. They looked into the darkness to their left and then to their right.

'A boat!' The lips of both figures moved, but only one voice emerged as they ran to a low, concrete shelf, jutting out from the wall where the circle of shingle beach came to an abrupt end. She came back to Michael and once again pulled his limp body to its feet.

'Come on, Michael, we can get out of here without having to risk a trip through the garden.' The familiarity of that voice, he thought again, in the mist of his weary brain. She half-dragged him towards the boat, but as they reached it she could hold him up no longer and he fell forward into it, his head making sharp contact with the piece of wood that acted as a seat. She folded his legs into the boat, loosened the knot that fastened it to a rusted, iron ring on the wall and, the water soaking her shoes and the bottoms of her jeans, pushed it off the shingle and out into the water. When its bottom was floating free of the shingle she jumped in, fitting the oars into the rollocks, and, with difficulty began to row the boat away from the beach towards the centre of Lake Como.

13

Something was sliding slowly across Sandro's face, leaving a trail behind it that felt sticky and faintly disgusting. At first he was unable to do anything about it. He was drifting, somewhere out on the edge of consciousness, the sun splashing down warmly on him between the branches of the trees that were all around him. He could feel that, at least. It felt good, the sun hitting his face like spots of rain, being diffused by the branches above him. He tried to raise his left arm and, to his surprise, found that he could not. There was no feeling in it. In fact, he felt as if he did not have an arm at all. This was a curious feeling and he turned his head to make sure that his body did, indeed, still exist. Gratefully, he could see the arm stretched out beside him, but it was bent at an unusual angle that he was certain was wrong. It looked like a child's drawing of an arm.

With increasing horror, he felt the thing on his face slither towards the corner of his mouth, which was open and which, given that his body did not appear to working as it should, he worried he might not be able to close. He turned his head to the right and tried the other arm, with more success this time, although he could only raise it with difficulty and not without considerable pain. Haltingly, he raised it to his cheek and pulled away whatever it was that was crawling across his flesh. He looked at his fingers and saw between them a large worm, almost a snake, in fact, bulbous at one end and gleaming darkly in the sunlight. Suddenly tiring, he allowed his hand to flop to his side, dropping the worm amongst the mulched leaves on which his body lay.

He had regained something approaching consciousness some time before, although, in reality, he had, at first, thought that he was actually dead. This thought – that he was dead – had entered his head and had not seemed at all strange or even worrying. He had lain there, not feeling anything for a while and either unwilling or simply unable to move – he did not know which.

Gradually, as the sun climbed higher in the sky, feeling began to re-enter his increasing consciousness. It came back at first only in surges of pain, especially down his left side. Pain shot up and down his arm and there was a sharp ache in his side, in his ribs, if he breathed too deeply. His left leg, too, throbbed painfully with almost every beat of his heart, as if the blood that was being pushed through his veins was too great a quantity for them to hold.

With consciousness and pain came thought, and, eventually, and worst of all, memory. He moaned, horribly, when his facility for memory returned, turning his head to allow tears to roll from the corners of his eyes, down the side of his face and into his ear where the salty water entered a cut he had, causing him further pain.

He closed his eyes and saw it all again. The faces of all his comrades floated in front of his vision and then spun off, leaving only the face of the German officer, smiling.

How often in his life would he relive this dawn? How many times would he stage the scenes he had witnessed like a perverted film director in his own private cinema? Who could he possibly tell what he had seen? Who would believe him?

They had seemed to be running short of oxygen as the night wore on. Their breathing became shallower and for Sandro it felt as if his heart was going to burst the very ribs in which it was caged. As the Germans drifted off to sleep one by one, changing sentries every couple of hours, the partisans became more alert, alert to the slightest changes in the light as dawn approached and with it, who knew what? One thing was clear to them, however – they were unlikely to survive the day that was about to begin.

A watery sun rose excruciatingly slowly over the far mountain peaks, throwing long shadows across the rotting leaves that carpeted the earth. A thin gossamer curtain of mist hung amongst the trees.

'*Steh 'auf!*' shouted the officer, rising to his feet and spraying commands around the waking bodies of the soldiers as they began to throw off their blankets and clamber to their feet.

The officer spoke for some time to one of his men, gesticulating now and then towards the partisans. Sandro looked around the men, whose eyes were sunken and lined. Carlo's nose was swollen, both his eyes were black and his face was caked in dried blood.

They picked one of the older men first – Guiseppe Montella, a man of the far side of the Valtellina who had fought in Ethiopia and then in North Africa. Finally, like many others, he had deserted and, returning to the mountains he knew, joined the partisans. His ropes were untied and he was dragged unsteadily to his feet and held by three German soldiers while the officer spat questions at him in Italian. Where was the group's camp? How many of them were there? Where were the other groups located? What operations were planned?

Montella was a hard man who had seen a lot of life and he stared relentlessly and deeply into the German's eyes while the questions were thrown at him. Then, the German approached him and struck him hard across the face with the back of his hand.

'Tell me!' he screamed.

Montella smiled, spat in the German's face and said as calmly as if he were in an argument in a bar, 'Go fuck yourself.'

By the time they had finished with Montella, he was barely conscious. His crumpled body was returned to the seated group of bound partisans and another was cut loose and faced the same barrage of questions.

Five of them underwent this routine of questioning and beating before the German tired of it. No one answered his questions. All of them stared contemptuously at him while the blows rained on them. Sandro breathed a sigh of relief when the German gave up on this approach, as he would have been next in line for a beating.

The officer spoke briefly once more to his second in command and then stood in front of them again, his face red from his exertions and his anger, his hands held tightly behind his back.

'You obviously didn't listen to me last night when I urged all of you to consider certain things.' He took several paces to the right and stared out across the valley which stretched a couple of thousand feet below him. 'Such a beautiful sight, this valley of yours and such a shame that you will not wake up to see it ever again. Unless you re-consider.' His voice had risen as he had spoken, but then he spoke very quietly. 'Let's see if we can encourage that, eh?'

There was another fusillade of commands in German and a scurry of activity. The soldiers went to their packs, which were scattered around the clearing, took out the small shovels they carried and started to dig seven holes about three feet apart.

They dug for twenty minutes or so, sweating as they encountered tangled roots and large stones, while Sandro and his comrades looked on with puzzlement. Puzzlement because at first, naturally, they thought that they were watching their own graves being dug. However, it soon became evident that the holes that were being created were not wide enough to hold a body and were very deep.

Eventually, one by one the soldiers clambered out of the holes and threw their shovels down, using their hands to brush the dry earth from their uniforms.

More sharp words issued from the officer's mouth. The soldiers took Carlo, untied his legs and dragged him to the nearest hole. They dropped him into the hole, his legs doubled up painfully behind him and began to fill it in. At first, a shudder ran through the partisans' bodies as if they were somehow connected on a grid, as they began to think that Carlo was going to be buried alive. Then the soldiers stopped piling earth in on his body at the point where only the top of his shoulders and his head showed above the ground. The Germans then proceeded to do the same with all the other partisans, the officer barking commands at them as they did so.

Sandro was the last to be taken, but as they started to move him towards the final hole, his colleagues staring at him from their hellish positions, the officer stopped them.

'*Nein, nicht dieser junge Mann!*' And then in Italian, 'I think it might be useful if this young man reported back to his other colleagues just what we Germans do when we are disappointed.' A slow smile spread across his face and he instructed a couple of his men to tie Sandro to a tree about fifteen yards away from his compatriots.

Sandro watched as the German stood in front of the strange crop of heads sticking out of the earth.

'One last chance, gentlemen. Is there one of you who would like to give me the information I require? I'll give you thirty seconds to consider your situation.' He strode across to his second-in-command and spoke quietly to him.

The seconds passed like a slow train. Carlo struggled to escape from his heavy tomb, but with his hands tied behind his back deep in the ground, was unable to do anything more than loosen some of the earth around his shoulders. Sweat broke out on the foreheads of the others and tears rolled down the face of one of the younger partisans. Several closed their eyes and their lips moved in silent prayer.

'Oh you are such fools!' shouted the officer, 'Such fools!' He then walked away from them and came over to Sandro. 'Now watch carefully, young man. You owe us that, at least, for sparing your life, don't you think?'

Once again he walked over to his second-in-command who handed him a grenade and it suddenly dawned on Sandro and the beleaguered partisans what was about to happen.

Sandro's life ended in that moment just as much as his colleagues' lives ended. He saw their eyes widen, their mouths open, and heard screams and curses and prayers. He screamed himself, the sound escaping from his body, having become animate and almost visible. He closed his eyes as the officer nonchalantly pulled the pin from the grenade and lobbed it like a tennis ball into the centre of the group of heads. He did not even watch, half-turning as he threw it, not reacting when the ground shifted under the force of the explosion, merely walking towards Sandro and kicking him high on the leg and then punching him hard in the ribs. He then picked up a piece of wood that lay nearby and mercilessly beat him until a red cloud descended slowly and mercifully over Sandro's eyes.

He was looking at his house, smoke gently rising from its chimney in the early dawn. He had little idea how he had got there and even less idea why or even what he was looking at. There were only vague memories of intense pain cracking his body as he rolled helplessly down slopes, or dragged his injured leg across the ground, half-hopping, half-crawling like a wounded animal on all fours. His leg was grotesquely swollen in several places. It felt as if the bones were trying to burst through the blue, black and yellow skin that covered them. His arm flopped at his side, sending razor-sharp messages of pain to his brain whenever it swung against his side. Each time he fell and the air was jarred from his lungs, forcing him to inhale deeply, his shattered ribs made him scream, the scream itself vibrating painfully inside his broken frame.

It had taken him all day and most of the night to get here. Sometimes he had passed out and each time he awoke he was unsure as to exactly how long he had been unconscious. Now he watched, delirious, not really understanding where he was. It had been as if he had been gripped by a homing instinct, had been following an invisible cord that had led him back to where his life had begun. And now, in a moment of shocking clarity, he realised once more how that life had ended. Once more he saw the faces of his comrades, detached from their bodies, swimming through the space inside his head and he retched dryly into the long grass that hid him from view.

And another face swam across his fogged vision. A dark, handsome face with just a hint of cruelty to it. Tears began to roll down his face. This time they were not tears of pain. They were tears of helplessness and anger.

'*Falcone,*' he croaked, 'Luigi. Why?'

14

17 November, 1999
Lago di Como
North Italy

Michael came to in the half-light of early dawn. He was being gently and pleasantly rocked and the sound of water was still with him.

At first he thought he was still in the room and that someone was trying to shake him awake. He expected to look up and see the familiar reflection of both his dream and now reality, rippling the ceiling. But when he looked up he saw nothing but sky. Puffy, white clouds spotted the blue, which presaged a beautiful day.

He sensed someone near him and, rolling painfully over onto his back, looked up from what he now saw was the bottom of a rowing boat at a figure, the figure of a woman, slumped over a pair of oars, her long blonde hair hanging lankly forward over her face.

'Who . . .?' His voice was croaky and caught in the back of

his throat to the extent that he thought he might throw up. He coughed and her head stirred and began to rise.

'Who are ...? He stopped in mid-sentence and almost burst out laughing at the absurdity of it. There she was in front of him, with those same brooding eyes and dark eyebrows and that same lambent smile that he had first appraised across the reception desk of the Lighthouse Inn.

'Good morning, Michael.'

This time he did laugh – until tears began to roll down his cheeks. 'I thought to myself, why not? I'd burned my bridges with the Lighthouse Inn, and, anyway if I saw another piece of bloody lighthouse memorabilia, I was going to turn into Grace Darling!' She laughed, raising to her lips the bottle of local beer she held in her hand. A jolly, rubicund Tyrolean character with a stein of frothy lager leered at Michael from the label. 'I decided not to wait for you to get in touch.' She smiled as she said this, 'I didn't phone because I knew you'd try to put me off – you English are so damned reserved. But it was obvious when I got to your flat there was no answer. So, I decided to try the newspaper.'

Michael grabbed a handful of crisps from the giant bag that lay on the table in front of him, and stuffed them into his mouth. They, along with the beers, had been all that they could find to eat and drink in an all-night petrol station once they had landed the rowing boat close to Beldoro in the early morning. They had then walked back to the hotel in the back streets of town that Helen had booked into on her arrival, and he had sneaked upstairs to her room while she distracted the night porter who was gratefully coming to the end of his shift.

'So I phoned the *Post* and after a load of trouble got through to a lovely Welshman who told me you were here, in Beldoro, but he wasn't sure exactly where you were staying.'

She took another swig of cold beer, sighed deeply and went on. 'To tell you the truth, I was curious, Michael. I fancied an adventure – perhaps not quite as much of an adventure as this one, mind you.' She stared into his eyes, 'And I kind of like you. My mother says I always have a soft spot for people in trouble. I have this terrible urge to help them. She swears it'll get me into serious trouble one day.'

'I think we could safely say it almost got you into serious trouble tonight, don't you think?' he asked, smiling broadly.

'Oh, I can't imagine how breaking into a strange building, dragging a drugged, semi-comatose man that I have known for about six hours through a houseful of armed thugs and rowing him in a tiny boat across a huge lake in the middle of the night could be construed as getting into trouble.' She laughed again.

'But how did you find me? That's what I don't understand.'

'I packed my bags next morning and booked a ticket to Milan – honestly, Margaret, my friend, thought I was insane. Unlike me, she's really sensible. Anyway, I hired a car and drove up here but when I arrived in town I realised it wasn't going to be that easy to find you. But I started to ask in all the hotels. Not difficult at this time of year, of course, because there aren't that many open. And, in fact, on my first day, I walked right past yours because it looked closed. There was scaffolding on the outside and it was obvious they were decorating. It was only when I had exhausted every hotel in town that I realised it was actually open. The guy at the desk told me you were here but I explained that I wanted to surprise you. He was reluctant at first but he's Italian, appreciates a bit of romance like they all do, and let me know what room you were in. So I went upstairs and was walking along the corridor to your room when I saw these two guys in the corridor ahead of me, standing in front of your door. I didn't want to share the moment with them so I stepped into this kind of alcove and peered out. God, Michael, I couldn't believe what I was seeing. They poured something onto this cloth they were holding.'

'I think it must have been chloroform or something,' said Michael, his nostrils filling once again with the acrid, chemical smell.

'Whatever it was, it stank. It made my eyes water even that far along the corridor. Anyway, when the door was opened – I presumed it was you – I couldn't see – there was a kind of scuffle. One of them looked back down the corridor to check if anyone was coming, I guess, and they went into the room. I waited a minute or two and was just about to head back downstairs and scream blue murder, thinking they were mugging you or something, when the door opened again and they came out. One, the big one, was carrying you over his shoulder like a sack of coal. And the other had a large envelope in his hand. They didn't come past me, but headed towards the fire escape at the other end of the corridor. I followed . . .'

'Bloody hell, you were brave!'

'Stupid, more like! But thank heavens I did. I don't think they had your best interests at heart in that house. Anyway, they took you down the stairs and out through a door that opened onto an alley at the back of the hotel. I watched them from a window on the first floor. They put you into the boot of the car and drove off. Now, luckily, my car was round the side of the hotel, not far from where I was and they had to go right round the front and past the road my car was on to get anywhere. Also, there was a set of traffic lights on the corner they had to take to turn into the promenade and I knew from my brief time in town that those lights only seem to turn green on Mondays, Wednesdays and Thursdays, if you get my drift. I took the stairs three at a time – you should have seen the look on the face of the guy at the desk! – and tore round the corner to my car. Just as I got to the bottom of the side street I was parked in, their car went past, heading out of town along the lake. I caught up with them at another set of lights and followed at a discreet distance until they pulled into the drive of the house I found you in. They closed the gates and I decided to wait just down the road where I could get a good view of the way in. I managed to keep myself awake through the night and through the next day, but as nothing was happening, I decided to explore once it got dark. So I jumped the wall, and made my way down onto that little beach. I hadn't been there very long when one of them came and opened the back door – they must have been cooking because the smell of the food was driving me wild.' She dug deep into the shiny crisp bag and started to talk again through a mouthful of potato chips. 'I had to get you out of there, so I climbed the stairs and found that there was no one in the kitchen. They were in another room eating by that time, I presumed, so I tried a few rooms, staying away from the one where I heard the television. Eventually, hey presto, there you were, all tucked up in dreamland. And here we are.'

'My God Helen, you took a hell of a chance. But I don't understand why you didn't just call the police.'

'Well, this is where it gets really interesting, Michael. That was exactly what I planned to do as soon as it got light. I didn't want to let the house out of my sight in case they moved you in the night. But there was a petrol station within view of the house and I went over as soon as it opened to buy some water. I was going to ask to use the phone there. But, as I was passing the newspaper stand there, something caught my eye. The front page was all about the kidnapping as far as I could see, pictures of the girl and her father – a right evil looking old bastard he is, too. What got my attention was a picture of you, too. It's a rotten one – you look like an international terrorist in it. Here, have a read. My Italian isn't quite as good as it was in third year at school.

She handed him the paper. Sure enough, it was all about the kidnapping, but in a box at the bottom, there he was. He read the small headline out loud.

English Journalist Missing

The police are concerned about the whereabouts of a missing English journalist, Michael Keats, aged 33, who is known to have spoken to Ignazio Mazzini before his death.'

The piece went on to talk about the tragic death of Rosa.

Michael shook his head and then began to translate the main part of the story out loud.

'The picturesque tourist town of Beldoro, nestling at the confluence of the Lago di Lecco and the Lago di Como, recently traumatised by the kidnapping, in broad daylight, of Teresa Ronconi, 35 year-old daughter of multi-millionaire, Luigi Ronconi, was further shocked today by the brutal murder of one of the participants in the events of the 10th of October. Police in Lecco have announced that the death on Wednesday of Ignazio Mazzini – the Beldoro farmer who confessed that he had, in fact, perpetrated the attack on disgraced shopkeeper, Bonfadini and not the kidnappers of *signorina* Ronconi – was now being treated as murder. It had initially been suggested that Mazzini had committed suicide by jumping from a cliff, but a post-mortem now reveals the cause of death to be what is described as a severe blow to the head and that the deceased was, in fact, already dead before plummeting one hundred metres. Police are interested in the whereabouts of *signor* Keats.'

'Christ!' Michael let the newspaper fall to the bed.

'Are you alright?' Helen grabbed his arm. 'You've turned white as a sheet!'

His head fell dejectedly to his chest and then he began to laugh.

'Well, can you blame me?'

'What do you mean?'

'They've missed one out.'

'Michael what are you talking about, missed what out?'

'Two murders. There ... have ... actually ... been ... *two* ... murders.' He spoke the words slowly and clearly, not looking up.

'Two?' she repeated. 'Who's the second ...?'

'Claudio Scatti ...'

'Who the hell's Claudio Scatti?'

'Claudio Scatti worked in the bar where Teresa Ronconi was kidnapped and I suspect that he was part of the gang that did it.' His voice went quiet as the acrid smell of Claudio's death flooded his senses once more. 'I went to talk to Claudio – I found out he was holed up in a summer chalet in the mountains, ostensibly so that he could avoid the press – and, I'm afraid, by the time I got to him, he was well and truly dead. His throat had been cut.'

'God, Michael, that's awful!'

'You're telling me. I've never seen anything like it.'

'But, by whom? Who's doing this?'

'At the moment I'm not sure, but the guys who grabbed me can't be a million miles away from it. I just don't know who is giving them orders, or why.'

'But, look, why is this other murder ... the barman ... not in the paper?'

'Because, Helen, they don't yet know. Claudio went up into the mountains to get away from it all; the chalet's pretty isolated and there isn't a phone. And, consequently, I presume no one has stumbled upon his body yet. But they will and I'll be in the frame again.'

'But why didn't you go to the police as soon as you got down from the mountain?'

'I don't know.' He shook his head, helplessly. 'I don't know. I had a feeling, you know. And I guess I was also very scared. I kind of thought, 'no one knows I came up here; there was an old guy who gave me directions, but I could easily deny that I followed them. I didn't pass anyone on the way up or down; no one uses the chalets at this time of year. Why get involved? But, in all honesty, I just wasn't thinking straight.' He stared at the wall, seeing once again the stony stare in Claudio's eyes and the gaping slit in his neck. 'Later, of course, I realised I should have gone straight to the police, but by then it was just too late. It would have looked suspicious. Especially as shortly after I found out that Ignazzio Mazzini was also dead.'

'So you left the poor bastard up there?'

'I left him up there wearing a halo of flies and a stench that will stay with me forever.'

'Michael! Where the hell are you? What's going on?'

Michael had had trouble getting through to Bruno – he was 'unavailable' – and, of course, Michael was unable to tell them who he was. However, when he had told them to tell Bruno that it was 'Homer' on the phone, Bruno had come at once. Homer and Buck were the names they had given each other when they were touring the States together and Michael knew Bruno would instantly realise who was calling.

'Bruno, none of this has anything to do with me.'

Michael! What do you take me for? Of course I know

it's nothing to do with you, but according to my sources up there they're building up evidence on you. Your fingerprints are on the ashtray that was used to beat the farmer to death – they've compared the prints on the ashtray with the prints in your hotel room.'

'Well, of course there are prints in the kitchen; I interviewed him there.' He recalled the faintly rotting smell of the kitchen and saw, in his memory, his hand reaching out to push a large, heavy green ashtray to one side to make space for his tape machine. 'But, he was alive and kicking when I left him, Bruno.'

Bruno recognised the desperation in his voice.

'I know, Michael, I know. Look, they're also struggling with it because, of course, they haven't got a motive. So, I don't think they really believe you did it.' He broke off and said something in Italian to someone. 'But look, I'm sorry, I have to go. You dragged me out of an editorial meeting. What are you going to do? You going to give yourself up?'

'What can I do? I don't want to give myself up just yet. I want to find out what's going on. My best chance is to stay on the run and try to find out who is behind all of this.'

'Okay, but please promise you'll stay in touch – I'll keep my ear to the ground. And, Michael, be careful. These guys obviously mean business.'

The line went dead. *They mean business, indeed*, thought Michael. He stood by the window, far enough back so that he could not be seen from outside. Helen had gone out to get supplies of food and drink for lunch and they were going to work out what they were going to do next.

Outside, the car ferry from Menaggio was slowly arriving at the jetty, almost empty apart from a couple of cars. A man stood at the rail, smoking a cigarette and staring towards the town. Something about him seemed familiar. Michael looked around for the opera glasses that were left in the rooms of this hotel to allow guests to enjoy the view across the lake in even more detail. He picked them up and put them to his eyes, allowing a moment for them to adjust to the different perspective of the glasses.

'Pedrini!' he gasped.

Vito Pedrini leaned on the rail looking almost directly at Michael. Michael instinctively ducked behind the curtain, but realised immediately that he was, of course, too far away to be seen. Pedrini wore a dark coat and a cigarette hung limply from his lips. He stood up straight, pulled his coat tightly around him and smoothed his hair, evidently feeling the cold breeze that was rippling the fronds of the palm trees along the promenade in front of the hotel. He turned and quickly descended the stairs to the only car on board – a sleek, silver, five series BMW. He opened the door and climbed in, disappearing behind windows opaque with steam.

As the ferry began to pull out towards the centre of the lake Michael grabbed the pen that lay on the table beside him and scribbled the car number on the back of his hand, raising the glasses to his eyes to check that he had it absolutely right.

The ferry swung ponderously to the right and disappeared behind the rooftops of the neighbouring hotels.

15

The streets of Sondrio were slick with summer rain. They shone darkly in the late afternoon. The rain was keeping people indoors, not that there was much reason to be on the streets. Such shops as were open, whose owners had not been killed in the war or who had not migrated to places of greater safety, did not offer very much at all. Desultory displays sat moodily in shop windows and an atmosphere of pointlessness hung over the entrances to such establishments. On the whole, though, businesses were mostly closed down, their markets and suppliers having dried up or their services having been rendered redundant by the hostilities.

Sandro leaned close in against a wall, which offered scant shelter from the rain. Taking a deep draw from a damp cigarette, he smiled to himself, emphasising the deep lines that were now etched incongruously on his young face. He felt close to some kind of resolution.

This satisfying thought was confirmed by the sight of a figure emerging from the gate of the building opposite where he was standing. It was an old school building which the Germans had turned into their headquarters. The figure, clad in the grey uniform of an *Obersturmführer*, stopped outside the gate, as he did every evening, and removed a silver cigarette case from his inside pocket. He opened it, took out a cigarette and tapped it several times on the lid of the case, looking up and down the street, as if expecting to see someone he knew. The cigarette lit, he took it from his lips and turned left, his shoulders hunched, walking into the teeth of the rain, which was now driving quite hard down onto the town from the peaks of the surrounding alpine massifs – the Bernina, the Disgrazia, the Adamello and the Redorta.

As he had done for the past week, Sandro turned in the same direction and began to follow at a distance that was unlikely to cause concern to the grey-clad figure ahead of him. This was made all the easier because he knew exactly where the German was going.

Sandro's partial recuperation had taken almost two months. His arm and leg were still not fully healed and, in fact, he was unsure if they ever would be. He walked with a limp in his left leg, unable to straighten it fully when he took a step. As for his arm, he could not raise it more than a few inches from his side. Both still caused him pain, especially at night and he slept only fitfully. His face, too, bore the scars of the beating he had taken that day in the hills. It had left a pronounced depression in his left cheek and he was no longer the handsome young man with whom Angela had fallen in love. Angela, who had long since disappeared from his life, but whose memory remained clear in his mind.

His mother had nearly fainted when she opened the door to her son's almost lifeless body that night. She had tended to him without a break for four days as he hovered deliriously in some distant place, mouthing obscenities and telling her the story of the preceding few days, but telling it with the wrong words in the wrong order, so that she understood nothing. Finally, some strength seemed to return to him. Then he would not talk. He had disappeared to a place somewhere deep within himself. It was a place peopled by ghosts. Visions of that moment of the explosion in the hills that had ripped apart his comrades' bodies troubled both his waking as well as his sleeping moments, until he could no longer tell the difference between being awake and being asleep. The faces of his dead colleagues floated across his eyes; the abject horror of those hellish moments never left him.

He had been visited after a few weeks by a partisan commandant who stared stonily at him as he retold his story, calmer now, accepting that it had actually happened. As he ended it, an uneasy silence hung between the two men.

'As you say, it would seem someone has been informing. Those good men have been lost because someone has gone over to the side of the Black Brigades.' The Black Brigades were a Fascist paramilitary group.

'But who?' answered Sandro, not voicing his own suspicions that it had been Luigi who had informed on them.

'We are investigating,' the commandant said abruptly, but there was something about his way of saying it. Just for a moment the commandant's gaze flickered away from Sandro's and he knew then that he was the one under most suspicion, simply because he had survived. 'You will receive further visits from us as we attempt to ascertain what exactly happened.'

215

The commandant had left, but Sandro had an uneasy feeling. They obviously had doubts, or else they would already have taken action against him. However, he was resigned to the fact that finally they would not believe him and that they would probably also link him with the San Giorgio catastrophe.

But had it been Luigi? Why would he have done it; why would he have given the Germans details of the partisans' operations? The only reason was that he had obviously become deranged by the loss of his wife and son. Luigi blamed himself for it, blamed the life he had chosen to lead in the last six months. Perhaps he blamed the bloodlust that he had discovered within himself. Perhaps Luigi had wanted to revenge himself on the person he believed had informed on him and if that meant that the whole battalion of partisans was to be wiped out in order to eliminate that one person, then so be it.

There were no further visits for the next few weeks. One evening, however, Sandro was walking in the woods not far from the house. He was watching a deer grazing amongst the trees. She nuzzled the ground, stirring the damp leaves with her snout, her large, dark eyes gleaming.

Suddenly she had looked up, her body frozen to attention, her ears twitching and her nostrils flaring as she searched for the direction of a scent or perhaps a sound. Then, all of a sudden, she was gone, kicking up dirt and dust, which spun lazily back to earth through motes of fading sunlight. Something had spooked the deer and Sandro's chest immediately tightened. He slid behind a bush and scrutinised the spaces between the trees in the opposite direction from the one which the deer had taken. *It could be hunters*, he thought. But hunters of what? Deer or men?

He moved silently from tree trunk to tree trunk. He may have been incapacitated by his injuries, but this was his territory and he understood it like an animal would. He knew where and how to place his feet on the earth, knew how to move without attracting attention, knew how to use the light and shade of the forest to swallow his movement. He became a mere shadow.

After a few moments he saw them – a large man, followed closely by a much smaller man, moving through the trees about twenty metres distant. One of them, the large figure, he recognised instantly – Cavalcanti, a giant of a man with a huge beard, clad in a goatskin waistcoat, which exaggerated his girth even more. He carried a rifle and a bandolero of bullets was wrapped around his body from shoulder to waist. He was known as *l'Assassino* and was used by headquarters, as his *nomme de guerre* suggested, to take care of embarrassments, to permanently remove those of the cause who had transgressed.

Sandro had never seen the other man before. He was thin and weedy, wore spectacles on the end of his nose and a fur cap that sat awkwardly on his head. His clothes seemed wrong for the terrain, too considered, too stylish. The two men moved slowly and carefully through the trees, the last remaining flashes of sunlight spraying onto them like rain in a spring shower.

Sandro knew at once why they were here. Somewhere far away, in Milan probably, the evidence, such as there was, had been amassed and a decision had been made by a roomful of men. He fully understood. In the absence of any substantial evidence it had to have been him who had informed. Why had he appeared to have been ill in the days leading up to the incident, if not to have escaped the consequences? Why had he alone survived? Injured admittedly, but in all probability that was only to make it seem that he was not involved. In the absence of anything else, surely it would be far better to do something than to make no decision at all. It was good for morale. It would teach a lesson to anyone considering such activity. Send *l'Assassino* to take care of this ugly business as quickly and efficiently as possible.

Sandro had taken to the woods up above his mother's house after dinner simply for a smoke and some gentle exercise. He was, consequently, unarmed. But he feared for his mother although he was certain they would not harm her. Their instructions were to kill him and they would never hurt an old woman, even the mother of an alleged informant. He knew what would happen. They would burst into the house and ask her where he was. When she said he wasn't there, they would then disappear into the night again, as if they had not been there. There was little he could do, because if he showed himself, he was a dead man. And, at any rate, they were now very close to the house and there was no opportunity for him to get back there to warn her before they announced their presence.

His chest tightened even more. He could barely breathe as he watched them slide across the clearing that led up to the house, the house where he had played as a child, where he had clambered around his mother's skirts as she hung out washing, where he had helped his ailing father in his work; this clearing which he had crossed on so many early mornings, a smile of anticipation on his face, on his way into his beloved mountains, such a short time ago, it seemed.

Suddenly, he had a presentiment that something terrible was about to happen and, without thinking of the consequences, started to move. They, meanwhile, stood in front of the door, looked at each other and then threw it open. Sandro was running now, or, at least, running as much as his bad leg would allow, but he was still quite a distance away and the house was lost from view behind the undergrowth. He shouted as he heard the first shot, his voice lost in the echo of the gunshot as it ricocheted around the forest. He had stopped dead in his tracks by the time the second and third shots rang out, his mouth frozen in the act of screaming silently.

At that moment, he fell to the ground. His body had still not properly healed. He lay there for an instant, catching deep breaths. There was silence from the house as, he presumed, they searched it for him, and then they re-appeared at the door. They stopped and looked around, rifles raised, scanning the surrounding forest. He stopped breathing for a moment as their eyes turned in his direction, but he was well hidden, low down in the evening shadows. After some moments, they turned and quickly disappeared into the trees on the other side of the clearing from where he was positioned.

Sandro stood there for what seemed like a long time, the dampness of the early evening beginning to seep upwards from the earth into his boots and his trousers. It was as if he had taken root and would remain there forever. In fact, he did want to remain there forever, because the alternative – moving, finding out what had happened in the now silent house – was just too terrible for him to contemplate.

Mist began to tumble through the branches of the high trees, falling down the sides of the hills drenching everything in its path like an avalanche. Branches trembled as droplets formed on them. Bird sounds faded into silence and the billion noises of the forest melted away as the sun slipped behind the peaks.

Finally, he had regained the ability to articulate his muscles and tendons. First one leg, very slowly. Then the other. And then he was plunging through the trees. He again stumbled and fell to the ground at one point, ripping his trousers on a branch, felt the jagged point stab his thigh like a sharp knife. The pain, however, did not touch him. He had gone beyond feeling anything in the last few weeks. He clambered to his feet again without even reaching down to touch the sticky hot flow of blood that ran down his leg inside his trousers. He ran on, through the clearing, through the door and into the house.

And there, where she had cooked and cleaned and knitted and sewed and cared for his father and for him, he found his mother, the essence gone from her, spread around her in the pool of drying blood which haloed her head. One of his shirts was draped across her shoulders. It had hung across the back of a chair and she, feeling the cold, must have put it on as she worked in the kitchen. They had run in, Cavalcanti and the other man, had seen a figure with its back to them, clad in a man's shirt, had presumed it to be him and had shot his mother.

He knelt beside her and did the only thing he could – cradled her lifeless head in his hands. Softly, he began to hum the old valley song that was one of his first memories. The song that one of his doomed comrades had been whistling on that fateful day when they had set out to their deaths just a few short months ago. The song she had sung while hanging clothes out to dry.

Outside, a sharp burst of a solitary birdsong rang out in the distance before fading away until it was only an echo. The silence of twilight cloaked the forest.

He sat there until dawn, reliving every moment of his life, humming now and then. And, as the sun clambered up above the high peaks, casting long shadows across the valley below, he dug a grave behind the house and placed his mother's body carefully in it, kissing her on the cheek and brushing the hair off her forehead, as she used to do unconsciously as she stirred the contents of a cooking pot on the stove, or darned one of his socks. He then shovelled the dirt over her body, sprinkling it with great care over her face, which he had covered with a handkerchief, as if he was putting make-up on her. That done, he went back into the house, packed a haversack with a few things, took the small roll of bank notes and fistful of coins that his mother kept in a box under her bed, locked the door and walked across the clearing without once looking back.

It would be fifty years before he would see that house again.

16

Obersturmführer Erich Weber was a creature of habit. Each night, he would leave the old school building and walk towards the eastern end of town, where the houses and buildings became slightly shabbier and the streets narrower and darker. He visited a woman, a girl, really.

Sandro had followed her, too, during the day when Weber was busy. A young prostitute, living with her family, but seeing her clients in the empty house next door to the one in which her parents lived. She was neither beautiful nor plain. He had noted the exhaustion in her face as he sat a few tables away from her one day in a cafe, where she had stopped to meet a friend.

One night, he lingered in the street outside her house long after Weber had emerged and lit his customary cigarette before disappearing back towards the centre of town.

He walked up to her door and after once raising his hand to knock and taking it away, finally banged loudly. The sound echoed and there was a pause before he heard footsteps coming from above.

She peered out around the door, her body hidden.

'Can I help you?' Her voice was soft and sounded young. He had not realised quite how young she was. For a moment he stood there, unable to say anything.

'Can I help you?' she repeated, slightly irritated by the seemingly dumb figure before her.

In truth, he had almost forgotten how to speak. He had been in Sondrio for more than three weeks now and, during that time, had spoken little more than to ask for a coffee in a bar or to buy some food. His voice, therefore, came huskily from his throat and surprised him with its sound.

'I . . . I was looking for some company.'

'Some company, is it you were looking for, lonely boy?' she said, emerging now from behind the door, the shape of her body, wrapped in a sleek, silk dressing gown, taking him by surprise. Provocatively, she placed her right hand on her hip, leaning with her other hand on the door. She smiled.

'Well, I'll tell you, I can't afford to be charitable and my company doesn't come cheap. I hope you've got the where-withal, lonely boy.'

Sandro reached into his coat pocket and pulled out a wad of bills, the money his mother had saved all those years.

'Well, I never.' There was sarcasm in her voice now, but it was not in any way vindictive. She was older than her years, however; so much older and it saddened Sandro. He thought again of Angela, never far from his mind. This girl would not be much older than her, but Angela's eyes had been alive with optimism and anticipation. This girl's eyes were dead with the exhaustion of living in these times.

'Who would have thought a boy from the hills would have so much money? I hope you came by it legally, lonely boy.' His accent, strained by years of speaking dialect, had betrayed his origins. 'Oh, all right, then. Come on in and let's see if we can cheer you up, eh?'

He entered a hallway lit only by the light of the full moon, which tumbled in through a window at the top of the stairs they climbed.

Her room was as luxurious as the straitened times would allow. A gas lamp flickered eerily, shedding light on a sofa which sat up against the wall on one side, a threadbare blue sheet thrown over it. In front of the sofa was a chipped oak table and on it were a couple of wine glasses and a bottle of wine with about a third of its contents remaining. The bed that stood against the other wall was unmade, its sheets trailing onto the floor and the pillows still showing the indentation of a head, probably Weber's.

'Make yourself comfortable. Have a glass of wine.' She poured what remained of the wine into the two glasses without washing them. He then raised his glass to his lips, knowing that Weber's lips had possibly touched its cool surface just an hour or so ago.

She sat down beside him, stretching her hand up to his neck and tugging at the hair at the back of his head.

'Don't have much to say, do you, lonely boy?' She smiled, throwing back the wine in one swallow. Her words were slurred and he realised now that she was, in fact, quite drunk. She sat forward, with a look of mock horror on her face. 'Wait a minute! Don't tell me you're a virgin! Well, don't worry, lonely boy. Virgins are my speciality – *la specialità della casa*!' She raised her glass, as if making a toast. 'All these German boys, they're like you lot up in the hills. Pure as the driven snow. Until they come to see Domenica, that is.' She stood up, unsteadily and went over to a cupboard by the bed, taking out another bottle of wine and attempting with some difficulty to remove the stopper.

'Come on, then, be a gentleman and help a girl, can't you?' He stood up and limped across to her, trying to take the bottle, but realising that with his bad left arm, it was going to be equally difficult for him to remove the stopper. She looked at him curiously and then held the bottle while he tried to pull the stopper out. Finally, amidst her giggles as she tried to hold the bottle, it edged free and she fell back.

She picked up the glasses and brought them over to where he was standing, pouring some wine into each on top of the cupboard. She then seemed to become sober as she picked up her glass.

'Where did you get that, lonely boy?' She reached her hand up to his damaged cheek, feeling the indentation where Weber had hit him with his pistol butt. 'And your leg and your arm. You've been through it, haven't you?' She moved close, staring up into his eyes. He looked down at her, noticing how liquid her eyes seemed, and wanted to drown himself in them.

She reached behind his neck and gently pulled his head down towards hers and brushed her lips tenderly against his. She pulled away and looked deep into his eyes and then kissed him.

She pulled him down onto the bed and he pulled apart her robe, its silky coolness unfamiliar beneath the calloused skin of his fingers. Her skin was smooth and warm and her lips were generous, her tongue exploring his mouth, the scent of wine on her breath. Her dark hair fell back from her forehead as he kissed her and all at once she was a young girl again. The exhaustion dropped away from her and innocence and the hunger of youth filled her eyes.

Above him, he thought he heard once more the song of the birds exploring the sky and thought that he felt rain fall down onto his naked back. Beneath him, it felt as if the grass of the clearing was shifting once more under the weight of the raindrops.

The next night he waited outside Domenica's house again. This time, however, it was different, for he knew now where Weber was, what his surroundings were. He knew the sofa where they would start out, a glass of wine in their hands as they kissed. He knew the scrap of carpet by the bed that he would stand on to remove his boots. And he knew the bed that they would fall on and on which they would make love, its slightly soiled off-white sheets, its four pillows.

The moon had slipped behind dark clouds by the time the door opened and Weber stepped out into the night. As ever, he engaged in his ritual of taking a cigarette from his silver case, tapping it on the lid and lighting it. He then turned and set out once more back in the direction of the old school that housed the German headquarters. He was in the habit of returning there every night and, as he never emerged again, Sandro presumed he must be billeted there.

Sandro fell in behind him, invisibly as ever. It was more difficult in a town to become one with the shadows, he found. Had he been following Weber in the hills that he knew so well, he would have found it easy. He would have been as invisible as a breath of wind, but down here amongst these buildings and geometric shadows that varied in intensity, it was more difficult.

A few streets further on, Sandro deviated from his usual route, striking out quickly down an alley at the bottom of which there was a wall which he climbed, sliding down the other side quietly and crouching for a moment at the bottom to catch his breath and let the pain in his injured leg subside. He then stood up and slid along a wall at the end of which he stopped, his ears listening out for the familiar footsteps that would signal the arrival of Weber, for his short-cut had brought him to this point ahead of Weber by a few minutes.

He heard the harsh sound of the German officer's boots on cobble stones approach and pulled from his waistband the pistol that he had put there before setting out this evening. The cold steel made his fingers numb at first, but soon the natural warmth of his hand entered the steel and it felt like an extension of him.

His breathing became faster and his heart pounded like a piston as the footsteps came closer. Then, as they drew level, he slid out from his hiding place, making almost no sound, placed the barrel of the pistol roughly against the German's temple, knocking him slightly sideways and hissed hoarsely:

'Keep your hands away from your pistol and stand absolutely still or you're a dead man!'

The German froze, his head pointing straight ahead, but his eyes swivelling as far round in their sockets as they would go, trying to see who his assailant was.

Sandro looked round to ensure that no one had seen his attack, but the buildings in this street were all empty, their owners having fled the war. He then hissed once more:

'Take out your pistol – hold it by the barrel!' His useless arm made it impossible for him to hold a gun to the German's head and take the pistol out of his holster at the same time. 'Now put it in my pocket!' The German did as he was told. 'To your left is a building. Turn and walk towards it, open the door when you get inside, climb the stairs and, remember, I will have this gun pointed at your head every step of the way. One wrong move and your brains will be decorating the pavement. Now go!'

The German turned stiffly, his eyes darting to first one side and then the other. He reached the door, turned the handle and they entered the building. A gas lamp, lit earlier by Sandro, cast light onto the stairs. The German hesitated, but Sandro hissed once again, 'Go on!' and they began to climb.

They climbed three flights of wooden stairs, all the way to the top of the house and at the top Sandro instructed Weber to climb a ladder that led from the topmost landing up to an open hatch door. He followed, the gun still trained carefully on the German.

'Don't turn around!' he told the German once they had both climbed into this attic. He quickly turned the pistol round so that he held the barrel in his hand, raised it above his head and brought it down sharply on the German's head. His body folded immediately and he fell heavily to the floorboards.

Sandro breathed deeply, raising a hand to a nearby beam for support. He had known it would not be easy to kidnap a fully fit man when he had only one useful arm to work with, but he had succeeded and now he had some work to do before Weber awoke.

He was out for longer than Sandro had anticipated. Perhaps he had hit him too hard; there had certainly been a great deal of blood flowing from the wound, but, of course, there was little that could be scientific about a blow to the back of the head with a pistol butt.

Weber's eyes eventually opened. His first feeling was one of severe pain, at the back of his head where it lay on the wooden floorboards of this room he was in. His second was one of confusion. Where was he? All he could see above him were the planks of a wooden roof with sunlight seeping between them where it was in need of repair. There was no sound from outside, even though it was evidently daytime. His third feeling was cold. He was very cold. He was wearing no clothes. And he was unable to move his arms or his legs. They were restrained in some way.

He turned his head painfully to the right and saw that his wrist had been tied with a thick rope that was secured to a beam. His left hand and his ankles were similarly tied. Sandro had prepared these ropes earlier with some difficulty, given his disabled arm.

There was a sound from the hatch and Sandro's head appeared at the top of the ladder. He had been checking on the German every fifteen minutes or so.

'*Teufel*!' spat Weber, followed by a stream of German, his anger almost making him choke. Then, in Italian, 'Why don't you just kill me? Why go to this trouble?' There was a break in his tirade as he strained to lift his head to get a good look at Sandro. 'Who are you anyway?'

'Ah, you don't recognise me, *Obersturmführer* Weber?' Sandro climbed up through the hatch and leaned on a roof beam, picking at his nails with a knife.

'No, I don't believe . . .' He stared hard at Sandro's face.

'Perhaps you will remember if I ask you to recall a morning about ten or so weeks back, up in the mountains, not far from Monte Santo. There were seven of us.'

A look of sudden understanding and a small smile crossed Weber's face.

'Ah, I see it's coming back to you now. You must remember me, Weber. I do look slightly different, I suppose, to the way I looked before you had some fun with your pistol butt on my face.'

Weber laughed before his head fell back to the floorboards, a look of sheer exhaustion filling his eyes.

'Oh, just kill me, why don't you? Get it over with.'

'No, no, no. That wouldn't do at all. At least, not until you tell me something, or confirm what I think I already know.'

'Oh, anything. You know, I don't care anymore, about the war, about Hitler, about Germany. I hardly exist as it is, so what do I care about any of it. I have done things I never thought I would be capable of. We all have ... even you.

'There are times, you know, when I find it all overwhelming. It's often just before the sun comes up over the mountains after another sleepless night. It suddenly strikes me, what I have become in such a short time. Do you ever feel that, my friend? Are you as ashamed as I am?' He looked Sandro straight in the eye, abject desolation clouding his eyes for a moment.

Sandro looked away from the German's gaze. 'I don't have as much to be ashamed of as you do, my *friend*.' He spat the word out with hatred. 'Enough of your regret. I want one simple answer to one simple question. Who betrayed us? Who told you where we were going to be that night?'

'Oh, is that all you need to know? That's easy! I was a bit surprised at first though, but not when I found out why he did it. You are all so damned emotional, you Italians. You are swayed too much by your feelings. The trouble with Germans and with Nazis, in particular − no, for your information, I am not a Nazi, never have been. I pretend so that I can get through this damned war. The trouble with them is they are not at all swayed by feelings. As you know, I am sure, they see them as something of a weakness. Anyway, your betrayer was a very angry man; he was made unstable by his anger, I would say.'

'But who ...'

'Well, I won't waste your time. It was *Il Falcone*. The one the children sing songs about in the streets of Sondrio − if they only knew! In the beginning he was trying to trade

231

information in exchange for the return of his wife and child who had been sent to a camp in Germany.'

Sandro's heart skipped a beat.

'But there was nothing we could do. They were long gone and probably already dead by the time he came to us. No one survives in those camps very long.' His eyes were dead as he uttered the words, as if he had shut himself off from all of the suffering they held. 'So, he asked who betrayed them. We told him it was one of you, but we did not know exactly who. He then swore that he would take his revenge and told us about your monthly meeting to replenish your stocks of ammunition. Hey presto, we made your acquaintance and here we are you and I, having such a fine time together.'

'And Luigi ... *Il Falcone*, what became of him?'

'We gave him safe passage into Switzerland. I have no idea what he is doing now or even if he is still there.' A silence settled between the two men. 'But, hey, if that's all you wanted to know, then put me out of my misery. Or let me go ...' He smiled. 'No I suppose that's not really on the cards, is it? After all, I did treat you all rather badly, didn't I?' He laughed, his body shaking in the flickering flame of the gas lamp. 'The look on your comrades' faces as they realised what I was going to do, as I pulled the pin out of the grenade. I'm fascinated by that moment, you know. The sudden realisation that it is all going to end. That the world will go on, but without you. That is the ultimate moment, don't you think? The power to do that, to be instrumental in that ... Magnificent in a way, eh?'

'You're insane, Weber.' Sandro stood up straight. 'I can't imagine what it must be like to *be* someone like you. People like you shouldn't be walking the earth. The worst thing is you make your victims as evil as you. War is difficult enough, but it's almost not enough for your kind. You have to invent new abominations, new cruelties all the time. And I do, too, in order to satisfy this overwhelming urge that I have to not just kill you, but to make you suffer as much as or even more than my comrades suffered. Perhaps I can enjoy that, as you call it, *ultimate moment*.'

'Hmm, I am interested to know what you are going to do. Do tell me.'

'No, I think I'll let you use your imagination for a little while, Weber.'

With that, he stepped down into the hatchway and disappeared from view. The flickering light of the gas lamp animated the shadows of the beams and highlighted the limpid gleam of the German's eyes as they stared blankly at the wooden ceiling.

The smell of the rancid meat that swilled in the bucket almost made Sandro gag as he pushed it ahead of him up the ladder with his one good arm. He had scoured the bins behind the only butcher's shop in Sondrio that remained open.

'*Gott im Himmel*, what is that?' The acrid smell reached the German's nostrils. 'That smell alone is almost enough to kill a man!'

'Sandro smiled. 'Oh, don't worry, there is much more than just that.' He clambered up into the attic, picked up the bucket and approached the German. He raised the bucket about a foot above him and carefully upended its contents onto the naked body, making sure he covered most of his top half with the contents – fat and offal and a bloody liquid.

'Bearrgh!' the German gasped in disgust as a fresh and stronger wave of the nauseous stink invaded his senses and Sandro stepped quickly back to prevent any of the filthy substance coming into contact with his boots.

'Oh, that is disgusting. Where did you get it? From your

mother's pantry? Is that the kind of filth you Italians are eating these days?' He smiled, but his eyes were screwed up as the smell filled the room.

Sandro also smiled. But it was a smile of anticipation. He stepped back towards the hatch and lowered himself carefully down onto the ladder, briefly disappearing from view.

Again, with difficulty, he pushed a container up the ladder ahead of him. It was a wooden box, much more awkward and heavy than the bucket and its weight kept shifting as its contents seemed to move around inside.

'Oh, I'd rather die than put up with this stink. Hurry up, get on . . .' The German had become very animated, but then, all at once, was silenced as Sandro removed the top of the box and the scraping and scratching of clawed feet could be heard from within.

'Oh, no, not that. Not that!'

Sandro put the box down and picked up a strip of elasticated cloth from the floor. He went over to Weber and wrapped it with difficulty around his head, gagging him. The Germans' eyes pleaded with him all the while and he struggled violently, trying to loosen the ropes that bound his wrists and ankles.

Sandro returned to the box, Weber's muffled cries behind him and set it on its side, allowing the twenty or so rats that were inside to spill out onto the floorboards. They emerged cautiously at first, their snouts twitching as they tried to acclimatise themselves to this new environment. The smell struck their senses immediately with the impact of a glass of whisky on a drunk, however, and they began hungrily to seek its source, skittering across the floor in every direction, climbing over each other in their filthy hysteria.

'Oh, by the way, Weber,' said Sandro, 'They haven't eaten

anything for a couple of days. You should keep them going for a while though.' He watched for a moment as the rats suddenly, as one, realised where the smell was emanating from. They turned and descended in a wave upon Weber's body. The last thing Sandro looked at in the attic were Weber's eyes, which were prised open in horror.

'The *ultimate moment*, my friend, the *ultimate moment*.' he said, before dropping down onto the ladder, pulling down the hatch door and fastening it above him. At the foot of the ladder he stopped for a moment. Above him he could hear the manic scratching of claws on the wood of the floorboards and the thumping of Weber's terror-struck body as it flailed about as much as its restraints would allow.

Stepping out into the street, Sandro gulped lungfuls of fresh air and held onto the wall to steady himself. It was late afternoon by now and the clouds that had been obscuring the peaks of the mountains all day were beginning to break up. The heat of summer hung in the air now, seeping into the walls of the empty buildings around him.

He slept that night in a tiny woodcutter's shelter in the hills just above Sondrio. He needed the smells of the hills in his nostrils, the scent of the earth and the trees to clear out the awful stink of the afternoon. He was almost delirious, however, and he could not clear out the memories. Luigi and Angela troubled his sleep all that short night. He would wake at regular intervals, lie there thinking of them and then drift into another brief period of restless slumber in which they would once more visit him in the many insane forms that his mind seemed capable of devising.

At the end of it, in the early morning, with the mist rolling down the sides of the hills towards the empty streets of Sondrio, he resolved to tell no one. Luigi had suffered enough and, anyway, he was gone and unlikely to be seen in this area again. Sleeping dogs should and would be allowed to lie. This war had already brought enough horror and death.

He stood up, rubbing his dead left arm, which throbbed gently, as it always did in the morning. He picked up his bag and without stopping to look back on the lands of his youth, limped off down the track that led to the south.

He took the first steps that began a journey that would take him far away from the Valtellina for a long time.

17

17 November 1999
Northern slopes
The Valtellina
North Italy

The silver BMW glinted in the sun as it disappeared around yet another bend in the road that clung to the side of the lake. A few miles further on, the road would climb away from the lakeside and become a modern highway, built a few years back as a conveyor belt for those who wanted to ski in Bormio. For decades before that, traffic would be strung for miles along the old road, moving at a snail's pace. Now the shiny new *autostrada* cut through the mountains in long, dark, dripping tunnels, cutting journey times in half and bringing the Valtellina, and, more importantly, the ski slopes, within easy reach of the *Milanesi* whose shiny, high-powered chariots scornfully brushed aside local traffic and sped on to the north and west.

Helen had returned just as the ferry had disappeared from

view and Michael had thrown down his opera glasses, grabbing her by the wrist and shouting 'Where are you parked?' He had dragged her out of the hotel, her breathless questions unanswered.

'Where are we going, Michael?' she shouted at him as he pulled the car keys from her hand and started the car, which was parked in the street that ran along the side of the hotel.

'Hang on,' he answered, negotiating the lights at the corner of the promenade and speeding away from town along the coast road that led to the north.

'I saw Pedrini . . . on the ferry,' he said at last, breathlessly, snatching at the gears as he threw the car around a bend. 'I'm hoping he's headed for Verdanno. If we go like the clappers we can get there before him.'

They reached the small lakeside town of Verdanno with time to spare. As he parked the car under the plane trees that lined the car park next to the ferry slipway, they could see the boat ploughing steadily through the water, the thrum of its engines audible from a distance through their opened windows.

A policeman stood by the slipway, talking to a man who was ready with a rope to moor the ferry when it arrived. They laughed at something, relaxed and happy in the warmth of the early afternoon. Michael instinctively slid down his seat. He presumed his photograph was being carried by every policeman in Italy. Helen looked at him nervously, but the policeman was not interested in anything beyond his conversation.

Once the ferry had moored at the jetty and the metal ramp had come down, the car engines started up and they began to move forward. As the BMW manoeuvred its way up the ramp, the window on the passenger side came down and there, visible for all to see, sat Vito Pedrini, sniffing the air as if it belonged to him.

'It's him, alright,' hissed Michael, turning the key in the

ignition and swinging the car round into place a couple of cars behind the BMW, which stopped at the junction with the main road, awaiting a change in the traffic lights. It then swung left away from Verdanno and followed the curve of the lake to the north and onto the *autostrade*, the passing scenery reflected in its dark, tinted windows.

At the eastern tip of the lake the road curves away into the beginnings of the Valtellina, at right angles to the Valchiavenna, which runs northwards towards the Swiss border. If you do not take the road to Switzerland, then you find yourself heading in an easterly direction towards Sondrio and then, further on, the winter sports resort of Bormio.

The BMW sped on into the Valtellina, on a normal, two-lane road now, which made it difficult to follow Pedrini as he overtook other cars moving too slowly for him only to find another slow vehicle in front.

Modern villas spewed down the valley side to the road. Vineyards stitched the slopes here and there and smoke drifted intermittently from chimneys into the sky. Michael knew what it smelled like, the air here. It was scented with burnt wood and it possessed the memories of many long, hard winters.

He drove on in silence, concentrating on not losing Pedrini. About ten miles into the valley he began to pass familiar landmarks and then he spied his brother-in-law's house, overlooking the road from the valley side. He imagined life carrying on as normal inside, Giovanna bustling around the kids, trying to persuade them to do homework, the television booming from the corner of the living room, as if playing for a houseful of people who were hard of hearing; he imagined dust settling on Rosa's things hanging in the wardrobe of the bedroom they always shared when they visited.

And then he was passing the spot where it had happened,

where all this began – the spot where she was struck by the blue car. It was the first time he had been back here since the unimaginable horror of that day. The thought of that particular moment, running towards her broken body, filled his head for an instant before he came upon a tractor moving at about ten miles an hour and was forced to brake hard.

'Overtake, Michael! Overtake or we'll lose him!' Helen shouted, leaning forward as far as her seat belt would allow, attempting to peer around the tractor and follow the BMW's progress.

'Okay, okay, I'm doing my best!' he retorted, irritated that she did not think that was exactly what he was trying to do.

The road cleared in front of the tractor and he crunched down into third gear, pulled out and overtook it.

Ahead of them the road was straight and empty. There was no sign of the BMW.

'We've lost him!' Helen banged her fist down in frustration on the dashboard in front of her.

'Damn! Bloody tractor!' he cursed, looking around for side roads Pedrini might have taken. 'There!' he shouted, almost causing a huge pile-up as he turned sharp left into a side road.

'Where?' asked Helen, covering her eyes with her hand to obscure the sun's glare. And then they both saw it together, the BMW, emerging from a clump of trees, climbing a zig-zag mountain road about two hundred feet above them.

Michael put his foot down and sped off in pursuit, comfortable in the knowledge that such roads did not offer the driver too many options. He could drive at a safe distance and still remain in touch with his quarry.

'There's nothing up here, you know,' Helen observed several minutes later, a map spread on her knees in front of her. 'After that last village it carries on for a few miles and then peters out into nothing as far as I can make out.'

'Strange,' said Michael, once again catching a glimpse of the car up above them.

On they drove, the edges of the road beginning to close in on what looked like ancient asphalt. The road plunged deeper into the hills and there were no longer the precipitous drops that had kept them on the edges of their seats for the last twenty minutes. Outside, the air was crisp and increasingly cool. They couldn'tsee the BMW ahead of them any more. The road ahead was obscured by tall pine trees and it began to bend and curve every twenty or thirty yards. Michael slowed down, worried that the BMW might have stopped up ahead of them and that they might come upon it suddenly.

They passed a turn-off that was no more than a dirt track, but which was certainly wide enough to take a car, even a big one like Pedrini's. Michael stopped the car, reversed, pulled up and got out, looking at the ground.

'What is it, Tonto? Have you found a track?' Helen sniggered, standing at the side of the car, speaking across the roof.

'Very funny, Matthieson, but look – and I know you'll think I'm crazy – but if you look at this wheel rut ...' He pointed at the ground, at a deep furrow in the road filled with water. '... you will notice that the ground is wet on either side of it. Hence, a car must have turned down this side road not five minutes ago. I, ahem, rest my case.'

She walked around the car to the spot where the rut was.

'My God! I *am* impressed.'

'I should think so, too!' He stopped, becoming serious. 'Look, do you think they're very far from here?'

'Well, you certainly wouldn't want to drive a posh car like that too far on a surface like this.' She gazed into the trees where the track disappeared from view, noting the rough terrain that it presented – a rutted, muddy dirt track.

'I agree. So, I think we should abandon the car and walk in. That way they won't hear us.'

'Unless they already have, of course.' she said, looking around for any sign of life.

'That's a chance we have to take, I suppose,' he replied. 'Why don't I drive the car into the trees up ahead to keep it out of sight. Then we'll walk for a bit and see what we can find.'

He parked the car about ten yards into the trees at the side of the road, far enough away from it for it to be invisible to anyone passing who was not specifically looking for it. Then they set out down the track.

The afternoon was not warm and they shivered after the shared warmth of the car. The trees closed in on them, shielding the sky and a silence hovered over them. All that was audible were their footsteps tapping out their rhythm on the ground. Michael wondered what he was doing here. How had he got into this situation? What was he hoping to find? And who was this girl he was walking with? He had met her one night and, somehow, amazingly, she had saved his life.

All at once, a sound in the distance disturbed his thoughts: it was the sound of a car coming towards them.

'Quick! Off the road!' Michael half-shouted and half-whispered.

They leapt to the side of the track they were on, plunging down a bank into clumps of bushes that grew there. Kneeling down under the cover of the bushes, they waited. A few moments later, the engine noise reached them and a navy blue Porsche Boxster with blacked-out windows passed them, slowly picking its way along the ruts of the track, its engine whining in complaint at the slow pace that it was making.

'Fancy car,' said Helen, standing up after it had passed, brushing earth and twigs from her knees.

'Yes,' Michael replied, following the sound of the Porsche engine into the trees with his eyes. 'Come on. Let's see if we can find out where he came from.'

They walked on for ten more minutes and had decided to walk for another ten or so when, through the trees, they began to discern something. The grey-green hues of a stone-built construction became visible.

'Aha!' said Michael, falling to his knees behind a large bush. 'What have we here?'

'This must be it,' whispered Helen, already on her knees beside him. 'Yes, look . . . there's the car.' She pointed to the left of the building where the silvery sheen of Pedrini's BMW could just be seen.

'Maybe it's his holiday hideaway,' Michael said.

They settled down on the slightly damp grass, staring at the building thirty or so metres in front of them.

It was fairly ancient, but had had a considerable amount of work done on it of late. This was obvious, not only from the varying colours of the stone that made up the walls and the brand new, grey slate roof that gleamed in the late afternoon light, but also from the construction materials that lay around – piles of stones and slates and a concrete mixer as well as a small bulldozer.

Smoke climbed lazily in a straight line from the chimney that sat at the apex of the roof. The house itself was big enough to have two storeys. Two rows of windows, one above the other confirmed that. Their view was of the back, as far as they could make out. There was a sliding patio door, which was curtained with something white, and to either side, small windows. The patio door was open, even though it was becoming quite cool as the sun slid down towards the tops of the mountains that surrounded the house.

'God, it's chilly,' Helen whispered, shivering and wrapping her arms around herself to keep warm.

Michael put an arm around her shoulder, feeling her bones through the thin jacket she was wearing.

'Look, Michael, someone's there.' Helen pointed at the house.

The curtain was pushed to one side exposing a dark triangle that was filled with two figures, one a man in a dark suit who was immediately recognisable as Vito Pedrini, and the other a woman, slim and young, with long blonde hair and clad in a white t-shirt and dark tracksuit trousers. Pedrini walked very close to her and was talking very earnestly. She stopped and turned to face him and, although Michael and Helen were too far away to hear what was being said, it was obvious from the body language that an argument of some kind was taking place. She used her hands expressively, raising them to emphasise whatever points she was attempting to make. He, on the other hand, stood there, his shoulders hunched and his eyes directed at the ground. An instant later, however, and he became animated again and the debate seemed to have taken an entirely new direction.

'Who's she?' Helen hissed at Michael.

Michael looked at the long, blonde hair of the woman and recalled the photographs he had in his files as well as the pictures that had been everywhere in Teresa Ronconi's bedroom.

'You know, Helen, I think we're looking at none other than Teresa Ronconi, the woman who was kidnapped.'

As they looked on, the couple seemed to come to some kind of consensus on what they had been discussing. They laughed and turned, Pedrini putting his arm paternally around Teresa's shoulders as they walked back to the house.

'That doesn't look to me like the normal relationship a

kidnap victim would have with her kidnapper!' whispered Helen.

'I know. How weird. What the hell is going on here? There's no doubt that Pedrini is a gangster. He *must* be behind the kidnapping.' He watched them enter the house and the triangle of inner darkness disappeared as the sliding door was closed and the curtain once again hid the interior of the room.

Michael glanced at the darkening sky.

'Look, I've seen enough. We should get out of here. It'll be dark soon and I don't really fancy driving that mountain road in pitch blackness.'

By the time they returned to the road, however, night had all but fallen. Michael executed a difficult turn on the narrow track above the turn–off, taking care not to reverse down the steep bank that lay just behind his rear wheels. They set off, gingerly at first, and then a little more speedily as the road became more substantial.

'Michael! Lights!'

They had been going for about twenty minutes and were now safely on the tortuous sequence of switchbacks that would take them down to the main Sondrio road. Helen was looking up the mountain and had spotted car lights swinging left and right on the roads above them.

'He's not that far behind us and he's moving fast. He must have seen our lights. He knows this road better than us. He's going to catch us in a minute!'

'Christ!' He started to brake, pulling to the side of the road where a space had been made to allow cars to pass each other. He quickly turned in his seat.

'Kiss me, Helen!'

'What! There's a bloody gangster who's probably armed to the teeth about to discover that we're on to his little secret and you want . . .'

'Sorry, no time to explain!' He put his hand behind Helen's head and pulled it towards him. Their lips met as the lights of Pedrini's car rounded the turn behind them. The car immediately slowed as it approached them. Michael kissed Helen even more passionately, lifting her hand to the back of his head to lessen further the chance of his being recognised.

They felt eyes peering into the darkness of their car as the other crawled towards them. They could each feel the other's heart pounding against the walls of their chests.

'Oh, God!' Helen mumbled through lips crushed against Michael's.

Michael took his hand from behind Helen's back, without turning round or removing his lips from hers, and middle finger extended, gestured at the passing voyeur.

Immediately, the horn of the passing BMW was sounded in response and its engine fired up again and roared away into the darkness.

'Just another courting couple. That's what he thought, dirty bugger, stopping to have a look. These hills are full of couples humping in parked cars every night.' said Michael as they both pulled away from each other and fell back onto their seats, a sense of huge relief flooding the car.

'God, I was scared then,' said Helen. 'That was bloody close.'

'We're not used to this kind of stuff, are we?'

'You're not wrong there. Hiding from gangsters, watching kidnap victims connive with their kidnappers . . . snogging a man everyone thinks is a murderer in a car on the side of a mountain in the middle of bloody nowhere. I can't speak for you, Michael, but I should say I'm not used to this kind of stuff! But, hey, I can't *believe* you pulled the old *kiss me to hide from the baddies* stunt!' She laughed. 'You're a pretty good kisser, though, for a double murderer!' He joined in with her and they laughed until it hurt, more out of a sense of relief than anything else.

'My brother-in-law's house is up there. It's not far and we can go that way to get back onto the main road. Let's drive past it so you can have a look at it.' He indicated to turn right and waited for a car to pass from the other direction before swinging across the opposite carriageway and bumping onto a badly surfaced side road.

'Are you sure? Shouldn't we be getting back to Beldoro to work out what the hell we're going to do?' answered Helen in a voice filled with concern.

'Oh, come on. It'll only take a few minutes to swing past it. He designed it himself – he's an architect – and just about built it himself, too. It really stands out from all the others around here. When you come in on the train from Milan to Morbegno, you can see it on the hillside in the distance. I remember how proud Rosa was when it was finished. It must have taken him three years, working in the evenings, at weekends. The kids spent their early years scrabbling about amongst the bricks and sand.'

Helen sat back and smiled, resigned to the detour as they followed the road past small houses, their shutters fastened tightly against the outside world.

'God, it's so dark and scary abroad when they have shutters, isn't it? It makes you even appreciate net curtains, the bit of light they let out into the street. This is just eerie, as if nobody was living in all these houses.'

Michael understood what she meant. The hillside was littered with houses and small villages were scattered across both sides of the valley, but there was hardly a light to be seen, apart from street lights. It was as if the world outside their car had ceased to exist.

'There it is. You probably can't see it very well. That white one there.' He pointed to a large modern building a hundred metres to the right of where he had stopped the car. It was fairly visible because its steep drive was illuminated by lamps that were mounted at intervals along the wall. Two stone lions sat on the pillars that guarded the entrance to the steep driveway.

'Strange they've got the lamps lit. They usually only switch them on when they have visitors.'

'It's a nice place, though,' acknowledged Helen, winding down her window and staring into the blackness. Ah, they *have* got visitors.'

The front door opened, exposing a rectangle of bright light, light with which Michael realised with a sharp pang he was very familiar. The figures of two men emerged. It looked like Renzo and another man. They stood talking for a moment and then shook hands and separated, Renzo walking back to the door and then turning to watch the departure of the other man, who took the stairs two at a time. They heard the sound of a car door slam and a powerful engine roared into life.

Michael switched off the lights of the car.

'Now look, Michael, if this is just another excuse for a kiss . . .' laughed Helen.

'Ssssh,' he hissed. 'Which way is he going? It might be someone I know, someone I met with Renzo or Rosa and I obviously don't want anyone to know I'm here.'

The door to the house closed and darkness clothed the facade of the building once again, as the lights on the drive were extinguished. The car engine became louder, coming in their direction.

'Keep down!' whispered Michael, wondering why on earth he was whispering.

They slid down against their seatbacks as the lights approached.

'I'm getting terrible *déjà vu*, you know,' muttered Helen between closed lips.

The car approached and then passed them, speeding up as the driver became accustomed to the darkness and the road. As the bright red of its tail–lights faded into the night, they sat up and turned to look at each other, puzzled.

'Michael, did you see what that was?'

'I did.' He was silent for a moment. 'It was the Boxster, wasn't it? The Porsche Boxster that passed us up on the mountain tonight. Coming from the house.'

'It was, wasn't it?'

'What the hell is he doing at the house? Is Renzo mixed up in this, somehow?' He sat back and closed his eyes, completely confused.

Helen reached across and cupped both his hands in hers and went on, 'I think we should just get back to Beldoro, and try to work this out, and work out what we're going to do. You can't carry on like this and if you're innocent you should get a fair hearing . . .'

'What do you mean, *if* I'm innocent? Don't *you* believe me now? And as for a fair hearing – how is that going to happen? I'm clearly the prime suspect for the murder of Ignazio Mazzini, and for all I know they may have found Claudio Scatti by now and I might have been fingered by the old guy who gave me directions. He might even have been part of all this, might have been told to follow me and give me directions so that I would be placed there at some time. God, my fingerprints are even going to be found all over that place.' He threw his head back on the seat headrest and stared out into the darkness. 'I'm dead meat, Helen, one way or the other. Either Pedrini and his henchmen find me and

I disappear – case closed. I am a fugitive, people think, and, therefore, guilty; or else the police get me and I go down for both murders, fingerprints, witnesses, the lot. They've got me.'

'We'll get out of this, Michael. And of course I believe you. You don't think I'm putting myself through all this just for the hell of it, do you?' She smiled. 'Let's get back to Beldoro.'

He smiled too and sat up, rubbing his eyes with the palms of his hands.

'Okay. Sorry. Beldoro it is.'

They waited for a few moments, looking down across the flickering lights of the valley beneath them, before he turned the key in the ignition, the engine fracturing the silence as it burst into noisy life. He eased the car back onto the road, down towards the last series of bends and the passing cars on the main road. Soon they were driving alongside the lake, palaces huddled together like huge, dark animals along its edge, their palm trees motionless in the approaching midnight.

18

3 September 1999
Morbegno
North Italy

The elderly man reached out his hand to stop the plastic cup sliding across the table, as the train tilted away from the lake and headed inland towards the yawning gateway to the Valtellina. He had just had a last gulp of the dark, bitter, lukewarm coffee it had contained and the cup, now almost empty, had insufficient weight to keep it still. He picked it up and looked around for a bin to put it in.

'Please, let me.' The young girl sitting across from him stretched out her hand to take it from him. There was a bin just to the side of her seat.

'Thank you,' he said, smiling.

She had the look of most kids nowadays, he thought. She was probably on her way back from college. Pretty, with long dark hair, and an attractive face, a Valtellina girl whose fore-bears would have been like his. But, how different her life would be to the generations of women who had gone before her. The fact that she was spending her days out of the valley; that would have been alien to those generations of women, and most of the men, too, who rarely left their villages, let alone travelled to the sides of the lake and beyond. People even commuted to Milan, he supposed, like those guys on the East Coast who trained in from Connecticut to New York every day. What a life! An hour and a half on a train there, and an hour and a half on a train back, with nothing to amuse you every day but the view – the same old same old, every single day.

Still, she appeared to be thriving on it. Smiling, he watched her lean back and stretch her limbs. The book she had been reading fell to the table and the pages flicked closed. *She will have to search for her place when next she opens the book*, he thought, thinking how fastidious his wife had always been about retaining her place in anything she was reading, had always kept the bookmarks that stores insisted on giving her when she bought those books that she used to lose herself in. The girl now reached into her bag, rummaging for something. Seventeen or eighteen, she would be, he thought, remembering another girl and another time.

He looked out of the window at the countryside rolling past. It was crowded. That was his first impression. There were lots of houses, lots of roads, lots of cars and lots of people. It seemed small, somehow. Much smaller than he remembered. The mountains had not changed, however, were unchanging. As they had come into view when the train exited the last of the series of tunnels that punctuated the view of the lake, he had expected to feel something special, some kind of call, like a priest long lost to the church finally being called back to his vocation. But, no, it was not like that. They were familiar, but only as familiar as the man-made peaks beneath which he had made his living these last fifty years.

She stood up, pulling her bag down from the luggage rack: a dark backpack of the kind worn by kids all over the world, the kind of bag he would have died for five decades previously, as he clambered up and down the valley sides between which they were travelling. They were coming into the station and the countryside had given way to modern housing. The train had begun to slow, rattling over points and crossings, bells ringing out and then fading.

His case was in the luggage rack near the door. He pulled it down and carried it forward, joining the queue of people, school and college kids and the first wave of homecoming office workers. The kids pushed and shoved each other, babbling away inanely. He liked that – the sound of young Italian voices – especially when they were tinged with the accent of the Valtellina. It had been so long since he had heard such sounds.

Eventually, after gliding slowly along beside the platform for what seemed like ages, the train screamed to a halt, its brakes protesting amidst the swishing of opening doors.

He stepped to the door and stood there, his case dangling from his right hand, his left hanging uselessly at his side. His face was old now, with lines carved into it just like his father's face had been, as if a sculptor had been set loose on it. The eyes were still deceptively young, though, still bright and handsome as they had always been – 'your secret weapon', his wife had always said. Beneath the left eye was the deep shadow of the depression caused by a German pistol butt a lifetime ago.

'*Signore!*' said an irritated voice behind him, a finger jabbing him in the small of the back.

'Oh, sorry . . . I mean *scusi*.' he replied, not turning round. His senses were invaded by the crisp mountain air and the feeling of being where he belonged. He clambered down, unsteadily, unable to balance properly as he did so, having no other good arm to hold on to the rail at the side of the door.

He put his case down and rested for a moment, looking down the platform to where people were crowding through the narrow barrier, on their way to the comforts of home and family. He felt, not for the first time of late, a pang of envy that caused him almost physical pain. Then, just beyond the barrier, he saw the young girl who had been sitting opposite him fall into the arms of a good looking boy in a leather jacket.

She stepped away from him, holding his eyes with hers and laughing with the sheer joy of the moment, a tiny splash of red colouring her face as she flushed with excitement.

She would be a little younger than Angela when he first met her, he thought. He tried to remember her face, her smell, the feel of her skin; tried as he had for the last fifty years, but it had long gone from him, had become mixed up with the smells and feelings of all of those years, had mingled to such an extent that only now and then, in a particular situation – a certain smell of wet grass, or a certain scent of pine trees could he retrieve any of that time.

He picked up his case and walked down the platform to the barrier where the crowd of passengers was beginning to thin and beyond which lay the town.

Sandro Bellini – or Giovanni Pavesi, as he had been known these last fifty-odd years – stood at the window of his rented apartment in Morbegno, stirring a cup of coffee and looking out.

He thought back to another window on another continent. A street – modern, concrete buildings and sodden, brown leaves stuck to the pavement, turning to treacherous mush beneath the feet of pedestrians. The odd car turning left into the hospital car park and rain beginning to fall once again. The wettest fall in years, the evening news claimed, blaming it on the erosion of the ozone layer or pollution or the melting of the Polar ice caps. Weather could not just be weather any more. There had to be a conspiracy, even about that. As if Kennedy and all the other conspiracies that had been dreamed up in the last twenty-five years were not enough.

He had listened carefully to the doctor, almost unemotionally, hearing his own death sentence.

'Inoperable, as we feared, Giovanni. Untreatable.' The doctor had leaned forward, blinking, adjusting the wire-rimmed glasses on the end of his nose. 'I'm sorry, but as you requested, and as I promised, I'm being quite blunt. There's no hope for your condition. For a man of your years and with the advanced state of your cancer, I fear any treatment would probably prove fatal.' He made a church-steeple of his fingers and placed them against his lips.

He had known it before the words were spoken, but, even so, a shudder went through his body. He realised he was afraid of death after all.

'Thank you, doctor, I appreciate your honesty. How long ... how long will it take?' To his surprise, his voice shook slightly.

'It's always difficult to tell, you know, and very often it is entirely in the hands of the patient. I would think, Giovanni, you have, at most, a year. As I say, though, we are sometimes proved wrong.'

It was at that moment that Sandro had looked out the window and, as most people in that situation did, lived a burning moment of intensity, experiencing the leaves, the people, the cars and the rain in the gutters almost more than he ever had.

He had shaken the doctor's hand and thanked him for

being straightforward about everything and had walked out of the hospital, his mind strangely empty.

Within a few weeks — weeks in which he had walked the city by day and drunk himself senseless by night — he had begun to see things more clearly and had begun to put some order back into his life, or what remained of it. His wife had been dead for three years now and, as they had never had any children, he was free to do as he pleased. Therefore, he had tidied up the loose ends and made his plans, arranging the rental of a one-bedroomed flat in Morbegno and booking his tickets.

It had been a bad week. The doctor had warned him that the rigours of the journey might do this to him. He had wakened late the day after his arrival and had been unable to get out of bed. For two days he lay there, sick and in pain. The medication he had brought with him did not seem to work until late in the second day when he was able, at last, to sip a few spoonfuls of *minestra*. Gradually, some strength returned to his body and the waves of pain receded. For the next few days he did not stray far from the apartment, venturing only as far as the shop in the next street to buy bread and fresh coffee.

Exactly one week to the day after he had stepped down from the train, he woke up, restored to something approaching normal health.

He packed some bread and a bottle of water in a small backpack and, locking the door, stepped out into a crisp early morning.

He walked briskly towards the outskirts of the town, which was beginning to stir from its slumbers. Street cleaners washed and brushed down the areas outside the boutiques and shops and people who had to get to work early staggered sleepily towards their destinations.

The mountain peaks rose dramatically around him into a cold-looking, clear, blue sky as he followed the road towards the bridge that traversed the River Adda on its way down to the lake. The river was low and white rocks, worn smooth by the water of centuries, gleamed from its edges. Crossing the bridge, he turned left, heading westwards on the road that ran between Lecco and Sondrio.

In the cool mountain air he felt as good as he had for some time. The morning was still with not a breath of wind. Autumn frost was still some weeks away, and this morning, though crisp, was very pleasant for walking. As the valley widened out, he was amazed and not a little dismayed by the amount of building that had taken place along each side of the road. The entire road from Morbegno to Dulcino seemed to consist of houses, where, when he was a boy, there had been nothing. The villages and their growing populations were pinned like brooches to the valley sides.

The early hours turned into the hours of the day when people did things. Buses filled with schoolchildren began to sweep noisily past him, creating eddies of wind that pushed him to the side of the road. After an hour he stopped and clambered down to the riverbank to eat some bread and refresh himself with a small bottle of water he had bought. He also threw back the first of the fistfuls of pills that he had to take every day.

He walked on, the sun climbing higher in the sky and his heart pounding as he moved closer to his goal.

Dulcino's heart had not changed. He rounded a corner and passed by a stand of trees and there it was, after fifty years still clinging to the side of the valley, a few hundred feet above the road. The buildings stood grey and dark amidst the gleaming white villas and bungalows that had grown around them during the last half century and which now completely surrounded them. In the centre was the church spire beneath which his mother had worshipped all her life. On this road, near where he was standing, would have been Luigi's garage; the house in which Luigi and Angela had shared the few years of their short marriage was in the village of San Marco, visible a few miles to the east and several hundred feet higher up the valley side. Now, these villages, once as separate as different countries, were linked by buildings that lined the sharply switch-backed road that still snaked up the mountain.

He turned off the Sondrio road and began to climb up past the turn-off to Dulcino. The houses everywhere made it difficult to recognise anything. There had once been thick forest here and now it was gone. He persevered up the slope for about fifteen minutes, sweat beginning to glue his white hair to his forehead.

Suddenly, he knew he was there. There was an unfamiliar building, but it had something about it, something akin to seeing a childhood friend after fifty years apart. The overall look is different – there are wrinkles, different coloured hair, the nose seems to have grown, the eyes are hooded – but there is something at the core, behind the eyes, that tells you that it is him. Indeed, this building had suffered a great deal of surgery. There was a conservatory at the side, the windows were different, the roof was new; but there was no doubt in his head that this was the house he had grown up in and in which his mother had been shot dead by Cavalcanti and his henchman that terrible night in 1944. It was no longer isolated outside the village, but was surrounded by other, newer buildings. He passed merely a few seconds assimilating the bright red climbing frame at the side of the house and the blue Mercedes with Milan plates parked on the steep drive. He turned his back on the house and thought back to that night. He remembered nothing except finding a spot in which to bury his mother's body. Across the road which now ran in front of the house was a fence and then a small stand of trees. It was there he thought he had dug a hole and there he thought he had interred his mother. Climbing the fence, he moved towards the trees, tears beginning to flood down his cheeks and stain his jacket. He lost his footing – his legs were tired after his long walk – and sat down on the dusty slope that led down to the trees. He held his head in his hands out of sight of the road and sobbed.

Sandro could not make sense of the centre of Dulcino. It seemed to contain the same buildings that it had all those decades ago, but there was hardly one which had not been tampered with. New windows, new roofs, a proper road leading down through the square in which the church stood, instead of the dusty track of his youth. It was familiar but very different. Cars – new and often with plates from other parts of Italy – were parked along the fronts of the houses. There was not the hubbub of sound he remembered from the past – the loud conversations between husband and wife, the rattling of cooking utensils, the screaming of children. It was silent, almost sanitised, he thought.

He was spent and in sore need of a coffee and perhaps something a little stronger and had ventured into town in search of a bar. He found one just off the little square, small and modern, with a chrome-topped bar, being polished, as he walked in, by a middle-aged man with a dark moustache. In the corner sat two elderly men who had begun staring at him as soon as he had entered and on the other side some teenagers were making a lot of noise with a pinball machine, slamming its glass top, lifting the whole machine and banging it down on the floor again.

''giorno, signore,' said the man behind the bar, barely looking up.

Sandro ordered a coffee and a whisky. He had acquired a taste for scotch in the States and it did, in fact, help him control the pain of his cancer sometimes when it was not too extreme.

He picked up a newspaper from the bar, went over to a table on the other side of the bar from the two old men and waited for his drinks.

'*Vacanza*?'

The voice was a deep growl and came from one of the old men to Sandro's right.

'*Scusi*?' he replied, lowering the paper. The barman silently placed his whisky and *espresso* on the table in front of him.

'*Vacanza*?' Are you on holiday, *signore*? We don't often see Americans in the village, do we Giuseppe? You are American, *signore*?'

'Indeed, yes, I am. Is it so obvious, then?' He turned to look at the two men. They could have been older than him, but it was very hard to tell. Their lives had probably been tougher than his, all things considered. They also had the weather-beaten skins of men who had spent most of their lives outside.

'No, it is not, *signore*. In fact, I might have said that you came from Dulcino, from your accent, or somewhere very close to it?'

It was a question and a menacing one. Sandro was immediately on his guard. He had spent the last fifty years as someone else. He had not even told his wife his real name. He had wiped that person out of history, not because of what he had done, but because of what he had kept hidden all those years ago – the truth about Luigi Ronconi. In doing so, he had become suspect and were Sandro to exist once more it might only lead back to those days.

'Oh, no. No, I am from Sondrio. Originally, that is. I went to America after the war and have lived there ever since.'

Their cloth caps nodded together, their minds processing every word he uttered. Nervously, but trying to hide his nerves, he picked up and threw back his whisky. 'But I must say, I am flattered that you think my accent is still strong enough to betray my roots.'

'And the war, *signore*?' asked the other one in a husky, breathless voice.

'The war?' He stiffened.

'Where did you fight? *Partigiano*?'

'*Partigiano*!' he laughed, 'No, not me. Wounded and captured in 1942 in North Africa.' He indicated his left arm, hanging, as ever, uselessly at his side – although for once it was serving a useful purpose. 'I was one of the lucky ones; spent most of it as a prisoner of war.' He smiled, trying to appear confident and casual.

The caps across from him nodded in unison again, but their gaze was steely, their moist, dark eyes boring into him. He was unsure, but he could swear that there was a momentary flash of recognition in the eyes of the original speaker and he was sure – afraid – that he also had recognised the other man and had failed to disguise this fact.

'Anyway, *signori*, it has been a pleasure. I must get on.' He threw back the whisky, stood up, throwing a few thousand *lire* on the table, picked up his backpack and left the bar without looking back.

As he walked as nonchalantly, but as quickly as he could, out of Dulcino, down towards the main road, he failed to notice the two old men scuttling as fast as their aged legs would allow, out of the bar and into the town. They separated, arms flailing as they gesticulated to one another, one following Sandro at a distance, the other, coughing and breathing heavily, heading towards a house at the edge of the village – a house with two lions guarding its entrance.

Sandro decided that he would have to take the bus back to Morbegno but as he waited a full forty minutes at the bus stop, he failed to notice a small Fiat arriving and parking round the corner, its driver nonchalantly reading the *Gazzetta dello Sport* with one eye, while awaiting the arrival of the bus to Morbegno with the other. Another young man stood to one side of the car, leaning on a fence, smoking and casting regular glances in the direction of the bus stop.

It was early afternoon and the gaps between buses were a little greater than they would be at other times when people were coming home from school or work. For Sandro, however, it was all the same. And anyway the view of the mountains – the mountains upon which he had not gazed for so long – could never become tiresome to him. He stared at them, picking out paths and trails that he had followed as a boy. He named all the peaks, like a god naming all the good things on earth.

Eventually, the bus grumbled its way around the corner and slowed to a halt at the stop. It swallowed Sandro up and pulled out into the road again. The driver of the Fiat put down his paper, leaned across the front seat, rapping with his knuckles on the passenger side window and turned the key in the ignition. The other threw down his cigarette, opened the car door and quickly climbed in. The car pulled out into the flow of traffic that had been created by the bus's ponderous progress and followed it in the direction of Morbegno.

Sandro had exhausted himself with his long walk of the morning. At the same time, however, he was also exhilarated. Walking back into his apartment, he was grinning and happier than he had been for a long time. He threw down his pack and sat on the sofa, stretching his tired legs and closing his eyes.

At first he thought it was a dream. He was running down a hillside, his feet thumping on the ground, somehow more noisily than they should be and making a different kind of noise, the wrong kind of noise. Gradually, consciousness began to seep into his head. Before he was fully awake, however, he could sense the pain in his gut: the same old pain that always heralded a few days out of the world, a few days lying in bed, searching for a place where it hurt no longer. A place in his mind or a place on the mattress, it did not matter; he just sought an escape from the pain.

Suddenly, he burst into consciousness. There was someone at the door. The knocking was gentle. It was not the officious knock of a policeman bringing bad news. It was more of an inquisitive knock, as if the person knocking were either unsure of whether there was anyone home or, indeed, if someone was home, whether it was the right door on which he or she was knocking.

He looked around. It was dark. He had been asleep for some time. He grabbed the small alarm clock that sat on the coffee table at the side of the sofa. *Eleven-thirty! Who the hell could be at his door at this hour?* And, anyway, regardless of the hour, he knew no one and no one knew he was here.

He hesitated a moment and then shouted out as the door once again rattled, 'Okay, I'm coming.'

He was yawning and running his hand carelessly through his hair as he opened the door. There facing him stood two young men, one with a small pistol pointing at him.

'Get your coat, old man. You're coming with us!' barked the one not holding the gun and nodding towards Sandro's coat, which lay across a chair.

'What . . . Why should I come with you? Who are you?' The one who had spoken pushed past him and grabbed the coat. He walked towards Sandro and took his arm, propelling him out of the door.

'Wait . . . I need my pills. I am ill. I need them for the pain.'

'Okay, where are they, old man? Quick! Go and find them. And don't try anything!'

Sandro was afraid and fumbled nervously with his one good arm at the bag that contained his various medicines.

'Come on, hurry up!' the one without the gun hissed again, looking nervously down the corridor in each direction.

They pushed Sandro ahead of them down the corridor after closing the door behind them. They went downstairs and he was bundled into the Fiat that was waiting just outside the front door of the building. A third man inside put the car into gear and drove out into the deserted road. Sandro sat blinking in the dark, feeling the barrel of the pistol making an indentation in his side.

They seemed to be travelling on roads with which he was unfamiliar, but at one point crossed a bridge over the Adda and turned onto the main Sondrio road, heading towards the lake. The two dark heads of the driver and the second man were outlined against the road ahead of him and he could feel the eyes of his third assailant boring into him from his left in the back of the car.

After a while, they turned off the main road and passed a sign indicating that they were entering the *commune* of Dulcino. At least he knew now where he was going. The question was, of course, why were they bringing him here? He knew inside himself the answer to that question, though. He had hidden from his past for fifty years, had wiped it away, had even changed his name. But, hardly a day or night had passed in all that time when he had not seen the faces of his six comrades in the instant before the explosion that had torn their bodies apart. Now, he knew it was time to face that past, to face the truth about himself.

The car pulled into the little square at the heart of Dulcino. He remembered the annual carnival that was held when he was a boy. The garish colours of the robes that clothed the heavy statue of the Virgin that the men would carry through the streets to the church. The tables would groan with food and wine, and music and dancing would go on into the depths of the night.

'Get out!' Sandro's memories were interrupted by the one with the gun, who had walked round to his side of the car and had thrown open the door.

Sandro slid out of his seat and stood up stiffly.

'Where . . .?' he asked.

'Over there. The church.'

The three men walked behind Sandro as he limped towards the dark silhouette of the church, which somehow looked menacing as midnight approached.

A dark figure leaned against the wall beside the door, the red tip of his cigarette illuminating his face as he inhaled a lungful of smoke. Seeing them approach, he stood up straight, throwing his cigarette away and knocked on the large church door. The door swung open and Sandro was directed to go in with a shove in his back.

The light inside was hardly better than outside. Large candles in recesses cast a dim, flickering light on the walls and a small, weak bulb splashed a pale, yellow glow down onto the pews.

The church was unchanged from when he had last been in it, all those decades ago. Behind the altar, the massive oil painting of the Madonna and Child that had hung there in 1940 still hung there, though the vivid colours he recalled were now a uniform brown and in sore need of cleaning. The gold of the ornate altar glinted as the candle light caught it and the ten or so rows of pews – it was a small church, barely big enough for this village now, he presumed – were filled with men, their heads all turned to face him as he stood at the door. This in itself was unusual. He remembered how, when he was a boy, the women would crowd into these pews and the men would wait outside, gossiping and smoking before pushing in at the door to stand at the back when the service began.

Again he felt a hand in the small of his back, pushing him towards the front. He turned to face them when he got there. In all, there must have been about fifteen of them, most of them young or middle-aged, but in the very front pews sat four elderly men, leaning forward and staring hard at his face.

'You are Alessandro Bellini?' The voice came from the back of the room. It was the priest and as he approached Sandro, Sandro noted that he was not a young man. A flick of white hair dropped down over his right eye and he reached up to smooth it back into place across the top of his head. 'I am *Don* Matteo, the village priest.'

'It is him, the bastard.' One of the elderly men stood up and pointed angrily at Sandro.

'Sit down, Marco, sit down. We have to establish a few things before we throw accusations around.' Another, younger man had stood up in the row behind Marco and put his hand gently on his shoulder, pushing him back down into his seat.

Sandro looked around the faces in the pews. The light from the candles gave them a manic glint as they stared at him.

'What is this?' asked Sandro, 'Why am I here?'

'Are you Alessandro Bellini?' asked the priest, ignoring Sandro's question.

'I haven't been for more than fifty years,' he blinked nervously in the dim light, 'but yes, I was born Alessandro Bellini.'

One of the old men at the front slumped back in his seat, placing his head in his hands.

'You are the bastard who informed on our partisan unit,

then!' Another of the elderly men half stood up, gesticulating at Sandro. Again, a calming hand from behind forced him back down onto the pew.

Sandro stared at him and felt a tear well up in his eye. He had slept next to these men in the hills in 1944, had fought beside them, would have gladly laid down his life for them. It was time for the truth.

'Could I have a seat, please? I have a bad leg and I am ill, I have cancer. If I don't sit down, I'm afraid I will fall down.'

The priest brought over a cane chair and Sandro lowered himself onto it with relief.

'Yes, I *am* Sandro Bellini, but I swear to you I did not betray the unit's activities to the Germans.'

'*Bugiardo*!' A shout came from the front pew.

'I am not a liar.' Sandro answered quietly.

'Well who did then, if it wasn't you? Who told them about San Giorgio and about our rendezvous, if not you?' The first old man, who Sandro realised was one of the two men from the bar earlier that day, was spitting these words, leaning forward, his hands gripping the front of the pew. 'How come you are the only one who got away? Doesn't it seem strange to you that you alone survived both incidents when so many died? You were the only one to survive the second. It certainly seemed strange to us back then. Your friends, the Germans, let you crawl off into the night like the snake you are. And then you disappeared before we got to you.'

'Is it any wonder I disappeared!' Sandro, himself, leaned forward in his seat. 'They tried to kill me but murdered my mother instead. I was innocent, but who was going to listen to anything I had to say? I knew the brigade was going to send someone after me and finally Cavalcanti, *l'Assassino*, came. But he killed my mother.'

'What is the truth then, Alessandro Bellini? If it wasn't you, are you saying you know who informed on the unit?' It was the priest, speaking from a dark corner on his right.

Sandro sat back in his chair, feeling a wave of pain and nausea. He suddenly realised how cold the church was. Its grey stone walls were radiating the chill of the night and his frail body, weakened by his illness, began to shiver.

He started to speak, hesitantly at first and then more and more confidently. He told them everything, about Angela, about Luigi's treatment of her, about the English captain and his discovery of his body with the single bullet hole in the back of his skull and, finally, about the German officer and how he had sought him out and left him for dead.

When he had finished speaking, the men's breathing was audible in the silence that followed.

'Why should we believe you?' asked the priest. 'Why didn't you tell this story back then?' Why leave it fifty years to make your peace and regain your reputation?'

'This story would have stayed with me; I would never have told anyone, if you had not found me. Luigi Ronconi was a broken man. He had lost everything and finally, I think, he lost his mind. It was not *Il Falcone* who told the Germans what our plans and activities were. It was a broken man convinced that one of us had betrayed *him* and cost him his wife and child. He couldn't work out who had done it, so in his confused state, he tried to take care of all of us. But he was still killing Germans, even then. His anger turned into an anger against the whole world. God help him wherever he may be now.'

'God help Luigi Ronconi? The other way round, you mean!' The priest laughed and a few of the others joined in, but not the old men at the front who continued to stare without expression at Sandro. 'You really don't know what became of Luigi Ronconi?' The priest looked incredulously at Sandro and then told him about the amazing success story that had been Luigi's life after the war.

'He's still alive?' asked Sandro, astonished at what he had been told.

'Yes, he is, but it is incredible that you haven't heard of such a man, even in America.'

'I kept myself to myself all those years. My wife and I ran a diner in New York. We worked morning till night for close to forty years. After the war I didn't have much time for the outside world.'

A silence descended on the room.

'I don't believe him. *Il Falcone* was a hero. He has been decorated by the government for his actions in the war,' said one of the old men.

'I agree,' said another on his left. 'Ronconi was our leader until his wife disappeared. He went off the rails and disappeared too, but any man would go to pieces in such circumstances. He would never have betrayed us.'

'I don't know,' said a third. 'Sandro was a good man, too. He was young and also went through a lot. I fought alongside him and thought highly of him.'

'But if this is true,' said a voice from the darkness, 'we have to do something about it. The world should be told about Luigi Ronconi.'

'If it is true. Pah! It's a lot of nonsense. He's had fifty years to prepare his story, just in case he got found out.'

Another silence enveloped the chill air of the church.

'You say you are ill?' the priest asked Sandro.

'I have cancer of the stomach,' Sandro replied. 'I came to the Valtellina to die.'

'The sooner and the more painfully the better,' muttered a voice from the front pew. Sandro threw a pained look in the direction of the voice and the priest glared at the speaker.

'How can you prove that what you say is true?' asked the priest.

'I don't think I can,' answered Sandro. The German, Weber, is the only one who can prove it for me. But I presume he died in that attic when I left him behind with the rats.'

'We need to talk,' said the priest to the figures in the pews. 'Take *signor* Bellini outside and wait with him.'

Sandro stood up. He felt that the priest was beginning to believe him. The fact that he called him *signor* was significant. The three figures who had brought him here appeared at his side again and they walked out into the cold night air. The door closed behind them and cigarettes were passed round. Sandro declined. He had not smoked since his illness had been diagnosed.

He leaned against the wall and looked up at the pinpoint stars that shone coldly in the heavens.

A shooting star fled across the sky and he made a wish, as his mother had always advised him to do when he saw one. The others stood stamping their feet and talking quietly a few metres away. He felt strangely still. It was as if he had emptied himself out and he now felt fresh and clean and even, he smiled to himself, pure. As for whether they believed him or not, that was up to each of them.

The door of the church opened and the priest stepped out, rubbing his arms to get some warmth into them.

'It is hard to arrive at a consensus, *signor* Bellini. Some of the men believe you and want to challenge Luigi Ronconi, take the story to the newspapers. Others don't believe you, especially your former comrades, and want you handed over to the authorities.'

'But what about you, *Don* Matteo? What do you think?'

'I became involved in this because I feared it would get out

270

of hand. There has been an unspent anger in this village since the war. So many families lost their men on the night of the San Giorgio incident and then, later, in the other incident which you survived. Everyone knew there was betrayal involved and your name has been demonised here for fifty years because you disappeared. It was even believed by some of the more bitter amongst them that you killed your own mother.'

'What?' Sandro could not believe what he was hearing. 'How could they believe such a thing?' He shook his head, his face creased with grief.

'Cavalcanti obviously never owned up to his mistake and it has been added to the terrible mythology that was created around you.'

'So, *Don* Matteo, what happens to me now?'

'Nothing, *signor* Bellini. We will return you to Morbegno. It's accepted that you are unlikely to disappear again after sharing your story with us. We need to discuss it – especially the older members of the community – and investigate what you've told us. We know where to find you.'

With that, he told the three younger men to drive Sandro back to Morbegno, which they did in silence, but this time without the threat of a gun. He climbed out of the car and made his way upstairs, a rising tide of pain beginning to engulf his body.

He fumbled with the key in the lock, and on entering his flat, collapsed on the bed, stretching his body in an effort to dissipate the pain to its extremities. It was unsuccessful, however, and he disappeared deeper than ever before into a world of pain, a world that made him hope that the wish he had made outside the church when he saw the shooting star would come true.

He had wished for death.

*

But death did not come.

These episodes of complete collapse and endless pain, were like a kind of labour. They had to be endured for a longer period each time, but the end would be death and not birth.

He lay on the bed for four days wearing the clothes he had worn that night at Dulcino, now and then reaching out for a fistful of pills and occasionally, with shaking hands and perspiring brow, holding a glass under the tap to drink some water. He drifted into corners of his being he did not know existed, hours passing like seconds and seconds passing like hours. Eventually, he awoke and the pain had subsided, like the tide leaving a beach after a wild and stormy night.

He staggered to the bathroom and ran a hot bath, barely able, in his weakened state, to twist the tap and make the water flow. He climbed in and let the filth that had gathered on his body seep away. A renewed strength entered him and he took to the streets to sit in a bar and watch this world go by, this world for which, having dispensed with his past, he felt a brand new affection.

Simple things touched him – a well-dressed, middle-aged woman, a young man roaring up to the pavement on a scooter, a dog sniffing lamp posts. The world was his again, after more than fifty years.

A couple of weeks passed in which he had mostly stayed in the flat, reading and watching television.

One night, he had been out, buying some pasta for dinner and had come upstairs with happy anticipation of cooking and eating, although his increasingly emaciated body retained almost nothing that he ate for very long.

Rounding the bend in the corridor at the top of the stairs, his heart skipped a beat as he saw the dark figures lounging against the wall. It was the same pair that had collected him in the middle of the night a fortnight ago.

'*Buonasera, signori*,' he said with false bonhomie.

'*Signor* Bellini, *il padre* says he would be very much obliged if you would accompany us to Dulcino.'

Sandro was struck by the difference in their approach compared to the last time they had arrived on his doorstep. They were courteous, deferential. Something had happened.

'Yes, just let me put this inside.' He unlocked the door, put the bags he was carrying on the floor and locked up again.

He was filled with curiosity as they sped along the road to Dulcino. They would have come to some kind of decision, he thought. But it would take some powerful evidence to convince the elderly partisans. He had not been able to come up with anything in fifty years except his own words and he thought it unlikely that they would have found anything.

They did not head for the church this time. Instead, they pulled up outside a long, low building that looked like it might be a village hall. Inside, men – the same men, it seemed – were seated haphazardly across the space of the hall. At one end was a table and seated on one corner of it was the priest, talking to a large, long-haired man wearing a leather jacket and jeans too tight for a man of fifty-ish.

'Ah, *signor* Bellini, thank you for joining us again.' He reached out his hand and Sandro took it. 'May I introduce to you Antonio Ronconi, son of Luigi Ronconi.' He indicated the man standing beside him. He smiled. 'I don't think you've seen him for quite some time.'

Sandro felt the ground shift beneath his feet. He saw a baby grizzling in Angela's arms, smelled once again the forest floor, heard the rain rattling on the boulder above them and felt Angela's skin beneath his fingertips.

'But . . . but how can it be . . .?' The priest saw the anguish pass over Sandro's face and placed a hand on his shoulder to steady him.

'*Signor* Bellini. *Padre* Gaspardi has told me what happened between my mother and you ...'

'But you are dead. I mean, the baby ... Antonio ... is dead. The camps ... How can it be you?'

'I was lucky, *signore*. My mother gave me away to a German guard whose wife was unable to have children. I wasn't Jewish or a gypsy, so I was a good find for them. They brought me up for a few years and my father, Luigi, who had been searching Europe for me, having heard that I had some-how survived, eventually found me and brought me back to Italy to live with him.'

'And Angela? Your mother?'

'She did not share my luck, I fear, *signore*. She died in the camp not long after she handed me over. My German father told me later.'

'And your father? Luigi Ronconi?'

'Like you *signore*, he is old, and he is also not a well man. He is probably in his final months.'

Just then, a couple of men entered the hall and nodded to the priest and Antonio Ronconi. The priest went over to them and they started a hushed conversation.

Sandro could not take his eyes off the man whose mother he had loved as much as he had loved anyone or anything in his life. He could see her face once again in front of him – the dark eyes and the large, sensuous lips. Even the long, dark hair reminded him of her. He felt almost faint as he stood there and had to lean on the table for support. Still, however, the eyes of the elderly partisans bored into his body like bullets.

'Okay, *signori*.' The priest addressed the men who gathered together around the room. 'You all know *signor* Ronconi. With his help we have discovered some unexpected new

274

information, or rather testimony which we think goes some way towards supporting what *signor* Bellini told us two weeks ago.' He nodded to the men at the back of the room and they disappeared through the door for a few seconds.

They re-emerged with another elderly man, a stooped figure with white hair and a severely disfigured face. His left ear was missing and he wore a patch over one eye.

'*Signori,*' the priest began. 'you will recall that *signor* Bellini told us that he had been told by a German officer – *Obersturmführer* Erich Weber – that Luigi Ronconi was the informant.' He stopped and looked around the room. A few heads nodded, but the old men sat impassively. 'Well, *signori*, the man standing in front of us now is *Obersturmführer* Erich Weber.'

There was a gasp around the room. Sandro himself almost collapsed. Weber. Yes, even with only one eye there was still that haunted look about the man. There was still a cruelty, even behind the red welts that landscaped his face.

'But I left him for dead! How . . .'

'Ah, it's you. The one-armed soldier.' He straightened up and stared hard into Sandro's eyes across the room. His Italian was broken, as it had been fifty years ago. 'How I have hated you all these years for not finishing me off that night.' His face, or at least, the half of his face that had not been rendered inhuman, broke into a sneer.

'But, the rats, how did you . . .?'

'Oh, the rats were doing their job, don't you worry about that. You see the results before you.' He laughed. 'I managed to dislodge the gag you put on me and screamed so loudly that they could hear me a couple of streets away. A patrol came and freed me, but it did take some time for them to find me, as you can see.'

The priest spoke again. '*Signor* Weber has promised to tell us what he knows about the informer in return for being allowed to return to Zurich where we found him and proceed with his life.'

There was a howl of protest around the hall.

'No!' The priest raised his voice. 'Quiet!' The room became silent. 'I gave my word that this would be allowed.'

'But he is the scum who killed our fathers, our friends. He can't be allowed to just leave. He deserves to be shot!'

'No! That will not happen. I have given my word, as a man of God and if any of you take the law into your own hands you will be acting against the will of God and I will see that you will suffer for it.' The voices were stilled. He looked around the room, catching the eyes of every one of them. He then hissed between clenched teeth, 'The war is over. It ended more than fifty years ago. Many men did things they are ashamed of. On both sides. This is the only way we are going to find out the truth.'

'Ah, the truth,' laughed Weber. 'I agree, it *is* time for the truth.' He walked away from the men who had brought him into the hall towards a chair. 'Please excuse me if I sit, *meine Herren*. My aged legs are not what they once were, when I used to run up and down these lovely mountains of yours like a chamois. In fact, it was on one of those runs that I first encountered the object of your attention, the informant. He knocked me over as I ran on a trail just above Morbegno. I remember it was pouring with rain and he was soaked and covered with mud. It was dripping off him, as if he had been rolling on the ground. Perhaps he had. I thought he was going to kill me then and there. I had been warned about my habit of running, especially as I was, naturally, unarmed – difficult to run with a pistol strapped to your side, eh? Anyway, he told me that in return for information he would in turn pass information to me.'

'What information could he possibly expect you to give him?' the priest asked.

'Well, *padre* as it was, of course, none other than *Il Falcone*, himself – Luigi Ronconi – there was only one thing in which he had any interest. Where were his wife and child and could he exchange them for information?'

Sandro looked around the room. Many heads were lowered. The old men had ceased looking at him and were staring now at the German who told this story as if he were in a bar, regaling his friends with a joke or a funny story. Antonio Ronconi looked on without expression or emotion.

'I asked him for something on account, as it were,' the German went on. 'He told me about the San Giorgio operation. I told him I would do what I could about his wife and child. We met again in the same manner a week later. His information had been good and so I lied to him and said that I could probably get his family back from Germany, if he would just give me some more information.'

'You never had any intention of returning his wife and child?' the priest asked him.

'No, or, at least, even if I did intend to do it, it would have been absolutely impossible. Once people went into those camps they were lost forever. At the same time, however, I wanted the information that *Il Falcone* was giving me. It was gaining me a wonderful reputation and I was heading for a big promotion if I could string him along a bit longer. So, he gave me the information about the monthly rendezvous and, well, *signori*, I think you know the rest.'

'*Bastardo!*' shouted one of the old men, tears of anger rolling down his face.

'We've heard enough. Take him away.' said the priest quietly to the men at the back of the room.

Weber turned as he got to the door and spoke directly to Sandro.

'Remember what I said about the look in a man's eyes in the instant before death, my friend? I see it in yours now as I see it in mine every morning. The shadow of death brings us together once again, it seems.'

A light drizzle played across the valley, obscuring the peaks. Sandro had set out before the town had wakened, his pack filled with a chunk of yesterday's stale bread and a bottle of Sassella, the local wine that he had always drunk in New York in the forlorn hope that it would give him a sense of place, of *this* place. It never did, however.

He had picked up his bottles of brightly coloured pills and had put them in his pocket. For all the good they did. The pain was evolving now. It was almost constant and could really only be dealt with by filling his mind with other things. Even that, however, was becoming difficult.

He had walked for half an hour before getting on the first bus of the morning. At the village before Dulcino, he got off and climbed a narrow, pot-holed road that led him up beyond the village. He stopped and gazed up at the jagged top of the mountain on whose lower slopes he stood, looking for familiar landmarks. Gradually, the memory of the mountain came back to him. He could once upon a time have mapped its every part.

He plunged off the road and headed steeply upwards, the trees shielding him from the drizzle, which was now turning into a heavier shower. He made slow progress as the morning wore on. The going was hard and he was experiencing increasing pain in his stomach. Every ten minutes or so he had to stop and catch his breath.

Eventually, he reached his objective: a large slide of gravel and rocks. He had last stood there, looking down on the Valtellina so long ago – how different it now was. Buildings and roads stretched across the valley floor and even up the opposite side of the valley. He took out a piece of bread and sat on a large rock, chewing it and surveying the view. After fifteen minutes, he picked up his bag and started heading back down the mountain in a different direction to the one by which he had arrived at this familiar place.

He rounded the boulder unexpectedly, just as he had the afternoon that he had bulldozed into Angela and had knocked her and the baby to the ground. Once again, however, the breath was sucked from his body and his legs trembled. He stopped and placed a hand on the rough grey stone that had sheltered them back then. He waited, but there was no sound save the constant Morse code of the rain battering the higher branches of the trees.

What had he expected? Angela bursting through the trees, rain dripping from her long, dark hair, her beautiful smiling face flushed and cold to the touch? He smiled at his ludicrous notion and then grimaced as the pain that had subsided for a few minutes returned with a vengeance.

He knelt down and crept beneath the boulder, lying on his side. Pulling his bag towards him, he took out the bottle of wine, held it between his knees and removed the cork. He looked out from his vantage point and once again he smelled the scent of the pine trees and the odour of the rain. For several minutes he lay there, taking long draughts from the bottle and examining the grass and stones around him for signs of his past self, for signs of Angela. He then put his hand in his pocket and took out the bottles of pills. He took another long drink from the bottle and unscrewed the tops of each of them, lining them up in front of him.

He poured the contents of the first into his cupped hands

and put them into his mouth, washing them down with the wine, now beginning to feel a little drunk. The contents of the second bottle followed and then the third.

He lay back on the slightly damp grass and closed his eyes. Around him, the rain shifted blades of grass, bounced off tiny stones that had not moved for decades and dripped from the boulder above him into tiny puddles that the earth swallowed up immediately.

She emerged from the bushes, untouched by the rain. Walking towards him, she ran a hand through her hair, pulling it away from her face and smiling, reaching out her hands to him. Slowly, he stood up and walked towards her, feeling already her cool, smooth skin under his fingertips, the movement of her body beneath his and the draught of her damp breath on his cheek.

Once again, he removed his jacket and laid it on the ground under the boulder, pulling her towards it. She lay down and he lay beside her, enveloping her with his arms. Slowly, their bodies began to melt into one another until they existed no more.

The only sound was once again the careless rattle of the rain, running in rivulets to the edge of the clearing, washing away memories.

19

17 November 1999
Beldoro
North Italy

'This doesn't fit you, does it?' Helen was holding up the jacket that the manageress of the Lighthouse Inn had sent Michael.

'God, no. It's the jacket your ... whatsername ... Stewart ...'

'Oh, Jacquie, you mean?'

'Yes – Jacquie – sent me. Remember, that was the reason I went to that stupid hotel of yours.'

'Christ, he *is* a big lad, isn't he?'

'Yes, and I haven't done much about finding out who he is.'

'Och ...' – he loved it when she said that – 'maybe that's a good thing.' She folded the jacket up. 'Don't you think?'

'Oh, I don't know, Helen. I just haven't had time to even think about it and it *was* the real reason I came back here. I guess I feel I need to know. I don't think I'll be happy until I find out. You know, closure and all that.'

'Have you thought about where the jacket was made? Who made it?' She stretched the soft, checked cloth out again across her arm, stroking the material. 'This is a beautifully made piece of clothing. You don't pick up this kind of quality at Burtons, you know.' She opened up the jacket in front of her, examining the inside. 'There's a label here.' She inspected it closely. '*Alberto Espagni, Sarto, Roma.*'

'Oh, I'm glad we have such a *precise* address,' he said with a sneer that came from the guilt that he felt for suspecting his dead wife, not realising at all how bad he sounded.

'Well, bloody hell!' she snapped, throwing the jacket down on the bed, 'Pardon me for trying to help someone the entire Italian police force are trying to arrest because they think he's done away with two people. Pardon me!' She put her hands on her hips and glared at him. She really wished there were another room into which she could make a dramatic exit. Instead they were within six feet of each other in her tiny hotel room, with absolutely nowhere to escape to.

He realized immediately that he had been in the wrong. This girl was helping him, after all. He stood up, and placed his hands on her shoulders.

'I'm sorry,' he said. 'That was very wrong of me. Look, I do appreciate what you're doing for me here. You don't have to, and you could be putting yourself in great danger.' He pulled her close. 'I sometimes wonder why you're doing it.'

Her hair brushed the side of his face as she buried her face on his shoulder.

'Well, I don't mean to get too cheesy or anything,' her voice muffled against his shoulder. 'but it might be because I think, you know, I quite like you.'

'Ah,' he said, smiling. 'Always dangerous. Your mother must have warned you about that.'

'Oh yes. She did. But I don't listen to everything she tells me.' She raised her head, looking into his eyes and kissed him. They staggered back against the wall and then fell slowly onto the bed, her hair falling over his face, her tongue exploring his mouth.

Outside, as the afternoon slowly darkened, the ferry began yet another journey across the lake.

He woke with a start. It was dark outside and Helen's bedside lamp was switched on. She was emerging from the small bathroom, dressed, brushing her hair. He blinked and looked at the clock that sat on the bedside cabinet.

'What are you doing? It's four-thirty in the morning, for God's sake. Are you running out on me?'

'Don't be daft, Michael.' She sat down on the side of the bed. 'What I'm doing is I'm getting the five-thirty train to Milan and from there I'm going to book myself on a flight to Rome.'

'To Rome!'

'*Sì, Signor* Keats. Roma,' she said, smiling and brushing his hair back from his forehead. 'I'm going to visit our little tailor friend, *Signor* Alberto Espagni.'

'Oh,' he said, understanding and relieved that she wasn't walking out on him. 'But when will . . .?'

'Oh, don't worry, I'll be back by this evening. I'm not going to buy postcards on the Spanish Steps, you know, attractive though that idea is.' She stood up and started to fold the jacket and put it into a small bag. 'I've already phoned Directory Enquiries for Rome – I think they were glad of the conversation in the middle of the night – and they've given me a phone number for *signor* Espagni. As soon as I get there, I'll phone him and get his address. If I show him the jacket, he'll probably be able to tell me who it belongs to.'

'God, you'd do that for me.' He fell back onto his pillow.

'Oh, don't worry, Michael, you can give me the money later.'

He smiled.

'And don't open the door. I'll tell the guy on the front desk that I don't want the maid in my room today. Get some rest. Watch TV and see what they're saying about you. But keep it turned down low. I'll try and call you later.'

And she was gone, even before he could tell her to take care of herself.

The station had been cold and deserted at five-thirty, only a few desultory early morning commuters littering the platform, yawning and adjusting themselves to another new day. She marvelled as the sun rose like a lion over the mountains to the east as the train pulled out of the station, but for most of the journey she slept soundly, oblivious to the beginnings of Milan's urban sprawl spreading across the train window.

From the station she jumped into a taxi to Linate Airport. Time was of the essence, as she did not want to leave Michael alone for too long. Why, she did not know, but it felt right.

She managed to get the last seat on a flight at nine-thirty and, two hours later, found herself in a cab driving past the Colosseum. She smiled at how ridiculous it all was and thought about phoning Michael, but as she had that thought, the taxi turned into a narrow side street and pulled up in front of a dark shop-front. Above the blacked-out window was printed the legend, 'Alberto Espagni, Sarto.'

She slid along the seat and climbed out of the taxi, paying the driver and then standing, blinking in the bright sunlight. It was noticeably warmer in the capital and she regretted the thick pullover and puffer jacket she had thrown on in the cold, northern early morning.

'*Buongiorno, signorina,*' said an elderly man standing in

what was effectively a workshop, as she opened the door and stepped in.

'Good morning,' she replied, attempting to adjust to the gloom of the room. '*Signore*, do you speak English?' She had, of course, neglected to consider what would happen if no one in Alberto Espagni, *Sarto*, spoke English.

'Ah, I . . . speak . . . ay leedle beet,' he replied.

She began to take the jacket out of the bag.

'I'd like to know who this jacket was made for.'

He looked at her as if she had just stepped out of an alien space ship.

'Dees *giacca*? . . . Who? *Per chi*?'

He shook his head and clicked his tongue against the roof of his mouth, muttering something in Italian under his breath.

'*Signor* Espagni,' he came out from behind the desk at which he had been standing. '*Signor* Espagni . . . bar . . . *Parla . . . inglese*.' Nodding constantly, he took her by the arm and led her to the door, opening it and pointing down the street to a bar on the opposite side.

'Ah, *grazie, grazie*,' she said, smiling and putting the jacket back into the bag.

She walked out into the street again, the traffic noises once more filling the air and, looking back and smiling at the elderly tailor who still stood nodding in the doorway, walked in the direction of the bar.

It was an ancient, dark establishment that had, in all likelihood, not changed in many years, if not many decades. A television flickered silently in the corner, being watched by a bar empty of people except for one elderly man staring at a newspaper, a tiny cup of steaming coffee in front of him.

'*Signor* Espagni?' she asked politely, for she presumed it must be him.

He looked up slowly, pushing his small, rimless glasses down his nose, the better to see who was standing in front of him.

'*Chi vuol sapere?*' His eyes were small and narrowed by years of stitching. His back was hunched, presumably through bending over the same stitches that had narrowed his eyes.

'You speak English, I am told, *signore*,' she asked, not daring to sit down until asked, but feeling distinctly uncomfortable looking down on him.

'Yes, English. I speak a bit.' His accent was still laced with an Italian inflection, but she was relieved to hear that he obviously spoke and understood English pretty well. 'How may I help you?'

'I am trying to find the owner of a jacket.' She indicated the bag. 'May I sit down, please.'

'I am sorry. How rude of me. Yes please, take a seat.'

'Thank you,' she said, pulling the seat out, sitting down and placing the bag on the table.

'Alfredo!' He waved his arm in the direction of the bar. And then to her, 'What will you have to drink, my dear?'

'Oh, a mineral water would be good,' she said as an elderly barman with a bored look on his face approached.

'*Acqua*, Alfredo, *e un altro caffè,*' he threw in the general direction of the barman without even looking at him. Years of familiarity had obviously bred extreme contempt. The barman turned on his heels and shuffled back to his domain behind the bar where he busied himself with the order, staring all the while at the silent TV.

'I do love finding an opportunity to exercise my English,' he said, leaning forward across the table. 'I lived in England for many years, you know. I worked in Saville Row in London, as a tailor, of course, and take every opportunity I can get to remind myself of the Queen's English.' He laughed.

'You speak it very well, if I may say so. The Queen would be very proud of you!' Helen replied, smiling, but impatient to show him the jacket.

'Thank you,' he answered, bowing ever so slightly. 'But you say something about a jacket?'

'Yes, *signore,*' she said, taking the checked jacket from the bag. 'This jacket. Would you be able to tell me for whom it was made?'

'I might, *signorina,*' he said, leaning back on his chair, spreading his hands out in front of him, and then removing his glasses, 'but why should I? I do not know why you need this information. I made this jacket for a client, and, believe me, my clients are my lifeblood. I would not wish to divulge – *divulge* . . .' he pushed the word around his mouth carefully, 'that is the right word isn't it . . .?' She nodded and he continued. '. . . *divulge* information about any of my clients to the wrong people, if you understand what I am saying.' He picked up his coffee and threw it back in one swallow, grimacing as he noisily placed the tiny cup back on its saucer.

'Oh, *signor* Espagni. I don't know how to explain this. It is very embarrassing.' Where, she thought, had she found this capacity to make up lies – no, entire histories – on the spot? She heard herself saying it just before she said it, but had no idea where it came from. 'Look, I am a student here in Italy. I am studying art and I met this man in a club a few nights ago. He was very handsome and, well, I liked him a lot. Well, one thing, as they say, led to another . . .' she looked down at the table as coyly as she could, '. . . and he spent the night at my place.' She felt his eyes upon her, the eyes of another generation, jealous of the freedoms of the generations that have followed it. 'But we fought the next morning.' She cast her eyes down at the table again and attempted to look as sad as possible. 'It was stupid. I threw him out, not realising in my anger that he had left his jacket behind. He banged on the door for ages but I hid in the bathroom until he went away.' She affected a sniffle as if she was crying, taking a tissue from her pocket and holding it to her nose. 'The trouble is,' she blew her nose, noisily. 'The trouble is . . . I think I . . . I am in love with him. And I don't even know his name.' She amazed herself by spontaneously bursting into floods of tears. 'I think I am in love with him and I want to find him again.' She looked up imploringly. 'Please help me find him.'

He reached across the table and took her hand.

'Ah, *signorina*, The madness of youth. I understand. Don't worry. In these circumstances, of course I will help you. Let me see this jacket.' She handed it to him and he held it up. 'Ah, we made a good job of this one. There are not many made of this material. Come with me back to the shop and I will check my records.'

They stood up and he led her with exaggerated courtesy from the bar back to the dingy light of his shop where his colleague smiled beatifically at her as she preceded *signor* Espagni through the door.

Michael had lain in bed for an hour longer than he needed to, conscious that there must be no noise in the room while Helen was gone. He got up and read a few chapters of a book to pass the time until mid-morning and then decided to switch on the television, keeping the volume as low as possible, while still being able to hear what was being said.

Italian newsreaders are impossibly glamorous compared to their English equivalents and this morning's version was no exception to the rule. Her hair radiated from her head in a golden halo and her clothes looked like they were from one of the more expensive fashion emporia.

Her words dismayed Michael. Claudio Scatti's body, with

its gaping, smiling neck had, at last, been discovered and, as Michael had anticipated, the police had learned from Claudio's brother and from the old man at the bar who had given him directions, that he had gone to see the dead man. His face filled the screen, looking out of a photograph taken some time ago for an *Evening Post* brochure. He lay back against a pillow as the item ended. *What must Renzo and Giovanna be thinking of all this?* he wondered.

An all-pervading feeling of hopelessness overtook him. He rolled over onto his side and pulled Helen's pillow towards him, clasping it tightly, pulling his legs up to his chest like a child, his eyes screwed shut, keeping the world out. He had to solve this mystery now. Going to the police would only stop him from digging deeper. But, at the end of it all, he would have one hell of a story to tell. He smiled as he thought about that part of it.

Opening his eyes again, from where he was lying he could just make out something on the floor behind the chest of drawers – a large brown envelope. He slid across the bed and swung his feet onto the floor, bending down to pull the envelope out from behind the chest.

He recognised it. It was the one from John that contained Rosa's last batch of photos. It had been taken from his hotel room by Pedrini and his henchman and had then been picked up by Helen as she had rescued Michael from the house by the lake. She had obviously thrown it onto the chest of drawers when they had come back to her room that morning and it must have slipped down behind it. They had then forgotten all about it.

He unpeeled the flap of the envelope – it had stuck itself down again. Inside were half a dozen contact sheets, each containing a couple of dozen shots. He pulled them out, feeling a pang of sadness at the thought that these were probably the last photographs Rosa had taken. He sat on the bed, spreading them out in front of him. They mostly depicted landscapes and buildings – ramshackle, old Valtellina hovels, made of irregularly shaped stones and clinging perilously to the sides of the mountains. They were very beautiful, but why was Pedrini so keen to have them that he had broken into his room?

In the middle of the fourth contact sheet, however, the reason for Pedrini's interest became suddenly apparent.

Michael threw the sheets down and walked to the window. It was getting dark and still there was no sign of Helen. But why endanger her further? He pulled on his shoes and threw his jacket on, pulling a baseball cap down as low as he could on his forehead in order to hide his face. He scribbled a quick note for Helen, leaving it on top of the television, folded the contact sheet and put it in his inside pocket. He then opened a drawer and took out the gun that Helen had stolen from Pedrini and his gorilla. He examined it carefully, not really knowing what to do with it should the occasion arise and then put it in his pocket, where its weight sat uncomfortably. Carefully he opened the door, looking up and down the corridor in both directions before stepping out. The desk clerk was in the middle of a telephone conversation with someone and was staring at a computer terminal in his office, probably making a booking and Michael was able to slip the few yards across the foyer to the door of the hotel without being noticed.

Outside it was getting chilly and a strong breeze was rippling the palm fronds and pulling at the sacking that cloaked the giant palm tree on the promenade. He pulled the collar of his jacket tightly round his neck, zipping it to the top so that very little could be seen of his face. He turned and with hunched shoulders walked into the teeth of the wind.

*

Helen returned to the hotel at around nine o'clock. Luck had not been with her and she had to wait a couple of hours to get a seat. The plane she was booked on then developed a fault on the runway and they sat there for an hour before it was ready for take-off. The inevitable wait for a slot followed and by the time she turned the key in the lock and opened the door to her room, she was exhausted.

'Michael?' She looked in the bathroom and found no sign of him. She immediately thought the worst – Pedrini had found him, or the police – but her eyes caught sight of the note on top of the television and she snatched it up.

POPPED OUT. WON'T BE LONG. DONT WORRY!
                                          LOVE M.

'Michael, you idiot!' she muttered to herself, sitting on the bed and beginning what she knew would be an agonising wait for his return.

The chill wind had driven the inhabitants of the small lakeside town indoors. The streets were quiet, a quiet interrupted only occasionally by the muttering of a television behind a pair of shutters. Anyone who was out was concentrating on staying warm as they bent into the wind.

Michael climbed the sloping streets, walking away from the lake towards the outskirts of Beldoro, where the mountain began to rise ever more steeply and on whose slopes building must be ever more difficult.

He walked past the entrance to Palazzo Ronconi, its gates shut fast against the outside world and the red roof of the palazzo just showing beyond the rise of the driveway. Walking on for a further thirty yards or so, he stepped off the road and down a bank to the foot of the eight-foot-high brick wall that protected the property from prying eyes. A tree grew just beside the wall at this point and Michael quickly glanced along the road in either direction before leaping up high enough to grab a branch about six-and-a-half feet up the tree. He swung his legs round onto some small branches that acted as steps and was soon seated on the branch, looking down on the top of the wall and the beautiful, sloping parkland that stretched beyond it. There was broken glass embedded in the concrete at the top of the wall, and so he carefully removed his jacket and dropped it down on top of the glass. Gingerly, he slid along the bough until he felt it would be unsafe to venture further. He then lowered himself slowly onto the jacket. He could feel the glass against his legs under the jacket, but it was not penetrating the thick wool. He then leapt from the wall, grabbing his jacket as he did so and tumbling onto his back as he fell. He rolled onto his front and stayed still, listening for any evidence that his entry had been seen. He had no idea if there were closed circuit cameras or sensors or anything else to detect intruders. These guys were, after all, seriously rich and anything was possible.

He lay there for a couple of minutes, his heart pumping against the wall of his chest, but there was silence all around.

Slowly he raised his body into a crouch and began to creep towards the house, wondering exactly what he was going to do when he got there.

Arriving safely at the side wall of the building, he flattened himself against it in order to regain his composure. He felt safer now, as bushes were placed intermittently around the building, affording him some shelter.

What now? He could not very well ring the doorbell and demand to see Antonio Ronconi. Perhaps, at least, he could find Antonio's office. That would be a start. He slid along the wall and round the corner to the rear of the house. Most of the rooms were lit and passing the windows was, consequently, a difficult process. However, every window he passed showed a room beyond, empty of people. He rounded the back and there in front of him was the large glass extension that contained Teresa Ronconi's butterflies.

Suddenly, just in front of him, a door swung open and the white-coated figure of a woman emerged. She left the door open, walked off into the landscaped garden and leaned against a tree, taking a packet of cigarettes from her pocket and lighting one. She then turned and looked, away from where Michael was standing, down towards the lake where the lights of Menaggio could be seen, twinkling dimly in the distance. She inhaled deeply and breathed out, the wind immediately tearing the smoke away.

Michael slipped silently along the wall to the door and crept inside.

It was a double door. The interior door led straight into the butterfly house. He gripped the handle, turned it and opened it, feeling sweat prickle the back of his neck as the damp heat of the interior struck his skin. Inside was very dimly lit, but he immediately caught sight of another white-coated figure working at a bench about fifteen feet away. He stopped for a second, crouching behind some large shrubs, getting his bearings. Around him he could hear the rustle of thousands of wings and every now and then a wing would brush against his face and then take its owner off on a desperate flight of panicked escape. In this crouching posture, he made his way towards the end of the line of shrubs he was using as cover.

The door to the interior of the house was now only ten feet away. He crossed the path and, hidden by another group of shrubs, reached it. Slowly, he turned the handle and left the conservatory. He opened the other door and gratefully left behind the sweltering heat.

He was now in the house, in a corridor very close to Antonio Ronconi's ground floor office, if his memory served him well from his one visit here.

Voices. He heard them around a bend in the corridor. He flattened himself against the cold wall and listened. It was a voice he recognised – that woman, Ronconi's assistant – the one with the distinctive American accent.

He stretched his neck around the corner of the corridor and there she was, standing at the door of Antonio's office. The conversation was quiet and he could not make out any of it, but the woman said '*Buonanotte*,' and walked away towards the grand staircase, closing the door behind her. He heard her footsteps mount the carpeted stairs and fade away towards the top.

Michael put his hand in his pocket, touching the cold steel of the pistol that lay there. He shuddered as his fingers ran down the barrel in search of the butt. He pulled it out, blinked at it, held it out in front of him and stepped out into the corridor, edging towards the door to Ronconi's office.

He pressed himself against it, listening, and then looked around before turning the handle and quickly opening it.

Antonio Ronconi was so startled he almost blew away several million lire's worth of cocaine that lay in a thin white line on the desk in front of him. A fifty thousand lire bill was stuck in his nose and his face was a mask of concentration and anticipation. Michael was unsure who was more surprised – he with the sight that lay before him, or Antonio Ronconi, seeing the English journalist that half of Italy was looking for, standing before him with a gun in his hand.

Staring at Michael, Ronconi removed the banknote from his nose absently, as if he were taking a cigarette from his mouth.

'Easy . . . now!' hissed Michael, looking round the room to ensure no one else was in there.

Ronconi stood up spreading his arms wide in disbelief that this was happening.

'Mister Keats! Are you here to kill *me*, now?' he said calmly.

'No, of course not. I'm not here to kill anybody ... I haven't killed anybody ... *yet*, that is.' He motioned to Ronconi to sit down behind the large desk. 'And keep your hands on top where I can see them, please.'.

'So, why then do the police think you are responsible for all these deaths? They have sufficient evidence, of course. And by the way, walking in here with a gun, well, it doesn't immediately suggest to me innocence of these crimes.'

'Ah, yes, the gun,' said Michael, regaining his composure. 'Well,' pulling himself together now, 'the gun actually belongs to a friend of *yours* ... was borrowed from this friend – well, stolen actually.'

'A friend of mine?' Ronconi leaned back in his large chair, putting his hands behind his head and stretching. 'I'm not sure I have any friends who would possess such a weapon.' And then, leaning forward again, 'You know, I am quite worried about you, about your health.'

'Pedrini? Vito Pedrini? He's the friend I'm talking about. You mean you don't know him?'

Just for a beat, Ronconi was knocked off his stride. Michael sensed it. It was a mere flicker of an eyelid, an irregularity of his breathing, but Michael knew he had unnerved him. Ronconi shifted in his seat, visibly discomfited, smiling no longer, but still saying nothing.

'Wait. I have something here that might just jog your memory.' He pulled the folded contact sheet containing Rosa's photographs from his inside pocket and opened it out. He threw it down on the desktop.

Ronconi, still with his hands behind his head, looked down at the photographs. He saw black and white pictures of a house in the mountains, in front of which stood a group of people, laughing. Those people were clearly visible as Vito Pedrini, Teresa Ronconi and her brother, Antonio. The house was the one in front of which Michael and Helen had seen Teresa Ronconi with Pedrini the night before.

'Look, Antonio; two men are dead and, believe me, no matter what the police think, I didn't kill them. But somebody did and I think it was your friend, Pedrini. Is that what you want to be associated with? Why don't you tell me what's going on? Why are you pretending your sister was kidnapped?'

Slowly, Antonio took his hands from behind his head and placed them very deliberately on the table in front of him.

'Mr Keats, I would suggest that you leave this house immediately. If you don't' – he reached out a hand to the telephone sitting on a corner of the desk – 'I will call for help. I wonder who the police will believe – you, a man wanted for two murders, or me. As for the photographs, well, they could have been taken any time. Oh and . . .' he smiled, '. . . I don't think you are going to use that gun.' He picked up the telephone receiver and held it in front of him.

'Okay, Antonio, I'm going, but I'll get to the bottom of this, I promise you, if it kills me.'

'Be careful, Mr Keats. It may just do that.' He placed a finger on the push-buttons of the telephone.

Michael stared at Ronconi for a long few seconds. His bluff had been well and truly called, as he had half-expected it would be – there was, of course, no way that he was going to use the gun. He picked up the contact sheet from the desk, folded it over, stuffed it quickly into his pocket and left the room, walking down the short corridor and exiting by the front door. At the bottom of the drive the gate was open when he arrived there. As he walked away from the house, he heard a car engine start up behind him. A few minutes later the Porsche he had seen with Helen the other night, drove past him and into the night. At least by signalling that he knew something was going on, he might have flushed him out, forcing his hand in some way that would be of benefit.

He walked on, watching the Boxster's tail lights blaze red as it slowed down for a corner before fading into the blackness ahead.

When he returned to the hotel, he was relieved to find the foyer deserted. He climbed the stairs on tiptoe.

'Where have you been? I've been worried sick!' Helen had jumped up and run to the door on hearing his quiet knock.

'I've been to see our friend, Antonio Ronconi.'

'Really? Why would you do that?' she asked.

'Because of these. We forgot about the envelope you lifted from Pedrini's place that night.' He stopped for breath. He had taken the second flight of stairs two at a time. 'It contained Rosa's photos.' He handed her the sheet and she saw the two pictures of the group of figures standing outside the house in the mountains.

'That's the guy you said was Pedrini and Teresa Ronconi and . . . that's Antonio Ronconi.'

He looked up, surprised.

'How do you know it's Antonio Ronconi? You've never met him.' he said, a puzzled look on his face.

'That's where you're wrong, Michael. I have met him.' She took his hands in hers. 'I waited on him at the Lighthouse. That's how I know him. And the jacket was made for him – the tailor in Rome checked his records. Antonio Ronconi was Rosa's lover.'

20

There was no moon and the switchbacks came upon them without warning in the short stab of light that the headlights threw out. Once again, they followed the road as it cut deep into the high mountain valleys and no longer looked down on the floor of the Valtellina, where the lights of towns and villages blinked like stars in a cloudy sky.

They came upon the road leading off to the right that led to the house and, driving past it, they again abandoned the car in the trees about thirty metres further on.

Arriving at the start of the track, Michael took out his mobile phone and dialled.

'Bruno!' And then to Helen, 'Thank God, it works! I've got a signal! Yes, Bruno, it's Michael. Yes, yes I'm fine. Look Bruno, it's a very long story and I still don't really know what the real truth is, but I am up in the mountains above the Valtellina and I'm very close to the house in which Teresa Ronconi is being held. Yes! That's right. Look, if I give you instructions how to get here, I need you to pass them on to the police in Morbegno. Yes. Thanks . . . Yes, I'm alright. No, I don't have time . . . Look, you'll get the story. Just pass it on to the police.' He proceeded to give as exact directions as he could. 'Tell them I'm here. That'll make them come, but tell them to get here quick!' He closed down the call and put the phone back in his pocket. 'Come on then, let's see if we can find out exactly what's going on.'

They walked on, shivering at first from the cold, the wind having died down from earlier in the evening, but still leaving chill air in its wake. As they came closer to the house, they stiffened and walked carefully so as not to make any noise. This time, however, instead of hiding in the undergrowth, they walked on, climbing the wooden gate that led into the property.

'What are we going to do?' whispered Helen.

'I have no idea, which makes it the second time tonight that I've arrived somewhere with big intentions and then bottled it at the last moment. I really don't know. Maybe this is crazy. Pedrini's a gangster after all. I'm really not sure . . . '

Just as he said that, the door at the side of the house opened and the man who, with Pedrini, had kidnapped Michael, came out and walked towards them.

'Michael!' hissed Helen.

'Quick, in here!' He grabbed her arm and pulled her through a half-open door into the large barn-like construction that stood to the side of the house.

He quickly pulled her down behind the shape of a car covered by a dark, heavy tarpaulin. The man walked into the barn, throwing a switch that turned on a single, bare light dangling on a long wire from the roof. Michael and Helen crouched down even further. The man was collecting logs, presumably for the fire whose seductive wood-scent they had smelled as they approached the house. He threw the logs into a wooden box and picked it up, walking back towards the door. Just before he put the box down to switch off the light, Michael looked down and suddenly felt himself going cold. The back of the car, right in front of them, was uncovered. It was a blue car and he realized immediately that he had seen it before. He knew this because its blue was quite extraordinary; not the kind of blue you see very often. It had a metallic glint to it and was almost as if it had little slivers of silver mixed in with the paint.

The light flickered before going out and they heard the man grunt as he lifted the box before the door creaked shut.

'Michael!'

He did not move.

'Michael!' She elbowed him in the ribs.

But he was elsewhere. He was running out of a shop, change scattering in every direction, his heart pounding and his mind screaming, seeing his wife's broken body crumpled at the side of the road, blood pooling around her head, and beyond her the rear end of a blue car, engine racing as it rounded the corner on the road to Sondrio. The blue of the car glinted in the afternoon sun.

He stood up, pulling desperately at the tarpaulin.

'Michael, what are you doing? Stop it, he'll hear you!' She grabbed his hands, but he pushed her away. At last the tarpaulin was off and a blue Audi TT stood in front of them. Its beauty was flawed, however. Its front bumper and bonnet had been crumpled by an impact of some kind.

He ran round to the back of the car and there it was. He had got it wrong, however. The design on the back of the vehicle was not, as he had told the police, a bird. Rather, it was a butterfly, the silver outline of a tiny butterfly.

'This is it!' he cried, scanning the length of the vehicle.

'This is what, Michael? What are you talking about?' she sounded almost afraid of him.

'Helen, this is the car that hit her ... that killed Rosa! This is it!' It was those bastards who did it.'

'It can't be! How do you know?'

It's the colour, exactly the same colour. Look at the damage to the front. And it's got the picture on the back. I thought it was a bird ... I only saw it from a distance ... and it's quite small ... but it was a bloody butterfly. That means it must be Teresa Ronconi's car.'

'But why, Michael? Why, if Antonio Ronconi was having an affair with her would he kill her, or have her killed?'

'I ... I don't know ...' He tried to work it out. 'Perhaps the photographs. Perhaps they found out that she knew what was going on ... that Teresa and Antonio were complicit in this whole kidnap business.'

'Hmm, in fact that's not a bad piece of deduction, Michael.' The voice came from the door, emerging out of the darkness just before the light was switched on. There stood Vito Pedrini, holding a revolver and beside him, as always, his henchman. 'Before we go any further, perhaps you would do me the great favour of throwing down the gun I believe you are now in the habit of carrying.'

Michael took the gun from his pocket and dropped it to the ground. Helen moved towards him and held him tightly round the waist. He could feel her tremble.

'You bastard, it was you who killed Rosa,' Michael said quietly, but with a venom of which he would never have believed himself capable.

'Oh, you flatter me, Michael. I am not quite as clever or as devious as you imagine. What you find in my line of work is that no matter how much you calculate, no matter how far ahead you plan, everything can be undone by an act of passion, an act of the heart. People's fucking emotions. They just can't be trusted.' Pedrini stood to one side of the door, directing with his gun. 'Now, let's go into the house where we can discuss this properly. And where we can think about what we're going to do with you. We've got a bit of a dilemma, you see.'

Michael and Helen came out from behind the car and walked uncomfortably into the night, negotiating the short gap between the barn and the house.

As he left the barn, Michael stole a glance back to the tortured front bumper of the Audi.

They entered the house by the back door, Pedrini pushing the barrel of the revolver into Michael's back to hurry him along. From the kitchen they entered a hallway and were directed in through a door that lay open to their left.

'Michael! What the hell are you doing here?' Renzo stood up and seemed unconsciously to be retreating from the sight of Michael at the door. Michael and Helen stopped, but the imprint of a gun barrel in the back soon pushed them on into the room.

Antonio Ronconi sat on one side of a log fire, slim, black-jeaned legs nonchalantly crossed, hands folded in his lap. He did not make a move when he caught sight of Michael and Helen – as if they were neighbours dropping in for a drink. Teresa Ronconi, however, standing at the rough timber table in the middle of the room, immediately signalled her alarm at the name 'Michael' by knocking over a glass into which she had been pouring wine. It rolled across the table and smashed on the floor, its sound shattering the silence that was interrupted only by the crackling of the logs on the fire.

'I could ask you the same thing, Renzo, but then I did see

Ronconi there with you at your front door last night. So, I had a feeling you were somehow involved in this nonsense.' Renzo looked confused. He then turned to Pedrini.

'Put that gun away. Do you think we're in New York? This is my late sister's husband!'

'Shut the fuck up, Renzo.' Pedrini replied angrily, waving the gun in Renzo's direction. After all, Gianni and I haven't been paid yet. And there's the other guys that also have to be taken into consideration.' He leaned against the wall at the door and his silent partner added to the firepower by raising another gun to cover the assembled group.

'What the hell are you playing at, Vito?' Now Antonio sat up straight, his eyes blazing.

'Quite simply, I think this is all going to go to hell, Antonio, this entire fucking venture. I always felt it wasn't right. When it was explained it to me, I thought Di Livio had finally gone mad. And as it has progressed, I've become even more convinced of it. Never work with amateurs, my old boss in Sicily used to tell me, but, Christ, when you move north, my friend, that is just what you end up doing. The pickings can be easier, I have to admit, but you have to work with fucking idiots.'

'What's he saying, Michael?' Helen whispered, only to feel the side of Gianni's hand silence her question as it swiped across her face. She slammed against Michael's side.

'Shit!' screamed Michael moving towards Gianni. 'You can't . . .' He fell backwards as Gianni's fist slammed into his face for the second time in just a few days.

The whole place became a cauldron of sound to Michael. He could see shapes moving over him and came round with Helen and Renzo leaning over him. Beyond her he saw Pedrini and Gianni still holding their guns, Gianni by the door, Pedrini at the opposite side of the room.

'He knocked you out for a moment, Michael. You're

alright.' Helen looked down at him imploringly, the side of her own face red. 'For God's sake, don't antagonise them. These guys aren't messing about here.'

He sat up, his head spinning, feeling his face swelling under his left eye.

'Now, people, let's get a few things straight here, eh,' said Pedrini.

'What I want to get straight is who the fuck killed my wife,' said Michael, heaving himself up onto his knees. 'You might be interested in this, Antonio, as I know you were having an affair with her.'

'Please speak in Italian, *signor* Keats, so that everyone can understand.' Pedrini then translated what Michael had said into Italian.

'*Che cosa?*' exclaimed Renzo, who was standing in front of the fire. 'What are you talking about, Michael?'

'He and Rosa, they were having a bloody affair, Renzo. Helen here served them breakfast in their love-nest in the Scottish borders. Rosa bought him a diamond tie-pin worth hundreds of pounds. I was a fool, Renzo. Your sister, my wife, was screwing this fucker!'

Renzo looked at Antonio who was staring into the dying embers of the fire, unable to look Renzo in the eye.

'But I tell you what's even more interesting, Renzo,' He raised himself to his knees as he said this, 'is the fact that the car that hit Rosa — you know the one that killed your sister and then drove on as if nothing had happened? — it's sitting out there in the barn.'

It suddenly felt as if there was no oxygen, as if everyone had breathed in at once and sucked all the air out of the room.

Renzo stiffened.

'What are you talking about? What do you mean the car is out in the barn?'

Pedrini smiled and spoke, looking at Teresa. 'Be sure your sins will find you out, huh?'

From the other side of the room, Teresa began to cry softly, her sobs muffled by her hands covering her face.

'Let me take you back,' said Pedrini. 'Oh what would it be; it seems like months, but it's only weeks. Her car had been driven up here by Antonio because his was in the garage. He left it outside with the keys still in the ignition. Teresa was free to walk outside, naturally, and we were not here to guard her, after all because, as you now know, she was here completely of her own free will. We kidnapped her and made it look as real as we could. She was even manhandled a little bit which made her scream because she wasn't expecting it. But it all added to the reality of it if there were any witnesses. We even gave her the same chloroform treatment we gave you.' He nodded at Michael, recalling that night. 'Anyway, as I was saying, we were at the back of the house with Antonio and didn't hear her start the car. By the time we realized, she was long gone. We thought the whole thing had fucked up, but about an hour later she was back. We found her sprawled across the front seat of the Audi, dead drunk. The front of the car was fucked and, I fear, as we found out later, so was your sister, Renzo. Shame. She was a pretty girl, judging by the pictures in the papers. Naturally, after you described the car to the police, we had to have some papers forged so that when the police came enquiring Antonio could prove she had sold it just before she was, as it were, kidnapped, and that it had been taken abroad. It helped that you were adamant that there was a bird on the back of the car that killed her, Michael.'

As Pedrini talked, Michael felt his heart exploding and it was all he could do not to collapse to his knees. To have the death of the woman he had loved talked about so flippantly overwhelmed him. Shaking his head, hot tears beginning to well up in the corners of his eyes, he looked across at Teresa, who stared at the ground as if she wanted it to swallow her up.

'What are you talking about, Pedrini? Teresa! Antonio! What the hell's going on?' Renzo was agitated to the extent that Gianni felt the need to approach him and stick the barrel of his pistol close to his head.

Antonio's head turned slowly back from the dying embers of the fire. Sobbing came from the back of the room where Teresa had slumped over the table, her shoulders heaving.

'I'm sorry, Renzo. I'm so sorry.'

'You see, the trouble was ...' Pedrini smiled. 'Teresa and Antonio have always been *very* close as half-sister and half-brother. Some would say a little indecently close. But, hey, these things happen.' He smiled a sickly smile.

Antonio leaned back in his seat, the leather of his jacket creaking as he did so.

'Theresa became increasingly jealous of her brother's attentions. And when she found out about the PO box Antonio had concealed from her, and the little presents your wife had been sending him, well ...' That afternoon she drank too much gin, took the car and sat outside your house, Renzo. It seems she didn't know what the fuck she was going to do, but when she saw you and Rosa leave the house, she decided to get Rosa out of her brother – her lover's – life. You know the rest, I believe.'

'Teresa!' A look of horror creased Renzo's face. 'This isn't true. Tell me it isn't true.'

'We're waiting, Teresa,' said Pedrini, the same smile still on his face. 'Tell them that you didn't put the Audi into gear, follow them down the hill, wait until she was standing at the side of the road and put your foot down hard on the pedal, aiming the car straight fucking at her. Tell them you didn't feel a sickening thump as the car struck her and threw her into the air ...'

'Shut up! Shut up!' Teresa screamed, standing up but leaning forward, her hands on the table. Antonio rose from his seat and moved towards her, putting his arm around her and pulling her close to him. It was hard to say what the gesture cost him. They both looked grief-stricken, but Antonio's face was contorted by other emotions as well – anger, pain and regret.

'I wanted to die, too. I thought I was killing both of us. I was just going to keep on driving into the fence at the side of the road and down the hill into the river at the bottom, but I couldn't do it. I was too big a coward. I swerved back onto the road at the last moment and drove back here.'

Antonio embraced her, stroking her hair and whispering in her ear as the room went silent once again. Michael looked down at the floor, shaking his head in disbelief. Renzo had slumped down in his chair and was staring into the fire.

'But why all this? Why the kidnapping in the first place? I don't understand . . .' asked Michael, anxious to get to the bottom of it.

'Look, we have to fuck off out of here,' said Pedrini, looking at his watch, 'and, of course, we have to deal with all of you somehow first, but there is just time to explain this piece of nonsense to you. Perhaps you should tell them Renzo. Go on, tell them why Teresa was kidnapped.'

Renzo looked at Antonio and Teresa. He sighed and began to talk, his voice sounding exhausted.

'You don't know about this, Michael, but during the war, there was a terrible betrayal. Someone informed the Germans where the partisans were going to be on a couple of occasions and a lot of men were massacred as a result. There are many in Dulcino who will be unable to rest until the person who committed that act of betrayal is exposed. Fathers have passed to sons the hatred of this unknown person and it has become a kind of silent hysteria, festering in the minds of the people of the village. We felt it too in our family because we lost a couple of relatives as well. Most people believed that a young local man called Alessandro Bellini was the traitor; he survived when others died and then disappeared. What else would they think? But, a couple of months ago, they found out that the traitor was, in fact, Luigi Ronconi. I must say it was difficult to restrain a number of the older men, and indeed some of the younger ones, from travelling to Beldoro to kill him there and then. Of course, they knew they could not take the story to the press – Luigi's power over that is still immense and he has managed over the years to stifle any stories about him. And, anyway, they feel no one will believe them as they have little or no evidence. Just some uncorroborated stories. They feared the litigation that could ensue. It might ruin their families. So, we spoke to Antonio and Teresa, told them what we thought was the truth about their father and it was decided to blackmail him into admitting his crimes by pretending to kidnap Teresa. Antonio has connections in the south – a man called Massimo Di Livio – and that is how Pedrini and his friend became involved. They work for Di Livio.'

'It seems, you see that our father is a monster who stole money during the war – money that he used to set up his businesses.' Antonio picked up the thread of Renzo's story. 'He killed an English officer who was carrying a considerable sum of money. And we believe he was not the only person he killed for money.'

'But how could you do this to your own father? asked Michael. 'Look at the efforts he made to find you after the war . . .'

'Ah, Michael. You don't know the man. Yes, he did find me after the war, but that was only because I was a possession

309

of his. As was my mother. He started out looking for her in Germany, but soon discovered she had died in the camps. So, he then shifted his search to me. He is a man who has never lost in his life, who has to come out on top in every situation. In fact, this is the secret of his success in business. He found me a couple of years after the end of the war, paid off the German couple who had taken me out of the camp and brought me back to Italy. But then he took no further interest in me. I was brought up by a series of nannies and rarely saw him. He had won by getting me back and that was the end of it for him.'

'And I was also one of his possessions.' Teresa spoke, wiping her nose with the back of her hand and rubbing the tears out of her eyes. 'He destroyed my mother in winning custody of me as a child. She could not stand up to the money, the lawyers, he could throw at a court case.' She stopped and sniffed. 'And he didn't even want me. He just had to win. Someone had stood up to him, had demanded something that he considered to be his and he couldn't let that happen. So he won custody and then became nothing more than a distant shadow in my life, a figure viewed from a distance. My mother, though . . .' she sobbed again. 'My mother killed herself.'

'He is a man who has destroyed lives.' Antonio spoke quietly, stroking Teresa's hair again. 'There are many, many instances . . . too many. It's time he was called to account.'

'Hey, but hang on a minute,' said Pedrini, sneering at Antonio and Teresa, 'Let's not forget, this is not all about altruism and fucking morality, is it? People might be interested to know that your father is about to cut you out of the family business, Antonio. All that money going somewhere else, eh? And Teresa, he was about to stop funding your little butterfly colony, wasn't he? This, you see, Michael, is not a purely charitable act on the part of Antonio and his sister.

310

The timing was just right for them to get their father into difficulties and take over the business, or get him to change his will. This, you see, is a complex kidnapping. Even Renzo gets something for helping out. He's not letting us use this place for free, after all. And his precious village even gets something – truth and revenge. So, you see, everyone gets something out of it. Everybody wins!' He laughed.

'Except the two men you've killed, Pedrini. They lost everything.

'Michael, I had no idea about any of that . . .' Renzo began to say.

'Oh, there's always a bit of collateral damage in this type of *business*, Michael,' interrupted Pedrini. 'Scatti was a fucking greedy weakling who was threatening to share what he knew with the police if we didn't pay him a bit extra. We couldn't let that happen.'

'Michael, I knew nothing about this part of it,' insisted Renzo. 'I just wanted the truth. And then when they started connecting you with the murders, I just couldn't understand what was going on.'

Michael merely shook his head.

'And what do you get out of it, Pedrini?' he asked.

'Oh, money, Michael. And lots of it. Antonio brought it with him tonight,' he nodded at a large holdall in the corner. 'But I fear it's not going to my boss, which is what everyone thought. No. Gianni and I are going to use it to set up on our own a long way from this shithole.' He beckoned Gianni back into the room from the door where he was standing. 'But look.' He glanced at his watch. 'It's been a joy telling you all this, especially you, Michael, because you've put so much effort into it, but it's time for us to fuck off. However, we have to, I'm afraid, take care of you first. Gianni will do the honours.'

The large man produced a length of rope from outside the door. He went round each of them, forcing them to the ground and tying their hands behind their backs and their legs together. As he did so, Pedrini stood guard, nodding approvingly.

As Gianni finished tying Helen's legs, Michael was thinking fast. Shards of the broken glass that Teresa had smashed when they entered the room lay all around them. He wrapped his fist around a large piece that lay nearby, quickly slipping it under his legs unnoticed, pressing his knees close together to hide the fact that anything was there. Gianni finished tying Helen's hands, and moved towards Michael. First he tied his legs. Then he bound his hands behind him, pulling so hard on the rope that Michael cried out in response to the sharp pain.

'Oh, sorry, Michael. You mustn't be so rough, Gianni!' Pedrini laughed. 'Still, it won't really matter in a few minutes. Okay, Gianni.' He nodded to the large man, who left the room. A moment later he returned with a large gas cylinder. Don't worry, you won't feel a thing.' A sickening smile spread across his face once more, as if he were a dinner host describing a dish to a roomful of guests. 'A little drowsy, perhaps, at first, but by the time the gas has filled the room sufficiently to be ignited by the lovely fire that Gianni has built for you, I am sure you won't be in any condition to be concerned. Pleasant dreams, everyone.'

'*Bastardo*, you won't get away with this,' shouted Antonio as Pedrini retreated to the door. Meanwhile, Gianni bent over the cylinder, turning the knob at the top. Gas hissed out of it. He took one last look around the room and disappeared through the door in Pedrini's footsteps.

As Gianni had been fiddling with the gas cylinder, Michael had shuffled forward until the piece of broken glass was within reach of his hands. Slowly – so as not to be noticed – he had leaned back until he could feel the jagged edge of the glass against his fingers. Gingerly he'd wrapped two fingers around it and lifted it from the floor. As soon as Gianni had left the room he hissed:

'Helen! Slide towards me and then turn round. Quickly!' She began to shuffle on her backside towards him.

The room was already starting to fill with the heavy, sickly smell of the gas.

'What are you doing, Michael?' Helen was now sitting back to back with him.

'I've got a piece of glass here . . . If I can just . . .' He took a deep breath and focused. Now pull your wrists away from each other as far as you can. Make the rope as taut as possible. '. . . If I can just . . . break it . . .'

'Ouch! Careful where you put it!' He had nicked her skin trying to find the rope. As the smell of gas in the room became increasingly pungent, he readjusted his position and sawed away at the rope with the sharp edge of the glass, feeling it give way a millimetre at a time.

'Hurry up, Michael. Hurry up!' Renzo and the rest stared at Michael's hands working away behind him. Suddenly, he felt the last piece give way. 'There!'

'You've done it, Michael. Give me the glass!' Helen leaned forward to slash at the rope that was around her ankles. It gave way.

'Quickly, Do mine now, Helen.' She cut away at Michael's and within another minute had cut through the rope binding his wrists. He then found another large piece of broken glass while she worked on Renzo. He cut through the binding on his ankle.

All of them were now starting to cough as the gas began to predominate in the room.

'Get out, Helen. Get out!' She was trying to open the shutters to let in some oxygen, but they were padlocked on the outside. She rattled them in desperation, moaning with frustration.

'I can't leave you, Michael!'

'Bloody hell! Go! Now! Get Renzo out and then and keep running once you are out of here! Go!' He stared at her until she was almost afraid of him, before hoisting Renzo to his feet and leading him from the room.

Michael moved towards Antonio, who was closest to him.

'No ... Save Teresa first! ... Quick! It won't ...' he coughed, '... last much ... longer!' Antonio screamed at Michael, his eyes bulging.

Michael changed direction and headed towards Teresa, who had collapsed onto her side. He picked her up, stumbling under the weight and gasping for breath. He was becoming confused as he staggered towards the door, his lungs scouring the atmosphere for air.

It was as if he was back in his old nightmare again. There was a rush of air, followed by a loud bang that seemed to make his ears explode. How he knew it he could not say, but he found himself lying on a bed which was flying through the air. The bed floated on a sea of flame – the heat was intense, but still, in spite of that, he could make out the familiar objects of the same old dream. As ever, blue was all he could see; a sea of dancing blue whose waves crashed against the walls beyond the flames and splashed against the ceiling.

There was the desk, a few feet from the bottom of the bed; the thick, leather-bound book; the jacket hung over the back of the same wicker chair in the corner.

Just on the periphery of his vision he sensed something massive and silent. Painfully – and now the pain was everywhere – his body was made of pain – he turned his head and once again discovered the familiar bulk of the ancient armoire with its massively mirrored doors.

As the pain crescendoed and he realised that there was, after all, a limit to the amount he could bear, the blue began to drain out of the room, along with the flames; together, they seeped under the door and oozed through the slats of the shutters, which lay fast against the light of the sun to his right, as if they were being sucked out.

The ceiling began to shimmer, as if a shutter were slowly being opened and light was being reflected onto it from the surface of a swimming pool. From outside came the sound of water lapping gently against stone.

Once more, he experienced the familiar sensation of watching rain fall on a watercolour. His vision dripped in long, slow elongations down the page of the room, and, just as he became aware that somewhere, in someone else's dream, he knew this room, his eyes opened and he knew, all at once, that he would never dream this dream again.

21

White.

White was all he had been able to see at first. He had been unable to move. Something had held his head in place and his entire body had felt like it was in splints, cool splints, holding him fast.

The white had, at first, been unblemished, a pure and unending absence of colour, stretching, for all he knew, from here to eternity; perhaps it was, indeed, the colour of eternity. Then, slowly, more had begun to leak into his cracked vision. A break in the lack of colour here, a stain there. A light bulb; the top of a poster. Sounds had leaked in like water gradually filling a basin. Gently at first, and then almost deafening. Offensive to his ears. Traffic, voices, the distant growl of a train, the scream of a plane about to land, the crashing of what sounded like dishes, the continuous hum of conversation, buzzing like a huge swarm of bees around him. He had wanted to reach up with his hands to his ears and block out the sounds but found himself unable to move.

Now, here he stood, six months later, unbelievably, on his own two feet, alive and mended, they said.

'Michael!' Harry Jones stalked towards him through the crowd like a predator homing in on its prey. It was his way.

'Michael! 'How are you, my boy?'

'I'm better than I was, Harry!' Michael said, reaching out a hand, pleased to see his old friend.

It could have been worse – a broken leg, and burns to his back. He had been unconscious when he had arrived at the hospital and his hearing had been damaged by the explosion, taking weeks to return to normal. But now the visits to hospitals and doctors were over. He had been luckier than the Ronconis, however. Antonio had not survived the explosion and subsequent fire while Teresa had suffered serious injuries and would never again chase butterflies around the garden as Luigi Ronconi had fondly remembered her doing as a little girl. Her spine had been damaged and the remainder of her days would be spent in a wheelchair, much of it in a prison cell. Saddest of all for Michael was the knowledge that Renzo was being prosecuted on serious charges and would be going to jail. In a letter from the prison where he was being held, he had confessed to Michael that he had got in way over his head, but had no idea what Pedrini was really up to. He admitted to becoming frightened of the others and what they were doing as time went on. It had all got out of hand but he had only become involved for the sake of his precious village and the expunging of its painful history once and for all. Michael could only hope that the judges might consider his loyalty to his community a reason for leniency, but only time would tell.

As for *Il Falcone*, he lasted no more than two weeks after the story broke. The stroke anticipated by his doctors had killed him as he sat in his wheelchair staring at the mountains of his youth, thinking who knows what thoughts. The story had come out, by that time, of course, slowly, and almost reluctantly at first, but within a short while it was everywhere. Meanwhile, Pedrini and his partner in crime, Gianni, had been apprehended on a yacht, heading for Albania. He was, apparently, singing like a veritable canary, and his boss Massimo Di Livio had been arrested a few days later.

'On the mend, boyo? On the mend?' Harry's eyes gleamed, staring deep into Michael's as he reached for an ashtray to stub out the cigarette he had been smoking, at the same time, putting down his wine glass and reaching into his pocket to extract another and light it.

'Yes, Harry. I get a bit tired now and then, but I suppose it's only to be expected.'

'Aye, but look at this, Michael.' Harry's eyes swept round the walls of the gallery. 'It's bloody marvellous. Rosa would have been so proud.'

'That she would, Harry. That she would.' He stared around the walls, walls adorned with the beautiful black and white, people-free landscapes that had been the last that Rosa had captured in her lens. They had a richness and a mystery, even in monotone, that Michael recognised as being the very essence of the Valtellina. He could smell the smells of the valley as his eyes moved from one image to the other.

Why he had persevered with this when he had been so betrayed by Rosa, he would never understand. It had happened and he had to leave it behind. Perhaps the glamour of Antonio Ronconi had been attractive to her. Perhaps he had let her drift away from him. It was just something he would never know.

'I've just been speaking to that young lady of yours, Michael – Helen. She's a fiery one.' Michael looked over to the far corner of the room where Helen was in earnest conversation with a couple of art critics. She looked up and caught his eye, nodding and smiling in his direction almost imperceptibly. They had been through so much and had now arrived at that point where they could share looks, glances and expressions without anyone else seeing them.

'Look, Harry, would you excuse me. I'm feeling a bit weary. I just need to go out onto the terrace to get some air. I'll be back in five minutes and you can tell me the latest gossip from the *Post*.'

'Of course, lad. I need to get myself a re-fill, anyway,' Harry said, raising the empty wine glass he held in his hand.

Michael excused his way through the groups of people that stood around talking and admiring the photographs and made his way to a set of French windows that led out onto a terrace on which stood some gleaming white metal chairs and tables. The early spring night was fresh with a gentle, cool breeze and he was relieved to see that the terrace was empty. It was still quite light and there was a view out across the rooftops of London's West End, ending in the ornate, massive, stone bulk of Harrods. He sat down at a table with a loud sigh and let his head fall back, at the same time running his hand through his hair.

Then he remembered the letter. He had found it on the doormat this evening when he had returned home to change, after spending the day helping to put the finishing touches to this show. The show was intended as a precursor to the publication of the book, a book now enveloped by the story that surrounded the kidnapping of Teresa Ronconi, a kidnapping itself enveloped in tragedy. He had had no time to do more than stuff the letter in his inside pocket as he left for the gallery with Helen, but his curiosity had been pricked by the fact that it had a Swiss stamp.

Reaching into his pocket, he pulled the letter out, tearing one corner and sticking a finger in, opening it carefully. He withdrew a few sheets of light blue, lined paper, opened them out, smoothing them where they had been folded, and began to read the confident, tidy handwriting.

Dear Mr Keats, it began.

'*You do not know me, but you certainly know my name – Erich Weber. I am the German officer involved in the story of Luigi Ronconi. I must admit, I followed the story with great interest while it was running in the papers. Yes, here in Switzerland, as everywhere else in the world, it was front-page news. I congratulate you on your work although I understand you were injured and hope that you are now recovered from those injuries.*'

'Michael!' Michael was interrupted by the voice of Helen from over at the door to the terrace. 'Are you alright?'

He turned.

'Yes, I'm fine, Helen. Just having a couple of minutes of peace and quiet. I'll be back in a minute.'

'Okay,' she said. 'I'll see you in a minute.' She smiled and closed the doors again.

Michael returned to the letter.

'*As I say, I have followed the story and, as you know have been instrumental in parts of it, for which I have suffered both physically and mentally ever since. There is one thing, however, in the story that is fundamentally wrong and I feel an overwhelming need to put it right. So, here is a part of the story that no other living person knows, apart from me.*'

'When I was based in the Valtellina – as you know I was an Obersturmführer in 16 SS Reichsführer Division – I always tried to remain fit. Therefore, I used to run in the hills around Morbegno. I was one of the fittest men in the division, and proud of it. I would run thirty kilometres a day, and more if I had time. On one of those days I ran in the direction of the village of Dulcino. I was close to the village when I ran into a clearing, just at the time that a young woman entered the clearing from the opposite direction. We both got a shock, but then found it very funny and laughed. She was beautiful and, somehow, for the first – and I am sad to say – only time in my life, I fell in love immediately I saw her with the force of a kick in the stomach. Any man would have fallen in love with this girl, I assure you. She was very beautiful. As you have probably guessed, it was Angela Ronconi, Luigi's – Il Falcone's – wife. She was engaged in her daily ritual of waiting for her lover, the partisan Sandro Bellini. He had not turned up for several months now and she, as I was to find out, was heartbroken about this. We talked – she was an innocent young thing – I think she believed there was inherent good in everyone and the fact that I was one of the enemy and a hated one, at that – the SS, after all – did not stop her, I think, liking me immediately. Naturally – I was more used to the cold hearts of the whores of Morbegno and Sondrio, remember, than a beautiful young girl – I returned regularly to the clearing and began to take the place of Sandro as her lover. She was very young and alone, apart from her child. She told me that her husband had been killed in the fighting in North Africa, but, of course, I did not believe her. That was what was said about any man missing from his home at that time in that part of the world. I presumed that, like the rest, he was probably somewhere in the mountains, fighting

322

with the partisans. This went on for several months. Sandro still did not appear and, I think – I know – she fell in love with me. It was impossible, of course, and I knew it. She, however, had fantasies of what we would do after the war, where we would live and so on. As time went on, I spoke of her husband and she told me the truth, that indeed he was a partisan, and how she hated him. He had beaten her all through their marriage. One day she arrived in the clearing with bruises on her body. He had visited her, got drunk and had beaten her as usual. But, more importantly, something seemed to have changed in her. It was as if a light behind her eyes had gone out. As he had done on many occasions, she told me, he had raped her. It was how he got his pleasure, it seemed, through others' pain. Through control. She wanted him dead, she said, and she was inconsolable at the thought of him returning home and picking up his life where it had left off, when the war finally ended. And so, she told me of a conversation she had overheard in her house. Another partisan who was also visiting his family, came to the house and Luigi and he drank. As she worked in the kitchen, she listened to what they were saying. She overheard them discussing an attack on the small San Giorgio garrison – she gave me dates, the number of men involved, everything. I was amazed. The beating had made her irrational, yes, but her hatred for him was such that she would carry out such a betrayal of the people around her, of the wives and families of the partisans who would surely be killed. But for her, the only thing that mattered was that Luigi be killed. As you know, Michael, the attack on San Giorgio was a disaster for the partisans because we were waiting for them en route. Unfortunately for Angela, however, Ronconi was one of the few partisans who survived. She was undeterred. She told me about the regular rendezvous to pick up ammunition – she knew about it because she had a cousin who was a member of the other group of partisans and Luigi carried family news between them when they met. By the time of this incident, however, Angela had been arrested and Luigi had disappeared. He was, consequently, not part of the group that we encountered in the hills that night. I was very angry that he was not amongst them, but she had warned me that Sandro Bellini would probably be there, and had described him to me, pleading that he be spared. I decided to let Bellini live that morning, which was possibly the worst decision of my life. But I did it for Angela, even though she was by this time, of course, lost to me. But his very survival was his undoing. They blamed him, just for living through it, because these were times when everyone was irrational, everyone was suspicious of everyone else.

Angela had been taken from her village and sent to Germany, which was entirely my fault. I told a colleague about her one night after too many drinks, and about her husband and the information she had provided us with. With the twisted logic of those days, he thought he could get Il Falcone to give himself up in exchange for the life of his wife and child. Angela and her son got lost in our bureaucracy and were mistakenly put on board a train heading for the camps.

So, Sandro Bellini, drowning in guilt for his betrayal of Luigi, his comrade-in-arms, took fifty years to tell people about him. And that was when I was brought back to the Valtellina, for the first time in half a century, to confirm that story in the village of Dulcino. As you have read, however, it was not true and I have thought much about it since. I want the truth known to someone at least, the truth being that the real traitor of those partisans was not Luigi, but Angela Ronconi. Luigi is, of course, not totally innocent. He was responsible for the death of the English captain and

324

the theft of the money he was carrying, after all, as well as other crimes from which he benefited financially. Above all, though, he was responsible for the destruction of Angela's innocence. But then, during those times, we were all guilty of acts that we would later – those of us who survived – abhor. I, lost my humanity. I was nothing but a machine that had been switched on in 1941, when I joined the SS, and which did not switch itself off until the war ended. When that happened, I was amazed, horrified by what I had done. It was like waking from a terrible, terrible dream. And yet, even though I escaped and have buried my true identity and tried to live a decent life for the last fifty years – yes, in spite of the horrors I had perpetrated, I believed I could redeem myself, somehow – I have discovered it is not possible. And never will be. For me perhaps it is more difficult. Every time I look in the mirror or see my reflection in the window of a shop, I am reminded of the war – my face, you may know, is very badly scarred, thanks to Sandro Bellini.

The writing and posting of this letter to you will be my very last act on this earth. I will fold it, put it in an envelope, take it to the post-office at the end of the street on which I live and on my return I will drink half a bottle of brandy and swallow a bottle of the pills I have to take to deal with the pain I have suffered for five decades – yes, even now, I feel it. I will have been dead for several days by the time you read this, although I have really been dead since 1944. I would ask you to do with this information as you see fit.

And I would finally ask one more thing of you, Mister Keats – I would ask you not to think too harshly of us; Luigi and Angela Ronconi, Sandro Bellini and me. We were not evil people. We were perhaps selfish, each of us, pursuing his or her own self-interest, whether that self-interest was coloured by love or tainted by money or hatred. Each of us

325

has inherited his or her piece of hell as a result of our actions;
Angela dying in the camp; Sandro in his gnawing guilt;
Luigi in the destructiveness of his life; me in my futile search
for peace and some kind of redemption. We were nothing in
the greater scheme. It was really a very small drama that we
played out against the vast backdrop of the war. Perhaps it
would be better forgotten. That is your choice.

I wish you well in your recovery. Farewell.
Erich Weber.

Michael lifted his eyes from the letter and raised them towards heaven. He remained thus for several minutes before picking up the pages, standing up and walking over to the metal railings at the edge of the terrace.

He looked down three floors to the empty street below him and then lifted his head, staring out across the rooftops to the tower of Big Ben, outlined against the darkening sky. The constant roar of city traffic filled the air from the streets below and the breeze was strengthening slightly.

He looked down again at the five pages in his hands and then, very carefully tore them in half and then into quarters. He held them up above his head and loosened his grip on them. They drifted out of his hand, down towards the street and then were caught by a gust of wind, which dragged them away across the rooftops towards the dark space of Hyde Park.

Michael watched them for a moment before turning and walking slowly back towards the French windows and the buzz of excited conversation that came from Rosa's exhibition.

Acknowledgements

One day last summer, I was idly scrolling through my emails when I noticed one from Sarah and Kate Beal of Muswell Press to whom I had sent the manuscript of a novel several weeks previously. My heart skipped a beat as I read that they liked the book and wanted to talk about publishing it. While on holiday for the following few weeks I was a very happy man indeed, and the excitement of that time has not left me. Grateful thanks, therefore, to Sarah and Kate for believing in The Partisan Heart and for lavishing so much care and attention on it in the months since. Thanks to them also for furnishing me with a wonderful editor, Laura MacFarlane, who brought her assiduous eye and keen intelligence to bear on my more purple passages and plot holes, for which I am eternally grateful.

A special thank you is due to my sister-in-law, Valerie Barona, and her husband, Michele, who have welcomed me and my family at their lovely home in the Valtellina for almost forty years. I hope the book does justice to that beautiful place in the mountains.

My brother, Bill, is probably the reason I have written all

my life and I thank him for his love and encouragement over the years. My oldest friend, Jack Mcgrane, spent an afternoon with me in Nice trying to come up with a list of titles for the book. None of them made the cut, but the wine was lovely!

Last, but, of course, by no means least, a huge thank you to my family, my wife Diane and children, Lindsey and Sean, for their love and unstinting support, and for putting up with this writing addiction from which I have suffered all these years.